# The Reluctant Carnivore

# The Reluctant Carnivore

## A Doctor Cooper Series Novel

## Warren J. Stucki

SUNSTONE
PRESS

SANTA FE

Sunstone books may be purchased for educational, business, or sales promotional use.
For information please write: Special Markets Department, Sunstone Press,
P.O. Box 2321, Santa Fe, New Mexico 87504-2321.
Body typeface › Bengulat Std
Printed on acid-free paper
⊗
eBook 978-1-61139-522-8

Library of Congress Cataloging-in-Publication Data

Names: Stucki, Warren J., 1946- author.
Title: The reluctant carnivore : a Doctor Cooper series novel / by Warren J.
   Stucki.
Description: Santa Fe : Sunstone Press, (2017)
Identifiers: LCCN 2017021613 (print) | LCCN 2017025148 (ebook) | ISBN
   9781611395228 | ISBN 9781632931887 (softcover : alk. paper)
Subjects: | GSAFD: Medical novels. | Mystery fiction.
Classification: LCC PS3619.T84 (ebook) | LCC PS3619.T84 R45 2017 (print) |
   DDC 813/.6–dc23
LC record available at https://lccn.loc.gov/2017021613

SUNSTONE PRESS IS COMMITTED TO MINIMIZING OUR ENVIRONMENTAL IMPACT ON THE PLANET. THE PAPER USED IN THIS BOOK IS FROM
RESPONSIBLY MANAGED FORESTS. OUR PRINTER HAS RECEIVED CHAIN OF CUSTODY (COC) CERTIFICATION FROM: THE FOREST STEWARDSHIP
COUNCIL™ (FSC®), PROGRAMME FOR THE ENDORSEMENT OF FOREST CERTIFICATION™ (PEFC™), AND THE SUSTAINABLE FORESTRY INITIATIVE® (SFI®).
THE FSC® COUNCIL IS A NON-PROFIT ORGANIZATION, PROMOTING THE ENVIRONMENTALLY APPROPRIATE, SOCIALLY BENEFICIAL AND
ECONOMICALLY VIABLE MANAGEMENT OF THE WORLD'S FORESTS. FSC® CERTIFICATION IS RECOGNIZED INTERNATIONALLY AS A
RIGOROUS ENVIRONMENTAL AND SOCIAL STANDARD FOR RESPONSIBLE FOREST MANAGEMENT.

**WWW.SUNSTONEPRESS.COM**
SUNSTONE PRESS / POST OFFICE BOX 2321 / SANTA FE, NM 87504-2321 /USA
(505) 988-4418 / ORDERS ONLY (800) 243-5644 / FAX (505) 988-1025

This book is dedicated to the many concerned citizens
of St. George, Utah and Washington County who struggle to
preserve the matchless beauty of this land and
our unparalleled lifestyle.

# Acknowledgements

Again I would like to recognize my wife Linda. As my first reader and critic, she has to put up with my razor-thin skin and often-inflexible attitude. She indeed does have thick skin.

Also, again thanks to Nick Adams for his superb editing and timely suggestions, and to Jim and Pam Hilton for the front cover photo.

# 1

In spite of my life's many failures, I was at peace, at least for the moment. Soaking in the sun and the ambiance of the season, I closed my eyes and let the slanted morning rays warm my eyelids and upturned face. If there was a heaven, which I mostly doubted, this could be it. This *should* be it.

When that final day arrives, this is all I could ask: to be in the morning sun, sitting before a postcard alpine pond, surrounded by the sights, sounds and smells of an autumn forest—the musky scent of fallen and decaying leaves, the nervous chattering of a tree squirrel, the gilded leaves and silvery trunks of a clutch of quaking aspen, a surprising flash of glaucous blue as the rising morning sun reflects brightly off a sequestered mountain pond.

At my feet, I felt Malachi, my aging chocolate lab, stir. Yes—I must add Malachi to that idyllic final scene. In contrast to my ex-wives, our relationship had been seamless and consistently pleasant. There was no one with whom I would rather share my final moments than him. Sighing almost inaudibly, I rubbed his soft floppy ears and reluctantly opened my eyes.

Suddenly, there he was, right at the forest edge, regal head held high and cautiously sniffing the gentle currents of early morning air. Softly, I patted Malachi's head as a sign for him to stay.

Patiently, we waited.

After a few more seconds of silent reconnoitering, the splendid buck took a guarded step forward, cautiously lowering his head toward the water.

Silently I raised the .30-06 rifle to my shoulder, sighting down the magnifying scope and counting the buck's horns, four points on the right side, three on the left. It was unusual, but not unheard for a buck to have asymmetrical points.

He was a large majestic creature, a male mule deer of at least two hundred pounds, maybe more, and five years old, perhaps older. Sporting typical "mule" ears, he had dark intelligent eyes, a light-colored face and a large cedar brown body. Due to my angle of sight, his signature white tail was not visible.

Readjusting my scope slightly, I placed the crosshairs squarely on his broad chest and immediately felt the old familiar adrenalin rush, the so-called *thrill of the kill.* As I cupped index finger around the perfectly machined concave steel of the trigger, my heart began to pound, my facial muscles tightened and my breath quickened. Slowly I began to squeeze. A milli-second later, I abruptly dropped the barrel downward a couple of degrees.

KA-BOOM!

Rocketing a potential missile of death forward, my rifle exploded, shattering the placid October dawn. Instantly, the gun's barrel bucked skyward, followed by a surprisingly small splash as the bullet plunked harmlessly in the water a couple feet from the male deer. Simultaneously, the air around me instantly lost its musky autumn smell and now reeked with the caustic odor of sulfur and combusting nitrates.

Immediately wary, the majestic ungulate raised his crowned head and glanced around the pond's periphery. Quickly, he located Malachi and me, then bounded effortlessly back into the dense and bronze-dappled foliage.

Silently, I hoped I had not scared him off into the direction of the other hunters, that I would see him again next year.

# 2

## One Year Later

To kill, or not to kill?

Didn't used to be an issue, but now, somehow, it was. Sort of.

Like cortisol cream, or testosterone gel, it somehow penetrated my protective skin barrier, squeezing past my ever-vigilant epithelial cells; then like crude oil from the ill-fated tanker *Valdez*, it somehow seeped into my venous circulation. Stealthily and insidiously, but nevertheless relentlessly, once it had invaded my veins it bubbled upward, like air from a scuba diver's mouthpiece, eventually passing across the blood-brain barrier and arriving at my brain's switchboard, the medulla oblongata. From there, it slowly edged its way upward, finally arriving at the mighty cerebrum. There, by some means I don't fully understand, it produced a series of electrolyte anion shifts, a bit like football fans doing the "wave" (except with charged atoms), thereby generating an electrical impulse. This fledgling electrical current raced down several tendril-like neurons and right through chemically mediated synapses before arriving at the prefrontal cortex where it was converted to conscious thought. Eventually, that nascent notion, massaged and modulated by life's experiences, grew and solidified into a principle, then further ossified into a moral conviction. All this took years and is not something of which I was very proud.

Nowadays it seems I brake or swerve to miss headlight-blinded jack-rabbits, or darting chipmunks, or distracted crows narrowly focused on their roadside carrion. Common pests, like mice, wasps, or spiders are often pardoned and relocated rather than summarily executed. And though I still eat some meat (beef, lamb and pork) I do so sparingly. Through the years, my portions have grown progressively smaller while Malachi's have ballooned correspondingly larger. More distant evolutionary cousins, like poultry and fish, I find less abhorrent, but nevertheless consume them less frequently and also in much smaller portions. More than likely I cook almost as much animal protein as ever, but I am embarrassed to admit I offer more and more of it to Malachi and satiate my own hunger with fruits, vegetables and grains.

I worry, however, if this most curious dietary metamorphosis may portend the onset of a similar personality transformation. Or, is it merely a modification of a single character trait? Did an isolated gene mutate, or the entire chromosome? More than likely, my ex-wives would be happy, even ecstatic at this most unexpected and paradoxical conversion, but I am not. I worry.

I truly hope it is not a progressive disorder, like ALS (Lou Gehrig's disease) or Parkinson's disease, and is self-limited, like post-streptococcal glomerulonephritis, or the common cold. But thankfully, so far it does not appear to be pandemic in nature; it has not yet infected my whole personality. So, other than being a somewhat reluctant carnivore and a less than enthusiastic hunter, I pretty much remain my usual annoying, recalcitrant and abrasive self. And at age fifty-two I have no burning desire to change.

Furthermore, Malachi likes me just as I am, and since there is no woman in my life (and after three failed marriages I'm certainly not looking for one) and I've given up on ever having children, I feel no biological, or social obligation to change my rather acerbic disposition.

No, I am mostly satisfied with my life. I have my work and a few friends. Any free time away from my surgical practice is consumed with maintaining my hobbyhorse ranch, plus a little golf and these seasonal hunting excursions (mule-tail deer, pheasants, turkeys, ducks and blue grouse).

My more solitary and sedate diversions include computer chess, studying Latin and divining the origin of surnames. I admit I love this to a fault and try to divine the origin of every new surname I encounter. For example my surname, Cooper, is English, an occupational name derived from the makers and repairers of wooden vessels such as barrels, tubs, buckets, casks and vats.

Also, I admit to a love for playing *Concentration,* also on the computer. Some say I have an eidetic, or photographic memory, but I do not. I have, however, pretty much mastered the art of association and consequently have a good memory, but maybe not quite so good as I grow older. Lastly, I am a stickler for good grammar and often correct friends and foes alike. Through the years, that most irritating habit has probably cost me more than one friend.

But lately, however, I have become a little uncomfortable with these annual hunts, an odd development because I am no stranger to hunting. I grew up with guns and had my own .22 rifle at age eleven. Hunting was a family tradition, a vacation and sometimes the only escape from the farm for the entire year. But more and more, just as I do with golf, I just go for the exercise and companionship, to be with friends and not so much for the actual hunting/killing or the swinging of a golf club.

During the hunt season, I concentrate more on the domestic chores, like cooking meals, cleaning and repairing the cabin. To keep up appearances I do take my rifle out, but if I happen to get game bracketed in my crosshairs I often readjust my aim high or low and fire off a harmless round, only later to cuss my bad luck to my companions. On the rare occasion I do kill something, I do not experience the ancient and tribal exhilaration of the kill, but rather a bilious nausea, and I try very hard not to think about what I have just done: ending an innocent life. Unless you believe in reincarnation, all living things have only one life and I just took it. I somehow feel dirty, like a murderer or an executioner, and even though I don't believe in ultimate justice, I do have a persistent nagging feeling that what I have done is wrong, robbing another fellow living being of their ultimate gift, *the gift of life*.

Now, even the charred-flesh smell of a grilling hamburger often turns my stomach just as much as the revolting sulfurous stench of rotten eggs or burning hair.

I am more than a little embarrassed by this newly acquired weakness, this recent sensitivity, and try hard to hide it from my hunting pals, particularly Tim Slade. I doubt any of them would understand, but certainly not Tim. Hell, even I do not understand it. I just hope, like a small kidney stone, it will eventually pass.

Timothy Daniel Slade, my hunting buddy, fellow surgeon and business partner of five years, would surely laugh and accuse me of going soft. He is a gun enthusiast, a dedicated hunter and literally a card-carrying member of the National Rifle Association. Even I am surprised and discomfited by this newly-acquired compassion for lesser life, but still I am unable to shake it. Like my shadow, it will disappear at times, briefly, but unfortunately it will always reappear. This is not me, at least not the Lawrence Addison Cooper of my youth, middle-years, or even five years ago—

"—So, how many place settings?" Ian McKenna (obviously Scottish, Anglicized from Gaelic) jolted me out of my prolonged brooding.

"Huh?" I heard the sound of his voice, but not his words.

"How many are coming?" Ian asked again, juggling ceramic plates, glass tumblers and mixed utensils over a rustic wagon wheel table. "How many should I set the table for?"

Dangling prepositions always drove me crazy and I almost lost my train of thought once again. "Oh, four," I finally answered, but wanted to add, don't dangle your *for*. But instead I added, "Tim Slade will be here sometime tonight." I laughed. "He's just the opposite of you, he's never on time."

"That's only three."

"Oh, yeah, and Wally Stroud (English, meaning marshy area) is coming with Tim," I replied. "They're both good guys; you'll like them." Silently I added, 'I hope'.

"Four it is," Ian beamed and began setting out the mustard yellow plates. He spaced them precisely an equal distance from each other, outlining a near perfect square.

Turning back to the burgers, in spite of a wave of nausea, I couldn't help but smile. I wouldn't be at all surprised if he produced a measuring tape and a protractor to check angles and lines of symmetry, but nevertheless I was glad Ian McKenna was here. We were more alike than even he realized.

Ian and I were college roommates years ago at Southern Utah University. Even though we were both nerds, Ian was a liberal nerd and I more conservative. It was a good and symbiotic relationship. Ian helped me survive the trauma of being dumped by Samantha Rose Jardine (years later to become my second wife) and I helped him survive Chemistry 101.

Right after college graduation, we separated. Ian went to Dartmouth Law School and I to the University of Utah Medical School and almost immediately we lost track of each other. Through the passing years, we had not maintained contact and I had no idea what happened to him. Then right after Giff called and canceled out for this year's deer hunt, Ian called and said he wanted to renew our friendship. I was surprised to hear from him, but pleasantly, and asked if he wanted join us on the hunt. He readily accepted.

Later, I found out Ian, as opposed to me, was married. And also as opposed to my less-than-enviable nuptial record, Ian had married later in life, had married only once and was still married. We were alike, however, in that neither of us was blessed with children.

Admittedly, Ian was a bit effeminate, not the rugged outdoorsy type. Certainly his brand new, right from the catalog L.L. Bean ensemble looked a little out of place for this deer hunt, and his obsession with perfection was a little irritating, but so what? None of us were totally free from irritating habits, least of all me. And after all these years, Ian appeared to be largely unchanged. He still was a bleeding heart liberal, an olive branch dove and still loved President Barack Obama.

"Hi, all!" Abruptly, the cabin door opened and Tim Slade, wearing an old checkered flannel shirt and faded Levis, entered. In both hands, he carried hard-shell rifle cases and also had an overnight bag wedged under his right arm.

"Sorry, I'm late," he growled. "Friggin' Ford trucks! Which bedroom's mine?"

I pointed with my stainless steel spatula. "The second one. There's two twin beds; take your pick."

Slade (middle English - meaning small valley) disappeared into the bedroom, apparently deposited his gun cases and overnight bag, then immediately returned empty-handed.

At that same moment, Wallace Stroud entered. Like Tim, he was weighted down with hunting gear. Wearing a typical Utah hunter ensemble--a bright orange cap and sweatshirt--he also carried a single rifle case and two sets of aluminum snowshoes. "Hello, Coop," he nodded. "Good to see you again."

Again using the spatula, I pointed each out as I introduced them. "Slade, this is Ian. Ian, this is Slade. Ian, this is Wally."

Wally enthusiastically shook Ian's hand; Slade was a little less enthusiastic.

"What's with the snowshoes?" I asked, turning back to the stove.

"Just a being prepared," Wally laughed. "Forecast is for snow this weekend. Maybe up to a foot. I had two sets of snowshoes, so I thought why not bring 'em?"

"I heard six inches and that was a maybe," I shrugged, "but who knows? They seem to change their minds with every broadcast."

"Where's Giff?" Slade arched a suspicious eyebrow, as he quickly broke free of Ian's wet-rag handshake.

"Remember, I told you," I flipped a burger, "he can't make it this year. His wife is expecting."

"That's pretty damn lame." Slade continued to eye Ian suspiciously. "Women have had babies without men for forever."

"Oh, you mean, like the Immaculate Conception?" Wally joked.

"What?" Slade looked puzzled. "No, I mean like the Indians. Drop 'em, pick 'em up and keep movin' on down the trail."

"It's not quite the same." I turned off the gas. "Nowadays, men are expected to be there to share the experience and bond with their kids."

"How would you know," Slade growled, then added, "well, then, what about Jacob Heinz? He's a lot of fun."

"Geez, Tim," I pulled a metal platter from the cupboard, "he's eighty-three years old. Let's eat."

"Right, I'm starved." Slade sniffed the air. "Smells like steak."

"More like burgers," Wally volunteered.

"It is burgers." I arranged the open buns on a metal platter, then used the spatula to transfer the burgers. "I can't afford steaks," I joked as I closed the buns over the patties, then set the tray in the center of the table. "Anyway, you guys don't deserve steaks."

"Like casting pearls before swine, huh?" Wally jested.

"What?" Tim growled.

"It's from the bible, Matthew chapter seven verse six," Wally explained with a lopsided grin.

"I know it's from the bible," Tim snapped. "The rest of verse is: lest they trample them under their feet, and turn and tear you in pieces."

"That's exactly what's happening today," Wally claimed, suddenly serious.

"You bet it is," Tim agreed, "just like in the Book of Revelations."

"Nothin' but superstitious tales," Ian said, "as seen through the eyes of illiterate goatherds."

"Careful what you say, Professor," Tim growled, his eyes narrowing.

"Help yourself." Like a referee, I quickly stepped between them. It was way too early to start fighting about religion or politics. "I'll get the fries out of the oven."

"Cheapskate." Tim Slade complained, but immediately grabbed a burger and started drowning it with condiments.

"I'll do that." Ian grabbed my spatula. "You go ahead and eat." He then found a pair of oven mittens and carefully extracted the hot fries from the oven, setting them next to the burgers precisely in the middle of the table. After rehanging the mittens, he joined us.

Just as I reached for the catsup, Slade blurted, "what is this—?" He stopped in mid-sentence, loudly sucked in air, coughed and choked. Wheezing loudly he got up from the chair, pointing to his neck. His face quickly turned red, then morphed to a cyanotic blue. He gagged again, hard.

Finally I realized he was choking. Jumping up from the table, I circled behind him, preparing to perform the Heimlich. Ian, however, beat me there. Looping and locking his arms under Tim's ribcage, he violently jerked upward. Nothing. Tim whole face was now a venous blue. Ian jerked again, even harder, briefly lifting Tim's feet right off the floor.

Tim gagged loudly, coughed forcefully and finally spat out a chunk of food the size of a quarter onto his plate. "W-what the," he gasped, pausing

14

to take in another lungful of air. "What is this shit?" He finally rasped, holding his burger up to the level of his eyes.

"Oh, you must have gotten Ian's veggie burger," I chuckled, then made a circular motion with my hands. "You two need to trade plates."

"A *veggie burger*!" Slade snorted. "On a friggin' deer hunt! That's kinda like taking a gay guy to a topless bar."

"Geez, Slade," Wally chastised as he prepared his burger, "maybe you could use a little less graphic metaphor, and anyway it's not that big of a deal."

"You should be thankful," I added quietly, "that Ian saved your life."

Slade looked at Ian, frowned, then without comment offered him his plate with the partially eaten veggie burger.

Acting as though nothing happened, Ian accepted Tim's plate, then immediately grabbed a paper napkin and attempted to remove Slade's saliva and food splatter. Finally, he gave up, washed the plate, then fished a steak knife from a cabinet drawer. Like a surgeon removing a cancerous melanoma, he carved out Slade's semicircular tooth imprint from the veggie burger, taking ample of margin, then he transferred the post-op burger to the cleaned plate, discarding the pathology in the trash.

With a jaundiced eye, Slade regarded the ongoing surgical measures. "So, what's your story, Ian?"

"Uh—well—it's not very exciting," Ian again joined us at the table, "Coop and I were roommates in college at Southern Utah University, then I went to law school at Dartmouth. Now I live in Salt Lake City and teach at the University of Utah Law School, but am considering going into private practice with Hansen, Zundel and Stamos."

"Danish, German and Greek," I blurted out.

Huh?" Ian stared blankly back at me.

"Oh, nothing," I mumbled.

"Coop's got this bizarre fascination with the origin of family names," Wally explained.

"Dartmouth—Big Green, huh?" Suddenly I made the connection. "This is like old alumni week. Isn't that where you went to school, Wally?"

"Yeah, but I was in the business school."

"What years for you Ian?" I asked.

"I was there from ninety-five to ninety-nine."

"That about when you were there, wasn't it, Wally?"

"Yeah, I was there from ninety-six to two thousand."

"So, you two," I pointed at Wally, then at Ian, "you two where there at the same time and never knew each other?"

"Nah," Wally said quickly. "It's a big school and we were in different scholastic departments."

Tim ignored my attempt to steer the conversation and like a pit bull refocused on Ian. "A lawyer, huh, and a vegetarian, and a college professor," he paused to take a bite of his real beef burger, then sarcastically added, "Let me guess, you must watch Fox News too."

"Yeah," Ian laughed, "but just for the babes."

"Yeah, I'll bet," Slade said without smiling.

I didn't like the direction this conversation was headed and again tried to change the subject. "Tomorrow's the big day."

"My first," Ian proclaimed excitedly, "I've never been on a hunt before."

Silently I gritted my teeth. What was it with Ian and his dangling prepositions?

"They don't hunt much up north, huh?" Slade continued to eye Ian suspiciously.

"Some do," Ian scraped off the excess mayo and catsup Slade had slathered on his bun. "But my family weren't hunters."

"Really! Big surprise there," Slade scoffed, then bragged, "It's my twenty-fourth. Never missed an opening day since I was sixteen."

"But how many times did you actually get a buck?" I finally took a small bite after stacking the burger with pickles, tomato, lettuce and onion, then covertly inching the patty off to the periphery, so I got only bun, pickle, onion and tomato.

"All of 'em." Slade bragged. Somehow, he managed to squeeze those words past the large bolus of food crammed in his mouth.

"All of them?" Wally looked skeptical. "How big?"

Discreetly, I pinched off a piece of exposed meat patty, offering it to Malachi who was expectantly waiting under the table. Obviously, we'd done this before.

"Nothin' smaller than a four-point."

"What's a four-point?" Now that Ian finally had his burger properly excised and sanitized he took a small nibble, then quickly wiped his face with a paper napkin.

"*What?*" Slade exploded, almost dropping his burger. "You don't even know that and you're goin' on a deer hunt?"

16

Thankfully, Wally stepped in. "A point is the tip of a horn branch. If you get a four-point buck that means there are four of those points on one side."

"Then eight total," Ian quickly calculated.

"*Wow!*" Slade blurted sarcastically. "You're a quick study, Professor."

Again I jumped in and changed the conversation. "So, where are you going to hunt tomorrow, Tim?"

"Uh, I don't know, maybe over by Summit Canyon. You?"

"Probably stay here, around the cabin." I finished my bun and Malachi had eaten the patty. "I've seen a lot of deer sign around here. How about you, Wally?"

"I've always had good luck over around Navajo Mountain."

"And what about you, Ian?" I added. "You want to hang with me?"

"Nah," he laughed. "I'd just get in the way. Go ahead and hunt. I think I'll go exploring. Familiarize myself with the area." Ian got up and started clearing the table.

"Don't get lost, Professor." Slade pushed back from the table. "There's some pretty rugged country out there. I remember one time, maybe fifteen years ago, me and a friend, Jim Riggs, were hunting on horses in this same general area. This was before I got my ATV. Steep terrain and lots of cliffs. Anyway, about an hour before dark, the fog started rollin' in. It got so thick visibility was not more'n twenty feet. As you might expect, we got lost and wandered around for an hour trying to find the trail. Then it got dark and even if you held your hand out, you couldn't count your fingers. One of the few times in my life I was truly afraid—afraid of stumbling over one of them fifty-foot cliffs. Unfortunately, we weren't prepared to stay the night, no flash-lights, coats, tents, food and very little water. It was like being blindfolded and trying to strike the *piñata*, but we pressed on. Riggs was in front leading his horse and I was walking behind. Suddenly, I heard Riggs scream as he disappeared. He fell right over a cliff."

"Did he die?" I asked to be polite, though I knew the answer.

"Jesus, Coop, you're a doctor, what do you think?" Slade didn't wait for an answer. "Anyway, you want know how I made it out alive?'

"Sure." Ian was wide-eyed.

Wally looked bored. Like me he'd heard this story many times before.

"Well, I looped the reins over the saddle horn, got behind the horse and grabbed hold of its tail, then slapped him on the butt."

Ian looked at me for validation.

I shrugged. "Horses do have a sixth sense. They can find their way home under almost any circumstance."

"Anyway, the point is, this ain't no place for greenhorns." Slade stood up and headed for the fridge. "Anybody want a beer?"

I nodded, as did Wally.

"How about you, Professor?"

Ian held up palms of his hands like a traffic cop. "None for me. I never developed a taste for the hops. I'll have a glass of the grapes."

"This ain't friggin' France," Slade grabbed three beers, then kicked the fridge door shut with his right foot, "there ain't no wine."

"Really," Ian laughed, "I could have sworn I passed through a *Beaujolais* vineyard on the way here."

"*Beaujolais?*" Slade asked, arching an eyebrow.

"It's a region in France," Wally Stroud volunteered.

"Oh, really," Slade said sarcastically, "thanks for educating me, Wally."

Ian got up, went into the bedroom and returned with a bottle of *Bordeaux* and a wine glass. "How about you, Coop?" He held up the bottle. "This is really good stuff."

"Nah," I shook my head, "I'll stick with beer."

Wally, however, changed his mind. "Yeah, I'll try some."

Slade handed me a beer and kept Wally's for himself. "What you shootin' this year, Coop?"

"Still have my trusty thirty-ought-six."

"And you Wally?" Slade popped the tab on his beer.

"I'm still using my dad's old two-seventy Winchester. Was going to get me a new one this year, but have you seen the price on them lately?"

"Yeah," Tim laughed, "you almost have to be a lawyer to afford one."

"And," Wally continued as he patted a holstered gun at his side. "I don't go anywhere without my twenty-two Smith and Wesson."

Tim nodded and turned to Ian. "What about you, Professor? What you shootin'?"

"I'll show you," Ian replied enthusiastically, then got up and once again disappeared into the bedroom. When he returned he was carrying an expensive-looking camera with a telephoto lens. "This is my gun," he proudly patted the camera, "a Canon EOS Five D Mark Three."

"You've got to be friggin' kidding me!" Slade exploded again.

One more time, I stepped in and tried to defuse. "So, what about you, Tim? What you got this year?

18

"Huh?" Apparently, he still hadn't fully recovered from the shock of Ian's camera.

"What are you shooting this year?"

"Uh—oh, I still got my thirty-thirty," he paused, "but I did get a new gun. I'll show you." He got up, stopped at the fridge for another beer, then vanished into the second bedroom. When he returned, he was carrying one of the two gun cases he'd brought in earlier. "Look at this baby!" He unsnapped the latches of the hard case, then extracted an assault rifle, inadvertently pointed the barrel directly at me.

"Geez, Tim," I pushed the barrel aside. "Get the gun out of my face," then I quickly added, "is it loaded?"

"Takes a hundred round magazine," he said proudly, ignoring me. "Ain't she a beauty?" He shoved the gun into Ian's reluctant hands.

Ian accepted it like it was a diamondback rattlesnake. "What is it?" He held it as far away from his body as he could, eyeing it with nervously.

"A Bushmaster Nine-O-Six-Two-Nine Predator with, laser sights, a night vision scope and like I just said a hundred round magazine," Slade boasted, then proudly added, "that's a two-K gun!"

Ian quickly thrust the gun into Wally's hands.

"Nice gun," Wally said as raised it to his shoulder and sighted down the barrel through the night vision scope, then handed it to me.

Weighing in in my hands, I rotated the Bushmaster, looking at it from every angle. "Tim," I finally said, "it might be a two-K gun, but I wouldn't give you a Roosevelt dime for it." Immediately, I wished I'd kept my mouth shut.

"The hell you say!" Tim bellowed.

"It's pretty much worthless," I shrugged. "You can't do anything with it."

"I know you can't hunt with it," Ian jumped in. "That's a Class A misdemeanor. You could lose your hunting privileges for life and they could confiscate—"

"—What do you mean, worthless?" Slade abruptly cut Ian off and turned back on me. "If nothing else you certainly can protect yourself with it."

"From what?" Wally asked.

"From anything, from everything," Tim answered Wally while still glaring at me.

"Like what?" I asked, not backing down.

"Well, from home invaders, from foreign invaders and from our own friggin' government for starters."

"Right," I laughed derisively, "our own government."

"Go ahead and laugh," Tim sneered, "but this administration is hell-bent on gun control."

"I wouldn't call background checks gun control," I countered. "And for that matter, I'm in favor of banning these things too," I handed the Bushmaster back to Slade, "along with those high capacity magazines."

"*Jesus H. Christ!* Are you some kind of a friggin' socialist?" Tim bellowed.

Finally, I decided to keep my mouth shut.

Ian, however, jumped right in. "I think the Second Amendment is a little outdated," he paused, searching for an analogy, then added, "like the paperback novel."

"*What!*" Slade exclaimed, angrily swinging the Bushmaster around. "I can't believe you said that. The Constitution is—uh—uh—is sacred!"

"It was written a long time ago when the world was a different place," Ian replied calmly. "Like the Bible, only a small part of it is relevant today."

"*Jesus H. Christ!*" Slade bellowed again, his voice was now shrill. "Are you a friggin' atheist too?"

Ian shrank back from the glowering Tim Slade. "What's wrong with atheists?" He minced his words out meekly.

I should have stayed out of it, but I couldn't help myself. "Tim, does the Second Amendment give you the right to own a Sherman tank?"

We locked eyes.

"You damn right it does!" For emphasis, Slade slammed his fist down on the table, rattling the empty beer cans and toppling Ian's half-full wine glass.

Immediately Ian jumped up and grabbed a paper towel and started mopping up the spill.

"Come on guys," Wally laughed nervously. "Why don't we call it a night?"

"Yeah," I forced a laugh and turned away. "We've got to get up early. The hunt starts at dawn."

Slade also turned away. As he furiously re-cased the Bushmaster Predator, the barrel again unintentionally pointed at me, then Ian.

"Tomorrow, we'll see who the real hunter is," Slade challenged, looking directly at me, "see who bags the biggest buck."

Once again, I should have kept my mouth shut, but I took up a challenge I knew I would never win. "I suspect that would be me."

"Put you money where your mouth is!" Tim Slade slammed a twenty-dollar bill down on the table.

"I'm in." Wally also slapped down an Andrew Jackson.

"Yeah, okay," I pulled out my wallet, "the biggest, but not only just for tomorrow, but for the whole weekend."

# 3

Like summer nightfall in Fairbanks, Alaska, sleep was slow in arriving that night. In lieu of sleep, I listened to Malachi snoring softly on the bed beside me, and Tim Slade's louder and more strident snoring rising up from the adjoining bed.

I had originally planned to put Ian with Tim in the second bedroom, but after the way the night had unfolded, I suspected that would be like asking the lamb to lie down with the wolf. So, even though it was not my preference, I suggested Tim sleep in my room.

Ian, and even Wally, looked relieved and readily accepted the second bedroom. I suspect neither one of them wanted to bunk with Tim either. Fortunately they'd seemed to hit it off almost immediately and were certainly a better match than Tim and Ian.

Trying to take my mind off this loud nasal discord, I studied the cabin walls. Though I could barely see the logs in the dim light, I nevertheless tried to count them, twelve high per wall, then tried to discern which joints needed re-caulking. That was next to impossible without turning on the overhead lights.

Samantha Rose and I had built the cabin in happier and certainly more lucrative times. After a series of legal and financial setbacks, I had started doing surgery again and she was practicing law.

It was nothing fancy. The walls were constructed out of dried and milled white pine, cut in the Swedish cope style. At sixteen hundred square feet, the floor plan was a basic rectangle. The front two-thirds of the cabin was a studio-like space, containing an open kitchen, and a dining and living area. Two identical bedrooms occupied the back third and it also sported a half-loft, like a movie theater balcony, perched directly over the bedrooms. To keep the winter snow from accumulating, the roof was acutely gabled and finished with slick hunter green sheet metal, but the *coup de grâce* was the massive native granite rock fireplace. As a colorful contrast, a few chunks of fire and blue agate were randomly mortared in with the gray granite. Samantha Rose and I had spent some lazy, but perfect evenings, snuggled here in front of a warm fire; the cabin suffused with the strong aroma of pitchy pine.

22

God, how I missed those days! God, how I missed Samantha Rose! God, I missed them all, Kylie and Claire too, but probably Samantha the most.

Kylie was the first. That in and of itself was special. Fresh young love and trying to make a new life together, playing *house* for the first time. I was never much of a ladies' man and when I finally found someone to say *yes*, and Kylie did, I was convinced I could do no better. Now in retrospect, I must confess my motive for that marriage was not the best. Eventually, I became pathologically dependent on her, clinging to her like a small child clutches the pant leg of a parent who is about to leave, even though that parent may have been abusive. I even sent her subsistence checks for months after she'd run off with Roger Callister, an itinerant landscape painter. I realize this confession opens a previously darkened and locked room and shines some unflattering light on me, but alas the past is a matter of record and something I cannot change.

Samantha Rose was my second and I quite honestly thought she was the real deal, my soul mate, my death-till-you-part. As I mentioned earlier, I dated her briefly in college before she dumped me for a football jock. After that, I did not see her again for years until I became embroiled in three, and almost simultaneous, malpractice lawsuits. My malpractice insurance carrier had a retainer with her law firm and unbelievably she was assigned to defend me. Not only did she do a great job, I fell in love with her all over again. While it's true she, like me, had a hard time with commitment, I really don't think that was what ended it. Abruptly, one night she announced she had a doctor's appointment in Salt Lake City, packed up and left the next morning. I never saw her again, though I tried many times to contact her.

My bond with Claire Dubois, ex-wife number three, was forged in the fiery furnace of a near-death experience. By happenstance, some friends and I were on a horse-packing fishing excursion at the same time Claire's daughter Collette went missing from a Utah youth wilderness camp. One evening a young girl who had been assaulted and savagely raped stumbled into our fish camp. Though I tried every thing I knew to save her, with my limited medical supplies coupled with her extensive injuries I could not. Initially, we thought the dead girl was Collette, Claire's daughter, but thankfully as it turned out she was not. But as a consequence of all that churning and intrigue, Claire and I were immersed in a frothy caldron of wayward kids, sex slaves and illicit drugs. And I must admit Claire did have some mettle, some true grit, but unfortunately other than that experience we had almost nothing in common. Claire was a Wall Street banker and I a Utah country surgeon. She was an eastern liberal, me a western conservative. She loved the theater, the opera and nightlife, me a good book and a quiet evening. In retrospect, our marriage was doomed before it started.

Tim snorted in his sleep, then ceased to breathe. I counted the seconds, one Mississippi, two Mississippi—up to ten before he snorted and took another breath. Undoubtedly, he suffered from sleep apnea and also without question his body habitus, his morphology, contributed to the problem. As opposed to ectomorphic, or my mesomorphic body style, he was definitely endomorphic. He was big boned with a rounded face and belly, a heavy chest and large legs. He constantly struggled with his weight.

Even though we were a close facsimile of the *odd couple*, not only in body morphology but also personality and values, we somehow managed to get along. To date, we'd been partners at Southern Utah Urology for six years, actually longer than any one of my marriages had lasted.

After medical school at the University of Oregon in Eugene, Tim returned to the University of Utah for his residency and worked with Jacob Heinz. As it turned out, Jacob retired the very same year Tim completed his residency. Before hiring Tim, I consulted with Jacob. His advice to me: "Though he'll never be an all-star, Tim is a good and competent surgeon. His major flaw and strength are the same; he does things by the book. He is not an innovator, but on the other hand, he's not a loose cannon either."

But it irritated me Tim had shown no gratitude to Ian. With the Heimlich maneuver, Ian had literally save his life. You'd think Tim would have personally thanked him, or at least cut him some slack later, but— but—I finally dozed.

Quietly, almost surreptitiously, the door opened and I could see three shadowy figures huddled in he hallway. They whispered in low tones, but pointed at me with angry gestures. Eventually they flipped on the light and came right in the bedroom. Instantly on guard, I sat up in the bed and Malachi snarled, baring his fangs. A goateed man with a purple beret and wearing a painter's smock stepped forward; his thin, deeply lined face was contorted in anger.

"I want you to take her back," he hissed.

"Who are you?" I demanded, trying to calm Malachi.

"Roger Callister and I want you to take Kylie back."

"Why?" I was stunned at his audacity. Even though we had a history, I'd never met Roger before.

24

"You ruined her, she's damaged goods. You must take her back. It's the right thing to do."

"Why?"

"Because she's a spoiled brat. She throws a tantrum when she doesn't get what she wants and she's high, very high, maintenance."

"But—but I can't."

"Why?" he demanded, casting a fold of his painter's smock aside and placing his hand on his hips.

"Wait a second!" A second stranger interrupted us, pushing forward. He was wearing a helmet and shoulder pads and carrying a football. "I'm here to return Samantha Rose!"

"Look!" I barked, "I never gave you Samantha Rose, so I feel no obligation to—"

—"It don't matter," he cut me off, "I still want to return her."

"Why?"

"She lives in the past."

"In the past," I echoed.

"Yes, I'm tired of hearing about her life with you."

"Oh, well then—maybe I will—"

"—No!" A man with a New York accent, wearing a three-piece suit and carrying a briefcase, interrupted me. "No you don't! Not until I return Claire Dubois."

"Why?" I sighed. Suddenly I was getting tired of this.

"She's too stubborn, too overbearing, and that daughter of hers is impossible."

"Listen," I said, a definite edge to my voice. "I never asked any of you to take my wives. You did it on your own accord. I can't possibly take them all back."

"Why not?" Roger Callister demanded. "After all, this is Utah."

"But I've lived alone for so long, and—and there's Malachi to consider."

The New York man took another step forward. "Then choose one, and we'll dispose of the others."

"Dispose? Dispose!" I couldn't believe what I was hearing. "What do you mean by dispose?"

"Yes," the football player nodded his agreement. "Choose one. We'll take care of the rest."

"No! I—I can't possibly do that—"

—Suddenly some one was shaking me. I tried to push the annoying hand aside. The significant others of my ex-wives were irritating me beyond belief. *Dispose of!* We'll see about that. Forcibly, I shoved the hand away again.

"Look, you three—"

"—Coop, wake up." The hand shook me again, harder. "You're having a bad dream."

"Huh," I rubbed my eyes and like an over-weighted scuba diver struggling to the surface, I struggled to reclaim consciousness.

Suddenly, something wet and slick was licking my face. Rolling on my side, I located Malachi and hugged him. This was the technique he always used when I started thrashing in the middle of the night and it almost always worked.

"You were having a bad dream," Ian laughed, standing above me. "Anyway, its time to get up."

"Huh? What time is it?"

"It's after six."

I sat up and slowly exhaled. "Yeah, okay, I'll fix some breakfast. Tim's probably chompin' at the bit to get going."

"Nah," Ian shook his head, "he's already gone. Left before first light."

"What about Wally?"

"He's walking out the door even as we speak."

"Well, give me a minute," I struggled to get out of bed, "and I'll fix us some breakfast." I swung my legs to the floor. "I'm not in a big hurry anyway, not like those other two."

After dressing, I wandered into the kitchen, pulled some eggs and bacon out of the fridge and a fry pan from the cupboard.

"How you going to do the eggs?" Ian asked.

"The only way I know," I laughed, "scrambled."

"I'll cook breakfast," Ian appropriated the fry pan from me. "Do you like omelets?"

I nodded, then watched with fascination as he rummaged through the cabinet drawer until he found an old sunflower-pattern apron that once belonged to Samantha Rose. After strapping it on, he rifled through the fridge and produced some cheese and onion left over from last night's burgers. As he grated the cheese and chopped the onion, I turned a chair around, sat down and watched. I must admit I had mixed emotions, him wearing Samantha Rose's apron.

"So, you finally got married, huh?" I eventually asked.

26

"Eight years ago." Ian placed bacon strips in the hot cast iron pan and instantly the sizzling aroma filled the cabin. Though now pretty much a vegetarian, I still loved the smell of frying bacon—virtually the only frying meat that did not turn my stomach.

"That long, huh? How come I've never met her?" I chided. "And why wasn't I invited to the wedding?"

Ian laughed. "No one was invited. It was a private wedding." He sat the spatula down and pulled out his wallet. "Here's a photograph."

I accepted the snapshot, then my jaw dropped. She was drop-dead gorgeous. With shoulder length raven hair, she had a fine oval face, flashing black eyes and a dynamite figure. Somehow she managed to look like a rare and exotic mixture of a Harvard graduate, a gypsy and a Paris runway model. Not someone I'd expect a nerd like Ian to end up with. "She's beautiful!" I gushed, handing the photograph back. "What's her name?"

"Katherine Kozlov McKenna."

"Kozlov her maiden name?"

Ian nodded as he replaced the photo back into his wallet.

"Russian," I announced, immediately recognizing the origin of her maiden name. "Shortened from Kozlovsky."

"Yeah," Ian nodded, "second generation."

"What does she do?"

"She's a psychiatrist in private practice." Ian located a whisk and started beating the eggs. "But like me, she also doubles as a part time professor at the U. of U. medical school."

"Where did she train?"

"University of Utah, then did her residency at Columbia Presbyterian in New York City."

"Why Colombia?" I jested. "There's no crazies in the Big Apple. When was she at the U.?"

"Uh, let me think. Nineteen eighty-eight to ninety-two."

"That's when I did my residency under Jacob Heinz. I'm surprised we didn't meet."

"Yeah? How often do the surgery circles and psychiatric circles overlap at the U.?"

"Not that often," I laughed, "but maybe they should. Most surgeons suffer from a God-complex and could probably benefit from a little mandatory psychotherapy."

"That could apply to lawyers as well," Ian also chuckled as he continued to beat the eggs.

"No," I joked, "lawyers tend to be narcissists."

"And doctors and even Gods are not narcissists?" Ian argued.

"Touché," I acknowledged. "Does your wife do any inpatient work?"

"Sometimes, but she'd like to give up her hospital practice. Too much night work, too demanding."

"Yeah, tell me about it," I agreed. "Any children?"

"Nah," Ian added a little milk to the eggs, then picked up the whisk again. "We didn't get married until we were in our late thirties and I guess the biological clock just passed us by."

"Did you ever consider private practice?"

"Yes, I in fact I am going to give it a spin." Ian removed the bacon and poured the egg slurry into the hot pan. "I just signed a contract with Hansen, Zundel & Stamos."

"And quit teaching?"

"I don't know," he put the fry pan back on the gas flame, "teaching's in my blood. So, for now, I'll still teach one class per semester, maybe at night." Ian broke the bacon into to small bits. "You're not married?" he asked.

"Nah," I shook my head. "Three strikes and you're out."

"Not seeing anyone?" Ian added the bacon bits, chopped onion and grated cheese to the rapidly solidifying egg slurry.

"No, not even looking. I may be a slow learner, but I finally realized I am not the domestic type. Better for me to live alone. Anyway, I've got Malachi."

"There's nothing wrong with Malachi," Ian agreed as he folded the floppy egg-disc over. "Hand me your plate."

I gave him my plate and watched as he ferried a golden brown omelet, oozing melted cheese from its seams, onto my plate. Then he started over again, making another one. "Go ahead and eat," he urged, "before it gets cold."

"So, do you want to tag along with me today?" I asked between bites. The omelet was terrific; exponentially better than my rubbery scrambled eggs. Even the bacon bits didn't nauseate me, though I picked most of them out and gave them to Malachi.

"Nah," he shook his head. "I'll just poke around the cabin a little with my camera this morning and Wally is going to take me out this afternoon."

"Don't get lost," I smiled, trying to hide my disappointment. I was looking forward to taking out Ian to show off my mountaineering skills while showing him the mountain. And since neither of us was serious hunters, it would also give a chance to get caught up with each other's lives. Well what the heck, if he'd promised to go out with Wally, so be it. "Have Wally take an hour or so to get you familiar with the local landmarks in case you get separated."

Ian laughed. "Don't worry about me, Coop. I'll be fine. Actually, I'm pretty good in the mountains."

Somehow, I doubted that, but held my tongue. Discreetly, I shared the second half of my omelet with Malachi. When we were finished, I announced, "I'll do the dishes, then we can go."

Ian would have none of it and shooed me out of the kitchen. After donning my hunter orange shirt and cap, and locating my .3006, I called to Malachi and headed for the door.

I knew if Tim were still here he would chastise me for taking a dog on a deer hunt and if I were an avid hunter, I would have to agree. It probably was not a great idea; dogs often chased the deer and deer saw them as predators, as wolves. They were more spooked by dogs than by man. But, I was not an avid hunter and Malachi was not a predator and we both loved the outdoors. In fact, Malachi was much more excited to start hunting than I was.

In early morning, I knew the deer often watered at a small pond at the foot of a steep hill, about a quarter of a mile below the cabin. Carefully, we picked our way down the nearly sixty-degree grade toward the pond. The forest was jungle-thick and almost impassible. Majestic balsam, blue spruce and foxtail pine, as well as heaps of jumbled downfall, made the going slow, circuitous and potentially treacherous. As usual, Malachi ranged ahead of me, his head down with his nose close to the ground.

Suddenly, there was whir of wings as a large bird launched and soared up to the top branch of a tall foxtail pine. Instinctively, I swung my rifle to my shoulder, then realized it was a ruffled blue grouse. Lowering my gun, I congratulated Malachi for flushing the bird; after all he was a bird dog. But there was no doubt he seemed disappointed I had not fired my gun and there was nothing for him to retrieve. It was in his DNA.

For another twenty minutes, we patiently picked our way through the mountain jungle. At last I could see a flash of Artic blue through the trees. Slowly I worked in closer. At that moment the sun crested. The brilliant reflection off the placid pond water nearly blinded me. Shielding my eyes, I circled north to get a better angle and away from the sun glare. I located a suitable granite rock and sat down. Carpet-thick, knee-high grama grass grew right up to the water's edge and the pond's shallows sported an exuberant growth of reeds and maturing cattails. Festooned in gold and circling the pond was a ring of coin-leafed, silver-trunked quaking aspens. Occasionally, a moss green conifer, or a flaming red cut-leaf maple wedged in and interrupted the quakies' golden circle.

Using a nearby quaky as a backrest, I settled in with Malachi; I was in no hurry. The October morning air was crisp and the nascent sun warmed my upturned face. Permeating the frosty air were customary smells of autumn: musty fallen leaves, the fragrance of damp sage and the pitchy wood smoke drifting down from our nearby cabin. Off to the northwest, I noted a low gray carpet of clouds that had slowly bled into the blue horizon, moving stealthily toward me and threatening the season's first snow.

In spite of my life's many failures, I was at peace. Soaking in the sun and the ambiance of the season, I closed my eyes. If there was a heaven, which I mostly doubted, this could, this *should*, be it. If this were my final day, this was all I could ask, to be in the morning sun, sitting before an alpine pond with my loyal dog and surrounded by the sounds and smells of an autumn forest.

Malachi stirred at my feet. I sighed softly and opened my eyes.

Suddenly, there he was, right at the forest's edge, regal head held high and sniffing the air. I patted Malachi's head, a sign for him to stay.

After a few more seconds of reconnoitering, the splendid buck took a cautious step forward and slowly lowered his head toward the pond water. Raising the .3006 to my shoulder, I sighted through the magnifying scope and silently counted his horns, five points on one side, four on the other. It was unusual, but not unheard of, a buck with symmetrical points.

My pulse quickened. Could this be the same buck from last year? Now a year older he had added more points, instead of a 4x3, he was now a 5x4. It was! It had to be. I was overjoyed to see him again. Pleased he had survived another year.

Through my scope, I studied him. Indeed, he was a majestic creature, a male mule deer of at least two hundred and fifty pounds and five years old, probably older. I adjusted my scope slightly, placing the crosshairs right on his chest and I felt the old familiar adrenalin rush; the so-called *thrill of the kill*. My heart raced and my breath quickened as my index finger cupped around the cold concave trigger. Slowly I tightened my finger. At the last second, I dropped the barrel down a couple of degrees, then pulled the trigger. The rifle exploded and the barrel bucked upward, followed by a surprisingly small splash as the bullet plunked harmlessly in the water. The caustic smell of sulfur and burning nitrates oozed rapidly into the surrounding air. Instantly alert, the huge buck raised his crowned head, looked around, spied me, then effortlessly bounded back into the deep forest. Silently, I hoped he was not headed in the direction of Tim Slade or Wally Stroud and that I would see him again next year.

Though Malachi and I continued to hunt and saw approximately twenty more doe, often with their six-month old fawns, we did not see another buck. Occasionally, the forest's solitude was shattered by the staccato pop-pop-pop of gunfire, typical of opening day, but none of it was close. About four o'clock, I called it quits and headed back to the cabin. As we climbed the thick plank steps to the cabin deck, I noted the gray carpet of clouds had moved much closer, now shrouding and blocking the angled rays of the evening sun.

Although Ian, Wally and Tim were not back yet, I started dinner promptly at six o'clock. With the thickening layer of clouds, darkness would come early this evening and I expected the three of them would walk through the cabin door at any moment.

Fifteen minutes later, Wally did walk in. "What's for dinner?" he asked as he deposited his rifle in the bedroom.

"Steaks." I put the fry pan on the burner and turned up the gas. "Any luck?"

"Nah, but I did see a lot of doe and passed over a couple of forked horns."

"Oh, well, there's always tomorrow. Where's Ian?"

"He wanted to spend a little more time at the Overlook taking photos and I wanted to hunt," Wally answered, then when he saw the worried look on my face he added, "actually Ian's pretty good in the mountains. He'll be okay."

"I sure hope so," I said, turning back to check the heat on the fry pan.

"You need any help?"

"Yeah," I held up a ten-pound plastic bag full of potatoes, "you could peel five or six of these."

Wally accepted the bag along with the potato peeler, then washed his hands and started in.

At dusk, the door opened and Tim, dressed in hunter orange, walked in.

"How did you two do?" he asked us after he deposited his already-cased gun in the bedroom.

"Didn't fire a shot," Wally complained.

"Nothing," I added, cutting the peeled potatoes into slices, then starting on the onions. "I did get one shot at a nice buck," I continued, though I knew it wasn't really a shot, "and missed. You?"

"Yeah!" His face was flush with excitement. "I got me a nice buck."

"Good for you." I said insincerely as I added the cut potatoes and onions to the hot buttered fry pan. "Where?"

"Over on that point overlooking Summit Canyon."

"You hang it up out back in the shed?" I retrieved the steaks from the fridge.

"Nah, it was getting dark," Slade shifted his eyes from mine to the floor. "I dressed it and hung it up in a tree. Tomorrow, I'll go back and get it with the four-wheeler."

"Geez, Tim!" I placed a second fry pan on another burner. "You know better than that. Tomorrow, you'll have no deer. Cougars, or coyotes, or both will get it tonight."

"That's the chance I'll have to take. Like I said, it was getting dark."

"And it might snow tonight," Wally added.

Tim shrugged. "I can't control the weather."

I sighed and shook my head, but nevertheless added, "tomorrow you can take Ike if you want."

"Nah, me and horses don't get along. I'll take my four-wheeler."

"Horses do better in the snow."

"Not much," he laughed, "I'll stick with my four-wheeler." He shuffled in closer and peeked over my shoulder. "What's for dinner? Smells good."

"Rib eyes for us. A veggie steak for Ian."

" A veggie steak, huh?" Slade snorted. "Made outta what? Tofu?"

"No," I held up the packaging information, "it looks like it's cornmeal and gluten. Why don't you set the table?"

"I'll help," Wally volunteered.

Slade shook his head in disgust, but nevertheless he and Wally began throwing the plates on the table, but not nearly as precisely arranged as Ian's were last night.

"Where's the professor, anyway?" Tim asked. "I don't want to have to go out on a night like this and search for his sorry ass."

"Don't worry about Ian." I stirred the potatoes. "I told him dinner was at seven o'clock. He'll be here. He's never late."

32

"Yeah, well it's seven o'clock and—"

—At that very moment, Ian, also now decked out in a checkered brown and orange shirt, with his camera strap slung around his neck, walked in.

"Hi, all." Ian took his camera from around his neck and carefully placed it back in its protective leather case.

Wally looked at his wristwatch and grinned. "Right on time."

"Time for what?" Ian asked, hanging his camera on a coat rack peg.

"Time for dinner." I looked up from the stove. "You have a good day?"

"Yeah," he frowned. "Got some very curious photographs."

"Curious, huh?" I turned the steaks over with a fork. "Curious is not an adjective that immediately comes to my mind when describing a day in the mountains. What happened to incredible, or fantastic?"

"No, I think I'll stick with curious." He paused like he was carefully considering his next words before speaking. "Did anyone get a deer today?"

"I did," Slade instantly bragged. "A real trophy!" He spread his hands about three feet apart to simulate the horn spread.

"Four points one side and five one the other?" Ian asked.

"Yeah," Tim shrugged.

Tim looked mildly puzzled, but I was furious. Apparently, he'd killed the very same magnificent buck I had spared earlier. Suddenly, I felt sick, nauseous, but had to bite my tongue. After all, I had to remind myself, this was a deer hunt.

"You must have had trouble with it," Ian continued, poker-faced.

"Trouble?" Tim asked cautiously. "What do you mean?"

"Did you wound it, or something? Have to chase it?"

"No, not me," Tim scoffed. "One shot right through the heart. They don't call me Slayer Slade for nothing."

Like a bloodhound locked on a scent, Ian was tenacious. "You hang it in a tree on that outcrop overlooking the canyon?"

Slade hesitated, looked out the window, then back at Ian. "Yeah, well, I guess I did."

"I counted seventeen holes in it!"

"Seventeen holes?" Now Wally looked confused.

"Yeah, bullet holes!" Ian said tersely.

"Jesus, Tim," I exploded. "Did you use that friggin' assault rifle?"

Slade went silent. Instead of further speech he glared first at me, then at Ian.

Ian got up and retrieved his camera. "Here, I'll show you."

Wally, Tim and I gathered around as Ian sat down on a dining chair. We leaned over his shoulder as he replayed the grisly digital photos on the camera's small screen. He had panorama shots as well as some disturbing close-ups. Indeed, the once regal buck now looked like bloody Swiss cheese with half its skull blown off.

When done, Ian shut off the camera, but did not return it to the coat rack. Instead, he held it close as if he were protecting it from aggression.

Silence followed, a jittery nervous silence.

After few tense seconds, Ian stood up and fished in his coat pocket. "Well, anyway, I also found these." He held out a plastic baggie containing three or four spent cartridges.

"Geez, Tim," Wally finally blurted, "what the hell were you thinking?"

"You just had to try out the Bushmaster, huh?" I growled, shaking my head.

Red-faced and with fists clenched, Tim got in Ian's face. They stood chest-to-chest, jaw-to-jaw. Though Tim towered over the smaller Ian, he still refused to back down. Wally immediately sided up next to Ian, standing beside him as a sign of solidarity.

Sick to my stomach, I remained rooted by the stove with fork still in hand.

Suddenly, charred-protein smoke billowed up, rapidly filling the room. "Damn!" I exclaimed as I jerked the smoldering fry pans off the burners. "Damn!"

# 4

After another restless night, I woke early. At first I couldn't figure out what had roused me, then finally I decided it was the sound of a slamming door. Obviously, someone was pissed.

Struggling out of bed, I looked out the bedroom window just in time to see Wally, in his snowshoes and carry a rifle, stomp off in the snow.

Yes, there was snow, roughly four inches of fresh powder, the first of the season. Though I am no longer a religious man, there is something inspiring, almost reverent, about the first snow—a symbolic cleansing, a new beginning, earth's annual baptism of gentle white. Standing before the bedroom window, I gazed out at the pristine, almost magical landscape. And for a few welcome seconds, I forgot the ugly scene of last night.

In retrospect, it was a mistake to invite Ian on a deer hunt. In my defense, I really didn't know him that well. For example, I was unaware he was a not a hunter. When I invited him and he accepted, I naturally assumed he was a hunter. We hadn't seen each other in years and I had no idea throwing him in with Slade would be a bit like mixing diesel fuel with nitrate fertilizer. At the time, it seemed like a perfectly logical thing to do. Giff had canceled out, Wally still hadn't committed and to be frankly honest I've always felt a little uncomfortable to be alone with Tim Slade. We were so different. So when Ian called and asked to renew our friendship, it seemed like the perfect solution, so I'd asked, "what are you doing the third week in October?" It bothered me not at all when he showed up with a camera instead of a gun and his own vegan food, nor did it seem to bother Wally Stroud, but it obviously did Tim.

Sure, I now had to admit Ian McKenna was a bit effeminate. I'm not necessarily saying he was gay, but he did not seem to possess those annoying masculine qualities of belching, cussing, farting, genital scratching and telling of off-color jokes. In truth, he was more like my gay fly-fishing friend, Harvey Peck. Like Harvey, he was well-dressed, well-educated, had perfect enunciation and was a precise neat freak. And, I had to admit, he had, though probably unintended, an air of superiority so common to sophisticated and educated urban dwellers.

That's not to say Tim Slade was uneducated. He was highly educated.

Like me, he had a doctorate degree in medicine, a year of internship and five years of residency in urology. But our schooling was more like the apprenticeship of a plumber or an electrician. We had a lot of on-the-job training, but almost no exposure to the liberal arts. Tim was smart, even street smart, but he was not liberal in any sense of the word: not in education, not politics and not in personal philosophy. He was, in fact, what I would term a religious redneck, so common to this area. His personal creed was surprisingly simple and straightforward: if it wasn't in the Bible, or the Constitution, it was of no consequence.

Still gazing out the window, I guessed the sun had crested, not because it was reflecting brightly off the snow--a residual thick cloud layer prevented that--but the gray flat light had lightened some, allowing me to see more details of the forest. The glacier-white carpet of snow was still unblemished, not yet tracked by humans or forest animals, and the conifers' limbs were weighted low, stacked with little mounds of heavy snow. Somehow, the scene calmed me and I felt at peace. There would always be another tomorrow, another snow, another chance.

But, I was also happy Wally Stroud was here. He served as kind of a buffer between Tim and Ian, and Tim and me.

Wally, a Merrill Lynch investment broker, was also an interesting study in contrasts. Like Tim, he was an ardent hunter, but like Ian he was more refined, more neat and definitely not a bigot, or a country redneck. Also, unlike Tim, Ian and me, he had children--two, a boy and a girl. He and his wife reportedly were having some marital discord, but what couple didn't? Also, as improbable as this sounds, Wally was reported to have a legendary temper, which I'd never seen, and was even enrolled in court-mandated anger management counseling. Around me, however, he'd always been civil, friendly and under control. The only temper tantrums I'd seen were from Tim, not Wally. But I guess just because I'd never seen that side of Wally didn't necessarily mean it didn't exist.

It was an odd coincidence, however, that Wally and Ian had both attended Dartmouth. And peculiarly strange they would finally meet in my cabin in southern Utah and not at Dartmouth College in New Hampshire? In spite of what Wally said, I knew Dartmouth was not that big of a school. Oh, well, why not? There were several, even dozens, of doctors on the staff of Dixie Medical Center that I had not yet met.

Suddenly, there was a mechanical coughing, followed by a discordant sputtering, then the loud pulsing roar of a piston engine. Though I could not see it--it was just outside my line of sight--the thunder of the eight-valve engine shattered my quiet morning musings. Instead of letting the engine idle and warm slowly, the unseen operator continually revved it, like he was on the starting line of the Moto Grand Prix. A few seconds later, Tim Slade roared into my field of vision, riding his CanAm 976 cc, V-twin, liquid-cooled, SOHC, 8-valve ATV, making ugly parallel tire tracks in the previously unspotted virgin snow.

I wanted to open the window and scream, "stop", but it was already too late. He was headed down the hill and a moment later he was out of sight. Obviously, he was going to retrieve his trophy mule deer, my 5x4 point regal buck. What a damn shame! He was so much more magnificent, more trophy-like when alive, rather than riddled with seventeen bullet holes and looking like picked-over roadside carrion. I sighed so loudly I woke up Malachi. Yawning and stretching, he got up and joined me at the window. I petted his head and stroked his ears for a moment, then as we turned from the window and started for the kitchen, we immediately bumped into Ian McKenna.

"You want some breakfast?" he asked, without smiling. He sounded glum.

"Sure. I'll get dressed and whip something up."

"It's almost ready," he said almost morosely. "French toast okay?"

Once again, he was wearing Samantha Rose's apron and holding a kitchen whisk in his right hand, but he mood seemed down, almost de-pressed. It was probably just a hangover, the residual from last night's row with Tim.

"Yeah," I nodded, "French toast sounds great. I'll get dressed. Where's Wally going?"

"I have no idea," he muttered, then quickly added, "he just took his snowshoes and left."

"Did he take both sets of snowshoes?"

"No. Why?"

"You ought to try them," I said. "They're actually a lot of fun and they sure make hiking in deep snow easier."

"Maybe I will," Ian replied, then immediately fell silent.

'What's going on here,' I wondered. Ian acts like he's pissed at Wally. "Even though Wally's a hunter, he's not fanatical like Tim," I volunteered, guessing that was the problem, then added, "I really like Wally."

"You're not much of hunter either, are you, Coop?" Ian finally asked as he cracked a couple of eggs into a mixing bowl.

"Is it that obvious?" I laughed.

"Yeah, kind of." Ian added a little milk and started whipping the eggs. "You're not impatiently waiting, gun in hand, for the crack of dawn."

"To be honest, I'm getting a little tired of guns," I held an index finger up to my lips, "but don't tell the others."

"Your secret is safe with me," Ian said without smiling. He started dipping the bread.

"I appreciate that. I don't think the others, or at least Tim Slade, would understand."

"Two slices or three?" he asked.

I held up two fingers.

Five minutes later, I was stuffing my mouth with Ian's golden brown French toast, drowning in a sea of maple syrup. "So, what's on your agenda today, Ian?" Not waiting for an answer, I added, "looks like a good day to curl up in front of the fireplace with a good book."

"Are you kidding?" McKenna forced a laugh, "that's not for me. This weather's perfect for photography, actually a shutterbug's dream."

"Yeah, I can see that." I nodded and shoved another bite into my mouth. "The first snow seems to always make for some spectacular scenes."

"How about you?" Ian sat down to his breakfast, one slice of French toast. "Are you going out?"

"Yeah," again I shared my breakfast with Malachi. As it turned out, he had a sweet tooth and loved maple syrup. "Yeah, I'll take my gun and poke around a little."

"Why pack a gun around if you don't intend to use it?"

"I don't know, habit I guess," I laughed and mopped the last puddle of syrup with a large chunk of French toast.

"Well, you don't have to pack a gun to be a man," Ian insisted. He also finished his single slice of toast.

"You're right," I agreed, fell silent for a couple of seconds, then added, "Why don't you stay away from Tim today?"

"I'll be okay," Ian took off and folded Samantha Rose's apron. "But there should be some terrific winter shots looking down that canyon. What did you call it?"

"Summit Canyon," I sighed and rinsed the residual syrup off my plate, "but stay away from Tim, okay? And please don't try to take any more photographs of his deer."

"Okay," Ian shrugged. "I really don't need any more. I have plenty, plus I have the spent shells."

"Of course, you can do what you like, Ian, but my recommendation is to drop the whole thing."

"I don't know," he said vaguely. "What Tim Slade did is plain wrong."

While Ian got dressed, I put away the dishes. I had to admit it was kind of nice having Ian around. Usually, I had to do all the cooking, as well as the dishes and cleaning.

By the time I pulled on my Sorel snow boots and found my Carhartt fleece-lined jacket, Ian had already departed. I called to Malachi, opened the door and stepped out onto the deck, tracking through four or five inches of new snow. It was not enough to make walking too difficult and certainly not enough to need snowshoes, but it was enough to flock the trees a fluffy white and pile-carpet the bare cold ground. By afternoon, barring more snow, it would probably all be gone. This time of year it was not unusual for the first snow to last on the ground no more than a half day.

Immediately, Malachi began frolicking in the snow. With him it was genetic. The only thing he loved more than frolicking in frozen snow was swimming in liquid water. For a minute, I watched him bury his nose in the snow, then roll on his back. I tossed him a couple of soft snowballs. Jumping high, he would catch them in his mouth where they would almost instantly disintegrate and melt.

When Malachi tired, I headed over to my aspen pole corral to feed, water and check on my Kentucky spotted saddle horse, Ike. Catching sight of me, he neighed loudly, probably not so much from the joy of seeing me, but more likely from anticipation of being fed.

Ike was a pleasure to ride. Like his close cousin, the Tennessee walker, he was a tall gaited horse. As opposed to the walkers, however, he had black and white spots, could lope and was fairly surefooted in the rugged terrain. After filling his feeder with a bucket of alfalfa cubes, I topped off his water trough, then decided against taking him out that morning. With the new snow, the rocks would be slick and with the ground covered the terrain would be uncertain. I did not want to risk fracturing a leg.

Turning from the corral, I located my .3006, called to Malachi and headed out into the forest, again vaguely in the direction of the pond. Why I always took my rifle, I had no idea. It really was habit, or maybe peer pressure. Like Ian had said, I certainly had no intention of using it.

As we hiked through the silent forest, over-hanging quaky limbs with golden leaves bending low with heavy snow would occasionally, and without warning, discharge their downy load. The snow slid off my orange cap and shoulders, some filtering past my shirt collar onto my bare back and shoulders. There it quickly melted from the body heat, leaving my skin and shirt damp.

Again, I started down the steep slope, my Sorel boots making almost perfect tracks in the carpet of unblemished snow. Malachi's paw prints looked a lot like and were about the same size as a cougar's, but there were subtle differences. I could see Malachi's claws embossed clearly in the snow; this was rare with a cougar. They had retractile claws. Also, a cougar's heel print was trilobar, whereas Malachi's was bilobar.

The going was slow, but I was in no hurry. I had the whole day to kill. Thankfully, after tomorrow it would all be over. We would pack up and leave the mountains. Ian would head back to Salt Lake City and Tim, Wally and me back to St. George. Tim and me back to our waiting surgical practice and Wally to his investment house.

Suddenly, I tripped, falling headfirst into a pillowy drift of snow. My head torpedoed downward through the snow, thudding against an unseen balsam log. The pain was immediate and excruciating. With my head spinning, hazy fog immediately seeped through my bony skull down the poorly lit corridors of my mind. I fought to remain conscious. Rolling over, I lay spread-eagle on the snow, tilting my head slightly downhill to encourage more blood flow. Concerned, Malachi was instantly at my side, licking my face.

Slowly, the cobwebs began to clear. Using my rifle for a crutch, I struggled back to my feet, then searched for the cause of my accident. It was obvious. I had tripped on a quaky stick submerged in the snow, no more than an inch below the surface. After rubbing my head for a few seconds, I started down the hill again, but decided I needed to be more careful. I could kill myself on this slope.

A half hour later we were back at the pond. Looking a bit like the crust of a banana cream pie, the banks were rimmed white with snow. A thin disc of ice, also sporting a mound of snow, floated in the center of the pond. Occasional concentric and enlarging dark water ripples heralded the presence of feeding trout. Last spring, I'd planted a couple hundred fingerling rainbows, now I silently hoped the pond was deep enough they wouldn't winter kill. A small inlet stream originating from a nearby spring hopefully would provide enough oxygen and food, but I was not absolutely sure. In the throes of winter, the ice would probably get at least two feet thick.

Sitting down on pillowed granite rock, I surveyed the feeding trout ripple rings. As I watched, they seem to increase in number and were now nearly constant. It was mesmerizing. Apparently the trout, sensing an early arrival of winter, were engaged in a feeding frenzy.

As I focused on the water, in my mind's eye I could almost picture the regal buck lowering his head for a drink. Damn, what a shame. To be spared by me twice, and an hour later to be butchered by Tim Slade and his Bushmaster assault rifle. It made me sick. What was wrong with Tim? That was more than the ancient tribal call of the hunt. It was downright morbid, sadistic, almost sinister. An assault rifle on a deer hunt!

To erase that grisly picture from my mind, I got up, called to Malachi and began working my way around the pond. I knew I really should make my way over to the top of Summit Canyon and help Tim retrieve his trophy deer, but I didn't want to. He didn't deserve my help and I didn't think I could stand looking at that dreadful carnage, the riddled carcass of the once magnificent buck.

By noon, to my surprise, it turned colder and started snowing again, certainly not typical for this time of year. The snow, however, was a light and grainy, and really did not add much to the existing depth, but on the other hand it prevented what snow that had already accumulated from melting. The little snow pellets stung my eyes, and my hands were cherry red and cold, made even colder from gripping the metal housing of the .3006 rifle.

It was not at all uncommon for these mountains to get their first snow in late October, but seldom was it a major storm. Usually, it dumped a few inches, almost always melting before the arrival of the season's second storm. I fully expected it to get warmer and this snow to be gone by late afternoon, but apparently that wasn't going to happen. Since I wasn't really hunting, just killing time, I called to Malachi and we headed back up the hill.

At the cabin, I toweled my gun dry and stowed it in my gun cabinet, then located my axe and started splitting logs. During the summer, I had chainsawed a large stack of quaky logs and another smaller pile of pine. I hauled and stacked them on the deck, but had not yet split them. Whole logs, I knew from experience, did not burn well, not enough surface area and acute angles. Since it was too early to start dinner, I decided to split logs. Balancing a quaky log in the upright position, I swung my axe downward—crack!

The physical exercise warmed me and about halfway through the stack I had to remove my Carhartt jacket. After I'd finished, I used the axe to shave off some kindling slivers, then carried the split logs and kindling inside, stacking both on the fireplace hearth.

Wadding up newspaper, I crisscrossed kindling on top of it and struck a match. Within minutes, I had a roaring fire and within an hour the cabin felt warmer. Since I was by myself, I discreetly made a small salad for lunch, gave Malachi some beef jerky, then settled down in front of the fireplace with my e-book. Malachi joined me and we snuggled down on a throw rug in front of the fire. Not a bad way to spend an afternoon, I decided, certainly better than killing innocent animals. I checked my wristwatch. Around six, I would start dinner, providing Ian hadn't returned before then to relieve me of that chore. Turning on my e-reader, I managed to read a full page and a half before falling asleep. The mixture of food, the fire and a lazy afternoon all combined to create a very potent sedative.

When I woke up a couple of hours later. I was still alone, no sign of Ian, Wally, or Tim. On a hunch, I checked the guest bedroom; both sets of snowshoes were gone. Apparently Ian had decided to go snowshoeing after all.

Walking outside on the deck with Malachi, I checked the weather. Though it was not presently snowing, the cloud cover looked even thicker and had dropped considerably lower. Darkness would come early tonight. More than likely the guys would also call it quits early. Back inside, I added a couple of more logs to the fire, then rather than opening my book again, I decided to go ahead and start dinner.

Tonight, we would have pork chops, green beans and mashed potatoes. Ian would have to settle for another one of his veggie steaks, as I had nothing similar that was pork flavored. The meal was not as ambitious as it sounded. The mashed potatoes were instant buttery Idahoan flakes straight from the foil pack and the green beans were right out of the can.

An hour later, I had the table set and dinner was ready, but still no sign of my companions. Again, I walked outside. It was mostly dark with just a hint of light making its way through the dark clouds on the far west horizon. Anxiously, I checked my wristwatch, almost seven o'clock. Where were they? This was not a night to be caught outdoors. Like a parent with an overdo teenager, I started to worry. I couldn't help myself.

Back inside the cabin, I picked up my e-book and tried to read, but couldn't concentrate. Sighing out loud, I sat the reader down and began pacing. Should I go out and look for them? Where would I start? Probably over at the Summit Canyon Overlook would be as good a place as any. Could I even find my way in the dark? With the solid cloud cover, there would be no moon or stars to use for direction or to light my path. Of course I would take a flashlight, but it gave only a narrow limited beam, which essentially resulted in tunnel vision. The terrain between here and the Overlook was rugged, peppered with granite rocks and strewn with almost impassible downfall. Traversing in the daylight was difficult enough, but at night it was next to impossible.

I continued to pace and check my watch. At eight o'clock, I gave up, put on my Carhartt coat and Sorel boots, found a flashlight, then with Malachi at my side headed outside. After making sure my well-stocked first aid kit was still in the pickup, we hopped into the cab. I fired up my Dodge Cummins diesel engine, turned on the headlights and headed down the steep hill from the cabin.

Within minutes, it started lightly snowing again, this time big lazy floating flakes. The headlights' bright beams seemed to both multiply and magnify their size. Concentrating on Dry Lakes Road, I tried to block the snow from my vision as I steered the pickup, heading mainly south. I knew this section of the road ran roughly parallel to the Overlook, but unfortunately never got closer than about a half of a mile. At the point where it had angled closest, I pulled the Dodge off the road and killed the engine. Buttoning up my jacket, I grabbed my flashlight, then called to Malachi and headed in a roughly westerly direction toward Summit Overlook. As I had predicted the flashlight did not provide much light. The huge snowflakes deflected and scattered the weak battery-generated photons, limiting my visibility to roughly six dimly lit feet, maybe less.

Stumbling on in the snow, I tripped over downed logs and half submerged rocks. It was difficult to maintain a constant direction with all the obstructions, and made even more difficult with no visible stars or landmarks for guidance. I soon became unsure of my direction, but nevertheless continued to wander for another thirty or forty minutes, not seeing any sign of my three friends. Furthermore, Malachi did not seem to pick up any meaningful scent either. Though we continued doggedly to search, we never actually found the Summit Canyon Overlook or any of our three hunters.

Meanwhile the temperature continued to plummet and the snow started coming down even harder. Finally, I had to give up. There was no way we were going to find them tonight, not in this evolving blizzard. Anyway, more than likely we'd missed them and they were already back at the cabin, warming themselves in front of the fire and wondering were we were.

Also, with weather conditions continuing to deteriorate, I felt we would be lucky to find our way back to the pickup and without Malachi's help I probably wouldn't have. With head down and flashlight trained on Malachi, I followed him. After a few minutes, I realized he was following my boot prints, even though the heavy snowfall was already beginning to cover them. As long as it didn't obliterate our scent, Malachi should still be able re-trace our path. I picked up my pace as much as possible, considering the jumbled and uncertain terrain.

After fifteen more minutes, I'd lost all trace of boot prints beneath the continuing onslaught of snow and had to rely solely on Malachi's nose. Panic started to rise in my throat and I fought for self-control. I took a deep breath. Slow down, I told myself, and trust Malachi. Take your time and don't thrash about blindly and get yourself killed.

Suddenly, there it was, the gray looming hulk of metal right in front of us. Breathing a sigh of relief, I hugged Malachi, then we scrambled into the cab. The trusty Cummins engine fired up on the first try and headed back for the cabin.

As we climbed the steep hill to the cabin, I put the Dodge in four-wheel drive, then anxiously looked for signs the others had returned. The lights in the cabin were on, but I couldn't remember if I'd left them on—probably I had. After parking the pickup, I hurried up the steps to the deck, then as I grabbed the doorknob, I smiled sheepishly at my runaway angst. Undoubtedly, Ian would have on Samantha Rose's apron, rewarming the dinner I'd cooked earlier. Wally would smile and ask me about my day. Tim would be pacing the floor, scowling at his wristwatch—not so much out of worry for me, but as a way of scolding me for being late and making them wait on dinner.

Throwing open the door, I rushed in. The fire had burned low; the orange coals were now crusted over with a gray ash. The ceramic yellow plates still sat undisturbed on the table and the pork chops, along with Ian's veggie steak, were still in the fry pan, untouched and now cold. And unfortunately, there still was no sign of Tim Slade, Wally Stroud, or Ian McKenna.

Once again, I checked my wristwatch, now a most disconcerting 9:35 p.m.! Serious disturbing questions seeped into my head and flooded my anxious mind. Where were they? What had happened to them? It was a wild night out there. Had they fallen over a cliff in darkness and lay somewhere maimed, or dead? Or, were they wandering about lost, numb and freezing? Or, had they already succumbed to the cold, frozen solid like downed quaky logs? Should I get back into the Dodge and head down the mountain to the Iron County Sheriff Department and report them missing? Probably, they would not qualify for missing person status yet, not until they had been gone for at least twenty-four hours. I looked at my watch again. How long had they been missing? I suppose I should start counting from when they didn't show up for dinner, not from when they left the cabin earlier this morning. Either way, it was doubtful the sheriff would, or could, mount a search in the middle of the night, not on a night like this! Reluctantly, I decided sit to tight and wait it out.

Sitting tight was just a figure of speech; actually I continued to pace aimlessly, frequently check my wristwatch, then pace some more. Finally, I re-fueled the fire, remembered to feed Malachi and Ike and paced some more. What else could I do? Right now it appeared there was nothing else I could do nothing.

At precisely 10:07 p.m. the door burst open and Tim Slade slouched in. Wind blasted and covered with snow, his eyebrows and moustache were now frozen white. With his coat, hat and jeans also similarly plastered, he bore more than a passing resemblance to *Yeti*, the abominable snowman. Tim closed the door and without greeting or comment he headed straight for the glowing fire, sloughing layers of snow as he went. Once at the fireplace, he unslung the rifle from his shoulder and stood it upright in the corner.

"Are you okay?" I quickly joined him at the fire.

He nodded and with teeth chattering mumbled, "j—just c—cold." Then he fell silent.

"Geez, Tim, where were you?"

"I took the four-wheeler over to Summit Overlook to get my deer." He took off his gloves and blew warm air onto his cold hands, then extended them over the fire.

"And?"

"You were right." Next he took of his coat and tossed it on the couch, scattering more snow, then inched even closer to the fire. "It wasn't there."

"That's a big surprise." I couldn't keep the sarcasm out of my voice.

He shrugged, but didn't answer.

"You see Ian or Wally in you travels today?" I asked, frowning.

"No, why?" He did not look me in the eye. "Aren't they back yet?"

"No!" I snapped, unable to hide my concern, then added, "it's after ten and Ian's never late."

"Wally's probably okay," Slade mumbled, still facing the fire, his back toward me, "But this one is on you. You should have never brought that friggin' gay greenhorn up here."

# 5

Tim finally turned away from the fire and locked eyes with me.

For the moment, I was rendered speechless. And even though my tongue refused to move, my mind was working overtime. Was I really responsible? Was he telling me everything? Did he know more than he was saying? Was it possible he had something to do with Ian and Wally's extreme tardiness? Had something bad happened?

Finally I blurted, "He's not gay, he's married."

"That don't mean nothin'."

"Are you sure?" I finally mumbled.

"Yeah, I'm sure, Coop. He's gay." Tim walked over to the kitchen and started eyeing the food.

"No!" I snapped. "Are you sure you never saw Ian and Wally."

"Jesus, Coop, yes, I'm sure," Tim bristled. "I would think I would know if I had seen them."

"Which way did you go?"

"The only way you can with a four-wheeler. Down Dry Lakes Road for a couple of miles, then I turned off and headed due west till I got to the Overlook."

"How did you get a four-wheeler through all that downfall?" I challenged, remembering Malachi's and my failed attempt of a couple of hours ago in the darkness and snowstorm.

"Why the twenty questions, Coop?" he snapped back. "Someone bulldozed a path over there last summer. You just have to know where it is."

"And you never saw Ian or Wally? No boot tracks in the snow?"

"No!" Slade barked. "Enough questions. Enough of the accusations!"

"You take the Bushmaster?" I persisted, even though I could plainly see it where he'd just set it in the corner next to the fireplace.

"Jesus, Coop, there's no law against that." He stubbornly thrust his chin forward. "I could take it into Wells Fargo Bank if I wanted to."

"And no sign of Ian and Wally?" I asked for the fourth time.

"No!" he slammed his palm down on the kitchen counter. "Why are you grilling me?"

"When Ian left this morning, he said he was headed over to the Summit Overlook to take pictures."

"Well, so? It's a big area and the greenhorn got lost."

"Don't you get it?" My voice also rose an octave. "Getting lost on a night like this could very well mean death!"

"I didn't friggin' tell him to go out and wander in the wilderness." Tim got in my face. "You're the one who invited him. You're the one that let him run around unsupervised."

I started to say something, then bit my tongue. Tim was right about that. I was not totally blameless in this—whatever this turned out to be. It was more than a little irresponsible of me to assume Ian had sufficient wilderness skills for these mountains, particularly on a night like this. I had not even taken the time to show him the lay of the land, point out pertinent landmarks, or check to see if he had mastered even the basic Boy Scout fundamentals of survival. In retrospect, by his demeanor and the way he dressed, he probably didn't possess any of those skills. Rather, he seemed like someone who would function well in City Creek Mall, but probably not so good in the Ashdown Gorge Wilderness during a blizzard.

Wally, on the other hand, I knew did posses those skills. Like Tim and me, he'd grown up in southern Utah and had spent a good deal of time outdoors hunting, fishing, camping and enjoying the wilderness. I silently hoped Ian was with him. If he was, he might have a fair chance, even on a night like tonight. But I had no way of knowing if they were together. When they left this morning, they had headed out in opposite directions. Ian had mention that he and Wally might go snowshoeing. The overriding question, had Wally returned to pick up Ian? But hadn't I encouraged Ian to try them by himself? As far as I knew we had two separate missing men and one with no survival skills.

Grabbing my fleece-lined jacket, I headed for the door with Malachi at my heels. "They're in trouble!" I shouted at Slade. "We need to go look for them."

"Slow down, Coop, use your head," Tim quickly scooted his linebacker body over to block my exit. "It's a friggin' blizzard out there. Like you said, this is the kind of night that can kill you."

"But, if we wait till morning," I sidestepped him, "the snow will cover up any sign, like their boot or snowshoe prints." I wanted to add, and or, any sign of struggle or spilled blood, but once again I held my tongue.

"Believe me, the snow's already covered them," Tim argued. "If they're still alive, they'll make new tracks in the morning."

"Then what do you suggest?" I snapped.

"Hell, we've got no choice; we have to wait till morning," Tim said firmly. "But you could call the Sheriff's Department and alert them. We'll probably need Search and Rescue first thing tomorrow."

"There no cell service up here," I growled. "You know that."

"Oh, yeah. Well, there's no way you can drive down the mountain tonight." Tim removed his orange hunting vest. "We have to wait till tomorrow." He hung up the vest on a coat peg and yawned. "I'm going to get some sleep."

In stunned silence, I watched Tim retrieve the Bushmaster, grab two cold pork chops from the fry pan, take a bite from one of them, then without another word he headed toward our bedroom, the pork chops in one hand and the rifle in the other. Not wanting to be around Tim at that moment, I stayed in the kitchen. Somehow, I managed to choke down half of Ian's cold veggie steak and gave the remaining two pork chops to Malachi.

With Malachi following, I started for the bedroom, then abruptly stopped. I did not feel like sleeping in the same room as Tim Slade, not tonight, and I sincerely doubted Wally and Ian would be back. Turning on my heel, I headed straight for their bedroom.

As I undressed, I again thought about the snowshoes. Undoubtedly, Wally had returned and he and Ian had set off together. Whether it was true or not, I had no way of knowing, but it did make me feel a little better. At least with that scenario both of them had some means to maneuver in the deep snow. If they hunkered down tonight, perhaps dug a snow cave, the snowshoes would give them the tools, no matter how deep the snow, to mush back to the cabin in the morning.

Needless to say, I did not sleep a wink; instead I paced, occasionally flopped down on the bed, checked my watch, then got up and paced some more. Sometimes, I ventured outside to check the weather. About three in the morning, it quit snowing and by four o'clock I noted a few stars winking through the rapidly fleeing clouds. By five o'clock, the thermometer had plummeted to a very chilly sixteen degrees. Retrieving my yardstick from the closet, Malachi and I measured over a foot of new snowfall on the deck. It would make searching for Ian and Wally difficult at best. Now there was enough snow to make walking difficult, even exhausting, but with no real base it might not be enough for cross country skis or snowmobiles. Snowshoes should work fine.

I wondered how Ike would do in the snow--not good, but probably better than me. His legs were longer and he had four-wheel (foot) drive. Footing, however, could be treacherous, but if I could find that bulldozed trail Tim mentioned, it shouldn't be too bad. Unfortunately, there were no great options; I decided I would saddle up Ike at daylight and give it a try.

However, most of the night I spent worrying about Ian, even more than Wally. To be honest, I didn't really know Ian very well. Again I wondered if he had any wilderness survival training? I doubted it. He looked more like the type who might have some proficiency in surviving Black Friday, the chaotic shopping day after Thanksgiving. Would he even know the basics of cold weather survival? Shelter, water and food, and in that order. Would he realize he needed to start planning and constructing a shelter way before nightfall? It was almost impossible to build adequate shelter after dark. Water, food and navigation could easily wait until the next day, because of course, they would be pointless if one did not survive the night.

I tried not to think about it, but in my mind's eye I could see Ian crouched down in a frozen meadow, slowly freezing to death. Even worse, briefly I pictured him bloodied, wounded (looking a lot like the buck) and unable to move or find shelter. Those macabre visions made me shudder, so instead I tried to concentrate on tomorrow, how to organize my day. First we would have to alert the authorities and help them organize their search. Probably, we'd start searching over at the Summit Overlook. I knew that was where Ian was headed, but I had no idea where Wally went yesterday. So after the Overlook there would be a lot of other ground to cover—actually over seven thousand acres of rugged forested wilderness. It would take months to cover it all.

Somehow I made it through the night by pacing, planning and checking my wristwatch every fifteen minutes.

Fortunately, Tim and I had taken a long weekend off from work for the hunt. We both had Monday off, but we both were due back at work on Tuesday. Furthermore, I had to start taking hospital call on Tuesday morning, covering both the E.R. and hospitalized urology patients. My call rotation was supposed to start on Monday, eight in the morning, but I had begged Dr. Keyes, a non-hunter, to take that day. Reluctantly, he had agreed, but I had to trade a whole weekend in return, a Friday, Saturday and Sunday in the future for one Monday. Some trade! That's what happens when you are desperate.

Finally at six o'clock, trying to anticipate everything, I got up and fed and watered Ike, so he'd be ready to go at the crack of dawn. Back in the cabin, I put a pot of coffee on to perk, scrambled some eggs in the fry pan, then burnt and buttered four slices of toast. I was not hungry, but I knew Tim would be, and we did need fuel for the day ahead, which I suspected would be arduous at best. By then, to the far east, a promising smudge of orange appeared on the blackened sky. At last, it was time. Quickly, I set the table, then headed into the bedroom to wake up Slade.

He was sound asleep, snoring deeply like a man with a clear con-science or at least an untroubled conscience. That bothered me. He seemed to have little or no concern for Ian and Wally. Sure he and Ian had clashed and were on opposite ends of the political and religious spectrum, but I thought Tim would have more concern for the welfare of another human being; after all he was a doctor. Did their petty differences allow Tim to simply write Ian off? Did Tim's lack of concern in someway incriminate him? Or simply reflect his moral character, or lack thereof? Certainly, it would not be enough to convict him in a court of law, but I must admit I found his attitude most disconcerting.

"Tim! Tim!" I shook him.

"Huh?" Instinctively, he pushed my hand away and rolled on his side.

I shook him again. "Come on, Tim, get up. We've got to get going."

He grunted and cracked a bleary eye. "Going? Going where?"

"We need go start looking for Ian and Wally, and alert Search and Rescue."

Groaning, he sat up and swung his feet to the floor. "How about some breakfast first? We didn't have any dinner last night, you know, and I'm starving."

I wanted to say you had two pork chops, but I bit my tongue. "Breakfast is on the table," then I impatiently added, "come on, get up. Let's get going."

As Tim sat down at the table, I poured the coffee, then sat down opposite him. I had to force myself to eat. The eggs were over-cooked and tasteless, and the toast tasted and smelled of charcoal, but the coffee was acceptable. It warmed and helped calm me.

"So, how do you want to do this?" Tim Slade asked. It still amazed me how he managed to force words out around a huge bolus of food.

"I thought we should split up." I cupped my hands around the warm mug. "You head on down the mountain and get hold of the sheriff and help organize the Search and Rescue. I'll saddle up Ike and head out see if I can find anything."

Slade scooped some scrambled eggs onto the toast. When he tried to fold it, the toast snapped like a brittle twig. Undeterred, he made a crusty blackened sandwich out of it. "Makes more sense for me to go look for the Professor and Wally." He paused for a bite. "You don't even know where that dozed trail is."

"I'll find it." I set my jaw. There was no way I was going to let go him hunt for Ian. That was a bit like letting the prisoners out to help find the escapee. I knew I was being a bit unfair, if not blatantly presumptuous, but I did not care.

"Whatever." Slade washed down the dry sandwich with a draught of coffee. "You just as well take the four-wheeler. Covers ground faster."

"Nah," I shook my head. "It can't go where a horse can go. I'll stick with Ike."

But if the truth be told, I didn't like four-wheelers. They were noisy, intrusive and smelly machines. No, I much preferred the clip-clop of a horse to the roar of a combustion engine.

"Suit yourself," Slade shrugged. He pushed his plate aside and got up, but made no effort to take his plate to the sink. "Where do you want Search and Rescue to start?"

"Same place I'm going to start," I snapped. "Over at the Summit Overlook."

Without another word, Tim got up, grabbed his hat and coat, then opened the door, slamming it behind him. More than likely I'd ticked him off, but I didn't really care. I took the rest of my breakfast, actually I had eaten very little and even Malachi didn't want it, and stuffed it in a plastic baggie. Cold scrambled egg and burnt toast would be my lunch. After gathering up the dishes, I put them in the sink to soak, then grabbed my hat and coat. At the last minute, I remembered to change my snow boots for cowboy boots, then called to Malachi and walked out the door.

As we stepped out onto the deck the sun was just cresting Brian Head Peak, slinging its eye-blinding photons toward the frozen earth. The angle of the rays was so acute, so oblique, and the sky so clear, I could almost see individual photons as they zipped laterally through the frosted air, impacting the snow on the cabin deck. When I exhaled the plume of water vapor instantly turned to fog. It was one of those perfect winter mornings that almost made you forget how terribly wrong this day really was. I exhaled a frozen cloud again, then stepped off the deck back into predawn shadows. For the next few minutes, the photons would zip over my head until the rising sun had risen sufficiently to change their angle of fire.

52

As Ike finished the last of his alfalfa cubes, I hurriedly brushed and curried him, then lugged my prized Dan Jensen saddle from the utility shed. Just the smell of leather and saddle soap brought back a flood of memories. Samantha Rose had given me this saddle as a birthday present shortly after I'd lost my father's saddle in a tack shed arson-fire.

With my mind elsewhere, I saddled and bridled Ike, then with Malachi leading we headed down the steep slope from the cabin, following Tim Slade's pickup tire tracks. At the junction with Dry Lakes Road, Tim's tracks turned left, heading down the mountain. I reined Ike to the right, up a gentle incline of the quaking aspen-lined road. In this direction, the snow was untracked and undisturbed. Once again, wisps of snow sprinkled down as overhanging leaves and boughs unloaded their white burden. Other than that it was a peaceful morning, almost eerily silent. Even the clomp of Ike's steel-shodded hooves was muffled by the twelve-inches of new snow. Fortunately, Ike was having no trouble at all with the snow, but of course this was on a graded and graveled road. It might be a different once we headed into the backcountry.

However, the pace on a horse was slow, maddeningly slow. Also, Malachi was struggling as the snow came up to his chest. Quickly he learned to follow behind, using the same trail Ike was breaking. I tried to channel my thoughts and plan my upcoming search, and not to think of the grim possibilities: Ian and Wally lying in the snow, maimed, or injured, or near death from hypothermia. Again I wondered if they were together, or were they missing separately? But I had to admit Tim was right about one thing, I could have covered more ground and faster on his four-wheeler.

It took us just over an hour to reach the point where I figured Dry Lakes Road angled as close to the Overlook as it would get. My tire tracks and boot prints from last night were completely covered, but where I turned the Dodge around I did notice where my tires had crushed an occasional two-foot blue sage. This told me I was in the right place.

Patiently, we worked the area in an ever-widening circle, looking for any sign of the bulldozed track Tim claimed ran from Dry Lakes Road to the Overlook. If I could find it, it would certainly make it easier and less treacherous for Ike, Malachi and ultimately me. Just as I was about to give up I noticed two oddly parallel lines of boulders and downed logs, roughly ten to twelve feet apart and heading roughly in the direction of the Overlook. I could almost imagine someone had taken a D9-Cat and bladed through the forest, leaving the boulders and logs in its wake. Undoubtedly, this was

Tim's trail and I must admit I was surprised. I thought I knew this country every bit as good as Tim, but I was totally unaware of this bladed track. It must be new, probably from last summer. Silently, I hoped it did not herald a new mountain subdivision planned for the Overlook. Sure, it would be a fantastic view, but it would be a travesty, a damn shame to place cabins over there.

I reined Ike onto the dozed track, heading roughly west. Without question, the going was certainly easier than it was last night when I was trying to fight my way though the almost impenetrable forest, jumbled downfall and undergrowth. By the time we reached the Overlook, the sun had risen to about forty-five degrees, halfway to zenith. Feeling its warmth beating down on my shoulders, I noted the last night's snowfall had already started to melt. I reigned in Ike right at the Overlook and took a moment to appreciate the vast panorama. From this height, nine and a half thousand feet, I could see all the way down to the valley floor, some four thousand feet lower and three miles away as the crow flies, but about a dozen miles if you used the meandering Dry Lakes Road. Going straight down, however, was impossible, unless you could fly. Even on foot, it was impassible without rappelling equipment and sufficient mountaineering skills.

Summit Canyon itself was an impressive chasm. Carved by wind and water, primarily into up-thrust gray granite, it also possessed distinctive splashes of crimson, signifying the eons of erosion had also exposed some iron-rich sedimentary rock. Now, all the gunmetal gray cliffs, granite buttresses, crimson pillars and ribbony canyon walls were flocked white with fresh snow. Almost like a layer cake, a series of terraces descended downward, giant step by giant step, to the distant valley floor. Ian McKenna was certainly right about one thing; it would make for fantastic photography.

Sighing to myself, I turned back to the task at hand. Nudging, then reining Ike to the left, we began systematically searching the area close to the Overlook. Beginning right at the rim, we worked slowly to the east and back from the edge in a zigzag pattern. Now, Malachi was again out front and leading with his nose. As the sun climbed higher, so did the ambient temperature and the snow began melting more rapidly. Soon what remained tended to be in the shaded areas and was becoming pretty well-tracked by small rodents and other mammals. From atop Ike, I noted multiple deer tracks, rabbit and squirrel trails and even thought I spotted the print of a cougar.

Suddenly, Ike's ears shot forward. He hesitated, then started slowly backing up. Simultaneously, Malachi bolted forward, nose inches from the ground; obviously he was on a scent. I stopped Ike from retreating, then with the heels of my boots coaxed him forward again. As we busted through a thicket, I immediately spied Malachi ahead, circling and sniffing, then I spied what had caught his interest and what had spooked Ike.

There was blood everywhere! It was captured in crystalline ice stipules and splashed across a large patch of shade-protected snow. It was a shocking red contrasted on a bed of Artic white snow and looked like some kind of bizarre Rorschach pattern. My pulse quickened and at the same time my sense of dread soared. Would I find a bullet riddled Ian McKenna, or Wally Stroud, or both in the next thicket of scrub oak? I steeled myself, drew a deep breath and nudged a still-reluctant Ike forward. Malachi had already disappeared into the next thicket.

As we inched forward, I noticed snatches of fur everywhere. It almost looked like a sable fur coat had been fed through a Flotron leaf and branch shredder. Once again, Ike tried to turn back, but I forced him further into the thicket.

Now I could see bones and a carcass! Or what was left of it. Not only was it devoid of internal organs, but every muscle fiber had been stripped from the skeleton, leaving only the occasional flapping strap of a severed tendon still attached to its bone. Even the joints had been disarticulated and the skull was crushed. The cranial vault was empty; the convoluted soft brain tissue had also been removed.

It was a skull I recognized! Even with all the facial muscle, hair and soft tissue were gone, and the cranium smashed, the distinctive rack of horns remained, four points on one side, five on the other.

There was only one animal I knew who could generate this kind of mayhem, this kind of carnage. This was not the work of a man, even a crazed man, but of a cougar, a Rocky Mountain lion! With mixed emotions, I realized I had not found the body Ian McKenna or Wally Stroud, but the remains of my majestic deer, Tim Slade's trophy deer. The one he'd hung in the tree, thinking he'd return the next day, yesterday, on the four-wheeler to retrieve.

I shook my head in disgust. Sure, I was happy it was not Ian or Wally, but nevertheless this was a damn shame. Actually, it was a travesty. The magnificent animal I had spared ended up here, like this. Sure, I knew this was nature's way and nature was violent, and cougars were carnivores, but Tim's Bushmaster was no act of nature. At least if it had just been the cougar, the buck would've had a fighting chance. After all, he had successfully evaded cougars for at least five years now, maybe more. But what chance did he have against an assault rifle?

Sickened, I called to Malachi and turned Ike around. Pensively we exited the thicket to continue our search. I resumed my previous pattern of zigzagging, now roughly in a north by northeast direction.

Late October in the mountains often has wild temperature fluctuations from very mild to very cold. Likewise, now the cold of last night had been replaced by surprising warmth. The twelve inches of snowfall from yesterday had shrunk to no more than a couple of inches in the shade and none out in the open areas. In a way, I was sorry to see it go. Yes, deep snow made travel harder, but in some ways it was helpful. It was easier to spot red blood on a white background and likewise, it was easier to identify snowshoe or boot tracks embossed in the snow. And even though it was quite difficult to navigate in snow, it could become even more difficult once the snow melted. There was nothing worse than slogging through sticky clay mud.

Leaning over in the saddle with my head down, I continued to search for another hour. Nothing. Needless to say, I was getting discouraged. I checked my watch. It was about time to take Tim's bulldozed track back to Dry Lakes Road and rendezvous, hopefully, with the Search and Rescue Unit from Cedar City.

Suddenly, off my left, at the base of a blue spruce, on the northwest side and still protected from the sun, something caught my eye. At the same moment, Malachi caught the scent and dashed over. With the snow rapidly disappearing it was it was hard to say for certain, but it sure looked like the crisscross pattern of snowshoe print. The snow was slushy, almost watery, and quickly losing any kind of pattern. Dismounting, I kneeled down for a closer look. If I used my imagination, I could still make out the signature grid pattern of a snowshoe. After tying Ike to a sturdy quaky, Malachi and I followed the fast-fading prints as best we could on foot.

The tracks continued on past the spruce tree, then I lost them as they crossed an open area, now flooded in warm sunshine. After searching for a few seconds, Malachi picked them up on the other side of the clearing. They headed straight for a dense grove of balsam and then finally stopped underneath the circular outstretched branches of a twenty-foot mature tree. The branches hung low, almost touching the ground, creating kind of a hollow. It would be a great place for concealment, or protection from the weather, forming almost a perfect umbrella tent. Still following his nose, Malachi darted under the branches. To follow him, I had to kneel down to squeeze under them. Here the snow was tracked and matted down with boot prints, like someone had taken off the snowshoes and rested here. Also, I noted the concave rounded imprint from a body, created from either siting or lying down or both, in the snow.

Calling to Malachi, I started to move on, looking for tracks exiting this copse of balsam trees. Malachi, however, wouldn't budge and started scratching. As I turned back to him, something caught my eye. Nudging Malachi aside, I carefully scraped away a shallow carpet of fallen snow from the underlying cones and pine needles.

And there it was! Another splotch of shocking red captured by, and highlighted in the ivory white snow.

# 6

Of course it was blood! But whose blood? Animal? Human? If human, which human? Ian? Or Wally? Unlike the previous bloody site, there were no other obvious clues, like a skull or fur, to indicate this might be an animal.

And furthermore, those were definitely human boot and snowshoe prints, so I could only surmise the blood was human. But again, which human? I knew of only three possible people in this area yesterday, Ian, Wally and Tim, and I very much doubted it was Tim's. Wait a minute! Slow down! I'd better not jump to conclusions. It was certainly possible there were others in the area as well; after all it was opening weekend of the very popular Utah deer hunt. And if I was being strictly objective, it was also possible it was Tim's. He could have cut himself cleaning the deer, even though last night I didn't see a laceration. But on the other hand, I wasn't really looking either.

It might be helpful, even critical to get a sample of that blood. I could have Hank Bettis (English - a variant of Betts), my pathologist friend at Dixie Medical Center, do antigen blood typing and DNA analysis. That way perhaps I could find out for sure whose blood it was.

Calling to Malachi, I finally coaxed him to leave. I retraced my steps, crawling back under the low-lying limbs and eventually back to Ike. From the canvas saddlebags, I fished around until I found the baggie containing my egg and toast lunch. One more time, I tried to eat the rubbery egg and burnt toast, but gagged, then tried feeding it to Malachi. When he refused, I ended up dumping it on the ground, while seriously hoping it would not harm any of the indigenous fauna or flora. After stuffing the baggie in the front pocket of my Levi's, I whistled to Malachi and we wriggled our way back under the balsam boughs.

Cupping my hands like the clamshell jaws of a river dredge, I then scooped up the bloodstained snow, transferring it into the plastic baggie. After resealing the baggie, we headed back to Ike where I deposited the specimen safely into my saddlebag, then swung back up into the saddle.

Shielding my eyes, I checked the sun's position, then my wristwatch. It was almost eleven thirty, time to head on back to Dry Lakes Road. In my mind, I figured it would take Tim till about noon to mobilize the Sheriff's

Department and Iron County Search and Rescue, then get them up the mountain. Hopefully, about right now they were staging on Dry Lakes Road.

Following Malachi, we retraced our path back to Summit Overlook. This time we easily found the dozed trail and headed due east. By now, not only was the snow mostly gone, but the ground had also thawed, allowing Ike's hooves and Malachi's paws to sink deep into the wet sticky mud. Fortunately, I did not have to walk it.

It was shortly after noon when we arrived back at Dry Lakes Road. To my dismay, nobody was there! Surely Tim had enough time to get down the mountain and on to Cedar City, and surely Search and Rescue had adequate time to assemble and return. After all, they were known for their fast response. So, why were they not here? Had Tim met with trouble getting down the mountain? Or, maybe for some unknown reason Search and Rescue took longer than usual to get organized. Swinging down from the saddle, I decided to wait. Though I was very worried about my friends, I forced myself to be patient. Tim and Search and Rescue would surely be here any minute.

An hour later, they still had not arrived and my patience was growing thin. Once again I got up and began pacing. We were wasting precious daylight hours. What should I do? Should I continue to wait? Should I strike out on my own once again and continue to look for Ian and Wally? Or, should I go back to the cabin, fire up the Dodge and go looking for Tim and Iron County Search and Rescue? Again, I glanced up at the sun, already starting its downward arc. This time of year darkness came early, particularly in the mountains. Our best hope of finding Ian and Wally alive would be today. With the low-pressure front now passed, probably currently over Colorado, and the cloud cover gone, temperatures tonight would undoubtedly plummet. It had dropped down to sixteen degrees last night; it would surely get into the low teens, if not the single digits, tonight. I knew Wally and Ian were not prepared to stay outdoors in those extreme temperatures. Sighing out loud, I once again looked at my wristwatch, then decided to give them another fifteen minutes.

The allotted time passed and still there was no sign of the Iron County Sheriff and no Search and Rescue. Finally, I made up my mind; I go would check on Tim and the Search and Rescue squad. By myself, I could cover very little ground. I needed help, a lot of help.

Remounting Ike, I nudged him with my heels into his trademark seventeen-mile-per-hour walk for which his breed was famous. Poor Malachi had to run to keep up. As Ike glided down the road, clumps of mud flipped up from his hooves, like mud from rear tires of a truck with no flaps. This time instead of taking an hour, we were back at the cabin in thirty-five minutes. Hurriedly, I unsaddled, curried and grained Ike, then rushed into the cabin. There was nothing from Tim, no note and no indication he had returned all day. His Bushmaster and overnight bag were still untouched in the bedroom.

After changing my cowboy boots for snow boots, I located my keys and with Malachi rushed back outside and scrambled up into the Dodge. I coaxed the Cummins engine back to life (it was still cold from last night), then we started down the steep hill from the cabin and onto Dry Lakes Road. From here, the road zigzagged steeply down the mountain with multiple "S" and some hairpin turns. Fortunately, the Dodge did have mud flaps, but nevertheless mud splatter still managed to get everywhere, including the windshield. I turned on the wipers, which only managed to smear and streak it.

Peering between the curvilinear mud streaks, I went as fast as I dared. On the short straightaways, I punched down on the accelerator, then stomped on the brakes when I approached a curve. Within five minutes, I had nearly slid off the road into twenty-foot ravine and also nearly hit a roadside fir tree. Deciding the better part of valor was prudence, I eased off on the gas feed and finally remembered to flip on the switch for the four-wheel drive. Obviously, that helped considerably.

Up ahead and about halfway down the mountain, there was a particularly acute descent, which ended in a couple of "S" curves. Here the gravel had been graded, or eroded, away leaving an exposed road base of slick purple clay. As I approached, I slowed the Dodge down, shifted into low and inched forward down the steep decline. With my eyes glued to the road, I rounded the first sharp turn. Out of the corner of my eye, something caught my attention. The roadside sagebrush had been tire crushed. Initially, I shrugged it off and continued on. This was a bad place to stop. A couple seconds later, I thought better of it and carefully applied the brakes. Coming to a complete stop, I shifted into park and killed the engine. As soon as I opened the door, Malachi flew out of the truck and sprinted back up the hill. Slipping and sliding, I followed as fast as I could.

When I got back up to the top of the hairpin turn, it was instantly obvious what had crushed the roadside sagebrush. Tim's Ford pickup rested some forty feet below me. Apparently, after running over the sagebrush, the truck had slipped off the road, then skidded down to the bottom of the forty-foot ravine, coming to rest in a thicket of blazing red maples. With the truck pointed down the hill and away from me, I could not see what damage the front end had sustained, but I could see the hood was up and driver-side door had apparently sprung open.

Where was Tim? Was he still inside the truck? Was he hurt? Maybe even unconscious? With Malachi leading the way, we slid down the hill, varnishing my Levi's with a layer of tacky purple clay. By the time I got to the pickup, Malachi was already circling and sniffing the truck. I took a deep breath and peeked in the open driver-side door.

Inside Tim was lying prone across the center console, head and chest resting on the passenger seat!

Was he dead? Oh, God, I hoped not!

As I reached out to touch him, he flinched and I nearly jumped out of my snow boots. Slowly, he twisted around and sat up, holding an adjustable wrench in his right hand.

"Oh, Coop! I'm glad you're here."

"Are you okay?" I blurted as I rapidly performed a visual physical exam; after all I was a doctor. In just a matter of a couple of seconds, I noted the windshield was intact and there was no bloodstain on it, or on the dashboard. I eyeballed Tim again, more slowly this time. There were no open wounds, no blood, no overt bruising and no cranial lacerations or goose eggs.

"Huh?" He climbed out of the truck still holding wrench. "Oh—yeah, I'm okay. I just slid off the road and now I can't get this bucket of bolts started."

"What?" I almost screamed.

He shrugged. "It won't start. I should've got a Dodge."

"You mean," I could barely control myself, "you mean you've spent all morning here, trying to get this truck started!"

"Well, yes. What else could I do?"

"For starters, you could have hiked down Dry Lakes Road to the highway, it can't be more than two or three miles, then hitchhiked into town."

"Yeah, well," he said defensively, "it was a judgment call. I thought it would be faster if I could get the truck started."

"Even if you did get it started, how were you planning on getting it back onto the road?" I demanded.

"I have four-wheel drive."

"Geez, Tim!" Now I was incredulous. "Do you honestly think you could just shove it in four-wheel drive and back up," I paused and pointed toward the steep slope, "up that hill and back onto the road?"

"Well, it does pretty good in rugged terrain—"

"—Don't you realize," I cut him off, "we have two men missing, probably in very bad shape, and every minute counts!"

He glared at me, but didn't answer. Instead, he walked around to the engine and leaned over the fender with his wrench.

"Forget that, Tim!" I snapped. "Come on, let's get in my pickup and go on to Cedar City. While I talk to the sheriff and Search and Rescue, you can arrange to have your pickup towed."

He hesitated.

I shook my head in frustration, called to Malachi and struggled back up the almost vertical hill. As I opened the door to let in Malachi, Tim opened the passenger door and slid onto the bench seat. Still steamed, I fired up the Dodge and once again started down Dry Lakes Road. At first Tim said nothing, but I didn't care. At this moment, I didn't feel like talking to him or anyone else. In lieu of conversation, I concentrated on getting the truck down that treacherous stretch of road. When the road finally leveled out, the silence rapidly morphed from being mildly uncomfortable to moderately painful. Nevertheless, I still focused on the road; I was not going to speak first.

"Can't you put him in the back?" Tim finally broke the silence.

"What?" I asked without looking at him. "Who?"

"The dog. Can't you put him in the back, in the cargo bay, like most people do?"

"Why?" I gritted my teeth.

"He's tracking mud everywhere, all over my clothes."

I glanced over. Sure enough, Malachi had soiled almost everything with his muddy paws including the bench seat, the backrest, the dashboard, Tim's jeans and even the front of his flannel shirt. I wanted to say, "I'll let you get in the back if you want, but Malachi stays up here."

What I did say, however, was, "Malachi never rides in the back. The one time I tried it, he jumped out. Fortunately, I wasn't going very fast and he wasn't hurt."

"You're not going very fast now."

"He stays!"

After that sharp exchange, the silence again thickened and eventually ossified like prehistoric fossils or petrified wood. We rode the rest of the way to Cedar City in this stony silence. As I promised, I let Tim off at the Ford dealership, so he could arrange to get his truck towed, then I headed over to the sheriff department.

The Iron County Sheriff Department was located on the far end of town on Main Street, close to the north freeway interchange. Along with the Search and Rescue and the Iron County Prison, the sheriff department was also housed in a single story building constructed of slate gray brick and exposed teal metal girders. The rambling complex had three distinct pods, the prison, the sheriff's department and Search and Rescue. I parked in public parking in front of the sheriff's section.

After instructing Malachi to stay in the truck, I entered that pod. At the reception desk, I stated my business and asked to see the sheriff. The red haired bespectacled receptionist nodded and disappeared. A minute later she returned and led me back to Sheriff Axel Klein's (obviously German— meaning small) office.

At first glance, Sheriff Klein's given name was clearly an oxymoron. He was anything but small; in fact he was huge and not just in girth. Towering over me at least six foot four, maybe five, he weighed close to three hundred pounds. Though he had some body fat, he was certainly not grossly obese and looked like he could still walk out on the gridiron and play defensive tackle for the local college football squad.

"Hi," he thrust a huge paw forward, "I'm Sheriff Klein, but most people call me Tiny."

"Hi," my hand got lost in his, "I'm Doctor Lawrence Cooper, but most people call me Coop."

"Well, what can I do for you, Coop?" He withdrew his hand and sat down behind his surprisingly small oak desk. Or, maybe it just looked small because he was so big.

I pulled up a chair and sat down opposite him. "I've got a lost deer hunter, actually two."

"Huh? Why don't you fill in the details?" He rested his elbows on his immaculate desk. Unlike my desk, there was no clutter, no folders, no flyers and no fast food wrappers. I couldn't help but wonder if he did any work, or if he was just a figurehead. Somehow I had trouble trusting anyone with a desk that neat.

"Well," I paused, trying to figure out where to start, "I have a cabin up in the Brian Head area, actually up Dry Lakes Road."

Sheriff Klein nodded. "I know the area."

"Anyway, there were four of us hunting this past weekend," I paused again and corrected myself. "Actually, there were only three hunters and one photographer."

"So, the photographer was not hunting?"

I nodded. "And it is he and one of the hunters, uh men, who are missing. The photographer was—" I quickly corrected myself from past to present tense, "is from Salt Lake City and is not familiar with the area."

"How about the other one? The missing hunter?"

"He's from St. George," I replied, "and has hunted that area several times."

"How long have they been missing?"

"Since sometime yesterday. They didn't show up for dinner last night."

"Were they together?"

"I don't know," I admitted. "They weren't when they left the cabin."

Tiny looked at me sharply. "How come it took you so long to report it?"

"Well," I hesitated, "well, there's no cell phone service up there and as you know we had a blizzard last night. I did send the other hunter down here the first thing this morning, while I continued to search, but he didn't make it."

"Didn't make it?" Tiny frowned and locked eyes with me.

"His truck slid off the road. He got stranded." I hated making excuses for Tim, but I wasn't ready to voice my suspicions yet. "When Search and Rescue didn't show up by noon today, I stopped my solo search and headed back. About halfway down Dry Lakes Road, I found Tim. His truck had slid off a steep section of the road. As soon as we got into Cedar City, I headed straight here."

"Tim?"

"Tim Slade, the other hunter, also from St. George. Ian McKenna is the photographer who is lost and Wallace Stroud is the lost hunter."

Tiny paused for a second and wrote this down. "Yeah, it was a wild night up there last night," he agreed. "Did this Stroud fellow, or McKenna have any wilderness training?"

"Stroud did," I said, then shook my head. "But I don't think McKenna did. He was—uh—is pretty much of a greenhorn."

"And you let him wander around in the mountains by himself—in this weather?" Sheriff Klein looked incredulous.

I gulped and wanted to say I didn't think the mountain and wilderness were the problem, that Tim Slade was the problem, but I bit my tongue. "I thought he could handle it," I answered defensively. "I showed him some landmarks on the first day and he did fine."

"Uh—huh," Tiny was silent for a moment, then added, "you know there's a fair chance this will be a recovery operation and not a rescue one."

"Well, can we at least try?"

"Sure. Where specifically? Dry Lakes Road is a big area."

"On Bear Flat, where the road gets fairly close to the Summit Overlook."

"Sugarloaf Mountain area?"

"No, before that."

Tiny nodded and glanced down at his wristwatch. "It's already after five. There's no way we can get organized and up there before dark. Meet me here at five in the morning. We'll get up there by the crack of dawn and start searching."

"That won't work," I objected. "I've got a horse up on the mountain that needs to be cared for. Why don't I meet you at the junction of Highway 143 and Dry Lakes Road at six o'clock? It'll take you about an hour to get up to the search area from there."

Sheriff Klein considered this for a moment, then nodded. "Okay, but you better be there. And bring that Tim fellow too."

I nodded and started to leave, then turned back around again. "Are you going to notify the wives?"

"Notify them about what? They don't even legally qualify as missing persons yet." Tiny stood up and loomed over me. "Anyway that sounds like something a friend should do."

"But—" I started to object, but again bit my tongue. I was going to say, but I don't even really know them. Yes, superficially, I knew Wally's wife, but I had only seen a photograph of Ian's wife. However he was right; I should talk to them. They were my friends, it was my hunt and it was my responsibility.

Feeling a little bit chastised, like I was leaving the principal's office, I ducked my head and left Sheriff Tiny Klein's office. Once back in the Dodge, I found my cell phone and flipped through my directory until I found Wally's home number, then punched it in. The phone started ringing. No answer. I tried again.

"Hello." The voice was grumpy and female.

"Misses Stroud?" I was somewhat taken aback by her tone.

"Yes, this is Susan," she growled.

"Uh—uh, this is Coop."

"Who?"

"Uh—Doctor Cooper. You know Wally's friend."

"Oh, yeah," she said without enthusiasm, "his hunting buddy."

I paused, trying to figure out how to tell her, then just blurted. "Wally is missing!"

"Missing?" She was silent for a couple of seconds. "What does that even mean?"

"Uh--he went out to hunt on yesterday morning and never came back."

"So missing since yesterday?"

"Yes, but Search and Rescue is going to start looking for him in the morning."

"That figures."

"What?" I didn't think I'd heard her correctly.

"It's just that tomorrow we had a fact finding meeting with our lawyers to disclose our finances and assets."

"What?"

"We are getting a divorce. Didn't Wally tell you?"

"No."

"Well, I guess that's all on hold now?" she laughed bitterly, then added, "Unless they find a body."

"What?" I repeated. This conversation was going straight over my head.

"Then I can collect on his life insurance. Double indemnity if it was an accident."

I paused, trying to think of the word that was the opposite of accidental. I couldn't. "And, if it wasn't an accident?"

"If it's natural causes, then the face value of the policy. If it's murder—nothing."

"Oh!"

"And it's hard to divorce a missing person. Very hard."

"Oh," I said again.

"They have to be missing for two years before I can be adjudicated as a widow."

"Huh?"

"They have to be missing for two years before the court will declare them dead."

"Oh, how—how do you know all this?" I asked.

"How else? I looked it up on the internet."

"Why?"

"Believe you me, I expected something like this might happen."

I didn't know what to say. "Uh--I'm sorry." Sorry for what, I wasn't quite sure.

"Me too," she said curtly. "You'll keep me informed?"

"Yes," I nodded, hanging up the phone.

Confused, I looked at the smart phone as I rotated it in my hands. That certainly was an odd conversation. It's not like Wally and I were confiding, secret-telling friends, but he had never said a word about his family problems, or the impending divorce, at least not to me. And certainly, Susan did not seem terribly broken up about his disappearance, only by the inconvenience of it all. But did that change anything? No, not really. Wally was still missing and the circumstances surrounding his vanishing were still a little suspicious. And if he were still alive, the present circumstances, mainly the weather, did not bode favorably for his continued survival.

Sighing, I turned on the phone again and dialed information for Salt Lake City. Unfortunately, there was no landline number listed for Ian McKenna. I then checked on a number for Katherine McKenna and even tried Katherine Kozlov. Again, nothing. Next, I called the University of Utah Psychiatric Department, but got a recording they were closed for the day. I left a message on their voice mail for Katherine McKenna to call me, then in desperation I scrolled down through my phone directory until I found Ian's cell phone number and impulsively dialed it. It rang and rang, then finally diverted me to his voice mail. I felt like a fool, but nevertheless I left a message, "give me a call as soon as you get this message."

Next, I called my office. It was after five o'clock. I got the after hours recording: *"This is the office of Doctors Lawrence A. Cooper and Timothy D. Slade. Our office hours are from nine to five Monday through Friday. If this is an emergency, call nine-one-one, or go directly to Dixie Medical Center emergency room. If you would like to leave a message press eight."* I pressed eight, then started to leave a message. Suddenly the tape cut off and returned to a dial tone.

Frustrated, but not knowing what else to do, I started the Dodge, and along with Malachi headed back to the Ford dealership. After talking to several people in three different departments, I discovered Tim had talked the tow truck driver into going up the mountain and retrieving his truck this evening. And Tim, of course, had gone along to show the driver the way.

By now, the snow would be gone and Dry Lakes Road should be in much better shape. I had no doubt the tow truck would succeed. I'd used them once in a similar situation and knew they would easily winch the pickup back up the hill onto the relatively firm and flat surface of the road. Then they would simply load it up on the flatbed and haul it back to the dealership. If all went well, they would probably get back to Cedar City shortly after dark. Unfortunately, I couldn't wait that long.

I tried to call Slade on his cell phone, but he did not answer. He must already be in the mountains and out of the service area. I left a message on his voice mail, then to make sure he knew our plans, I gave the receptionist at the service department a note to give him.

> *Tim,*
>
> *Search and Rescue will be leaving Cedar City about five o'clock in the morning. I will meet them at six at the junction of Dry Lakes Road and Highway 143. You can either come up to the cabin tonight, or stay in Cedar City and hook up with Search and Rescue in the morning. But make sure you come.*
> *Coop.*

The receptionist promised me she would make sure he got the note tonight. If they were not back by the time she left the dealership, she would call the tow truck driver and make him aware of the note. I thanked her and headed back to the Dodge and Malachi.

By then, it was well after six and I really did not want to cook tonight. Anyway, there wasn't much food left at the cabin. We weren't planning on staying this long. I pulled into a fast food restaurant and without thinking ordered two double cheeseburgers, one each for Malachi and me. Though I was ravenous, the smell of meat still nauseated me. Was I becoming Ian and turning into a vegetarian? It sure seemed like it. Forcing myself not to think about it, I managed a few nibbles while I hand fed Malachi his burger. But for me, it didn't work. I couldn't help but picture cute little calves frolicking in a green meadow. Needless to say, I ate mostly bun and fries, and gave the two patties to Malachi.

As we ate, I noted the truck was a mess. Malachi was still caked in dry mud and I wasn't much better. He had managed to soil the seats, the passenger door and dashboard. Fortunately, they were leather and should clean up okay, but without question we both needed a bath before we went to bed.

Malachi and I finished our sandwiches just the sun was sinking behind Iron Mountain. Firing up the Dodge, we got back on the freeway, heading north toward Brian Head and the cabin. A couple of miles this side of Parowan, we passed a tow truck with Tim's pickup, heading south toward Cedar City. It looked like at least that rescue was successful.

It was well after dark when we arrived back at the cabin. Again, I fed and watered Ike, then gave Malachi a bath in the tub. When finished, I drained the water, refilled the tub and hopped in. After finishing my bath, I took the wet towels outside and cleaned the cab of the pickup.

Exhausted, I finally tumbled into bed and closed my eyes. I was so tired, intern tired, I thought I would immediately fall asleep. Fluffy up my pillow, I turned on my side and tried to relax. My mind switched to autopilot, began to wander and I started to fade. Abruptly, my eyes opened wide again. I tried to force my mind to return to its meandering and the land of sweet oblivion, but now it was impossible. Unfortunately, now my mind found a mission and began working overtime, processing the events of this strange and this possibly horrific weekend.

I really didn't know for sure what to make of Tim Slade, but I had my suspicions. He certainly didn't seem at all worried about Ian and Wally. Was his apparent lack of concern due to Ian's less-than-subtle threat to turn him in for using an assault rifle on the buck? But what about Wally? He and Tim had been friends for several years; maybe not close friends, but friends. There was, however, no question about it, Tim was clearly unconcerned as manifest by his blasé attitude about their vanishing and his total lack of enthusiasm in joining the search. Was he in some way responsible for their disappearance? Had he harmed them? If so, why harm Wally? Hell, why dance around the word? The word was *murder!* Had he murdered Ian and Wally? Not only murder, but premeditated murder in the first degree! Then hid the bodies.

Murder them in the first-degree? That seemed like a bit much. Ian's threat to turn Tim in for illegal hunting did not seem sufficient motivation for murder. And again, why Wally? Had he been a witness to the murder of Ian so Tim shot him to keep him quiet? But the whole thing didn't seem to add up. The act didn't seem to justify the action. On the other hand, in the long and dark annals of murder, certainly people had been killed for a lot less. That thought, however, was too horrific for me to dwell on, so I forced my mind in a slightly different direction. Maybe the blood sample I'd collected earlier would help.

Blood sample! Suddenly, I remembered I'd left it in the saddlebag. Outside it would freeze. Jumping out of bed, I rushed outside to the utility shed and located my saddle and saddlebags. Rummaging in the dark, I finally found the plastic baggie and hurried back into the cabin. Shivering uncontrollably, I placed the baggie in the propane fridge and climbed back into bed.

Once again my mind started to drift. What would happen when we got home? Without question our relationship, Tim's and mine, had already suffered considerably and that could prove awkward since we assisted each other in surgery and shared a medical office. Not only shared an office, but Tim's wife, Ronnie, worked as our receptionist and that could prove to be uncomfortable if not down right dicey.

About a year ago, right after our receptionist quit, Tim suggested his wife for the job. Initially, I was staunchly opposed. It was never a good idea to have family working in the office, let alone a pampered doctor's wife. I had assumed, since they had no kids, she was bored and just wanted a hobby. If so, there was almost unlimited volunteer work available in the community, or she could take oil painting lessons or even go back to college. Certainly, working in a medical office was not a hobby and I doubted very much she had the patience, skills or dedication for the job. And I knew for sure she didn't need the entry-level paycheck.

Immediately, I could foresee a couple of potential problems. When it came to scheduling patients, would she be fair? Would she give all the good patients, the ones who would likely need surgery (that's how we made the bulk of our money) and the ones that had insurance to Tim, and give me all the enuresis (bedwetters), urinary tract infections and the uninsured? And how could I possibly critique her work, or even discipline her, let alone fire her if that ever became necessary?

But as it turned out, none of that was needed and all that the worry was needless. She was great! Surprisingly, she was competent, efficient and could actually multitask, a skill essential for that position. Not only did our receptionist have to greet and check in patients, but she also had to answer the phone, make appointments, enter new patient data into the computer and schedule office procedures. Within the medical community, the conventional wisdom was a receptionist could make or break your medical practice. Without question, Ronnie made ours. And even though she was a blonde, and loved to play up the "dumb blonde" role, she was actually quite smart, had a good sense of humor and was very kind to the patients. They loved her. Also, she was fair with me and subsequently our practice flourished.

Ronnie Wilson Slade was a natural blonde with Miss-America looks, a bikini figure with an unexpected quick wit, though she often pretended otherwise. She was a runner-up Miss Utah and I often wondered how an urban redneck like Tim Slade managed to woo her. They seemed, at least to me, a bit of an odd couple, a mismatch. But after a year on the job, I had absolutely no complaints about her—well, maybe one, a tiny one. She was a bit of a flirt. I should have put a stop to that months ago, but I must admit I kind of liked it. Yes, I confess, I am a red-blooded male starved for female attention.

Anyway, regardless of all that it would be tense around the office for a while. But if we found Ian and Wally, and if they were healthy, then my suspicions of Slade would be totally unjustified and things at the office should eventually smooth out. I would simply apologize to Tim, and hopefully he would accept, and life would return to normal, or as normal as it ever was.

Suddenly my mind flipped channels back to Katherine Kozlov McKenna. I felt bad about not getting hold of her, but why hadn't she tried to call us, tried to find Ian? Briefly, I wondered what he had told her about how long he would be gone and when she should expect him back. Maybe Ian had told her he wouldn't be back till Tuesday, so she wasn't worried. Nevertheless, I felt bad that she had no idea of what was going on, but if we found Ian tomorrow, and he was alive, then there would be no need to alarm her.

My mind then drifted to Wally's wife. I must admit Susan Stroud surprised me. I had no idea of their marital problems, but how could I? Wally hadn't told me. But Susan didn't seem at all broken up about Wally's disappearance and unless I was reading her wrong, she was hoping for an accidental death and double indemnity. That was cold, real cold. I suppose I should call Wally's office and alert them he would not be back to work, at least not by tomorrow.

Work! I suddenly remembered I was supposed to take both E.R. and hospital call tomorrow. This definitely was not good. I made a mental note. Tomorrow, not only did have to try again to get hold of Ian's wife, and Wally's work, but I also had to get hold of the hospital's Medical Director, Dr. Jeremy Faux (French) and explain my absence. Faux would not be happy.

Unfortunately, I had done this sort of thing before, but just like this time it was due to circumstances beyond my control.

A few years ago, I got stranded with some buddies in the mountains on a horse packing fishing trip and missed a call rotation—

—I awoke with a start! Apparently, I had slept after all. What time was it? I flipped on the lamp beside me on the nightstand. It was five-thirty! I was supposed to meet Sheriff Axel 'Tiny' Klein at six o'clock. Throwing back the covers, I clambered out of bed, threw on some clothes, found a can of dog food for Malachi, then rushed outside to feed Ike. Geez, it was cold! I had to take an axe and chip through two inches of ice in Ike's water trough.

By the time Malachi and I climbed into the pickup, it was five minutes to six. No doubt I was going to be late. Sheriff Tiny Klein would not be happy.

I gunned the Dodge down the hill from the cabin, then on down Dry Lakes Road, heading north toward the highway. Suddenly, a doe with her nearly grown fawn jumped in front of the pickup, then abruptly stopped, blinded by my oncoming headlights. Slamming on the brakes, I whipped the steering wheel hard to the left. I barely missed the deer by mere inches, but smacked into a small quaking aspen sapling, snapping it in half.

Jumping out of the Dodge, I checked the damage to the front end. Other than a vertical imprint of the tree in my bumper, there was not much. Surely, nothing that would keep me from driving. Hurriedly, I returned to the pickup and started down the road again, this time at a more moderate speed.

When I arrived at the junction of Dry Lakes Road and Highway 143, there was a early blush of apricot orange on the dark eastern horizon. My dashboard clock flashed a very tardy 6:19 a.m.! There were at least twelve vehicles randomly parked alongside the road. Quickly, I searched through the convoy for Sheriff Tiny Klein. He was not hard to spot. Standing in front of his sheriff's cruiser with arms folded across his massive chest, he was several inches taller than everyone else. As I pulled up, he looked over and scowled.

After advising Malachi to stay, I got out of the pickup and approached the group.

"You're late!" Tiny barked.

"I'm sorry." I immediately decided to be honest. "I—I overslept."

"You overslept!" Sheriff Klein was incredulous. "Your friends are missing, possibly hurt, undoubtedly hypothermic, and you overslept?"

"I'm sorry," I repeated. "I was exhausted. I didn't sleep much the last two nights."

"Haven't you ever heard of an alarm clock?"

"Actually, I don't have—"

"—Forget that," he cut me off, "let's get going. You lead the way."

He started to turn away, then stopped. "Where's that friend of yours? That Tim fellow?"

I quickly looked around. "He's not with you?"

"Why would I be asking you if he was?"

# 7

Once again I awoke late. Glancing over at the alarm clock, I groaned out loud. I had a busy night on call for the E.R. and had a busy day ahead. I hated to start it by rushing to catch up. First, I had a meeting with Dr. Jeremy Faux and the Surgical Peer Review Committee, then I planned to head up to Salt Lake City, hopefully to find and talk with Katherine Kozlov McKenna. Pitching back the covers, I got up and threw on yesterday's clothes. With Malachi following at my heels, I put coffee on to perk, then hurried outside to feed the horses.

It was chilly, but certainly not as cold as the last few days on Brian Head Mountain. Though the unseen sun had not yet ascended high enough to illuminate Diamond Valley, its upward-angled rays nevertheless had spotlighted the lofty snow-capped peaks and sheer granite face of the Pine Valley Mountains.

My five horses, including Ike, were waiting in their stalls, neighing and impatiently pawing the ground. Stumbling into the barn, I dumped a two-gallon bucket of alfalfa cubes into each of their feeders. The pungent aroma of stale urine and fresh horse dung assaulted my nostrils. Pausing, I took a moment to appraise the condition of their stalls. Without question, they needed a good cleaning, but I had no time now. Considering my hectic and often erratic schedule, I really should hire a fulltime stable boy, perhaps the Snow kid from across the valley. I already occasionally employed him to feed and care for the horses when I went out of town, like this recent deer hunt and my planned trip to Salt Lake City for later today. Maybe I'd pay him a little extra to clean the stalls while I was gone.

Back in the kitchen, I fed Malachi, wolfed down a charcoal toasted bagel, inhaled my black coffee and headed for the shower. The warm water both soothed and calmed me. I leaned against the shower wall and closed my eyes. As the tepid water tumbled over my head and shoulders, I couldn't help but think about the recent ill-fated deer hunt and my still missing friends.

Unfortunately, the last two days with Search and Rescue and Sheriff Axel "Tiny" Klein had turned out to be an exercise in futility. The supervisor for Search and Rescue, Tom Palmeri (obvious Italian, probably Sicilian) carefully dissected the Summit Overlook area into a near perfect grid, then assigned each of us a section to search. As soon as the sun topped Brian Head Mountain, we were also joined by the rhythmic whack-whack-whack of an overhead Bell helicopter, also systematically combing the same area from the air. The terrain was too rugged for Ike, but I took Malachi and we searched our section on foot. Malachi had an excellent nose and I thought there was a fair chance he might pick up Ian or Wally's scent. Each team member worked his or her section till noon, then while we ate lunch Tom drew up a new grid, a little further to the south. By mid-afternoon, he drafted yet another grid, this time further to the north.

Unfortunately, none of this careful planning yielded much in the way of results. Tom surmised the snow cover on the day of Ian and Wally's disappearance had probably hurt us. With the snow cover, there would be no tracks imprinted on the bare muddy ground and obviously any tracks in the snow had disappeared as soon as the snow melted. So, other than my specimen of blood in the baggie, known only to me, there was nothing: no boot tracks, no more blood and no torn scraps of clothing, but thankfully no bodies either. And Malachi picked up no promising scent either.

With the sun starting to set and temperatures again beginning to plummet, I fired up the Dodge and with Malachi drove the three miles to the ski resort town of Brian Head, purchased a pizza, half vegan/half meat lovers, to go, then headed back to the cabin. By the time we'd finished off the pizza, it was still early, only eight o'clock. I knew I couldn't sleep, not yet, so I called to Malachi and we headed out into the starlit night and fired up the Dodge.

In the dark (fortunately the road had dried out) I spent the next forty-five minutes negotiating the "S" curves of Dry Lakes Road to S.R. 143, eventually arriving in small farming town of Parowan located at the base of the mountain. As I had hoped, I did have cell phone service down in the Parowan Valley. Touching the quick-dial icon, I punched in Tim Slade's number, then listened to it ring.

After six unanswered rings, I was transferred to Tim's voice mail. I left him a curt message:

*Tim, we missed you today! Where were you? The search will continue tomorrow with the staging area again at Summit Overlook. Please be there. Oh, and if you haven't already, please let the office and the hospital know what is happening. Thanks, Coop.*

After that phone call, I thought about calling Ian's wife in Salt Lake City again, but with no known phone number available that was not possible. Also, I remembered to leave a message at Wally's work.

Malachi and I spent another night at the cabin, then the next morning we again met up with Sheriff Tiny Klein, Tom Palmeri and their crew. This time we were on time. We spent another full and exhausting day searching. Palmeri expanded the search further and further away from the Summit Overlook. Once again, however, there was no sign of Ian McKenna and Wally Stroud, or of Tim Slade either for that matter. I could only assume he was back at work and hoped he had taken the initiative to have his wife reschedule my patients and call Doctor Jeremy Faux and explain my absence.

Unfortunately, as it turned out, the second day also yielded nothing. A third day was scheduled, then cancelled as yet another major late October snowstorm was expected.

Suddenly, I shivered; the shower water had turned cold. With a start, I pushed my mind back to the present. Geez, I had no time for a leisurely shower and this prolonged daydreaming. I had an eight o'clock appointment with the Surgery Peer Review Committee and Chairman Jeremy Faux hated tardiness. Sighing, I turned off the water and quickly dressed in blue jeans, cowboy boots, a checkered fawn brown and powder blue western shirt and then donned a sheep wool-lined suede leather jacket. Grabbing my suitcase and i-Pad, I called to Malachi and headed out the door. Fortunately, before I got out of the driveway I remembered the blood sample. Returning to the kitchen, I retrieved it from the fridge, put it in a Coleman cooler with some ice and rejoined Malachi at the pickup.

On my way out of Diamond Valley, I stopped at the Snow residence and talked fourteen year old Jess into feeding my horses. Unabashedly, I also dangled another fifty in front of him if he would clean the horse stalls.

Back in the Dodge, I roared down the ten-mile hill from Diamond Valley to St. George, an almost two thousand foot descent, arriving at Dixie Medical Center at 8:15 a.m. After parking in the patient loading zone and saying goodbye to Malachi, I then rushed into the hospital, flew down the stairs and arrived at the Zion Conference Room at 8:19 a.m. Peeking through the door's half-window, I could see the committee had already assembled. Half a dozen doctors dressed in starched white lab coats, including Jeremy Faux, were slouched around an oval oak table in various angles of impatience or boredom. Also, I was not at all surprised to see Mr. Cameron Hall, Esquire, hospital attorney, and Beth Myerson, medical staff secretary, both unobtrusively embedded in the sea of white coats. Hesitating for a moment, I took a deep breath, then opened the door.

Jeremy Faux immediately looked up, glanced down at his wrist, then held up his watch while tapping the crystal. "You're late, as usual," he barked.

I was in no mood for Faux's haughty attitude. "You could've started without me," I quipped.

"But you are the only item on the agenda."

"Nobody consulted me about scheduling a time."

"You are in no position to make demands."

We glared at each other for a couple of seconds, then Faux nodded toward an empty seat. "Take a seat, Doctor Cooper and we'll get started. Beth Myerson will take notes."

I shrugged and took an empty seat, but not the one he'd indicated.

"I see you dressed for the occasion." Jeremy disdainfully eyed my cowboy ensemble.

"Huh?" I took off my hat.

"Never mind, let's get started. In our profession, time is money." Faux switched to his formal voice. "Is Doctor Margaret Toolsen, Chairman of the Emergency Department, here?"

"Geez, Jeremy, you know I am," Toolsen growled. "I'm the only woman doctor in the room. And if we're going to be that formal, it's Chairwoman of the Emergency Department."

"Huh?" Faux looked puzzled.

"It is Chairwoman Margaret Toolsen of the Emergency Department. In case you haven't noticed, I am a woman."

"Oh," Faux turned red, then sarcastically rephrased. "Doctor Toolsen, *Chairwoman* of the Emergency Department, would you be so kind as to explain to the committee the problems you had in the E.R. over the last few days."

Still scowling at Faux, Dr. Toolsen stood and faced the group. "We've been incredibly busy and we definitely need more space, more doctors and more patient bays."

"No!" Faux barked. "Specifically, I mean your problems with Doctor Cooper."

"Oh," Toolsen said calmly without a hint of embarrassment. "Coop, uh—uh—Doctor Cooper was on call this week, starting with Monday, and was not available." Toolsen abruptly sat down again.

"*Doctor Toolsen*," Faux had a definite edge to his voice, "could you please give us a few more details. Did Doctor Cooper's unauthorized absence cause you any problems?"

Reluctantly Toolsen rose again. "Uh, yes, there were a couple of incidents."

"Please, enlighten us, Doctor."

Toolsen glared at Faux for a moment, then cleared her throat. "On Monday night we had a urinary tract bleeder. His bladder filled up with clots, he couldn't void, and we couldn't get a catheter in or the clots out."

"He must have been in agony," Faux editorialized. "So, what happened?"

"Well, we called all the other urologists on staff and finally got Doctor Keyes to come in. He managed to get a catheter in and evacuate the clots."

"Anything else?"

"Well, yes. Tuesday we had a kidney stone come in septic. She was a diabetic, running a high fever and her CT scan showed an eight-millimeter stone in the right proximal ureter at the UPJ with hydronephrosis and complete occlusion."

"And?" Faux prodded.

"And, again we could not get Doctor Cooper, but his time we could not get a hold of any of the other staff urologists either. We eventually had to Life Flight her to Intermountain Medical Center in Salt Lake City."

"What is the present condition of this patient?" Faux looked as though he had his prey in sight and was ready to pounce.

Margaret Toolsen shrugged. "As far as I know, okay. She was taken to surgery and a stent was placed. She's presently in their ICU."

"So," Faux surmised, "if Doctor Cooper would have been available to take care of this problem in a timely fashion, more than likely she wouldn't have ended up in the ICU."

"I don't know if you can say that," Toolsen argued, "these patients get pretty sick, pretty fast. Most of them end up in the ICU anyway."

"Anything else?" Faux asked.

"No, just minor things we could take care of and Doctor Cooper was back on the job last evening." Margaret Toolsen sat down once again.

Faux cleared his throat, stood and faced the group. "As many of you know, this is not the first time Doctor Cooper has pulled a stunt like this. I

78

move we summarily strip Doctor Cooper of his operating room and hospital privileges."

"Can we do that?" Dr. Joe Carter, Chief of Orthopedics, asked.

All heads turned to Cameron Hall, the lawyer. He nodded his head as he stood. "Yes, you can legally do that. Doctor Cooper is still on probation and the provision for a summary suspension for any repeat offense was included as a prerequisite of his probation."

"Wait a minute!" Dr. Richardson, Chief of Surgery, was on his feet. "We haven't heard from Coop yet."

"We don't have to," Faux snapped. "He's already on probation for a similar offense. He's violated the terms of his probation, so a summary suspension is in order."

Richardson stood his ground. "I still want to hear from Coop."

"I second that," Doctor Oran Staples, Chief of Anesthesia chimed in.

All heads turned toward me.

Shrugging, I stood up and faced Dr. Toolsen and the others. "Didn't Doctor Slade inform you I was detained?"

Margaret Toolsen shook her head. "I haven't heard a thing from Tim— uh—Doctor Slade."

Immediately, I felt my blood pressure rise and fought to contain my anger. Not only had Tim not helped with the search for Ian and Wally, when he got home he hadn't bothered to tell the E.R. I was unavoidably detained. Surely, he would have informed the office, his wife, so patients wouldn't come in for their appointment and me not be there.

"Well," I gritted my teeth, "we lost two men on the deer hunt—" then I proceeded to give the committee a detailed report of the last four days.

When I finished Faux jumped to his feet. "The bylaws, which you signed when you applied for hospital privileges, specifically state you will take call and if you cannot it is your duty to find a replacement of equal skill and training." Faux opened a thick binder. "Let me read: *Members will take call in an equal and equitable manner based upon the total number of physicians (under age 65) in the division—*"

—As Faux droned on, I tuned him out. I knew perfectly well what was included in the bylaws and I also knew since Tim had not informed them I would not be back to take call I didn't have a leg to stand on. On the other hand, I also knew most of the committee members sympathized with me and most of them despised Faux.

Faux finally finished reading and set down the binder. "So, as you can see Doctor Cooper is in clear violation of the staff bylaws once again, as well as the terms of his probation. I move we summarily suspend Doctor Cooper's hospital privileges, including, of course, his operating room privileges. Do I have a second?"

To my surprise, not a single "aye", or hand rose up from the group. An awkward silence ensued.

"I think," Dr. Margaret Toolsen finally said, "we should—"

"—I'll!" I abruptly stood up, cutting Margaret off. "I'll second the motion!"

"You can't do—" Faux started to say.

"—I am still an active member of this committee, at least for the moment," I argued, cutting him off, "and still have a vote until I'm suspended."

All heads again turned to the hospital lawyer, Cameron Hall. "Yes," he slowly nodded his head, "technically he can still vote until he is suspended or otherwise permanently removed from the committee."

Next heads then turned back to Dr. Faux. I could tell Jeremy wanted to ask me why I seconded his motion, but was afraid he would lose his newfound advantage. Instead he cleared his throat and quickly proceeded, "I now have a second, so let's vote. All in favor of the motion say *aye*."

Immediately, I responded with a loud *aye*. The others looked confused, but hesitantly followed my lead.

"Are there any *nays*?" Faux asked.

There were none.

"So, be it," Dr. Jeremy Faux concluded. "Doctor Lawrence Cooper's hospital privileges are hereby suspended effective immediately." He turned to me. "You may appeal, it you desire, by sending a written letter to the Medical Executive Committee, or you may reapply for privileges after one year."

I acknowledged my understanding by a silent nod.

"Is there any further business to bring before this committee?" Faux asked formally.

There was none.

"I hereby adjourn this meeting of the Surgical Peer Review Committee." Faux gathered up his briefcase and immediately left.

As I turned to leave, Dr. Margaret Toolsen grabbed my arm. We waited until the others had cleared the room, then she asked, "What was that all about, Coop?"

"Now I'm officially off call."

"What?" She frowned.

"I have to leave for Salt Lake immediately," I explained, "I was still on call till Saturday, now I'm not."

"Why Salt Lake?"

"One of the men we lost was a friend of mine. His wife still doesn't know. We haven't been able to locate her."

Margaret slowly nodded her understanding. "Well, good luck, Coop." She started to walk away, then turned back. "You should appeal this, you know. There is such a thing as mitigating circumstances and I can guarantee you'll have the committee's support."

"Thanks," I said as we walked out together. "Probably I will, but I can't think about that right now. Right now I'm still in the middle of a major crisis. Wally and Ian are still missing and Ian's wife still has to be notified."

Back in the Dodge, I checked my wristwatch, 8:57 a.m. Before heading to Salt Lake City, I still had a couple of errands to run. I really should to stop by the office and see what kind of chaos was brewing there and I needed to get the blood sample to Hank Bettis of the Pathology Department. Since I was already at the hospital, I decided to dispose of the blood first. Hopefully, Hank was in the office by now, however, pathologists were notorious for their banker's hours. Retrieving the baggie from my iced Coleman cooler, I again told Malachi to stay and headed back into the hospital.

Hank Bettis' office was in the basement, not at all uncommon for pathology departments. By the time I arrived, it was a couple minutes after nine. Through the glass wall partition, I could see the office was well lit with overhead fluorescent lights, always a good sign, and the reception desk was manned. I opened the glass door and approached the desk.

"Is Doctor Bettis in yet?" I asked, then added, "I'm Doctor Cooper."

"And who shall I say is calling?" the receptionist asked brightly.

I gritted my teeth. She was pretty, but she wasn't even blonde. "I just told you. I'm Doctor Cooper."

"Well, you don't need to get huffy."

"I'm sorry," I said, though I wasn't, "is he in?"

"Who?"

"Doctor Bettis."

"No."

I bit my tongue. I wanted to ask her, 'so why did you ask me, *who shall I say is calling*,' but instead I said evenly, "When do you expect him?"

"At nine o'clock."

"It's," I checked my wristwatch, "it's now nine-o-seven."

"I have no control," she said curtly, "over when he comes in." She turned her back to me and pulled open a file cabinet drawer.

Fighting hard to control my temper, I turned to leave. At that moment the glass door opened and Hank Bettis strolled in. "Hi, Coops," he beamed, "what's up?"

"Hi, Hank," my anger immediately dissipated. "I see you're on time as usual."

"Dead people," he quipped, "don't really care."

"But eventually they do start to smell," I grinned. "Hank, I need a favor."

"Come on, Coops, let's go back to my office."

As I followed Hank, I noticed how toned he appeared and suddenly felt embarrassed by my own flabbiness and lack of exercise.

Hank pointed to a chair in front of his desk, then sat down opposite me. "How you been, Coops?"

"Nothing to brag about."

"Why don't you get a date and let's go out to dinner sometime. Jenny's always asking about you."

"I'm not seeing anyone right now."

"Surely, there's someone you could ask."

"No, not that I can think of."

"Well, then how about you just come over to our house for dinner?"

"Okay," I said vaguely. Actually, the truth of the matter was I really didn't care much for Hank's wife, Jenny. I hurriedly changed the subject. "Hank, I need a favor."

"You already said that."

"Could you do DNA analysis on this blood?" I held up the baggie.

"That depends—" Hank put on his reading glasses and examined the specimen.

"On what?"

"Well, as you know red blood cells have no nucleus and no mitochondria so it is impossible to do a DNA analysis on them, but if there are some preserved white blood cells in there, then it is possible."

"I kept it in the refrigerator, or on ice."

"Yeah, well then maybe," Hank paused, then added, "what's this all about, Coops?"

82

I took a moment to explain the situation.

Hank frowned. "Geez, Wally Stroud, he's my investment advisor. I sure hope he's okay."

"Me too," I nodded in agreement.

"So you think maybe a crime was committed?"

I nodded again. "I don't know. Maybe."

"You know just because we do DNA test on this blood it won't necessarily identify anyone."

"What?"

"We don't have every single American's DNA genome on file, a few criminals, but almost nobody else. If you are trying identify whose blood this is, we'll need something we can match it with."

"Oh, okay. What I really want to know if this is Ian McKenna or Wally Stroud's blood."

"Hmmm," Hank turned on his computer and logged onto the Intermountain Health Care website. IHC owned a majority of the hospitals in the state and with this website doctors could access lab or pathology reports from any of them. Hank scrolled from page to page. "Wally Stroud is easy. He had a skin lesion removed just a week ago. They should have some of that tissue on file." He scrolled some more. "And Ian McKenna—it looks like he had a prostate biopsy last year at IMC (Intermountain Medical Center) in Salt Lake City."

Wally's skin lesion was no surprise, but I was surprised about Ian. He hadn't bothered to mention a prostate biopsy to me and prostate cancer was my specialty. "Was it positive?"

"A Gleason grade VIII, on the left side only, in two of six cores."

"Do they save any tissue?"

"Always," Hank nodded, "with positive biopsies. They imbed it in paraffin wax and bank it for a minimum of twenty years."

"Could we get some of that tissue for comparison?"

"It would be a little unethical, since you are supposed to be the treating physician to access it," Hank said, "but yes. You just need to sign a tissue release form."

I didn't hesitate. "Get me one; I'll sign it." Silently I hoped IHC wouldn't send a memo to all its other hospitals stating I no longer had hospital privileges, and obviously Hank didn't know yet.

Hank rummaged around in his army green metal file cabinet, finally producing the form.

"You know," Hank said, as I signed the form, "we send DNA studies out of town."

"Yeah, I supposed you did."

"Boston Genetics," Hank continued. "It'll probably take a day, or two, to get the prostate tissue from IMC. After that, we can overnight the tissue to Boston, then it will take another week, or so, to get a report back."

I quickly did the math. "Then approximately ten days total."

Bettis nodded. "And unfortunately, since it's not our lab, I can't do this *pro bono*."

I gulped. I hadn't even considered this. "H—how much will it cost?"

"It varies a little," Hank replied, "but a legally binding test will cost you around seven hundred dollars. Times that by three since there are three specimens and we're talking about twenty-one hundreds dollars, more or less."

"Times by three?" I was still stuck on how many specimens I was paying for.

"Yeah, one for Wally, one for Ian and one for this specimen." He held up my baggie.

I paused, then nodded. Certainly, Ian and Wally were worth twenty-one hundred dollars. "Okay, Hank, let's do it." I stood up and held out my hand. "Unfortunately, I've got to run. I've got one of those days."

Hank laughed as he took my hand. "You should've gone into pathology." Then as he walked me to the door, he added, "remember the dinner invitation is always open."

Back in the Dodge, I hurriedly navigated the eleven blocks to the office and pulled into the small parking lot behind the building.

Our office, Tim's and mine, was a 1950's white brick house, which had been converted to an office. To give it a commercial appearance, a parapet was constructed around the periphery of the low gable roof creating the illusion of a flat roof. The entrance was modified from a single wooden door to a double glass door and we added a covered portico. Next, the carport was bricked in, then partitioned into three more exam rooms. Finally, after completely remodeling the interior and moving several walls around, we had a serviceable office. It sported a total of six exam rooms, a cystoscopy/minor surgery suite, a lab, a business office, two personal offices and a somewhat cramped waiting room.

Again leaving Malachi in the pickup once again, I entered the office through the back door and headed straight to my personal office, somehow managing to avoid all the staff. As usual, there was a pile of paperwork on my desk: advertising flyers from pharmaceutical companies, lab slips, x-ray and pathology reports and hospital memos. Quickly, I sorted through the stack, signing off on the lab, x-ray and pathology reports and throwing the junk mail in the wastebasket. Finally finished, I stood up and headed up front to the reception desk.

"Oh, my God!" Ronnie exclaimed, jumping up when she saw me. "Are you okay, Coop?" She never called me Doctor Cooper.

"Didn't your husband tell you?" I asked, while once again noting how beautiful she was. She was wearing a low-cut loose white blouse and dark, figure-flattering business slacks.

"Tell me what?"

"That I was detained and to reschedule my patients."

She looked confused. "Well, I did reschedule the patients each day after they sat here for an hour, or so, and you didn't show up." She grabbed for my hand, which wasn't that unusual.

"You mean," I was incredulous, "when Tim got home from the hunt, he didn't say a word about me?" I should have removed my hand from hers, but I was still feeling the tingly electricity of her touch.

"No, he just said he got a deer." She leaned forward and her blouse gaped open. "Actually, as you know, we don't talk much."

"Where is Tim?" I tried hard to keep my eyes away from her chest.

"I don't expect him in the office at all today. He's got a full day of surgery."

I paused trying to think of what to do. "Well, I've got to go to Salt Lake City right now," I finally said. "Could you cancel me out for the rest of the week and tell your husband, we, he and I, need to talk first thing on Monday morning."

"I will if I see him."

"Actually, type it in on both our schedules right now—for eight o'clock."

She nodded and removed her hand long enough to change her computer screen to the scheduling program and type in the information. Promptly, she grabbed my hand again. "Don't forget you and Tim have that county commission debate on Saturday night."

"Oh, I forgot," I groaned and tried to disengage my hand. She held on. "Sorry, I've got to go."

"Would you like some company?" she asked coyly.

"Huh—uh," I stammered like a tongue-tied teenager. Actually, I really wouldn't mind a couple of days in Salt Lake City with the gorgeous Ronnie Slade, but regrettably my rational side prevailed. "What about Tim?" I finally asked.

"Who cares," she shrugged. "I'm pretty sure he's having an affair anyway."

"Uh—uh, I have Malachi with me." Again, I tried, but not too hard to remove my hand.

Ronnie held on, then leaned across the counter, brushed her chest up against me and kissed me on the cheek. "Well, you take care of yourself, Coop."

"I—I will," I stammered.

Finally, she released my hand and blushing like a schoolboy, I hurried for the back door. Just as I put my hand on the knob, my office nurse, Ana Frehner (Swiss, I think—possibly German), stopped me.

"He may not have told her, but he told me."

"Huh—what?" Ana often confused me.

"Doctor Slade told me you wouldn't be back in the office for a day or two."

"Didn't he tell his wife that I wouldn't be back?"

Ana shrugged. "I don't know."

"So, why didn't you tell Ronnie," I demanded, "so she could reschedule my patients?"

She shrugged again. "I thought she already knew."

# 8

As soon as I left the office, I immediately began my three hundred mile trip to Salt Lake City to locate Ian's wife. More than likely it was an avoidable trip, I could have continued my phone search, or hired a private investigator in Salt Lake City, or waited for her to eventually find me, but I felt responsible for Ian's disappearance. And just as I hated telling my newly biopsied cancer patients their diagnosis over the phone, likewise I felt Katherine McKenna deserved more than just an impersonal phone call.

The trip, however, brought back a flood of memories, both good and bad. Fifty miles north of St. George and straddling Interstate-15 was Cedar City, home of the Tony award-winning Shakespearean Festival. It was also the home of Southern Utah University, where I'd obtained my bachelor's degree and where I first met my second wife, Samantha Rose Jardine. My smile soon faded to a frown as I remembered it was also where my good friend and mentor, chemistry professor Dr. Marcus Westover was killed, actually murdered in a laboratory fire. I sighed and shook my head. Though unwitting on my part, his death was nevertheless partially my fault. Damn! It was hard even now and I forced my mind in a more pleasant direction.

In Fillmore, about the halfway, I stopped to let Malachi out to stretch his legs, filled the Dodge up with very expensive diesel, then purchased a couple of sandwiches at a fast food restaurant for Malachi and me. Malachi again got a double cheeseburger and me a vegan burger. All three of my wives had tried, but not succeeded in breaking me of the fast food habit. However, they would have all been thrilled, maybe not Kylie, but the other two would have been thrilled about my new vegan trend.

Two and a half hours later we topped the sloping three hundred foot high gravel ridge, Point of the Mountain, which separated Utah Valley from Salt Lake Valley. To my left, the ridge sloped sharply down to the Jordan River and the Utah State Prison Complex in the rapidly growing suburb of Draper. To my right the ridge abruptly inclined, almost vertically, another thousand feet to the Salt Lake County Flight Park, a foothill bench area dedicated solely to the many para and hang gliders residing in northern Utah. Just above the Flight Park, I could pick out the almost perpendicular track of the famous Widowmaker Motorbike Climb, a death-defying annual event where dirt bikes attempted to climb another thousand feet at an unbelievable seventy-percent grade.

As I started my descent from the Point of the Mountain into the valley, my eyes immediately began to itch and burn. In the distance, I could see a gray/black particulate layer of smog, floating over and blanketing the Salt Lake Valley. With the absence of any wind and a stationary dome overhead of high atmospheric pressure, this was a common problem this time of year. The cold air and smog were trapped, squeezed between the Wasatch Mountains to the east and the Oquirrh Mountains to the west. As I descended further down into the valley, I kept an eye on the Dodge's digital thermometer. It dropped from forty-five degrees at the Point of the Mountain to a chilly thirty-one degrees at the valley floor, a classic temperature inversion, also typical this time of year.

The freeway was already congested even though it was only three o'clock in the afternoon. Thankfully the city fathers had the foresight to add extra lanes for the 2002 Winter Olympics or Salt Lake City more than likely would be suffering total gridlock now. As I dropped into the layer of smog, right at the interface I could see the tops of skyscrapers and the copper-domed Utah State Capitol Building in the distance. Their heads gleamed in the bright sunlight, while their bodies, below the interface and immersed in the blanket of smog were invisible. After reaching the valley floor, I still had another thirty minutes of driving through this thick soupy air before reaching downtown.

After exiting I-15 at 600 South, I pulled over and fished out my smart phone. I typed--no, pecked--in *Salt Lake County Vital Records*, which was not easy on the small virtual keyboard, then entered it into the Google search engine. Within seconds, I discovered there were two different locations: one at 288 North 1460 West and the other at 610 South 200 East. I decided to start with the latter, since it was only five minutes away.

The 610 South Vital Records location was a two-story building constructed of Sienna brown brick with the exterior walls recessed into an exposed framework of bare concrete. On both levels, the concrete roof overlapped the walls and windows by roughly four feet, creating the illusion of a completely encircling portico supported by well-spaced solid concrete columns.

After a few minutes of circling, I found a metered parking space and somehow managed to squeeze the Dodge into it. After instructing Malachi to stay, I hurried inside.

Manning the desk was a humorless lady submerged in a tent-like dress, sporting an ankle-length hemline and wrist-length sleeves, and looking like the quintessential librarian. She curtly informed me the only records kept at this facility were those from the County Health Department. All vital statistics, such as birth, death and marriage were housed at the other building. Frowning, I looked at my wristwatch, then thanked her and rushed back outside to the Dodge and Malachi.

When I arrived back at the pickup, a meter cop was standing on her tiptoes, trying to wedge a ticket under my windshield wiper.

"Ma'am," I calmly explained, "the ticket isn't necessary, I was just leaving."

"Sorry," she smiled almost apologetically as she finally secured the ticket.

"But I was only in there five minutes!" My voice raised just a single decibel.

"There's nothing I can do about it now." She shrugged and turned away from my pickup.

"What do you mean—nothing?" My voice rose another decibel. "You could tear it up."

"That's against the department regulations." She turned her back on me and climbed inside her side-by-side ATV painted identical to the much larger Salt Lake City PD cruiser.

"Geez, give me a break!" I shouted at her back.

She just waved and started her engine.

As she pulled away, I angrily tore up the ticket and tossed it in the gutter, then climbed into the cab. This trip was starting out just great! Was this some kind of a harbinger? Malachi, sensing my frustration, licked my face. Sighing, I finally gave him a hug and started the engine.

I took 200 East Street to South Temple, then headed east two blocks to State Street. At State Street, I again turned north for one block to North Temple, then headed due east again, crossing under the I-15 freeway and over the Jordan River. Finally, I turned north one more time at 1460 West Street. At the end of that street was the other Vital Records Department.

Once again, this records department was a rectangular reddish-brown brick building, but this time it boasted four stories and no concrete framework. Each story seemed to consist of nothing more than a continuous bank of dark sun-reflective windows.

After a bit of looking, I found a non-metered parking stall and hurried into the main entrance. At the reception desk, I waited ten minutes for someone to show up. Finally, I heard a toilet flush. A few minutes later a bespectacled male bureaucrat wearing a gray cardigan sweater and dark baggy slacks appeared.

"Can I help you?" he asked, without out looking up.

"That would be, *may I help you*," I blurted without thinking. I couldn't help it. I had a passion for both the study of English and Latin.

"Huh?" he looked up sharply.

"Never mind," I quickly replied, "but I do need help in finding someone."

Unfortunately, by then the damage was done. "Try the phone book," he growled, picking up the e-book he apparently was reading.

"I have. She's not listed."

"Maybe she has an unlisted number."

"Really?" I said sarcastically. "Gee thanks, I never thought of that."

"Look, Mister, we are not a telephone directory here."

"But you do have the records of births, deaths and marriage licenses don't you?" I fought hard to control my temper.

He paused, looked me in the eye and scowled deeply. After a moment, he spoke slowly and with seemingly a great deal of effort, like he had to force each word through a very tiny pinhole. "Do—you—have—a—name?"

I started to say no, but thought he wouldn't see the humor in that. "Katherine Kozlov."

"Middle initial?"

"I don't know."

"Can you spell it?"

I bit my lip, then began, "K-a-t-h-e-r-i-n-e," then "K-o-z-l-o-v."

He wrote it down, then finally turned on his computer, scrolled to the appropriate program and typed in the name.

"Nothing."

"What?"

"No birth, no death and no marriage documents. Nothing."

"Are you sure?" I didn't trust this guy. I had a feeling he would love to sabotage me.

"Come look for yourself." He pointed a way for me to get behind the counter.

Circling behind him, I looked over his shoulder as he cleared the screen and started over. He typed the name in correctly and checked the

90

appropriate boxes: birth certificate, marriage license and death certificate. Next he hit the enter icon again, then screen abruptly changed and a typed message appeared: *this person is not found.*

"Try Katherine with a *C*." I had assumed it was Katherine with a K, since Russians loved K's.

He typed in the appropriate changes. "No, still nothing."

Needless to say, I was both shocked and confused. After mumbling a hollow unfelt apology, I shuffled back to the Dodge and Malachi. What to do now? I needed a minute to think. None of this made any sense. I couldn't even find Ian's wife to tell her he was missing. This was nothing short of crazy. Crazy! Wait a minute. Hadn't Ian said his wife was a psychiatrist on staff at the University of Utah Hospital? That was it! I jumped back into the cab, started the engine, shoved it in gear, then headed east toward the Avenues and the University of Utah Hospital and Medical School, also my alma mater.

When I arrived at the university, I had to circle for fifteen minutes before finding a parking spot, then I took another fifteen minutes to let Malachi stretch his legs, urinate on a parking lot light pole and get a drink of water. With those essential tasks completed, I put Malachi back in the pickup, cracked the windows and headed for the entrance.

At precisely 4:25 p.m., I entered the foyer and stopped at the huge guest information desk, constructed in the shape of a large horseshoe. Four young people, I assumed to be students employed on a work/study grant, manned it. I chose the shortest line, then waited impatiently to talk to a clean-shaven, neatly dressed young man. As it turned out, it wasn't the shortest line. I impatiently abandoned it for another one, which then also promptly slowed down. A full fifteen minutes later, my Stetson in hand, I was standing before the desk and clerk.

"May I help you, sir," the young man politely asked.

Normally, I was reluctant to use my title for leverage, but on the spur of the moment decided it might help here. "I'm Doctor Lawrence Cooper here to see Doctor Katherine McKenna."

He looked at me suspiciously. "You're a doctor?"

Sighing, I looked down at my cowboy boots and hat, then pulled out my wallet and showed him a laminated card, a miniature replication of my diploma.

"Which department would that be, Doctor?" He handed my card back.

"Psychiatry."

"Let me check." He scrolled through several pages on his computer. "I'm sorry, Doctor Cooper, but I'm not finding a Doctor McKenna on the psychiatry staff."

"What about the general hospital staff?"

He turned back to his computer. "How do you spell the last name?"

Patiently, I spelled it out. "M-c-K-e-n-n-a."

"No, we have a Doctor Kenneth McKenney, but not a Katherine McKenna."

Now I was frustrated. "Could you please check again?"

"Doctor Cooper, believe you me, she is not here. Perhaps she recently left the staff. You could go over to the Psychiatry Department and check with them. Maybe they could give you some further insight."

"Yeah, okay," I nodded grudgingly. What choice did I have? "How do I get there?"

"They are no longer located in this hospital. They now have their own building over in Research Park, 501 Chipeta Way."

I thanked him and immediately left. Moving the Psych Department was certainly a change, one of many, since I was a student here. Fortunately, Research Park was not far, just north of the campus by Fort Douglas, but with the early rush hour traffic beginning, it still took me another fifteen minutes to get there.

The new University of Utah Neuropsychiatric Unit was a state-of-the-art four story, eighty bed, and one hundred and twenty thousand square foot cinnamon-red brick building. It was constructed like a three-legged mythical beast, probably appropriate for psychiatry, with the head serving as the reception and public entrance. The body of the beast was a long connecting hall and the legs were three annex wings coming off the body at right angles and probably containing the hospital wards and beds.

By now, my wristwatch showed it was straight up five o'clock. If I knew anything about psychiatric units, I knew they, like government buildings, closed to the public promptly at five. I shoved the Dodge's gearshift into park, cracked the window for Malachi, grabbed my cowboy hat and sprinted for the entrance.

A man in a starched white lab coat rushed out the front door just as I arrived. As he blew by me, I grabbed the open door before it could close and hurried in, stopping one more time at the lobby reception desk. This time, however, the curvilinear, alder wood desk was not manned or even lighted and sported a sign: *Closed. Will reopen tomorrow at 9:00 a.m.*

Frustrated, I started searching for a bell or buzzer or phone that I could use to summon someone. There were none. Getting even more irritated, I quickly checked the wall directory, rushed to the elevator, then punched the button for the fourth floor. According to the directory, the fourth floor housed the private physician (psychiatrists) offices. Exiting the central elevator, I wandered down the hall, checking the names engraved on the bronze plaques affixed to each door. First, I passed Jose H. Gutiérrez, MD (obviously Spanish, or Mexican), Lee Sambino, D.O (Italian, probably Naples), Tiffany Child, MD (Great Britain, most likely from England), Stephen Sandberg, MD (Sweden) and so on down to the end of the hall. But there was no Katherine McKenna or Katherine Kozlov or anything that resembled it. With growing disappointment, I hurried back to the elevators, then started down the hall, heading in the opposite direction.

Linda Nieto, MD (Spanish - nickname for someone descended from a prominent elder).

"Hey, Dude!"

I nearly jumped out of my cowboy boots. "Huh?" I quickly turned around.

"Hey, what ya doin' here, Tex?"

"Looing for a doctor."

"You know very well they've gone for the night." The man grinned, revealing yellow-stained ocher teeth.

He was of indeterminate age, perhaps thirty, or fifty, with a skinny refugee-like body. Oily tangled hair spilled down onto his thin bony shoulders; possibly the same color as his coffee brown eyes. His t-shirt was probably white at one time, now a faded pink (more than likely from mixing his wash), his jeans were faded and frayed at the knees, his Roman sandaled feet were without socks and his nails needed a trim. The only thing faintly officious about him, there was a large retractable ring of keys attached to his leather belt.

"How did you get out of lockup, Tex?"

"Huh?" This conversation made no sense to me whatsoever. "Name's not Tex. I'm Doctor Cooper."

"Yeah, yeah, I know," he laughed and grabbed my arm, "and I'm Jesus Christ or I used to be before I got back on my medicine." Then as he began steering me down the hall, he added, "let's head on back."

"Back? Back where?"

"Back to the floor." Then he grinned and winked, "your patients are waiting, *Doctor*."

"I don't think you understand." I abruptly stopped and refused to move. "I'm not a patient—"

—Not letting me finish, he changed his grip to my elbow, then once again began firmly steering me down the hall.

I was a head taller than him as well as forty pounds heavier and easily stood my ground. Latching onto his wrist with my other hand, I forcibly removed his hand from my elbow. "I'm not going anywhere with you, Stoner."

"Not been taking your pills, huh, Tex?" He grinned as he pulled out a cell phone from his front denim pants pocket. He punched a speed dial number, then held the phone up to his ear. "Yeah, security, I got an unco-operative up on the fourth floor by the doctors' offices." He turned off his phone and replaced it in his pocket. "Now, Tex, all we have to do is wait."

"There's no need for security." I instantly became more compliant and my voice was several decibels softer. "I'm just looking for a doctor."

"We'll find you a doctor, Tex, I promise, but first we've got to go back to the floor."

"Look, I'm not crazy," I blurted, though probably not everyone would agree with that, especially my ex-wives, "and I am not a patient here!"

"Oh! So you came in through E.R.," the Stoner grinned and grabbed me again. "Why didn't you say so? Come on, we'll go get you registered."

I was starting to lose patience with this guy. If anyone looked like he should be in lock up, it was him, not me. Again, I clamped onto his wrist, squeezing it has hard as I could. Finally, he let go, then I shoved him backwards out of my face and up against the wall. "Look!" I yelled at him. "You're not listening to me. I'm not a patient here. I'm Doctor Cooper!"

The smile finally disappeared and for the first time he looked worried, even frightened. "Whatever you say, Tex—uh—Doctor Cooper. Let's all just stay calm."

"Here," I reached for my wallet located in my back pocket, "let me show you. I have indentifica—"

—Suddenly, the stairwell door flew open, banging loudly against the concrete wall. Two blue-uniformed campus security guards were on me in an instant. The taller one grabbed my hand before it reached my wallet, then acutely twisted it upward between my shoulder blades. The pain was immediate and excruciating.

I whirled to the right, thereby untwisting my arm, then jerked to free it from the guard's grasp. As he grappled to get hold of my right arm again, I brought it up, executing a swift rabbit punch to the face. He staggered backwards, blood dripping from both nostrils. Pivoting on my heel, I turned to face the other shorter heavier guard. He lowered his head and charged. Like a capeless Spanish matador, I stepped aside, then as he passed dropped him with a vicious blow to the back of the neck. Once again, I quickly turned back to face the tall guard. With a blood-splattered hand, he pulled a Taser from a belt holster and aimed it directly at me. I knew instantly what it was and wanted none of it. Slowly, I backed off and very deliberately raised both hands high above my head.

"Where did you get this clown, Ziggy?" the tall guard growled, pinching his nose to stop the bleeding.

Ziggy grinned and shrugged. "Mike, I was checking all the floors and locking up, and he was just here."

"Where do you want him?" Mike, still pinching his nose, asked in an obstructed nasal tone.

Ziggy ignored him and continued to grin. "He sure gave you guys a battle, didn't he?"

"He just surprised us," the shorter guard said, "that's all. Usually your patients aren't violent."

Mike grunted, then as a test, he quit pinching his nose. The bleeding immediately started again. Scowling down at Ziggy, he then continued with a nasally twang. "Come on, Ziggy, I'm tired of this shit and I've got to get my nose taken care of. Where do you want this jerk?"

"Back down on the first floor, the lockup ward," Ziggy stopped smiling long enough to add, "safe room number two."

With Mike pointing the Taser directly at my chest, the heavier guard handcuffed me, then they escorted me to a nearby bank of elevators and on down to the first floor. We paused briefly at the door to the lockup ward where Ziggy used his ring of keys to unlock the steel door. Mike shoved me through the door, then followed along with Ziggy and the smaller guard. Immediately, Ziggy relocked the door.

We appeared to be in a spacious day/recreation room sporting a large Samsung 58 inch-screen T.V., a half-dozen overstuffed couches and chairs, and a well-stocked library. Also, I noted scattered around the room there were several game and recreational tables: Ping-Pong, chess/checkers, air hockey and a pool table. A few curious patients looked up as we entered and a couple of them edged forward for a closer look.

"Looks like they got you, huh, Tex?" One glassy-eyed man observed.

"You can put him in my room," a young lady with a pink Mohawk winked.

Ignoring them, Ziggy led our group across the room while I continued to eye the room and its inhabitants.

With her reading glasses dangling from her neck, secured by eyewear retention straps, a woman dressed in street clothes and carrying a clipboard rushed up.

"Beth," Ziggy was all business now, "Beth get me ten milligrams of Haldol stat."

"P.O.?"

"Geez, Beth what do you think?" Ziggy said sarcastically. "Look at him—no I.V."

Pivoting on the heels of her sneakers, Beth rushed off in the same direction she had just come.

With the patients trailing behind us, Ziggy and the guards ushered me from the dayroom, turning abruptly left and down a short hallway, stopping at a door simply labeled, "2." Again, Ziggy opened the door with a key and the guards shoved me in.

Stumbling forward, I tried to keep my balance, but nevertheless tripped and fell forward, face down. Surprisingly, I was not hurt. Fortunately, the floor was covered with soft white gymnastic mats and the walls were padded with a similar material. Immediately, the guards grabbed me by the arms and shoulders and helped me back to my feet. As I stood, I took rapid inventory of my surroundings.

I was in a mostly white room with no wood or plastic furniture, or other sharp objects for that matter. As I mentioned, the walls were padded and the bed, which appeared to be made of memory foam, had no frame and was placed directly on the padded floor. As best I could tell there was no bathroom and the only door was the one through which we had just entered. The only lighting was from the ceiling, and it was recessed and grated. There were no lamps or nightstands. There was, however, a single window, probably made of prison-strength reinforced glass, which over-looked a serenely landscaped courtyard.

Nurse Beth rushed in, syringe in hand. "Ten milligrams of Haldol," she snapped, sounding like a surgical nurse as she shoved syringe into Ziggy's hands.

After uncapping the syringe, Ziggy turned to the guards. "I need his arm like this." He demonstrated the correct position using his own arm.

He strapped the tourniquet tightly to my upper arm, then slapped my ante cubital fossa, trying to get a recalcitrant vein to surface.

With the strength of adrenaline, I fought back, jerking my arm away.

"Geez, you guys," Ziggy complained to the guards as he tried in vain to aim his needle at my still-moving arm. "Now hold him still!"

"No!" I shouted and jerked my arm again.

# 9

"No! Stop!" I screamed one more time and momentarily wrenched my arm free. "I—I have a dog in my truck."

"What?" Ziggy hesitated, the needle hovering inches from my recaptured arm.

"I have a chocolate lab in my truck. He'll die if someone doesn't care for him."

"Man, don't even joke about that," Ziggy mumbled. "I love dogs."

"I'm not joking!"

"He's lying," the tall guard, Mike, declared.

"No, he may be hallucinating," Nurse Beth argued.

"Maybe--I don't know." Ziggy seemed unsure. "What's its name?"

"It's not an it; it's a he," I responded quickly, "and his name is Malachi."

"Malachi," Beth repeated, "obviously this is some kind of a religious delusion."

"Huh?" Ziggy looked up at Beth.

"Malachi is the last book in the Old Testament," Beth said, then added, "for you Jews, I'm pretty sure it's in the Torah as well."

"I wouldn't know," Ziggy shrugged. "I'm not religious." Then he turned back to me. "A lab, huh?" Ziggy paused and seemed to be debating with himself. "Where's your truck?"

"He doesn't have a truck," Nurse Beth insisted. "I'm telling you he's a schizophrenic."

I ignored her. "It's a gray Dodge diesel pickup, parked in the second row right in front of this building."

Ziggy frowned and paused again. Finally he asked, "You got the keys?"

"If these Gestapo thugs," I scowled at the guards, "would release my arms, I would get them for you."

Ziggy nodded to the security guards. Reluctantly they loosened their grip on me, but remained close enough to seize me again if I decided to act up. Carefully, and making no sudden moves, I reached into my jeans pocket and fished out my ring of keys. It was substantially smaller than Ziggy's.

"Which one?" Ziggy asked as he accepted the keys.

"Probably," I replied sardonically, "the big one that has *Dodge* stamped on it." Once again, I couldn't help myself.

Ziggy ignored my jab and held up a silver key with the black plastic head cover with an attached remote control. "This one?"

I nodded and held my tongue.

Ziggy turned to the guards. "Keep him here while I go check this out."

"Damn it, Ziggy," Mike moaned and pointed, "my nose."

The heavier guard complained, "Ziggy, do you think we have nothing better to do than babysit your crazies?"

Nurse Beth immediately rebuked him. "Zack, we don't use that word around here."

Ziggy grinned at them. "Mike, Zack, I'll be right back." He handed the Haldol syringe to Beth, then with keys jangling exited the lockup safe room.

"Ziggy," Mike stopped him, "we're going to take the cowboy back out into the dayroom while we wait." Gingerly he touched his already swollen nose, then added, "Where there's some chairs."

"Yeah," Zack agreed, "my plantar fasciitis is killing me."

Ziggy shrugged. "I don't care. Just don't let him out of your sight."

We followed Ziggy out of the safe room, then as he left the dayroom we found some empty chairs over by two older gentlemen sitting at a chess table.

"You want me to take a look at your nose," I asked Mike after we were all seated.

"No," he growled, "keep away from me."

"It's up to you," I said indifferently, "but I do have some ENT training."

"ENT training?"

"You know," I replied, "as an intern I did a rotation on Ears, Nose and Throat."

"Keep away from me," Mike growled again. "You're not a real doctor."

"It's up to you," I said again. Shrugging, I turned my attention to the chess game. "Do you mind if I watch?"

"No, I don't mind," the bald man on my right said, "but I need to warn you, this match is a bit like pouring cold molasses from a Mason jar. It takes Al forever to move."

Nodding, I pulled my chair a little closer. I loved the game of chess and figured since we had a few minutes to kill, why not?

The bald man, wearing a yellow knit shirt, moved his white knight from G-1 to F-3, then waited for his partner Al to move.

After a minute, he gave a verbal nudge. "Al, it's your move."

Another minute went by and still nothing from Al.

"Al," the bald man persisted, "do you want to play or not?" This time he nudged him with his hand.

When again Al didn't answer, I looked at him more closely. His eyes appeared glassed over; he was salivating excessively; and suddenly developed bizarre movements of his tongue and facial muscles. Also now there was a generalized tremor of his hands and legs, and his neck strap muscles were rigid as a board. All this muscle spasm and rigidity prevented his jugular veins from draining and they bulged like a tourniquet had been placed around and was constricting his neck. Even as I watched, the cervical muscle spasm seemed to progress, resulting in extreme tightness of throat as manifest by difficulty in swallowing and breathing. And all this spasm was punctuated by the continual odd thrusting and oscillating motion of his tongue.

Then without warning, he abruptly fell face first right onto the chessboard, scattering pawns, knights and bishops, sending them flying and clattering to the floor.

Jumping up from my chair, I grabbed Al and gently transferred him to the hardwood floor. Groping his neck, I managed to find his carotid pulse. Even though it was rhythmic, it was also very fast with very little amplitude. I counted as best I could - approximately168/minute! From my internship, I remembered Haldol overdose often presented with *torsade de pointes*, a ventricular tachycardia with multiple points of electrical origin.

Just the opposite of his runaway heart, Al's breathing was labored, strident and very slow. I counted his respirations at 7/minute. With his generalized muscle spasm, I decided he had also developed severe bronchospasm. It was a bit like trying to draw air through a collapsed coalmine vent. With his lungs getting no air, obviously that meant his brain was getting no oxygen. I knew it only took about five minutes of anoxia before delicate cerebral neurons started dying and at a very rapid rate. I had to do something and I had to do it now!

"Nurse Beth," I barked, "do you have a crash cart on this floor?"

Still holding the Haldol syringe, she looked blankly at me but didn't answer.

"*Nurse!*" I grabbed her shoulders and shouted, "Where's the crash cart?"

"Uh—uh, in the med room," she mumbled.

"Well, go get it." She still didn't move. *"Now!"* I yelled.

Suddenly, she leaped into action and sprinted to the med room, returning only seconds later with the crash cart.

As she handed over the cart, I continued to bark out orders. "Get me some help, the medical resident on call for the hospital. And have them send an ambulance."

Quickly I sorted through the cart, finally locating a laryngoscope and a #8 endotracheal tube. After jerking the cushioned pad from an overstuffed chair, I handed it to Beth, then lifted Al up so she could insert the cushion under his shoulders. With his torso elevated, I could now lower his head far enough back to insert the laryngoscope. After cranking upward as much as I dared without breaking his dental incisors, I used the endotracheal tube, like a tongue blade, to depress the tongue down far enough to see the epiglottis and vocal chords. Like two sliding patio doors, they were firmly closed, tightly shut. Gently, I tried pushing the endotracheal tube through the vocal chords. They refused to open. I tried a little harder - still nothing. I dared not use even more force as I might permanently rupture or damage the chords. If injured enough, Al would never speak again.

Again, I searched through the cart till I found a vial of succinylcholine, then drew up 5 cc's. Al's jugular veins were still bulging so I simply shoved the needle in, drew back blood, then injected all 5 cc's. This was risky maneuver as succinylcholine caused temporarily paralyses (6-8 minutes) of all skeletal muscle, i.e. the patient would not be able to use his diaphragm or intercostal muscles to breath. But hopefully, the succinylcholine would relax the laryngospasm enough that I would be able to insert the endotracheal tube, then I could breathe for him. If I did not succed, the patient would be dead.

As I waited the obligatory sixty seconds for succinylcholine to work, out of the corner of my eye I noted Ziggy had returned with Malachi. Though Malachi immediately bolted for me I had no time for him now. Hurriedly, I patted his head, then indicated for Ziggy to take him back.

I checked my watch; sixty-two seconds had passed. After repositioning the laryngoscope, I gently pushed the endotracheal tube—still nothing. I pressed more firmly. I had to get the tube in or Al would die! Finally, the chords opened a little and I wedged the endotracheal tube between them. The succinylcholine worked! Carefully I advanced the tube down the trachea a couple more inches. Al may have a little hoarseness for a while, but at least now he could breathe.

As I located an Ambu bag in the lower drawer of the crash cart, I noticed Nurse Beth had returned. I attached the bag to the endotracheal tube and began rhythmically squeezing, roughly 16-18 breaths/minute. Undoubtedly, I'd have to ventilate Al until all of the succinylcholine had worn off and he could breathe on his own.

While I worked the bag, I again felt Al's carotid pulse, still 172 beats/minute and still regular; there were no irregular beats. It had to be ventricular tachycardia, which often progressed to ventricular fibrillation, which often progressed to asystole and death.

"Nurse," I turned to Beth, "fire up the defibrillator."

Surprising for a psychiatric nurse, Beth seemed to know how the defibrillator worked and seconds later had it charged up and ready to go. I accepted the paddles from her, placed them diagonally across Al's bare chest, then pushed the electrical discharge button. Unfortunately, my right knee was touching Al's chest. The current surged through Al's chest, then instantly jumped to me, nearly knocking me over. Quickly, I checked my pulse, thankfully it was still normal sinus rhythm, then I checked Al's. It was still V-tach!

"Again," I shouted at Beth.

When she gave the okay, I fired a second time. Al's chest bucked once again, but this time I did not bleed off most of the current to my leg. As I grabbed the Ambu bag again, I checked Al's pulse again - much slower, 92/minute and regular. Thank God!

Still thanking a God I didn't really believe in, I delegated the Ambu bag and respiratory care to Nurse Beth, then searched the crash cart for the necessary fixings to start an I.V. After tightening a tourniquet around Al's upper arm, I slapped his hand several times till a vein popped up. As I inserted a #18 angiocath in the vein, the medical resident and his intern arrived.

Securely, I taped the I.V., then gladly, thankfully, turned Al over to the medical resident and her intern. With our help, they lifted Al onto a gurney and wheeled him out of the dayroom toward the ambulance waiting outside.

After they were gone, I turned my attention back to Malachi, giving him his usual and more appropriate greeting - a big hug. He was ecstatic!

Wide-eyed and with mouth agape, Ziggy stared at me.

# 10

Finally Ziggy blurted, "Geez, Tex, I guess you really are a doctor."

I shrugged and nodded as Malachi began licking my face. "Or a damn good faker."

"So," Ziggy grinned, "where did you train—"

"—Ziggy!" Nurse Beth abruptly cut him off. "You know very well you can't bring a dog in here."

"Sure I can," Ziggy grinned. "We'll call it canine therapy. We do it all the time."

"But—but this dog hasn't been trained or checked out," Beth argued. "What—what if he has the mange or rabies?"

Ziggy shook his head. "I hardly think he has the mange, rabies or any other disease. Come on, Beth, just look at him; that dog has been pampered." He paused, looked at me, back at Malachi, then switched his gaze to the security guards. "Mike, I really don't think I'll be needing you guys any more." He nodded at the door. "Go ahead and get your nose looked at. I need some time to talk with Doctor Cooper and get this whole thing straightened out."

"He could be dangerous," Mike cautioned, re-examining his sore nose.

"Nah, I don't think so. Just look at that tail." Ziggy pointed at Malachi's furiously wagging tail.

"No, not him," Mike said suspiciously, "I mean the crazy cowboy."

Beth scowled and started say," Mike, we don't use—"

—"Nah," Ziggy cut her off, "I don't think so. I'll be okay."

"What do you want me to do with this?" Nurse Beth growled, holding up the unused syringe of Haldol.

"Just pick out a patient," Ziggy gestured around the room, "any patient and give it to them." Then with a straight face he added, "we sure as hell can't waste it."

Beth looked furious, but bit her tongue.

"If you don't want to do that, I suppose," Ziggy smothered a chuckle, "you're going to have to waste it."

Nurse Beth threw her hands up in frustration and stomped from the room. The two security guards looked at each other, shrugged, then followed after her.

Ziggy picked out an empty card table, sat down then motioned for me to do the same. Malachi immediately trotted over to Ziggy, lowered his head and shamelessly begged for affection. Ziggy grinned, stroked his head and rubbed his ears.

Annoyed with Malachi, I silently watched this gross breech of loyalty.

"So, have you got any identifications?" Ziggy finally asked, still petting Malachi.

"You should have asked me that thirty minutes ago," I growled, pulling out my wallet, locating my laminated diploma card and handing it to him.

He stared at it for a moment. "You sure don't look like a doctor," he finally said.

"Well, you sure don't look like—" I paused, "—you sure don't look like whatever you are."

"I'm a resident."

"Oh," I looked at him sharply, "that figures." Silently, however, I thought what's he doing with the keys? That's like having the mountain lion guard the deer herd.

"No, I'm not a resident patient," he chuckled, "I'm resident-in-training in psychiatry, fifth year, an MD like you."

No, not at all like me, I thought silently, then added. "I understood psychiatry residency was only four years."

"It is."

"So, are you doing a fellowship, or something? A subspecialty?" I had done the same thing, an extra two years to subspecialize in urological oncology."

"No."

"Then what are you doing here?"

"Man, I don't know. I guess I just like it here and they need the help."

"So," I instantly made the diagnosis, "you're afraid to go out into the big bad world by yourself and get a real job."

"Yeah, I guess," "he shrugged and grinned sheepishly.

"I hear there they are looking for a psychiatrist at my hospital in St. George," I said then almost instantly wished I'd kept my mouth shut. That was just hearsay and did I really want him to move to St. George?

"I don't know," Ziggy hesitated, "I guess, I'm a classical Peter Pan Syndrome."

"*Puer aeternus,*" I added

"What? Sometimes, I must confess, I just don't understand you Doctor Cooper."

"Likewise," I said, then added, "that's Latin for eternal boy."

"Well, eternal boy or not, my name is Elijah Ziegfeld," he held out his hand, "but I only answer to Ziggy."

"I can see why," I replied with a wry smile, then added, "Your parents must be orthodox."

"Very," he nodded. "How did you know?"

"Believe you me, it wasn't hard. Elijah literally means the lord is my god."

"Well anyway," Ziggy said disinterestedly, glancing at his watch. "My shift was over at six. I'm starving. Let's go get something to eat."

As if somehow cued by Ziggy's words, my stomach growled and I realized I hadn't eaten anything after we'd stopped in Fillmore for burgers. "Yeah, okay" I said agreed. "Malachi needs something. You got any dog friendly restaurants close by?"

"Yeah, but they're all outdoor."

"So, that's okay by me."

"Man, it's too friggin' cold," he shot back. "Why don't we pick up something and head over to my apartment?" He stood up from the card table.

I hesitated, I really didn't want to go to Ziggy apartment, but Malachi jumped up and followed Ziggy. Somewhat reluctantly, I tagged along. Doctor Ziggy Ziegfeld, fifth-year resident, led us from the dayroom and out into the hall, then he opened the front door and we nearly tripped over each other getting out into the parking lot.

"Where's your car?" I asked. "We'll follow you."

"I don't have a car." Ziggy grinned, immediately producing a pack of cigarettes.

"How do you get back and forth to work?"

"The Trax Train." He selected a cigarette, then lit it.

I shrugged. City living without an automobile was just another sign Salt Lake City was now all grown up. Or maybe it just meant Ziggy didn't have a driver's license.

"We can take your pickup." Ziggy held up my keys.

I sighed in resignation. "What kind of food do you like?"

"How about The Steakhouse? They have takeout."

"I don't eat red meat."

"Oh," Ziggy looked surprised. "The Market Street Grill downtown has great seafood."

"Are you buying?"

"Huh?" Ziggy took a drag on his cigarette. "Well, no. I'm just a resident."

"Well then, choose something cheaper," I growled. "I'm currently out of work."

"The Red Lobster?"

"Cheaper."

"Long John Silver?"

"Okay," I grabbed my truck keys from Ziggy. "Malachi loves seafood. Oh, and put out that damn cigarette before you get into my truck."

Ziggy took two more long drags, stomped out his unfiltered Camel, then followed Malachi into the pickup. "Long John Silver is on State Street."

As I started up the Dodge and headed out of Research Park via Sunnyside Avenue, the stench of stale cigarettes filled the cab. I fought back the urge to sneeze and cracked a window.

"Turn right on Foothill Drive," Ziggy instructed.

I complied. "You must be a recovering something, alcohol or sub-stance abuse."

"Why do you say that?" Rather than offended, Ziggy looked amused.

"Doctors don't smoke anymore and recovering addicts do."

"Very insightful," Ziggy congratulated, then added, "yeah, alcohol and cocaine, but mainly alcohol."

That certainly answered why he didn't drive. More than likely had no driver's license, punishment for a DUI. "You're sober now?"

"Four years," he bragged, "and counting."

"You better not have any crack cocaine on you right now," I warned, "or I want you out of this truck. I don't need an arrest right now for possession."

"I told you I was sober."

"What if I don't believe you?"

"Why?" Ziggy looked wounded.

"Addicts are also pathological liars."

"True," he admitted, "but I'm clean."

We drove the rest of the way to Long John Silver's in silence. After picking up three dinners with two soft drinks, including an extra order of breaded fish for Malachi and an extra coleslaw for me, we headed for Ziggy's apartment. No surprise here. It turned out to be just what I expected for a recovering alcoholic/addict, fifth-year psychiatry resident suffering from a severe case of Peter Pan Syndrome.

Located downtown in the middle of the block between 3$^{rd}$ and 4$^{th}$ South and 3$^{rd}$ and 4$^{th}$ East, it was an old, three-story California-style bungalow home which was sectioned into five separate apartments. There were two apartments on each of the first two floors and a single studio apartment on the top floor. Probably at one time it was grand, maybe even an elegant house, now it looked pretty seedy with equally shabby landscaping.

After we found a place to park, Ziggy led the way, taking the steps two at a time until he arrived at the landing of his third floor studio apartment. Fumbling with his retractable key ring, he finally found the right one, unlocked the door, then held it open for Malachi and me.

Inside was no better. Immediately, I stumbled over a faded green, overstuffed ottoman, perhaps a match to an infested-looking green chair with a grungy blanket thrown over it. A similar looking overstuffed, possibly brown, couch was positioned on the opposite wall. The two conceivably parasitic pieces were separated by a wood veneer coffee table, once stained and varnished, now painted a garish turquoise green, probably trying to match the pea green couch and chair.

Instantly deciding it would be better to avoid the living room altogether, I headed straight for the small kitchen area. The tiny area was mostly filled by what I guessed was a dining table. Constructed from tube-aluminum, it sported a faded yellow Formica top, which was unevenly balanced on wobbly legs. Accompanying the table were two tube-aluminum chairs. They were upholstered with a now frayed yellow vinyl and looked like they might collapse under my substantial weight. But what choice did I have? After locating the cleanest spot on the table to set the food, I gingerly sat down and held my breath. The vinyl-covered seat ripped a bit more and groaned under my weight, but held.

Totally unfazed, Ziggy sat down opposite me and Malachi found his usual position on the floor at my feet. I passed out the Styrofoam boxes, keeping three, one for me and two for Malachi. Initially we concentrated on our food and ate in silence. The aroma of hot grease, stale cigarette smoke and fried fish filled the room. It didn't take long till I felt bile rise up in my throat. Trying to fight off the nausea, I concentrated on the coleslaw.

"So," Ziggy finally asked between bites of golden deep-fried fish, "are you really looking for a psychiatrist?"

I nodded, my mouth too full to speak.

"Schizophrenia," Ziggy proclaimed with confidence.

"What?" I looked up and frowned. Psychiatrists were certainly a strange breed. To say I didn't understand them was a bit of an understatement. It was like saying I didn't comprehend the new *String Theory* of theoretical physics, which I didn't, or the third law of thermodynamics, which probably I should. In medical school, it was a totally different breed of student that gravitated to surgery compared to those who chose psychiatry. Usually, they were complete and total polar opposites. Surgery residents tended to be more aggressive, more confident and more assertive. Psychiatric residents, on the other hand, tended to be more introspective, more contemplative and more thoughtful.

"Huh?" I repeated.

"You're struggling with schizophrenia, probably with associated religious delusions and illusions of grandeur."

"What?"

"You said you were looking for a psychiatrist."

"No!" I exclaimed. "I'm not looking for a psychiatrist for me."

"Ah, but *the lady doth protest too much, methinks*," Ziggy winked. "I know, you're looking for a friend."

"Actually, that's right," I snapped, my temperature beginning to rise. "I'm looking to find the wife of a friend. And don't throw Shakespeare at me! I might be a surgeon, but I had a little sprinkling of liberal education."

"So, why don't you tell me about it," Ziggy smiled condescendingly.

"You know what the problem is with you psychiatrists?" I blurted.

"That we go into psychiatry to work on our own problems."

"Well, that too," I growled, "but you really don't listen. You conduct all this verbal psychotherapy and group therapy, but you only hear what you want to hear."

Ziggy paused for moment. "*Touché*," he raised his soft drink to me, "point well taken. So, why don't you tell me your story? I promise I will listen this time."

Frowning, I lapsed into moody silence.

"Come on, Doctor Cooper, I promise to be quiet." He dragged his fingers across his lips in a zipping motion.

Haltingly at first, then eventually more freely, I related the whole story. I told him about the deer hunt, about losing Ian and Wally, about the search with no results and about my inability to find and notify Ian's psychiatrist wife.

As I spoke, Ziggy pushed his empty Styrofoam box away and lit a cigarette.

"They're still missing?" he asked when I finished.

I nodded again.

"Man, that's some story, Doctor Cooper." Ziggy took a drag on the cigarette. "That's either a very elaborately constructed delusion from a profoundly disturbed mind or it is a great example of the paradigm, *truth-is-stranger-than-fiction.*"

"Geez," I sneezed and waved the smoke out of my face, "do you have to smoke in the house? And call me Coop."

"Yeah okay, Coop. What's her name?" Ziggy grinned, but ignored my protest about the cigarette smoke.

"Huh?" I got up and opened a window. The cold air felt good on my face and the smoke-free air felt good in my lungs.

"What's her name?"

"Who?"

"The psychiatrist."

"Oh, Katherine McKenna."

"I don't recall hearing that name." Ziggy assumed a pose that was a rough imitation of the *Thinker*, except he had a cigarette in the hand under his chin. "You sure she worked at the University?"

"That's what Ian told me," I sat down again amidst the cloud of smoke, coughed and immediately got up again, edging toward the window, "and I think he should know as she is his wife."

"Well, I've been here for five years and I think I've worked with every psychiatrist on the staff and I've never met her. I'm pretty sure she is not on the teaching staff of the U. of U."

Exasperated, I looked down at him. Was he playing games with me? He grinned, he was always grinning, as he blew a perfect smoke ring.

"You have any ideas how I can sort this out?" I finally asked.

"Well," he said, as he ashed his cigarette into his empty Styrofoam box (unfortunately this added the odor of burning polystyrene foam to residual cigarette stench), "it appears someone is not telling the truth, either me, or Ian. I suggest you start by checking us out."

I was surprised at the clarity of his logic. Of course, it was obvious, that's what I should do. "You got a phone book?"

Instead, Ziggy pulled out his smart phone. "What do you want to know?"

"Find me the address of Ian's law firm—uh—uh—Hansen, Zundel and something."

With a cigarette dangling from his lips, Ziggy worked his smart phone. "Hansen, Zundel & Stamos?"

"Yeah," I nodded, "I forgot the Greek. Where are they located?"

"They're downtown, not far from here, the Triad Center at the corner of Three Hundred West and North Temple."

Instantly, a lump formed in my throat. It was the very same building of Samantha Rose's old law firm. That was where she worked when we got married. Also, it's where we first made love. Hansen, Zundel and Stamos must occupy the floor below Samantha Rose's old firm.

"I'll stop by there tomorrow on my way out of town," I said. "See what they have to say."

"You going back to Saint George tomorrow?"

"Yeah, I've got to participate in a debate tomorrow night."

"A debate?"

"Believe it or not, I got railroaded into running for the county commission." I stood up and motioned to Malachi it was time to go.

"You can stay here tonight if you want," Ziggy offered, nodding toward the possibly infested olive green couch.

Through the lingering haze of cigarette smoke, I eyed the faded couch and decisively shook my head. "No thanks. There's a pet friendly hotel near here; I've stayed there before."

Ziggy walked me to the door. "I'll ask around about Katherine McKenna. If I hear anything, I'll give you a call."

I nodded and with Malachi stepped out onto the landing. Immediately, I filled my lungs with fresh and untainted air. Fresh and untainted were relative terms as we were talking about Salt Lake City air in the winter.

"I'll need your cell phone number." Ziggy followed me out on the landing. A cloud of cigarette smoke escaped through the open door and swirled past my face.

"What?" I sneezed and frowned.

"If I find anything, I need to be able to get hold of you."

I didn't like the idea of him having my phone number and it was pretty unlikely he would come up with anything worthwhile, but on the other hand how much of a pest could the little long-haired, chain-smoking, fifth-year-resident be? And if he did find something—well I really would want to know. Reluctantly, I gave him my number, which he immediately punched into his cell phone directory. I started down the stairs. Halfway down, I turned back around.

"You're still an addict, you know."

"Nah, man, I swear I'm clean."

"No, man," I mocked him with his own colloquialism, "it's the cigarettes, man. You've got to do something about those damn cigarettes."

He shrugged and grinned. "It's best to conquer one addiction at a time, Doctor Cooper."

Sneezing one more time, I turned around again and with Malachi headed for the Dodge.

We spent another restless night at the pet-friendly motel. I was never a good sleeper and when away from my familiar pillow-top memory foam bed, I almost never slept well. Malachi, on the other hand, had no trouble whatsoever. As I listened to him gently snore next to me, I attempted to collate, dissect and analyze the events of the day. Try to make some sense of it all.

First of all, I appraised Ziggy. I honestly didn't know what to make of him. He was more than a bit odd. I would have to say he was rather weird and strangely eccentric, but most psychiatry residents were. And the cigarettes were more than annoying and he smiled way too much, almost to the point I wanted smash that irritating grin with my fist. Probably that was a sign of my own insecurity. But did any, or all of that, add up to or expose him as a liar? Probably not. And, what possible reason would he have for lying to me? None that I could think of. Nevertheless, I decided I would check him out tomorrow as well. Probably, the way to do that would be to contact his residency Program Director. He or she probably would not divulge the details of his life, but they could, and probably would, at least tell me if I could trust him.

Next my mind turned to Ian. Was he lying to me about his beautiful wife? Why would he do that? To impress me? That was a bit juvenile. Regardless, it appeared at least he was lying about her being a psychiatrist, or at least a psychiatrist on the staff of the University of Utah Hospital. Was he lying about him being a lawyer as well? Was he ever even married? Really, how much did I know about Ian McKenna? The embarrassing truth, not very much.

And what about Wally Stroud? I knew he was an investment broker, but almost nothing else. I had heard rumors of his legendary temper, which I had never witnessed. Several patients of mine were also clients of his and they'd had nothing bad to say about him. His wife, however, didn't seem particularly broken up when I told her about his disappearance. On the other hand, why should I expect her to care? Apparently they were not getting along and were divorcing. But still, I thought she might at least show a little concern.

After a bit my mind turned to Tim Slade. He also had the reputation for a temper, which I had witnessed in the operating room. I'd seen him throw surgical instruments at nurses in anger or frustration. Try as I might, I just couldn't shake the feeling he had something to do with Ian and Wally's disappearance. Unfortunately, I had no concrete evidence, but there was no doubt he had butchered a magnificent buck with an assault weapon! What kind of person did that? It was obvious under these circumstances I could not continue to share an office with him, or continue to work with him. That is if I ever got my privileges back so I could work again. No, without question, we would have to separate. What a hassle that would be and expensive too. Not only would we have to appraise all inventories and equipment so one could buy the other out, but we also would have to dissolve our legal bonds as well. Southern Utah Urology was an LLC, a limited liability company, and would need to be to be legally dismantled.

Groaning, I turned on my opposite side, but my mind didn't miss a beat; it immediately turned to the subject of guns. If I were honest with myself, I'd have to admit I was a bit of a hypocrite when it came to guns. I still pretended to hunt, even enjoy it, when in reality I despised killing and more and more thought of guns as evil. This last deer hunt and the slaughtering of the buck was just a tiny tip of the iceberg. How many mass and random shootings had there been in the United States the last few years, not to mention the killings of terror, passion, in the commission of a crime or gang related? It was an all-American travesty, which left the rest of the world shaking its head. But talking about being hypocritical! How many guns did I own? Several. Not only my .3006 deer rifle, but I also had a .22 Winchester rife, a semi-automatic Browning shotgun, a Beretta over/under shotgun, a .45 Desert Eagle handgun and a 9-millimeter Smith & Wesson handgun. What the hell was I doing with an arsenal like that? Not only did it make no sense, it was reckless, deceitful and—and hypocritical. Silently, and just like I did with red meat, I decided to swear off guns. Looking to the heavens, don't ask me why, I made a silent vow. When I got home one of the first things on my to do list was to get rid of all those guns. I also swore to never pick up a gun again. Somewhere I'd read the St. George Police Department had a gun exchange program. If true, I would take advantage of that.

Finally my mind turned to the upcoming county commission debate. My more liberal democratic friends had pushed and pushed, until I had agreed to run for county commission. They claimed I had good name recognition, a good reputation and had a respectable vocation, but most of all I was a native southern Utahan and by birthright a *good old boy*. What they did not want to advertise was my liberal leanings and encouraged me not to mention them either. A Democrat rarely got elected to anything in southern Utah and to have a chance I'd have to run as a conservative, or at least as independent. Surprisingly, the early polls put me in the lead, slightly ahead of my partner, Tim Slade, who of course was running as a conservative Republican. We vowed, Tim and I, the county commission race would not get personal and would not affect our relationship no matter how it turned out. It appeared that vow was no longer relevant as our relationship was already thoroughly trashed. Silently, I wished there was some way for me to gracefully drop out of the race.

I sighed out loud and Malachi stirred, then settled down again. And what about Ronnie Slade? Geez, I hated to admit it, but I would miss her a lot. Just her presence was like adding a fresh bouquet of flowers to the office each morning. Not only did she add much needed beauty, but she was always cheerful and also a most competent employee. Indeed, I loved to banter with her. She had a quick self-deprecating wit, often by playing the dumb blonde, and if honest I would also have to admit I would also miss her flirting. I sighed deeply again. God, how I was starved for female company!

At some time, though I don't remember exactly when, I must have fallen asleep thinking about Ronnie. This I only know because when the phone rang it took me almost a full minute to get oriented. Where was I? Was I still on call? Was it E.R.? Or the surgical floor? Had someone on the floor crashed, or needed immediate emergency surgery? I hoped not. Fumbling around the nightstand, I finally found the cell phone, unlocked it with a swipe and slapped it to my ear.

"Hullo," I mumbled, eyes still closed.

"Hey, man, you wanna go to breakfast?" The voice was bright and cheery, and I could almost smell the cigarette stench coming through the phone.

"No!" I shouted and hung up the cell phone and tried to go back to sleep. But now I was fully awake. Silently, I chastised my supreme idiocy for giving Ziggy my phone number. What was the hell was I thinking?

Once again I attempted to go back to sleep, but now it was hopeless. Getting up, I showered, called to Malachi and we went out to a fast food restaurant for breakfast. Malachi had two sausage biscuits and me a ham, egg and cheese breakfast sandwich. I offered Malachi the ham, then washed down the dry biscuit and egg with hot coffee. By the time we finished breakfast, it was after nine and we headed back to the University and the Neuropsychiatric Unit.

Once again, I parked out front. Fortunately, at this early hour there were still plenty of empty stalls. Hoping not to run into Ziggy, I quickly scouted the entryway, then entered the lobby and approached the reception desk. At the desk, I asked the receptionist, again probably a work/study student, to see the residency program director. He eyed me closely if not suspiciously.

"I'm sorry sir, do you have an appointment?"

"No, but this is very important."

"And who are you?"

"I'm Doctor Lawrence Cooper."

"I don't mean to doubt you," he grinned almost apologetically, "but could I see some identification?"

Frowning to show my displeasure, I nevertheless handed him my miniature diploma card.

"I suppose around here everyone thinks they're either Jesus Christ, God or a doctor," I joked as he looked at the card.

"Yeah," he agreed, "around here that's our Holy Trinity." He smiled sheepishly, handed my card back, then joked, "You know the difference between God and a surgeon?"

"No, I guess not."

"God doesn't think he's a surgeon."

I did not validate his joke with a laugh, though it was funny and like all good jokes it contained a grain of truth, but it did not apply to me. As a surgeon, I did not think I was God; after all I was mostly an atheist.

When I didn't laugh, the receptionist hurriedly added, "the cowboy boots and hat threw me Doctor. I will go see if Doctor Christine Chen has time to see you."

Dr. Christine Chen (obviously Chinese) was a small, very attractive woman in her mid-forties with nearly perfect English. From her facial features, she was obviously of American-Chinese ancestry. Her office had just the bare essentials, a desk and two chairs. I was surprised to see no Chinese art on the walls, no replicas of Ming vases on the floor and no bamboo screens. Why did I always stereotype people like that? But in lieu of anything Chinese, behind her desk on there was an impressive collection of framed diplomas and professional awards.

I shook her small hand. "Hi, I'm Doctor Lawrence Cooper from Saint George and I would like to talk to you about one of your residents."

Instantly a worried frown settled on her delicate face. "Chris Chen, nice to meet you. Which resident are you talking about?"

"Ziggy."

"Oh, Elijah Ziegfeld."

I nodded.

"What has he done now?"

"Uh—oh, nothing." I laughed, then paused. I really hadn't thought this through. On the spur of the moment, I tried to come up with a cover story. "He's—he's—uh—applied for privileges at Dixie Medical Center and I'm just doing a routine background check."

"So, Ziggy's finally trying to get a job!" She looked relieved and was instantly more cooperative. "What do you want to know?"

"Uh—oh—just the usual. Is he a good resident? Does he have a good understanding of psychiatry? How is he with patients? Any disciplinary problems?"

"He's actually a very good resident, one of the best we've ever had. I sure he'll make an excellent clinical psychiatrist."

Somehow I doubted he was that good, but I kept my thoughts to myself. "Is he sober?" I finally blurted.

She looked at me sharply, almost quizzically. "So, you do know about his past? Yes, as best I can tell he's been sober ever since he entered the program, some five years now."

"Trustworthy?"

"We never had any trouble with him. Lately, he functions more like junior staff, than a resident. He even has the keys to everything."

"I know," I said absentmindedly.

"Huh?" Chen looked puzzled.

"Oh, nothing," I stood up. "What about the smoking?" I couldn't help myself.

"Well, that is a problem, not only with him, but with a lot of recovering addicts. Do you think that will hurt his chances in St. George?"

"I don't know, maybe," I said bluntly, then shook her hand again. "Thanks for your time. That really does help."

"I do hope you give him full consideration," she smiled again. "It's not that we don't like him, but it's a lot like having an adult child at home; it's time for him to move out of the house."

I started to walk away, then suddenly turned around again. "Do you know a Doctor Katherine McKenna?" I asked.

"No," she thoughtfully shook her head, "never heard of her."

As I left, the Neuropsychiatric Unit, I wondered if Dr. Christine Chen was single. She had such a pretty smile. Sighing, I rejoined Malachi in the Dodge's cab and we headed downtown to the Triad Center located at the corner of North Temple and 300 West.

Occupying the entire second floor, Hansen, Zundel & Stamos was one floor below Samantha Rose's old law firm. I had to forcibly restrain myself. I so much wanted to continue on up the stairs to Cannon, Jeffs & Hanks and ask if they'd heard from her lately, but showing great restraint I opened the glass door and entered the foyer of Hansen, Zundel & Stamos.

Like almost every other law office I'd been in, and believe you me I have been in a few, this one was richly furnished. It was the complete opposite of Dr. Christine Chen's office. Once again, I was amazed how lawyers could afford more lavish furnishings than doctors, or maybe it was they had a better sense of interior design, or maybe it was they did not need to be as practical, i.e. they probably did not have clients throwing up or leaking bodily fluids all over their floors and furniture.

Quickly, I crossed the plush rose-petal pink carpet and approached the impressive black walnut desk. An equally well-dressed and meticulously made-up woman glanced up at me with a forced cosmetic smile.

"May I help you, sir?" she asked, though she sounded like she really didn't care to help.

"Yes, ma'am." I removed my Stetson. "I need to talk to Mister McKenna's assistant."

"And you are?"

"Doctor Lawrence Cooper, a personal friend of Mister McKenna."

"And you are here to see who?

"I just told you," I growled, "and that would be *whom*." Sometimes I just can't help it.

"Huh?" For just a split second she looked flustered.

"Forget it. Could I just talk with Mister Ian McKenna's assistant?"

Her smile rapidly faded to a frown as she checked her computer. "Would you excuse me for a minute, sir?" She stood up and quickly left the room.

Wearing a form-fitting gray business suit, sheer nylons and high heels, I watched her walk down the hall and enter a backroom. What can I say; she had a nice walk. I passed the time trying to figure out what I would say to Ian's assistant. Have you heard from Ian lately? When do you expect him back? Or, maybe just a curt, where's Ian? Do you know his wife? How can I find her?

I did not have to wait long. A couple of minutes later the receptionist returned.

"I'm sorry, sir," she said curtly, though she didn't sound sorry, "there is no Ian McKenna that works here."

"Are you sure?"

"Yes, sir, I am very sure."

# 11

I was well within Beaver County, almost to the small farming town and county seat of the same name, when my cell phone rang, a barking dog ring tone. Malachi perked up his ears as I pulled over to the side of the road and fumbled to unlock my phone. To be honest, I really disliked smart phones, preferring my older, simpler and more user-friendly flip phone.

Finally, I succeeded in silencing the barking dog. "Hello," I growled.

"Hi, buddy."

"Oh, hi, Russ." I immediately recognized Russell Spielman's (German/ Jewish-occupation name meaning musician) voice. He was perhaps my only friend not employed in the healthcare industry and also thank goodness, he was not a hunter. Other than being a non- hunter, the other thing we had in common is we were both single, me divorced, Russ was a widower. His wife, Camille, died of a particularly virulent renal cell carcinoma. I had operated on her, but it was too late. That's how Russ and I met.

"How's it going?" I added.

"I could use a little more business," he laughed. "Want to sell your office?"

I hesitated. Silently, I said maybe. Who knew what would happen with Tim and me, but I didn't want to talk about that now. "I would in a second," I joked, "if I could get a job like yours."

"You couldn't live on my salary."

"I would like to try."

"Yeah, well, how about some racquetball tonight?"

"Can't. I've got the county commission debate tonight. How about tomorrow?"

He paused. "Yeah, okay, that works. How about two o'clock?"

"Two o'clock?" I echoed doubtfully.

"Yes, Coop, it's Saturday."

"Oh, yeah, call me tomorrow and remind me."

"Just put it on you smart phone calendar," Russ said. "The phone will remind you."

"I don't know how."

Russ sighed, then hesitated. "Uh, you know, Coop—"

118

"—Yes, Russ." I also waited.

"You really should change your position on the pipeline," he finally blurted.

He was talking about St. George's current eight hundred pound political gorilla, the billion dollar-plus pipeline. The town was badly divided on the Water District's plan to pump water from the Colorado River at Lake Powell (Glen Canyon Dam) and pipe it one hundred and forty-seven miles to St. George, Utah.

"Russ, you know my position."

"Yeah, but some of us have gotta eat," Russ countered. "Like I've heard you say before, if a surgeon doesn't cut he doesn't eat. Well, likewise, if a real estate agent doesn't sell he doesn't eat."

"Russ, I do favor some well-managed growth."

"Yeah, but not that much growth," he said bitterly. "Do you know how many real estate agents there are in town?"

"We'll probably never agree on this."

"Yeah, but you're on the wrong side this time, Coop, both economically and politically."

"Okay, Russ," I changed the subject. "I'll see you tomorrow morning for racquetball."

"Yeah, okay," Russ said glumly and hung up.

Sighing, I turned off my phone and steered the Dodge back on the freeway. The pipeline was something Russ and I would never agree on.

We, Malachi and me, had traversed all of Beaver County and were cruising through Iron County just outside of Parowan when my phone rang again. With growing irritation, I once again pulled off the freeway onto the asphalt apron.

"Hello," I barked.

"Hey, man, it's Ziggy."

"Yeah," I said curtly. Geez, was it even possible to get away from him?

"I'm calling about the job."

"What job?" Again I could almost smell the cigarettes.

"Doctor Chen said you might have a job for me."

"Oh," I said lamely, then silently added, that's what I get for telling lies. They always come back to bite you. "Oh, well, that's not up to me." Hurriedly, I fashioned another lie. "It's up to the committee."

"Well, man, could you put in a good word for me?" Ziggy bubbled with enthusiasm. "I need a job and I would love to live in St. George. The red rocks and all."

"Yeah, okay," I replied halfheartedly, then added, "are you smoking right now?"

"Yeah," he admitted sheepishly.

"I thought so," I snapped, then hung up. Of course, there was no committee and just a rumor of a job, but if there was one I was pretty sure I would not support Ziggy's application. Not that he wasn't a good psychiatrist, he probably was, but I doubted St. George was big enough for the two of us. And why did Chen have to go blabbing to him anyway? No doubt she was probably overly excited at the prospect of getting rid of him.

In reality, with its burgeoning population, St. George was in dire need of another psychiatrist. There was a critical shortage of both mental health-care professionals and facilities in southern Utah, but nevertheless I was not prepared to have Ziggy that close. If it happened, I would undoubtedly have to change phone numbers, maybe even addresses.

It was just after five o'clock when I pulled up to my office in St. George. All the cars were gone from the parking lot, so I naturally assumed everyone had gone home. Normally, I didn't take Malachi into the office, Tim insisted it was unsanitary, but when it was empty I often did sneak him in.

After unlocking the back door, I ushered Malachi inside and almost immediately bumped into an out-rushing Ronnie Slade.

"Oh!" She grabbed her chest as she nearly jumped out of her high heels. "Oh, it's just Malachi! I didn't expect you."

"I'm sorry." I tried to back Malachi off, but Ronnie was already hugging him. "I didn't see any cars. I assumed the building was empty."

"My car's in the shop. I'm waiting for a cab."

"Uh—uh," once again I became tongue-tied around the gorgeous Ronnie, "uh—I could give you a ride."

"That would be fantastic!" she exclaimed just as the checkered cab pulled up. Pushing past Malachi and me, she hurried through the still open office door, across the parking lot and dismissed the cab.

Malachi and I followed her. "So are you ready to go now?" I pulled out my keys.

"Sure," she smiled and my heart melted. "Riverside Mercedes, it's, of course, on Riverside Drive."

"Yeah, I know," I mumbled though I'd never been in the place. It was a bit too pretentious for me.

After closing the office door and unlocking the Dodge, I climbed into the driver's seat. Somehow, Ronnie managed to wrestle Malachi out of his usual position and sat down next to me on the bench seat. Without complaining Malachi took the window seat.

With Ronnie's perfect body next to me, it was hard to concentrate on driving.

"So, how was your trip?"

"Uh—uh—not—uh—very productive."

"Oh, I'm sorry. What were you trying to accomplish?"

I took a moment and explained, without casting undue suspicions on Tim, about the disappearance of Ian and Wally and vaguely about the deer hunt. Lastly I explained, my trip to Salt Lake City was to find and inform Ian's wife, and how I still had been unable to locate her.

"That's certainly a very strange tale, Coop," she said, then hurriedly pointed her perfectly manicured finger to the left, "that's it."

"Yeah, okay," I braked and we pulled into the dealership, "did Tim mention any of this while I was gone?"

"Not much, just that we would be leaving Urology Associates and the sooner the better."

"You mean," I blurted, "you mean he's said nothing about Wally and Ian?"

"No, just that we were moving."

I was both incensed and at the same time relieved. Angry that he could be so cavalier about two missing and probably dead men, but relieved that he was planning to leave. So, that meant I would not have to go! Suddenly my relief moderated to a scowl. But that also meant I would have to buy him out and—and Ronnie would be leaving. Buy him out? Buy him out with what? Right now I had no income and very little reserve cash. I really needed to appeal the Surgery Committee's suspension.

"But I still haven't decided what I'm going to do," Ronnie continued.

"What?" I looked at her sharply.

"I haven't decided whether to go or stay at Urology Associates." She laughed almost blithely, then added, "I guess it would be Urology Associate now."

"Don't you have to go with Tim?"

"This is the twenty-first century, Coop," she again laughed out loud. "Woman are no longer considered chattel."

"But what does Tim say?"

"He said if I stay, we're through."

"Well, uh—uh," I should have stopped there, but I added, "you certainly can stay if you want."

She grabbed my hand, then leaned in and pecked me on the cheek. "Thank you, Coop. You're so sweet. I'll let you know." Somehow she deftly slid past Malachi, opened the truck door and got out. "And good luck with the debate tonight."

I watched her walk away with mixed emotions. Certainly, I would love her to stay at Urology Associates, but what about Tim? As I mentioned, he had a well-known temper, particularly when he drank. But ultimately, it was up to Ronnie; I knew I would stand by her if she wanted to defy Tim. Our relationship, Tim's and mine, was already beyond repair.

Sighing out loud, once again I headed back to the office. I needed a few minutes alone to prepare my opening statement for tonight's debate.

This time the office really was vacant. With Malachi lying next to me, I sat down at my desk and opened my computer. Quickly, I typed a letter to the Surgery Committee to appeal the suspension of my hospital and surgery privileges. After printing it, I faxed it to Dr. Jeremy Faux's office, then found another blank sheet of computer paper and a ballpoint pen. Call me old-fashioned, but I think better with a pen and paper rather than with a keyboard, and I really needed to jot down a few thoughts for tonight's debate. Sitting back, I rested my feet on the desk and tried to think, but now the office was tomb quiet, almost too quiet and my thoughts started to stray from their assigned task.

More than likely Ronnie had already picked up her Mercedes and was now heading home to face Tim. I wondered what that would be like? She had led me to believe her marriage with Tim was on the rocks, was over, but she had also hinted she was afraid of him. Now, after the past week, I certainly could see why. Silently, I hoped she would be okay. I didn't know for sure if Tim ever got physical with her, but I did know he put seventeen bullets into a defenseless deer using an assault rifle!

I tried to force my thoughts back to the debate. Unfortunately, I had been "roped" into running for county commission, an undertaking completely out of character for me. For years, I had steadfastly remained out of the spotlight, out of public life, except for my medical practice. Purposefully, I'd tried to stay neutral on most things, so as to not alienate patients by being too vocal on political or religious issues, but now here I was, a candidate for county commission. Unfortunately, neutrality was not an option now.

Of course, the single most important issue facing the city's voters was the question of growth. Should we? Or shouldn't we? If so, how much?

How fast? All other candidates had expressed they favored growth in some form and certainly there were some industries, particularly the housing/construction sector, which relied almost solely on growth. In truth, most sectors of the economy, however, benefited in some degree by growth. But growth, of course, was not without its problems: crime, congestion and air pollution to name a few.

St. George was surrounded entirely by the Mojave Desert with an annual rainfall of roughly seven inches per year. So, in order to sustain our average growth, four percent a year, there needed to be a new source of water. Present water supplies were reaching their limit and increasing our focus on conservation would only buy a little time. The Washington County Water District had offered a controversial new plan. Basically, their proposal was to construct a billion-plus dollar pipeline to convey water one hundred and fifty miles from Lake Powell and the Colorado River to St. George, Utah. All other county commission candidates favored growth; consequently they favored the pipeline. There was no one to represent the opposing point-of-view, so I was drafted as the reluctant standard bearer. Why I let them talk me into it, I'll never know.

One point three billion dollars! That was an extremely daunting debt for a small town of one hundred thousand to shoulder, or at least it was in my view. And there seemed to be no credible strategy, no realistic blueprint, to explain how we would repay this enormous debt. Sure, new construction impact fees would be raised, as would the individual water user's rates. But unfortunately, if this huge debt could not be repaid, resulting in default, the residents would have to shoulder the consequences of that as well. And to add further fuel to the controversy, some recent studies on climate change indicated the Colorado River may not be the unlimited, perpetual source of water as it was once thought.

But enough of this musing. I checked my wristwatch and tried to force my mind back to the debate. I really should jot down an outline, so I would have some idea of what I was going to say. Otherwise, there was a real possibility I would come across as a stuttering fool. Usually the moderator had the candidates give a five-minute opening statement and regrettably as of yet, I had nothing prepared. In my defense, I really hadn't had much time. But the electorate expected the candidates to say something, and sadly I was not very good at ad-libing either.

Fortunately, small town debates, as opposed to national contests, were typically quite benign; no dredging up the past, ferreting old skeletons out of closed closets and no vicious or personal attacks. Almost universally, they were courteous and civil affairs. The moderator and/or audience would ask each candidate his, or her, position on a particular issue. The candidates would respond respectfully, then move on to the next question. Also as opposed to national contests, evasive or tangential answers were not the norm and everyone usually tried to truthfully articulate his, or her, position. Customarily, there was none of that cagey politicking, vague answers and not actually taking a position, but instead mechanically regurgitating what the candidate thought the audience wanted to hear—

—Suddenly, I heard the front door of the office open and close, then the soft fall of footsteps on the tile floor in the hallway. I frowned. Who could that be at this hour? A burglar? An addict seeking drugs? Ronnie must have forgotten to lock the front door when she'd left earlier. Looking around for a weapon, I seized the closest thing, a bronze letter opener, then holding it like a knife took a tentative step toward the hall.

At that moment, Ronnie burst into my office, her hands full with a couple of white paper bags.

Surreptitiously, I dropped my weapon, the bronze letter opener, back on my desk.

"Thought you could use some dinner before your debate tonight." She smiled her most dazzling smile as she set the bags on my desk. "I'll bet you haven't bothered to eat."

I started to say I wasn't hungry, but thought better of it. "Thanks, Ronnie, but you didn't need to do that."

"I know I can't think on an empty stomach."

Actually I could, though I wasn't doing a very good job of it tonight. "What did you get?"

"Oh, I just stopped at that new Japanese place east side. They have a great oriental salad and fresh sushi!"

I gulped, but managed to hold my tongue. If she'd asked my two least favorite foods, more than likely I would have said exactly the same thing. Somehow I succeeded in hiding my disappointment. Even though I was presently experiencing an aversion to red meat that certainly didn't mean I favored raw fish. And I liked salads, but not salads dotted with mandarin oranges. "Thanks a lot, Ronnie. You shouldn't have gone to all the trouble."

"You need a good meal." She smiled again, as she looked me up and down. "You look like you're losing weight."

Her charismatic smile made me change my mind. Yeah, okay, I decided, I would try to eat the sushi for her. "Are you going to the debate?"

"I don't know," her smile suddenly vanished. "I'm supposed to go with Tim, for appearances, but he's tied up in surgery."

I didn't know what to say. I'm sorry seemed both appropriate and inappropriate, so I didn't say anything.

"Anyway," she quickly added, "hope you enjoy the food."

She picked up the bags again and handed them to me. As our hands brushed, I instantly felt the electricity of her touch. For just a moment our hands lingered, prolonging the contact. Neither of us moved.

*"So, there you are!"*

I nearly jumped out of my socks. Quickly, I lowered my hands, sliding them down to my sides, while somehow still managing to hold onto the bags of food.

An angry Tim Slade stalked into the room.

Mostly as an attempt cover my schoolboy blush, but also because of the events of the last week, I glared back at him and said nothing.

"Come on, Ronnie," he growled, ignoring me. "Let's go get something to eat before the debate."

"I thought you were going to be tied up in surgery," Ronnie said coldly, not moving. She did not seem at all embarrassed by all the drama, or if she was she certainly didn't show it.

"The case was cancelled," Tim barked. Seizing her by the wrist, he began dragging her from the office.

Abruptly I bounded from behind my desk, making a threatening move toward him. Not to be left out, Malachi also lunged forward, growling and baring his fangs.

"Stay out of this, Coop," Tim snapped, his voice hard and hostile. "And call off your friggin' dog before he gets hurt."

"There's no call to get physical!" I said tersely, taking another step toward him, Malachi still at my side. "And don't even think about touching my dog."

Somehow Ronnie managed to jerk her hand free, then she angrily stomped out of the room.

We watched her leave, then Tim turned back to me. "Trust me, Coop, none of this is your business." Tim locked eyes with me, then continued, "our business, yours and mine, will be settled on Monday." He glared at me for another couple of seconds, then turned and stomped off.

"In case you're interested," I shouted at his receding back. "We still haven't found Ian or Wally."

Slowly, Tim turned back around again. "That's too bad," he said without emotion. "I really liked those guys."

I bit my tongue and remained silent. On the spur of the moment, I could not think of an appropriate comeback.

"And," he added still without emotion, "good luck at the debate tonight." He pivoted around again and was gone.

Trying to control my anger, I watched him walk out of my office. I felt both worried and sorry for Ronnie. What a mess she was in! I wished I could help her, but I didn't know how. Anything I did was only likely to make things worse. Unfortunately, this was something she was going to have to do by herself.

Sighing, I turned back to my dinner. Removing both Styrofoam containers from the paper bags, I opened the lids and cautiously eyed my oriental salad and assortment of sushi, seaweed rolls and white rice. The smell was almost nauseating. Pinching my nose, I took a tentative bite of a California Maki roll, gagged, then offered the rest to Malachi. He seemed to like it, but that was not a great endorsement. Malachi would eat almost anything. I settled for the oriental salad, topped with mandarin orange slices. After removing the oranges, I'll have to admit, it wasn't too bad.

Once finished with dinner, I again turned my attention back to my blank sheet of paper. I sat there for at least another thirty minutes and still didn't jot down a thing. Sighing, I cleaned up my mess, called to Malachi and headed out the door. It was time for the debate and if I didn't hurry I would be late.

Tonight's debate was to be held in the historic St. George Opera House, also known as the St. George Social Hall. It was a beige, box-like building, originally constructed in 1864 by the St. George Gardeners' Club as a wine cellar. When the demand for wine dwindled due to the Mormon's new prohibition on alcohol, the building was expanded to host theatrical productions. It operated in this capacity until sold to the Utah-Idaho Sugar Company in 1936. They utilized it as a place to process locally grown sugar beet seeds. In 1988, the St. George Neighborhood Redevelopment Agency purchased it and restored it to an opera house. Now it once again was opened to the public and was used for a variety of community events.

After ducking in a side door, I saw all the other candidates, including Tim, were already seated on folding metal chairs, facing a packed hall.

126

Quickly, I checked my watch. In spite of my best intentions, I was ten minutes late. The first candidate, Alex Segar (English: a variant spelling of Seager), was standing before the podium extoling the virtues of the Lake Powell pipeline. He explained it would allow for more growth, which meant more jobs. More jobs meant more money for people to spend, more spending certainly would help the local economy and an improved economy would certainly shore up our tax base—

While he droned on and as inconspicuously as possible, I slipped in behind him, sitting down on one of the two empty chairs. Silently I hoped the one I chose was not the one Alex Segar had just vacated. Shortly after I sat down, Alex finished with his opening statement and turned around to his chair. Now, it was immediately obvious I was in his seat. Red-faced, I scooted over three chairs to the next empty chair.

The moderator immediately reclaimed the podium, then introduced the next candidate, Doctor Lawrence Cooper. She gave a short resume of my accomplishments, then turned to me. A smattering of applause accompanied me as I strode to the podium.

Unfortunately, I still didn't have much prepared. I grabbed the podium with both hands and looked over the audience, then like a computer screen wiped clean, my mind went totally blank. Perspiration popped out on my forehead, my mouth felt dry and desiccated, and my tongue stubbornly refused to move.

After clearing my throat a couple of times, I managed to croak out a few words. "Uh—uh, hello, uh—my name is Lawrence Cooper, but you can call me Coop." I laughed nervously, but unfortunately the audience didn't laugh with me.

Somehow I managed to channel my thoughts. "Uh—I think the pipeline is a mistake, a big mistake—uh—for a couple of reasons. One, with a billion dollar plus price tag—uh—who will pay for it? That's uh—uh—over ten thousand dollars for every man woman and child living in the county. I see no viable way of repaying this without raising taxes—and I mean raising them big time. Not only will this be an enormous debt we have to service, but we will undoubtedly pass it on to our children and grandchildren.

"And—uh—number two. Most of us live here, because we like the lifestyle of a small community. Uh—the Washington County Water Conservancy officials estimate with the pipeline, uh—we would have enough water for a city of five hundred thousand—uh—that's a half a million people! Do we really want this? Think of all the problems that go with a city of this size, not the least is major traffic congestion and skyrocketing crime. I repeat, do we really want this? Uh—uh—thanks for your time." I turned, and with my face burning red, hurried back to my seat accompanied by almost no applause.

Once again the moderator walked to the podium and briefly thanked me, then in glowing terms introduced the next candidate, Doctor Timothy Daniel Slade. Even I was impressed by his list of accomplishments. I only wished my resume was half as remarkable.

As it turned out, Tim was an excellent public speaker. He made good eye contact with the audience and knew instinctively when to intensify, or lower, or modulate his voice. To keep things interesting, he varied the speed of his delivery and spiced his material with humor. Lastly, as opposed to me, he knew his subject.

Smiling, Tim loudly cleared his voice, then began. "Good evening, fellow citizens. I think most of us agree on the need for the Lake Powell pipeline, after all we live in a desert. So tonight, I'm going to direct my remarks to another issue, which I feel strongly about - personal integrity and family values. In this day and age, with society disintegrating all around us, I don't think we can stress this too much. Non-traditional marriage, divorce, couples living together without the benefit of marriage and single parent households are becoming all too common. In fact, data collected from the latest U.S. census survey indicated less than half of all Americans are now growing up in traditional two gender, two parent homes.

"The fallout from this is obvious. Murder is on the rise. Rape is skyrocketing, as is drug and alcohol use. Teen pregnancy and teen suicide are both escalating at an alarming rate. More and more people choose not to work, not to become productive citizens, but live on the dole, on a multitude of government handouts. In my mind, there is no question you can trace all these appalling national maladies right back to breakdown of the traditional American family.

"When choosing your next county commissioner, man or woman, I think you need to consider the integrity of the person and whether or not his or her life, his or her actions, exemplify traditional American values, traditional St. George values. It's that important.

"If these values are important to you, you should vote for me, Tim Slade," he paused and winked, "and if you do, I just might throw in a free operation, one of your choice, of course." He sat down to a chorus of laughter.

There were two more candidates, but I only half-listened to their opening statements. It was more of the same, pro-pipeline propaganda. When they were finished, the moderator again took control of the meeting. The next segment, she informed the group, would be a question and answer session. Anyone in the audience with a question should stand up, then when called on they could direct their question to any or all of the candidates.

Instantly, four or five people stood up and patiently waited.

The moderator pointed to a woman on the third row. Instantly I recognized her as the owner of a local public relations firm.

After clearing her throat, she looked me in the eye. "I would like to know how Doctor Cooper feels about family values?"

I stood. "I am in favor, of course."

She remained standing. "How do you feel about same-sex marriages?"

Immediately, I knew this was a loaded question, after all St. George was a very conservative Mormon community, but I had to answer. "Uh—uh—I don't think we should discriminate against anyone regardless of race, religion or sexual orientation."

She zeroed in. "So, does that mean you favor same sex marriages?"

"Uh—yes, I guess it does."

Her point made, she immediately sat down and the moderator pointed to another woman on the back row.

"So, have you been divorced, Doctor Cooper?" Her voice was ripe with righteous indignation.

This was starting to feel more like an ambush than a random question and answer session. "Uh—yes," I admitted.

"How many times?"

I paused as if I had to mentally count. "Uh—three."

She still didn't sit down. "Have you ever been arrested and if so, how many times?"

Undoubtedly, she'd been researching public records already knew the answer. "Uh—uh—three or four, but there was never a conviction."

"Four times! Wow, that's a lot for a family man," she exclaimed, then abruptly sat down.

I breathed a sigh of relief. Finally, I was off the hook.

The moderator pointed to a bearded man on the back row. I immediately recognized him from the office. He was a patient. He had seen both Tim and me.

"I would like to know Doctor Cooper's position on gun control," the man asked.

Again I stood. "Uh—uh—as some of you might know, I am a lifetime hunter." I did not modify that statement by adding, although now a most reluctant hunter.

"What about assault rifles?" he demanded, almost angrily.

"I must admit," I took a deep breath, then slowly shook my head, "I must admit I fail to see why the average citizen needs to own an assault rifle."

"So, you don't believe in the Second Amendment?"

"Well, yes, and no. It is a different world now. When the Constitution was written, the most common and most lethal weapon was a musket, an instrument hardly conducive to mass murder. I sincerely doubt the founders could foresee the very efficient instruments of killing we have today."

"So, you would be in favor of changing the Constitution?"

Instead of answering, I said tangentially, "Mass murders are becoming all too common in this country."

"Guns don't kill people," he literally shouted, "people kill people." Then he abruptly sat down.

Rising again, the moderator pointed to another person—

The question and answer period lasted another thirty minutes with two-thirds of the questions being directed, or hurled might be a better word, at me. Somehow, I couldn't shake the feeling this whole fiasco was carefully orchestrated to get me. But whether it was, or not, I knew there was no way I was going to win this election. Certainly I wasn't going to slit my wrist over that, but I can say I can't remember when I was so happy to exit a building.

Without staying to mingle, as the other candidates did, I rapidly walked out of the St. George Opera House and joined Malachi waiting for me in the Dodge. I fired up the Cummins diesel engine and in the almost complete darkness of a moonless night we started the ten-mile trip back to Diamond Valley and the ranch. Just as I passed the St. George city limits, my cell phone, the barking dog rang. Fighting to control my temper, I pulled off on the asphalt apron.

"Hello!" I snapped. Certainly I was not in a very good mood.

"Who is this?" a female voice asked.

This salutation always annoyed me, the caller asking you to identify yourself instead of them, when they were the ones calling and interrupting. "Who the hell are you calling?" I barked, my blood pressure instantly rising.

"Is this Doctor Cooper?" she barked back.

"Yes," I growled. "And who the hell are you?"

"This is Katya Kozlovsky," she replied icily.

"Who?" I asked again.

"Katya Kozlovsky. Apparently, you've been looking for me."

"No I haven't," I snapped. This conversation was really starting to tick me off. "I certainly have not been looking for you. I think I would know if I had."

"I am Ian's wife!"

# 12

"No you're not, " I blurted, getting even more irritated. "Her name is Katherine McKenna."

"Actually, Katherine Kozlov McKenna."

Finally, the mental light came on and I made the connection. All I could say was, "Oh!"

"Elijah and I are coming down to Saint George tomorrow."

"Who?"

"Who, what?"

"You are coming with who?"

"That would be *whom*," she quickly corrected me.

I gritted my teeth. Instantly, I did not like her. Of course I knew it was *whom*. I had been distracted with shock and anger and had slipped up. Big deal! Under the circumstances, it was completely understandable. I quickly corrected my grammatical *faux pas*. "Who is coming with you?"

"Elijah Ziegfeld."

"Who?" I frowned.

"Elijah Ziegfeld, you've met him."

"Ziegfeld? Oh, you mean Ziggy."

"We have reservations at the Marriott," she continued. "Early check in time is two. We'll expect you at two-thirty."

"What has Ziggy told you?"

"Be on time," she said abruptly.

Her attitude was more than infuriating, but after all, I rationalized, she was Ian's wife. With him missing and possibly dead, she merited a little empathy. For all I knew, she might now be a widow; so cut her a little slack. I bit my tongue and answered evenly, "Yes, ma'am, I'll be there," then I hung up before I said something I would regret.

Before I got halfway home, where the highway closely parallels red rock chasm of Snow Canyon, my phone barked again. Once again, I headed for the side of the road, crushing a straw-colored tumbleweed, bouncing over a football-size lava rock and banging my head on the Dodge's roof. While rubbing my sore head, I searched for the still barking phone, now on the resting on the pickup's floorboards.

132

My mood should have been better, after all I'd found Ian's wife, or rather she had found me, but my head hurt and I was still stinging from her haughty attitude.

"Yeah?" I snapped after finally locating my phone.

"Hey, man, it's Ziggy!" He sounded like an over-inflated helium party balloon about ready burst.

"Oh, hi, Elijah," I answered without enthusiasm.

"I found her!"

"Yeah, I know—and you gave her my number."

"Hey, man, we're coming down to St. George tomorrow."

"So, I heard."

"Maybe you could set up some job interviews for me."

"What? What interviews?" I had no idea what he was talking about.

"You know for the job."

"Huh? What job?"

"You know, you talked to Doctor Chen about it, the one at the hospital."

Silently I groaned. Was that Chen lie going to haunt me forever? "How did you find her?" I quickly changed the subject.

"Find her? Man, she's my residency Program Director."

"No, not Chen. Ian's wife."

"Oh, man, I worked with her."

"I thought you said you didn't know her?"

"I didn't know Katherine McKenna, but I do know Katya Kozlovsky."

"Ziggy," I said, gritting my teeth, "as usual you are making no sense."

"It was easy," he continued, apparently oblivious to my bad mood, "once I figured out Katya was really Katherine and Kozlov was short for Kozlovsky."

"Oh, yeah, Kozlovsky literally means related to Kozlov," I said, while silently chastising myself for not figuring it out. After all, the meaning and origins of *surnames* was my hobby. I added, "and Katya is a diminutive of Katherine."

"A diminutive?"

"In Russian, a diminutive is an accepted nickname," I explained. "Like in English Hank is for Henry, Chuck is for Charles and Jim is for James."

"And Ziggy is for Ziegfeld."

"Well diminutives are usually for first names, not surnames."

"Huh?"

"Forget it. How did you find her?"

"I started going through old university yearbooks, they're online now you know, looking at pictures of past faculty here at the Psychiatric Department. I never found a Katherine Kozlov, but I did find a Katya Kozlovsky. Actually, she was junior staff when I was a first year resident, so I did know her and she's still senior staff and lectures here from time to time. From there, it was easy. I found the number of her private practice in the yellow pages, then called her. She actually remembered me," Ziggy gushed.

"You're pretty hard to forget," I agreed tongue-in-cheek.

"And I guess I've met her husband too, though I didn't remember his last name was McKenna."

"You met Ian? Where?" I asked.

"At the department Christmas party. He's a great guy; talked to him for quite awhile."

'I'll a bet he couldn't wait to get away,' I thought, but verbally I agreed.

"Yes, he is a great guy."

"Man, isn't it strange how all the world is connected. I've met your friend that is missing and I know his wife. That must mean something. Some kind of karma?"

I ignored his *connected* comment, instead I asked, "why doesn't she go by McKenna?"

"Huh?"

"Her married name is McKenna."

"I don't know, man. You'll have to ask her."

"I'm afraid to ask her anything."

"What? No, man, she's okay."

"If you say so." I was rapidly tiring of this conversation. "All right, Ziggy, I'll see you tomorrow," I said and immediately hung up before he could make another weird comment or connection. As I steered the Dodge back on the road it occurred to me that what Katherine was doing was not all that unusual. A lot of women used their maiden names for their professional careers. It was kind of a way to keep their personal and professional lives separate.

Five minutes later as I was rounding the volcano, almost home, when my phone started barking again. I suppose it's from taking hospital call for twenty years and having to get up hundreds of times in the middle of the night to go either to the emergency room or the operating room, but

134

regardless of the exact etiology I have a strong revulsion of phones. Three calls in ten minutes definitely exceeded my personal acceptable limit. Pulling off once again onto the gravel shoulder, I angrily swiped the unlock icon on my smart phone.

"What!"

"Coop?" The voice was definitely female and sounded taken aback by my brusqueness.

"Yeah," I snapped.

"It's Ronnie."

"Oh!" Immediately, I poured a bucket of water over my bad mood. "I'm sorry, Ronnie. I'm not having a very good evening."

"Well, that's why I called," she explained. "I thought you did great tonight. Saint George is changing, you know. It's no longer the small, homogenous, conservative town it used to be. You'd be surprised how many people sympathize with you."

While I appreciated what she was trying to do, we both knew I wasn't great and there wasn't that much diversity in southern Utah. "Thanks," I replied lamely, then quickly tried to change the subject. "Are you okay?"

"Why?"

"Well, Tim seemed pretty upset when he left the office earlier."

"Yeah," she forced a laugh, "I'm okay. I can handle Tim."

"Anyway, please be careful." Briefly, I considered telling her about the slaughtered buck, the Bushmaster assault rifle and the inexplicable absence of Ian and Wally, but decided against it. I didn't want to contribute to the breakup of their marriage, particularly when I wasn't yet completely sure of the facts, so I added, "and if you need anything—"

"—I've decided to stay," she cut me off.

"Stay? Stay where?"

"At Urology Associates."

"Oh," I said, then added, "great! But you mean, Urology Associate don't you?"

"What?" She looked puzzled.

"With just me," I explained, "it will no longer be Urology Associates, but only Urology Associate."

"Oh," she said, "now I get it. After all, I'm a blonde."

"Yes you are," I laughed, then abruptly turned serious. "Ronnie, I'm not so sure that's a good idea or a great career choice. Right now I have no hospital or operating privileges."

"You'll get them back," she confidently predicted, "and you can still see patients in the office, can't you?"

"Well, yes," I nodded my head even though she couldn't see.

"Then, I'll see you on Monday morning," she said brightly.

"Please take care of yourself."

With mixed emotions, I hung up the phone, then turned if off. I was not on call, had no patients in the hospital and I'd had enough calls for one night.

But what about Ronnie? Certainly I was happy, even cautiously overjoyed, Ronnie had decided to stay, but on the other hand I knew Tim would not take the news well. What exactly he would do, I was not sure, but I did know of what he was capable. Suppressing a shudder, I put the Dodge back in gear and once again headed up SR-18 toward Diamond Valley.

Back at the ranch, I checked on and fed the horses (they seemed fine), then supplemented Malachi's meager meal of sushi and my even less-filling oriental salad with microwaved hotdogs for Malachi and some Mac and Cheese for me. After wolfing down our nuked dinners, we headed to bed. Though completely exhausted, I did not immediately fall asleep. My stomach almost immediately started to churn and I began tossing and turning. I knew better than to eat that late, particularly fatty heartburn-generating foods like cheese. Getting up, I mixed a cocktail of baking soda and water, drank it down, then I had to fight the acute gastric distension from the instant production of $CO_2$ gas.

Finally, the gas moved on and I climbed back in bed, but still could not sleep. There was plenty to worry about. One, I had a meeting with Katherine—uh—Katya Kozlovsky McKenna tomorrow, ostensibly to explain to her what had happened to her husband. That would not be easy, because even I didn't know what happened to him. Suddenly, I had a premonition that the meeting might not go well and I made a mental note to check with Sheriff Tiny Klein tomorrow before going over to the Marriott to meet Katya. It would be nice if he'd found something, if I had some answers.

A related worry was Wally Stroud. At least his wife was not pressing me for anything, but what had happened to him? Had he and Ian suffered the same fate? Just by the sheer weight of coincidence, both go missing on the same day, would make one think so. There was an old axiom taught in medical school: *for any given set of symptoms, don't look for two diagnoses when one will do.*

Then there was Tim Slade. I dreaded the breakup of our office and feared the splitting of practice assets would not go smoothly. Tim had a legendary temper, he was bigger than me and younger than me, and quite frankly I was a little bit afraid of him. I didn't know what he was capable of, but—but now it appeared he was capable of almost anything. I was, however, relieved he had indicated his willingness to move. That was one less headache for me. The hunting for new office space and hiring movers, or even worse trying to move everything myself, was an ordeal I did not want to face at this time.

Also, there was Ronnie Slade to worry about. Would she turn out to be my Helen of Troy? If she stayed would Tim declare and wage a Trojan-like War on me? Should I even let her stay? After all, I could say no. Was I thinking with some organ other than the one in my head? Sure she was a good employee, but I was not about to delude myself that was all there was to it. There was no question I was attracted to Tim Slade's wife. Yes, and I had to remind myself she was still a married woman. If I had any sense at all I would tell her *no*. Even fire her if I had to.

Finally, my thoughts turned to the election and debate. What a fiasco, a blind-alley trap, a box canyon ambush, an Iraqi roadside I.E.D. (improvised explosive device) that had turned out to be. Regardless of what Ronnie had said, I had not done well. It had been nothing short of disaster! Now my liberal leanings, as well as my less than stellar track record with marriages and run-ins with the law were exposed to the entire electorate. There was no way I was going to win this election. Not in southern Utah. Not in a million years. Oh, well, I decided as my consciousness slowly faded into sweet oblivion, there was a definite upside to all this, now there was absolutely no need for me to campaign. Nothing I did now could or would ever change the outcome. That made the debate almost worth it.

What I really needed was some advice, impartial, but friendly. Mentally, I made a note; tomorrow I would find the time to go talk to my old friend and mentor, Jacob Heinz.

The next morning I was awakened by my favorite sound, a ringing phone. While trying to shed my lingering sleep narcosis, I fumbled for my cell phone. Malachi instantly jumped off the bed and hid behind a Lazy Boy. He hated ringing phones almost as much as me, undoubtedly his reaction was from watching the way in which I'd dealt with telephones over the years, usually as flying projectiles. Finally, I realized it was not a barking dog ring, but a standard ring, and reached for the landline phone on my nightstand.

"Yeah," I growled, "this better be good."

"Hello, buddy, you told me to call and remind you."

"About what, Russ?" At least I recognized his voice.

"About our racquetball ball at two."

"You called at this hour?" I blurted, "for racquetball at two o'clock!"

"What?"

"You had to call this early!"

"Geez, Coop, it's after ten!" Russ Spielman sounded both flabbergasted and wounded.

I glanced at the electronic clock, also occupying the nightstand. Sure enough, it flashed a very tardy 10:07 a.m. "Geez," I'm sorry, Russ," I apologized. "I guess I overslept."

"Yeah, it's okay. You still good for two o'clock?"

"Yeah," I nodded. "I'll be there."

By the time I fed the horses, fixed breakfast for Malachi and me, showered and stuffed a batch of never-ending dirty clothes in the washing machine, it was eleven-thirty. I still had time for a quick horse ride. After saddling Ike, we headed into the hills south of the ranch. It felt good to be on horseback again. That's the one place I could truly relax.

By the time we returned to the ranch it was one o'clock. I threw my racquetball clothes in my old gym bag and called to Malachi. Fortunately, it was still cool enough outside he could wait for me in the pickup.

This time, believe it or not, Russ was the one who was late; he got tied up showing a client a house. Consequently, we didn't start our match until two-thirty, then we took the obligatory ten minutes to warm up by hitting the ball off the front wall.

"Let's play," Russ finally said after he had executed a perfect lob off the back wall, "I'll serve first."

He won a close first match and I won an even closer, tiebreaker second match. Always competitive, Russ insisted on a third rubber match. This match was not even close; I ran out of gas. Russ easily won 15 to 7.

We showered, then I looked for something to towel off with. Finding nothing, I finally squeegeed the water off my skin with my hands, then started putting on my clothes.

Russ looked over at me curiously. "No towel?"

"No, in my rush I forgot to bring one."

"What rush?"

"Forget it," I waved my hand dismissively.

"Okay." Russ changed the subject as he handed me his damp towel. "I went to the debate last night."

"I really don't want to talk about it."

"You got killed."

"You think I don't know that." I handed him his towel back. "And, yes, I know you warned me."

"No," Russ stepped into his slacks, "it was more than that. It was more than you were on the wrong side of the pipeline issue."

"Like what?" I asked, pulling on my polo shirt.

"It was like that whole thing was orchestrated, you know, masterminded."

"What do you mean?" I also stepped into my pants.

"Do you really think all that was spontaneous?"

"Well," I frowned, "I don't know."

"Believe you me it wasn't." Russ looked into a mirror and combed his hair. "Rumor has it, your buddy, Tim Slade, engineered the whole thing."

I acted surprised, though I wasn't. "You got any proof of that?"

"No," Russ admitted, then added, "but that's the conventional wisdom around town."

"Keep me informed if you hear anything else." I buttoned my shirt.

"It still doesn't change anything though," Russ added. "You're still going to lose."

"Yeah, I know," I struggled with my cowboy boots, "I think I'll drop out."

"It's up to you," Russ shrugged, "but that might be wise. Same time next week?'

"What?".

"Racquetball, the same time next week?"

"Yeah, okay, but call and remind me."

"You're not the most pleasant guy to call."

I waved goodbye, climbed in pickup and was immediately greeted by Malachi. Even though I made him wait, he still liked me. Dogs are simply amazing. I checked my watch; it was four-thirty. "Let's go talk to Jacob Heinz," I said to Malachi, "then we'll get something for dinner."

Now retired, Jacob and his wife Sophie lived in a Spanish/Mediterranean style house situated right on the seventh fairway of the Entrada Golf Course. Entrada was unique even for St. George golf courses. Though it also had spectacular views of a looming bank of red Navajo sandstone cliffs and canyons, it had the singular distinction of being built right on top of an old lava flow. Most of the fairway roughs were not tall fescue grass, but rather jumbled heaps of black lava rocks. Therefore, hitting a ball from the rough was next to impossible.

Before retiring, Jacob was the Program Director of my uro-oncology fellowship, which I did at the University of Utah after completing my five-year residency. We, Jacob and me, mentor and student, had become close, very close. Over the years, though now retired, he had continued to be my confidant, not only with medical problems, but also with life's difficulties.

Jacob was a pre-WWII Nazi refugee from Schlamending, Austria. His emigrant parents brought him to America as a pre-teen and though he spoke nearly perfect English, he still had a bit of trouble with *"w's"*, but probably not as much trouble as he pretended. He enjoyed pretending he understood very little English and claimed one could learn a lot by playing the dumb foreigner.

I pulled up in front of his house and parked. Calling to Malachi (Jacob loved that dog), we went up to the front door and rang the bell.

Sophie, Jacob's wife, answered the door. Though now well into her eighties, she still possessed a natural grace and a mature beauty. They had been married for less than five years, but I had to admit she had been perfect for Jacob.

"Oh, Coop," she exclaimed, "and Malachi! Come in. Jacob will be thrilled."

I pecked her on her withered cheek, then followed her into the dining room. The table was set and Jacob was just beginning to fill his plate. When he saw me, he smiled, stood up and motioned me in. Seeing Jacob, Malachi immediately bounded to his side and Jacob totally forgot about me, his meal and made a huge fuss over him.

"Oh!" I started to back out. "I didn't realize you were sitting down to dinner. I'll come back another time."

"*Schwachsinn*, nonsense," Jacob vigorously motioned me in.

"I'll get another plate," Sophie quickly added. "We have plenty of food."

Before I could continue to protest further, Sophie had set another place. Jacob somewhat shakily stood up, embraced me, then pulled a chair back for me. I was surprised how feeble he had gotten since I last visited.

"I'm sorry," Sophie apologized, "but we've pretty much gone vegan with Jacob's cholesterol and all."

"That's fine by me," I beamed and sat down. "It looks good." As Sophie pulled a tray of hot breadsticks out of the oven accompanied by a whiff of warm yeast and garlic, I added, "and smells good too."

Sophie served me a large square of tofu-spinach lasagna, garlic-flavored breadsticks and a tossed green salad sprinkled with raspberry vinaigrette. Then she went to find a package of turkey jerky, which they stocked specifically for Malachi. Without question, it was the best meal I'd had in weeks and, not to take away from Ronnie's good intentions, it was much better than her sushi and mandarin orange salad.

As we ate, the conversation bounced from Jacob and Sophie's declining health, to reminiscing about our time together at the University of Utah. Jacob revealed not only did he have coronary artery disease, but had recently been diagnosed with Parkinson's disease. Sophie had her own troubles as she had just finished her sixth round of chemotherapy for breast cancer.

I glanced at her closely. She laughed and removed her wig to reveal her bald head. Suddenly, it dawned on me; my friends were taking their last lap around the oval of life. I fought back a tear and managed to ward off a waiting wave of depression.

When we finished, I helped Sophie clear the table and load the dishwasher, then she served Jacob and me coffee in the family room. Through the French doors, I could see the seventh fairway of the Entrada Golf Course.

"You still play some golf?" I asked as we sipped coffee.

"*Nein,*" he held up a trembling hand. "*Ficken* Parkinson's. I can't hit the ball anymore, just hack up divots. You?"

"Nah," I shook my head. "I don't have the patience or the time."

"Vell, *mein Freund,*" he spilled a little coffee on the tile floor as he tried take a sip. "*Was stört Sie?*"

"What?"

"Vhat's bothering you?"

"What makes you think anything's bothering me?"

"*Ich kann sagen,*" He set his clattering cup down on the saucer. "*Sie beunruhigt schauen.*"

"Jacob, you're speaking German," I smiled. "And I've already exhausted my limited *Deutsch* vocabulary."

Jacob chuckled. "Vell, the older I get, the more I revert back the language of my youth."

I nodded.

"Vell?"

"You are right," I sighed, "I am troubled."

*"Erzähl mir davon—uh—uh—tell be about it."*

For the next fifteen minutes, I described in detail what had happened. Starting with the phone call from Ian right before the hunt, I explained how I'd invited him on the spur of the moment to join us, then described how Ian and Tim never hit it off, right from the start. Next, I related how Tim had apparently killed a deer with his Bushmaster and how Ian had documented the act with his photographs and had collected empty shell casings.

After taking another sip of coffee, I described how Ian and Wally had both disappeared on the same day and without a trace, well almost without a trace. I told Jacob how I'd found some blood and was presently getting DNA tests on it. Also, I described our search and rescue efforts and Tim's obvious lack of enthusiasm in helping. Scowling, I told him about my meeting with Dr. Jeremy Faux and the subsequent suspension of my hospital and surgical privileges. I concluded by telling him about Mrs. Stroud's unexpected reaction when I told her Wally was missing and my difficulty in locating Ian's wife.

"And that's about it," I sighed, taking another sip of coffee.

"That Tim Slade, he's a strange one," Jacob remarked. "I remember him from my days at the university."

"Yeah," I nodded. "I can't help but think he is responsible for their disappearance."

"Vell, you need to get vell away from him. Get a separate office."

"We are in the process of separating," I explained, but decided not to tell him how Tim's wife Ronnie had elected to stay with me. I already knew what Jacob would say about that.

*"Sehr gut,"* Jacob took another sip and a little spilled more coffee, "but I think there's more to this than just Tim Slade."

"Like what?"

"Vell, I think it's odd that both vives are not more emotional, more concerned, about the disappearance of their husbands."

"Yeah," I nodded, "certainly Susan Stroud showed no sign of sorrow. I'm not sure about Katherine McKenna's reaction, but she didn't sound terribly broken up either."

With his hand quivering badly, Jacob set down his cup. It rattled loudly against the ceramic saucer. "I think that might be a good place to start. Check out the relationships between both husbands and vives. Something damn *vierd* is going on there."

"You might be right," I sighed and checked my watch, "Well, my friend,

I've imposed on you enough and I've got to go." After finishing the last of my coffee, I gathered up both mine and Jacob's cups and saucers and delivered them to the dishwasher. I thanked Sophie for dinner and coffee, called to Malachi and headed for the door.

Using his cane, Jacob got up and hobbled after us.

"I'm sorry, Jacob, but I forgot to bring you more Viagra," I said at the door. Whenever I visited, I tried to bring Jacob samples of the little blue pill.

He waved is hand in a sign of dismissal. "Vell, don't bother. I don't use them any more. I should probably give the ones I have stockpiled back to you."

"Nah," I laughed, "I don't need them."

"Because you're vay too young or because you have no one?"

"Both."

"I'm sorry things didn't work out vith Claire."

I shrugged. "Some things are not meant to be." Then I embraced my old friend. "Take care; I'll come back soon." After calling to Malachi, we headed for the pickup.

By the time we arrived back at the ranch, it was after dark. As I fed the horses, I realized how exhausted I was. With chores finally done, I headed back to the house. Tiredly, I dropped my clothes on the bedroom floor and even though it was still early I flopped into bed. Malachi quickly followed, claiming his usual spot at the bottom of the bed. Sighing out loud, I closed my eyes and started to drift.

Suddenly, the doorbell rang.

Groaning out loud, I pulled a pillow over my head and tried to ignore it. Maybe, hopefully, it would go away.

The bell rang again, this time more persistently. Still, I ignored it. A moment later there was loud and relentless banging on the front door.

Cussing under my breath, I stood up and in my underwear (I don't wear pajamas), and stomped toward the living room. Fighting to control my temper, I threw open the door.

"What in the bloody hell do you want?" I barked at two vague shadowy figures, standing there on the dark porch.

# 13

"Where in the hell," the woman hissed, hands planted on her nicely rounded hips, "were you?"

Katherine McKenna, Katya Kozlovsky, was not at all what I expected. I really don't know what I expected, perhaps a vague female facsimile Sigmund Freud. I remember the classic photograph of the legendary psychiatrist, the one where he sports a gray goatee, is dressed in a frumpy three-piece business suit and smoking a large Churchill cigar. In that photo, at least in my estimation, he looked like the archetypal psychiatrist, but not so with Katya Kozlovsky, aka Katherine Kozlov McKenna. She was anything but frumpy and was not smoking a large Churchill cigar.

Instead, she was a tall raven-haired beauty with dark flashing eyes. Instead of a gray goatee, she sported salsa red lipstick to match her equally red turtleneck sweater. Her flattering figure was seemingly meant for the designer jeans she wore, and on her feet were stylish black strap heels. If possible, she projected both a raw gypsy quality blended with the haughty bearing of gentry. When she opened her mouth, however, all that wild charm disappeared replaced with the harsh tone and pugnacious manner of a Marine Corps drill sergeant.

"Where in the hell were you?" she demanded, hands still planted on her hips.

"Huh?" I was so taken aback I could think of nothing else to say.

"As I recall, we had a two-thirty appointment."

Instantly, I was flooded with both anger and shame. Yes, it was a bit unconscionable, with my friend, Ian McKenna, missing, maybe dead, that I would be out enjoying myself, playing racquetball to the point of distraction, and somehow forget my appointment with his wife, who as of yet did not know what was going on. That was pretty crass, even for me. On the other hand, her overbearing attitude was more than a little irritating. I was not used to being treated like an irresponsible teenager, though in this instance that was probably exactly what I was.

Dumfounded, I stared back at her nicely curved hips. Without question, she was really quite stunning when she was not speaking, but her demanding attitude and no nonsense voice quickly erased her good looks.

Still photographs, not talking videos, best served her kind of explosive beauty.

"I—I—uh—I forgot." I was so stunned I couldn't come up with a good excuse.

"You forgot!" She looked incredulous.

I shrugged and managed my 'oh shucks', my most disarming country-boy smile. It didn't work.

"I tried to call you several times and couldn't get you?"

"Oh," I said sheepishly, "I turned my cell phone off."

"Turned it off!" Visibly she struggled to control her temper, then she slowly measured her words. "From what Elijah tells me, we have things to talk about." She pushed past me into the living room and almost immediately ran into Malachi.

She was such a shrew I assumed Malachi would have nothing to do with her, maybe even growl and bare his fangs, but was I wrong! He went right up to her with tail wagging furiously and ducked his head, waiting to be petted. And even more shocking, rather than kicking him aside, or just ignoring him, Katya kneeled to stroke his soft ears and head. Then the less-than-loyal dog followed her to the walnut brown leather couch where he curled up at her feet.

Ziggy, on the other hand, still politely waited at door. I sighed out loud, then motioned him in. As he passed me, he smiled almost apologetically, then sat down next to Katya McKenna. The symbolism was not lost on me. It was two against one.

"They make other fabrics, you know," Katya barked as I sat down on my matching leather Lay-Z-Boy chair.

"What?"

"Haven't you ever heard of silk, vinyl or velvet?"

"What?" I frowned. This woman was making no sense to me.

"They have to kill cows to make leather."

Yes, I did know. Actually over the last few months I had become more and more attuned to the PETA philosophy and had even considered getting rid of my leather furniture, but I was not about to give her the satisfaction.

"You may stand, or sit on the floor," I growled.

"Humpf," she snorted, marched into the kitchen and returned with a padded wooden chair.

I wanted to say, 'they have to kill trees to make that,' but I kept my mouth shut.

After a long moment of painful silence, she continued, "So, why don't you tell me what you've done with Ian?"

I bit my tongue. I wanted to say I have done nothing with Ian, but instead I managed ask, "How much do you know?"

"Nothing."

"Apparently, you know he's missing," I blurted. I couldn't help myself, "otherwise you wouldn't be here."

"Let's stop playing these sophomoric games," she snapped. "Obviously, I just know what you told Ziggy."

"You haven't heard from Ian?"

"No. Have you?"

Continuing to bite my tongue, I tried to calm myself. I took a deep breath, ignored her question and began at the beginning. "A couple of weeks ago Ian called to renew our friendship; we were roommates in college. Since I was going hunting and had our regular guy cancel out, I invited Ian to spend a few days with me at my cabin and go hunting—"

"—I already know that," she abruptly cut me off. "Ziggy told me. But, I find that pretty hard to believe; Ian was not a hunter."

"He was, however," I countered, "a pretty damn good photographer."

She glared at me, then slowly and precisely meted out her words like I was deaf and had to read lips."I—know—that—but—I—know—nothing—about—his—disappearance."

Again I struggled for self-control. 'Calm down,' I tried to tell myself, 'she is not being unreasonable.' She deserved to know what happened to her husband. After taking another deep breath, I launched into my narrative, trying to be as clear, detailed and impartial as possible. First, I told her about Tim Slade and the suspected slaughter of the deer with the Bushmaster. Then, I described Tim and Ian's growing feud, including Ian's incriminating photographs of the bushwhacked deer and spent cartridges he'd collected for evidence. Next, I related the relevant facts associated with Ian and Wally's disappearance and the subsequent thorough search (at least in my opinion) by the Iron County Sheriff Department and the Iron County Search and Rescue. I made sure to mention I had tried to call her multiple times. Lastly, I told her about the blood I had found and the pending DNA studies.

"Man, that's pretty heavy." Ziggy reached for a cigarette.

"Not in this house!" I shouted. "No smoking."

Sheepishly, he replaced the cigarette back in its soft pack.

At first Katya said nothing and I almost could see the circular mental gears grinding, turning slowly with teeth meshing. Finally she growled, "sounds like a comedy of errors."

"Excuse me?"

"A veritable Laurel and Hardy, Keystone Cop routine."

"Hardly," I insisted. "I assure you we did everything possible to find him. And furthermore," I couldn't help myself, "Laurel and Hardy were never featured with the Keystone Cops."

"I'm sure they were," she said coldly.

"No, but Charlie Chaplin was." I stood my ground, then added, "Is something bothering you?"

"Is something bothering me?" She shook her head in disgust. "You take a man with absolutely no outdoor skills and turn him loose in the wilderness!"

"Uh—uh," I gulped. "I did show him around, uh—uh—the salient landmarks."

"That's like giving a medical student a one hour overview lecture on psychiatry, then have him chair a group therapy session."

"I don't think that's a valid comparison."

"So, what did the DNA studies show?" she demanded, abruptly changing the subject.

"Uh—uh," I gulped again. I had been so busy playing racquetball and visiting Jacob Heinz I had forgotten to call Hank Bettis, so I lied, "The results are not back yet."

Still she stared at me, started to say something else, then changed her mind. "He's not dead," she finally declared.

"What?"

"He's not dead."

"How do you know that?"

"I just know."

"Women's intuition?" I couldn't keep the sarcasm out of my voice.

She glared back and me. "At least women have intuition. Men have testosterone-fueled tunnel vision."

"Man, this is intense." Ziggy shifted nervously on the couch and instinctively reached for another cigarette. "What do we do now?"

"I don't know, ask Comrade General Svetlana," I said sarcastically, then immediately added, "and don't light that cancer stick in here."

"Tomorrow," Katya ignored my barb and continued with a voice of ice, "we, you, me and Ziggy, are going to see the pathologist, then we're going to get an update from the Iron County Sheriff and Search and Rescue, then we're going to head up to the mountains. I want to see exactly where Ian disappeared."

"Do you cross country ski?" I asked brusquely.

"Why?"

"Cause there's at least two feet of snow up there now. Maybe more."

"Two feet," Ziggy looked skeptical. "Really? There's none down here."

"That's at ten thousand feet," I barked, "a big damn difference."

Abruptly, Katya stood up. "Come on Ziggy, we're going back to the hotel." She turned back to me. "Pick us up at seven a.m. sharp. Absolutely no excuses this time."

"Yes, Ma'am," I said, then as she turned away I gave her a military salute, but she was gone.

Smiling sheepishly, Ziggy paused on his way out, unlit cigarette already dangling from his lips. "Hey, man, did you line up any interviews yet?"

"No!" I snapped.

"Well," he paused to light up his cigarette, then immediately started coughing, "well, I can be available at any time for interviews. Just let me know."

"You can't tomorrow," I growled. "Didn't you hear her?"

Seething, I watched them get into the Chevy rental car and drive away. What a friggin' bitch! Suddenly, I felt sorry for Ian. Not only was he missing, lost, injured, or dead, but he was married to her! His life must have been a living hell. As I turned away, another thought occurred to me, being married to her was enough to make any man want to disappear. Then a second disparaging thought snuck through my usually impenetrable firewall to reach my well-protected conscience. Was that why I was thrice divorced? Was I the male equivalent of Katya Kozlovsky? Is that why all my wives left? I couldn't help but shudder at the thought.

Accompanied by the traitorous canine, Malachi, I headed back to bed. As usual, Malachi jumped onto his spot on the bed and like someone with a clear conscience was almost immediately asleep. I guess it should come of no surprise that his sleep was unaffected by the Russian Baba Yaga; I think he actually liked her. What a little Benedict Arnold! As I fumed, it dawned on me tomorrow was Sunday. Hank Bettis' pathology office would not be open and we might have a hard time connecting with Sheriff Tiny Klein and Iron County Search and Rescue as well.

148

I breathed a sigh of relief, one more day of reprieve. Picking up the phone, I dialed the Marriot Hotel and asked to be transferred to her room.

When she picked up, I simply blurted, "tomorrow's Sunday."

"So?"

"So, the pathologists office is closed and we'll probably have a difficult time finding Sheriff Klein."

She was silent for a moment, then said tersely, "pick us up the same time on Monday morning."

"Can't. I have an important meeting Monday at eight. I can't miss it."

"A meeting is more important than finding Ian?"

"They are not necessarily mutually exclusive," I snapped. "There's no reason we can't do both."

"But your priorities speak volumes."

Again, I fought to control my temper. "I'll pick you up after the meeting. Wear something warm." I slammed down the phone before she could argue.

Once again, I did not sleep well. I tossed and turned, and worried about my early Monday morning meeting with Tim Slade. That should be unpleasant at best, but nevertheless necessary. We simply had to formulate a plan to separate our practices, divide common assets and dissolve our Limited Liability Corporation. But equally unpleasant was the thought of having to spend the rest of the day with the American Cossack, Katherine McKenna (to spite her, I'd decided I would call her by her American name and not the Russian diminutive of Katya), and her sidekick, the bantam, wannabe hippy, fifth-year resident, Elijah 'Ziggy' Ziegfeld. In the gathering fog of pre-sleep, I decided I would make a supreme effort to be civil to them on Monday—for Ian.

Sunday was actually quite pleasant. I spent the day cleaning the house, barn and horse stalls, and mending my pasture fence in a couple of places where the cedar post staples had popped out and the wire was sagging. After that, I still had time for a ride. I saddled up Ike for the second day in a row, what a treat, and with Malachi tagging along we headed out on a trail that ended up on the Three-Sixty.

The Three-Sixty was beige sandstone peak affording a three hundred and sixty degree view of the area. To the south, in the distance was St. George, spreading out two thousand feet below. The city circled now around the protruding buttes and mesas like dispersing floodwater. To the southwest, the huge red Navajo sandstone gorge of Snow Canyon. To the northeast, the small hamlet of Diamond Valley and my ranch. And further to the north, the lofty snow-capped granite ten thousand-foot peaks of the Pine Valley Mountains.

I dismounted and found a sandstone slab to sit on and was immediately joined by my two-timing buddy, Malachi. For the first time in weeks I felt a peace. This was my church, my sanctuary. This is where I felt close to—to what? Perhaps, to God, though I didn't really believe in him.

That night, for the first time in a long time, I slept, really slept. The last time I remember checking my clock it was just after nine. Either I did not hear my alarm clock when it went off at six-thirty, or I forgot to set it. When I finally did climb out of bed it was after seven! Tim would be chomping at the bit. He was never late for meetings. Unfortunately, I usually was.

As I hustled outside to feed the horses, I noted there was a colder nip to the air and a gray carpet of clouds had surreptitiously sneaked in overnight. It smelled and felt like snow. As fast as I could, I fed the horses and Malachi, then grabbed a bagel and a mug of hot coffee to go. As I headed out the door, I heard the telephone ring, but didn't stop to answer it. I was pretty sure I knew who it was and what she wanted.

It was eight twenty-five when I pulled up in the office parking lot. After cracking a window, I told Malachi to stay, then sprinted for the back door. After checking both my private office and Tim's, they were both empty, I hurried up front to the reception desk.

"Oh, hi, Coop." Ronnie greeted me cheerily with her usual luminous smile.

"Hi, Ronnie." I rapidly performed a visual examination. Thankfully, there were no discernable bruises or abrasions and as usual she looked terrific. "Where's Tim?"

"He left about ten minutes ago. Said he had better things to do."

"But—but we had a meeting," I protested. "Did he reschedule?"

"No, he said you would hear from his lawyer."

I groaned out loud. The last thing I wanted was for this to degenerate into a battle of lawyers. That's what happened with my first divorce. From that experience I knew dueling lawyers could get very expensive, too expensive for a doctor out of work.

"What did he say about you staying on here?" I finally asked.

"That I could choose, but it was either him or you."

150

"And?"

"And, I'm still here." Reaching out, she placed her perfectly manicured hand on my forearm.

*"You're late!"* a female voice thundered.

I nearly jumped out of my cowboy boots. Peering through the reception window, I saw Katherine McKenna and Ziggy Ziegfeld impatiently sitting in the waiting room. Both were dressed in denims, cargo shirts and hiking boots, but I admit, Katherine, in her tight designer jeans, once again took my breath away.

"They kept pounding on the door," Ronnie explained apologetically, "so I let them in. They said they had an appointment with you."

I sighed deeply.

"I can ask them to leave," Ronnie volunteered, almost eagerly.

"Don't even try, Barbie," Katherine growled as she approached the partition that separated the waiting room from the reception area.

"Don't call me Barbie, Elvira!" Ronnie shot back.

As they glared at each other, I couldn't help but notice, how totally dissimilar they were, but also how they were two of the most stunning women I had ever known.

"Are you really a surgeon?" Katherine barked, looking at me. She had now apparently decided to redirect her venom toward me.

"Why do you ask?" I replied evenly, remembering my earlier vow to be civil.

"Surgeons are notorious for being on time," Katya snapped. "Otherwise they lose their first hour surgery start time."

She was right, of course. In most hospitals operating time was at a premium and for nearly all hospitals the surgery department was their biggest moneymaker. They hated to see their operating rooms sit idle or operate inefficiently. And for surgeons first hour starts were highly prized. Without a first start, you were at the mercy of the O.R. Whenever they had an opening, anywhere from eight in the morning to eight o'clock in the evening, you had to immediately drop what you were doing, often seeing patients in the office, and head straight to the hospital. There simply was no way to plan your day without a first hour. Regrettably, in the past, before I had a first hour, I routinely had to cancel out patients, often three or four times.

At Dixie Medical Center, first starts were awarded by both seniority and productivity. If you were lucky enough to get a first hour, you guarded it like home-stored gold bullion and it took just three tardies and you were out, no more first starts.

"Are you really a psychiatrist?" I snapped back. Suddenly, all my good intentions of civility were forgotten.

"Why?" Katya demanded.

"Because most of the psychiatrists I know are masters of the art of audition and have an incredible gift for empathy!"

Instead of answering, she glared at me. In the waiting room behind her, I could see Ziggy grinning and signaling a two thumbs up, then he started coughing.

Ronnie laughed nervously and thankfully the phone rang.

"Well, let's get going," Katherine ordered, finally breaking the tension. "We've got a lot to do today."

With jaw still clenched, I broke off eye contact and turned back to Ronnie and waited for her to hang up the phone. "If you see Tim today apologize for me and tell him I really would like to keep the lawyers out of this. I will meet him anytime, anyplace of his choosing."

"But not today," Katya interjected from the other side of the partition.

Ronnie ignored her. "I don't know if I'll see him, but if I do, how can I get in touch with you?"

"I'll be on my cell phone," I replied, then added, "but we'll eventually be heading up to Brian Head so I may be out of service for the last half of the day."

"You still looking for your friends?"

I nodded and thought about introducing Katherine as Ian's wife, then thought better of it. There was no point in trying to mix oil with water. They, Ronnie and Katherine, like Katherine and me, would never be friends.

"Remember, you've got patients Wednesday morning starting at nine o'clock," Ronnie said, "then office procedures in the afternoon."

I nodded, left Ronnie's reception cubicle, then entered the waiting room through a side door. After collecting Ziggy and Katherine, we headed outside to the back parking lot.

"Well, hop in," I motioned toward my pickup, "let's get going."

Katherine stopped when she saw Malachi in the cab. "We're going in that? All of us?"

"Yeah," I shrugged. "Why not?"

Let's take my rental." She motioned toward her rental Chevy sedan. "It has more room."

152

I hadn't noticed it parked in the second row when I had arrived. "Does it have four-wheel drive?"

"No. I don't think so."

"Then we'd better take the Dodge," I pointed up at the threatening sky, "we may very well need the extra traction today."

Katya and Ziggy huddled over at their rental car. Apparently deciding I was right, they both grabbed a travel bag and returned to the pickup. I shrugged; I had brought nothing, but a coat and snow boots. I wasn't planning on staying the night. Probably a city thing; never go anywhere without a change of clothes. Without comment, I placed the travel bags back in the bed of the pickup.

Initially, there was some confusion with seating, like a comical and chaotic child's game of musical chairs. I assumed they were contesting the seat next to me; who would draw the short straw. Eventually, Katherine literally pushed the smaller Ziggy in first, then she wedged in next to the passenger door. Poor Malachi was suddenly displaced from his usual seat. After more shuffling, he eventually settled down, lying down across the legs of both Ziggy and Katherine.

"Let's check on the pathology report first," Commandant Katya advised.

"Yes, Ma'am," I replied as I put the Dodge in gear and headed east toward the hospital.

Once in the hospital parking lot, Katherine directed Ziggy to remain in the pickup with Malachi, then I led the way to Hank Bettis' office. After a short wait in the pathology department foyer, the receptionist returned and led us back to Hank's office.

When Hank saw me, he smiled broadly, took off his reading glasses, stood up and warmly hugged me.

"Hank Bettis," I turned to introduce them, "this is Doctor Katherine McKenna."

As Hank shook her hand, his mouth gaped wide open. He was not very subtle. Her beauty had obviously stunned him.

"Now," she smiled at Hank, as she corrected me, "now, I go by Katya Kozlovsky."

Smiled! Not only a smile, but a dazzling smile. Why did Hank Bettis deserve such a smile? In two days I hadn't gotten so much as an upturned corner of her lip. I tried hard not to sulk, but nevertheless dourly added, "this is Ian McKenna's wife."

"Who?" Obviously, Hank was not focusing on me.

"Ian McKenna. You know, the blood?"

"Huh?" His eyes were still glued on Katherine.

"The DNA tests!" I nearly shouted. "The ones I paid you over twenty-one hundred dollars for."

"Huh? Oh, yeah," he finally refocused back on me, "yeah, the DNA tests."

"Are they back?"

"Yes," Hank nodded, "we got them by Federal Express last Friday—"

"—When?" Katherine cut him off.

"Last Friday morning."

"So, you had them on Saturday?" Katherine gave me, then Bettis a withering glance.

"I—I tried to call Coop, but couldn't get—" Bettis said defensively.

"—Well, then?" I interrupted.

"Well, then?" Bettis looked confused.

"Well, then could we see the results?" I asked.

He finally took the cue, "uh, let me go find them."

Taking one last furtive peek at Katherine, Hank disappeared from the room.

"So," Katherine hissed, "you lied!"

"Remember," I said lamely, "I turned my cell phone off."

"I wonder what else you're lying about." She locked eyes with me.

I didn't reply. In uncomfortable silence, we eyed each other with mutual distrust.

"So, tell me," Katherine finally asked brusquely, "if it's not Ian's blood what does that mean?"

I shrugged. "It really doesn't mean much as far as Ian is concerned, but it could be Wally's."

Katherine scowled. "And, if it is Ian's blood, what does that mean?"

Honestly, I was not sure what it meant, but I tried to come up with something. "It won't tell us how badly, but it will tell us Ian was hurt."

"Or, he was faking it," Katya commented without emotion.

"What?"

Just then Hank returned with a manila folder. He opened it and extracted three standard 8.5 x 11 inch computer sheets, then paused. He peered over the tops of his +2.50 reading glasses and frowned.

"Well, Hank," I said impatiently, "let's have it."

154

Still he hesitated. "Well, there are the HIPAA laws—you know patient confidentially."

"So?" I asked.

"So, I can't just give out this information to just anyone." He turned back to Katherine. "If you are Ian McKenna's wife," he asked, "how come you go by Katya Kozlovsky?"

Katherine focused her hard brown eyes on Bettis' baby blues. "I go by Katya Kozlovsky because, I am not Ian McKenna's wife!"

# 14

"Maybe you'd better explain," Hank clutched the DNA test papers close to his chest, "before we go through the results."

"So, you're worried about HIPAA?" Katya asked.

Hank nodded. "Can't be too careful. The feds are very serious about it. This information is supposed to be confidential, even if the patient's been dead for forty years."

"What about him?" Katya nodded at me. "He's not family."

"He's the attending physician," Hank fibbed.

Katya was silent for a moment, then shrugged. "Ian and I were married for eleven years. We divorced a couple of months ago."

"So, why Katya Kozlovsky?" I bluntly asked.

Again Katya paused and appeared to be debating her answer. "Our divorce was not at all congenial, in fact it was quite contentious," she replied, scowling. "When the divorce was final, I couldn't wait to get rid of the name McKenna. Though my maiden name was Kozlov, historically it was Kozlovsky, shortened by my father when he emigrated from Russia at the beginning of the Cold War. Katya is the Slavic nickname for Katherine," she turned to Bettis and added, "as I assume Hank is for Henry. I've always preferred Katya to Katherine. I think I look more like a Katya."

Silently, I had to agree. She did not look much like the conservative-sounding Katherine, but more like a tempestuous gypsy, like a Katya. "So, why did you and Ian divorce?"

"Several reasons, general incompatibility and financial disagreements," she replied vaguely.

"So, then, why are you here?"

"Just because we are divorced," Katya face was like a mask, "doesn't mean I don't still have feelings for him, care for him. He—he's still like a brother to me."

"But, I though you said the divorce was contentious."

"What can I say," Katya shrugged, "siblings fight and make up."

"So, why did he show me a photo of you and say you were his wife?"

"How could I possibly know that?" she forced a laugh. "You'll have to ask him."

Silently, I thought, 'I certainly would if I could.'

Hank looked at me as if to say, what do you think?

I shrugged. "What the hell, Hank, let's see what you've got."

"Then we better fill her in," Hank said. He took a minute to explain how I had brought in the sample of blood, the need for comparison tissue and how he had located a previous prostate biopsy of Ian's. And Wally had a skin lesion removed."

"So, give it to us, Hank," I said, "that's more than enough prelude"

"They match," Hank said simply.

"Geez, Hank, whose? Wally's, or Ian's?" I asked, trying to grab the papers from him.

"The blood is both Wally's and Ian's."

I was silent for a moment, trying to analyze what this meant, trying to think of all the possibilities and permutations.

"So, does Ian have cancer?" Katya finally asked.

"What?" I tried to mentally change gears.

"Does he have cancer?" she repeated. "Did the comparison prostate tissue really show cancer?"

Hank nodded. "A Gleason Score eight."

"You didn't know?" I asked.

She shook her head. "Was it treated?"

"I don't know," Hank answered, then looked at me.

"Neither do I," I replied, "but we can find out."

Hank took the suggestion and immediately got on the computer. He logged into IHC's network program and started searching.

Katya turned to me. "A Gleason Score eight—as I recall from our two-day urology lecture in medical school, is pretty serious."

I nodded. "Gleason Score eights tend to be quite aggressive. Not as aggressive as pancreatic cancer, but they can certainly cause trouble within a year, or two."

"How long ago was the biopsy?" Katya asked.

Hank looked up from his computer. "It was two years last July."

Her face was inscrutable. I couldn't tell if she was worried about Ian's health or secretly happy that he had a potentially serious health problem.

"Was it treated," I asked.

"No," Hank shut down his computer. "No, not that I can tell. There are no op, or x-ray reports. No consults with an oncologist. If it was treated, he went out of the IHC system."

"So, if it hasn't been treated, what does it mean?" Katya frowned.

"Well," I explained, "if he really hasn't been treated, his window for a cure is rapidly closing."

With her face still unreadable, Katya changed subjects. "So, tell me, what do the DNA tests prove?"

"That it was both Ian's and Wally's blood that I found."

"I figured that much out by myself," Katya replied sarcastically, "but does it tell us anything about if he's injured or dead or just faking it?"

"Why do you keep bringing that up?" I frowned and shook my head. "What reason would he have to fake his own death?"

"You don't know him like I do," Katya said non-committedly, then abruptly clammed up.

Hank looked at me.

I shrugged and gathered up the papers. "Hank, do you mind if I keep these?"

"Go ahead," he nodded, "you paid for them. Anyway, I've got copies."

"Thanks again, Hank," I quickly shook his hand and prepared to leave.

"Yeah, thanks, Hank," Katya also grabbed his hand, "if we have questions, do you mind if we call you?" She smiled again at Bettis.

Stammering like a teenager, Hank stuttered, "s—sure, c—call me a—anytime."

Unexpectedly, I was hit with a pang of jealousy. Was the Volga River queen, the female Russian Cossack, actually flirting with Bettis? I frowned as I watched her turn away and head for the door.

"So, why don't you get a date," Hank whispered, winked at me and nodded at Katya's receding back, "and go out to dinner sometime with Jenny and me?"

"You've got to be kidding—with her?" I exclaimed, then turned and followed Katya out of his office.

Back outside, Ziggy was leaning against the pickup smoking. When he saw me he hurriedly put out his cigarette, then instantly started coughing.

"You really need to give up those damn things," I growled, then added, "that cough sounds terrible."

"Nah, man, it's not that," Ziggy responded between hacks, "I think I'm getting a cold or something."

"Either way, those cigarettes make things worse. Destroys the cilia in the trachea so you can't cough up the phlegm. Turns colds into pneumonia."

"I know, man, I know," he sputtered as he hacked again.

Back in the Dodge, and after more musical chairs, Katya turned to me. "What now?"

"Cedar City and Sheriff Tiny Klein," I responded as I fired up the Dodge, negotiated St. George's new double-diamond interchange and headed north on I-15.

"Did you lie to me about him too?" she asked coldly.

"Who?"

"Sheriff Klein."

I didn't answer.

For the first fifteen minutes, nobody said anything. Actually, it was very nice; I'd never found silence uncomfortable. In fact, in my opinion it was very underrated. But unfortunately, the solitude couldn't last. It was eventually slaughtered by Ziggy's screeching and whiny voice.

"So, what about the job, Coop?"

"Huh? What job?" My mind was miles away.

"Man, you know," he paused for another fit of coughing, then continued, "the psychiatry job at the hospital."

"What about it?" I snapped.

"I though you were going to line up some interviews."

"And just when have I had the time?" I snapped back, then was suddenly, hit with a pang of conscience. Why shouldn't I help him? He wasn't that bad, at least as far as psychiatrists went, and certainly a damn sight better than the other one sitting by to the passenger door. And—and the hospital really did need another psychiatrist.

"Geez, man, I'm sorry. I just thought—"

"—I will," I cut him off, then added more in a more gentle tone, "just as soon as I get a chance."

We drove the rest of the way in silence. As soon as we topped the Black Ridge, snow began to carpet the passing landscape, but fortunately the freeway remained clear. Overhead, the clouds continued to thicken and threaten more snow.

It was after eleven o'clock when we pulled into the parking lot of the Iron County Sheriff's Office. Once again leaving Ziggy to attend to Malachi, Katya and I entered the building. We checked with the uniformed deputy at the reception desk and were politely informed Sheriff Klein was in a meeting and could not be disturbed. Katya told the desk sergeant we would be happy to wait. Obviously taken by her, he smiled back, shrugged, then said amiably, "suit yourselves." Finally at straight up noon, we were escorted back to Tiny Klein's office.

I shook the sheriff's huge hand, then as I made the introductions I noticed he, just like Hank Bettis, couldn't seem to take his eyes off Katya.

"Sheriff Klein, this is Katherine McKenna, Ian's wife." Deliberately, I said nothing about being an ex-wife or her new name.

"I see you finally found her," Klein said to me, but his eyes were still fixed on Katya. "Good."

"I no longer go by that name," Katya started to say, "you see Ian and I —"

I side-kicked her, striking her ankle hard. She grimaced, but nevertheless stopped talking in mid-sentence.

"—Ian and I never go by your city," she quickly amended her statement while visually firing daggers at me, "without thinking how beautiful it is."

Tiny Klein nodded. "It a lot prettier in the summer, especially during the Shakespearean Festival."

"Sheriff," I immediately changed the subject, "we stopped by for an update. Anything new with the search?"

"Well, we've searched for them every day for a week," Sheriff Klein stated, then hesitated. "Starting today, however, we've called off our daily searches and have officially classified them now as missing persons and have entered them into the national database."

"Any new clues at all?" I persisted.

"Well, maybe one." Tiny Klein got up and left the room. A moment later he returned carrying an expensive camera along with a manila envelope. "Either one of you recognize this camera?"

Kaya shook her head.

"Sure," I nodded, "that's Ian's camera."

"Are you sure?"

"Positive. It's a Canon EOS Five D Mark Three." My nearly perfect memory served me well.

The sheriff checked the markings and nodded. "That's what it is, alright." He then extracted some photographs from the manila envelope. "Then, maybe you can explain these too." He handed the photos to me and Katya peered over my shoulder. "We got these of this," he held up Ian's Cannon, "from the camera."

Most of the photographs were of wintery landscapes: a frame shot down the canyon from the Summit Overlook, another of the frozen pond

160

and another of snow-weighted balsam boughs with their ice crystals shining like rhinestones in the bright sun. Lastly, there were a half dozen shots, taken from different angles, of a killed male deer. Close-ups showed the rack of antlers, five points on one side and four points on the other. Additional photographs documented the deer was shot multiple times, a total of seventeen.

My mind raced ahead as I looked at the photos. Should I now incriminate Tim Slade? Surely, the sheriff will ask about a deer shot seventeen times! And Tim was a suspect, the prime suspect, at least in my mind. I owed him nothing. Even if I did, I still couldn't withhold pertinent information from law enforcement. That could possible make me an accessory to murder after the fact. And even if I did finger Tim, it could not possibly damage our relationship any further. Or, could it? Probably not. It was way beyond repair now anyway.

"Let's sit down," I said reluctantly. I sank back down into my chair.

Tiny settled his big frame into his high-backed chair and even though there was another chair Katya remained rigidly upright.

For the next ten minutes, I explained the details surrounding the photo of the slaughtered deer, including the Bushmaster and the ongoing feud between Ian and Tim.

"I see," the sheriff said when I finished, then frowned. "Why did it take you so long to tell me this?"

"I don't know," I mumbled. "I just wasn't sure. I'm still not."

"So, how does Wally Stroud fit into that picture?"

"I wish I knew." I shook my head. "Maybe the two disappearances are not related.

"Maybe," Klein said, "but in criminology we were taught to never look for two theories when one will do."

"We have the same axiom in medicine," I agreed. "Never assign two diagnoses when one will explain everything.

Katya remained silent. I assumed that meant psychiatrists always looked for multiple personality disorders.

"Well," the sheriff continued, "I guess I'm going to have a discussion with Doctor Tim Slade."

"Wouldn't hurt," I agreed, then asked, "where did you find the camera?"

"Just off Summit Overlook," Klein replied, "right at the base of a hundred-foot cliff."

"But no sign of Ian, huh?"

"No," Tiny shook his head, "not yet, but we may very well find him in the spring after the snow melts."

"You'll never find him there," Katya blurted from behind me.

"Why is that?" Klein raised an eyebrow.

"Because he's not dead!" Katya declared, dark eyes locked in with Klein's hazel eyes.

"Do you have some special knowledge of that?" Klein finally asked. "Something you are keeping from us?"

"No," Katya replied, but unflinchingly still maintained eye contact.

Tiny didn't back down either. The room became uncomfortably silent.

"Woman's intuition," I laughed to break the tension.

"Well, if you do know something," Tiny finally said, "please let us know. We've already spent a ton of the county's money on this search and investigation."

"I would think," Katya replied coldly, "that saving two lives would be worth the cost."

Again, there was silence.

"Well," I abruptly jumped in, "thanks for your time, sheriff," I stood up, "but we've really got to go."

"Where you going?" Klein asked.

"Misses McKenna," I emphasized her name and simultaneously out of the corner of my eye saw her blanche, "Misses McKenna wants to see where her husband disappeared."

"Well, be careful," the sheriff turned to me, "there's a major storm moving in. Tomorrow's supposed to be pretty bad."

I shook his hand. "We should be off the mountain well before then."

It was one o'clock by the time we joined Ziggy and Malachi at the pickup; both were out of the cab. Once again Ziggy quickly stomped out his cigarette. After arguing about it for five minutes, we settled on pizza for lunch, one small vegetarian for Katya and me (at least we had something in common) and another small meat-lovers for Ziggy and Malachi.

Two hours later we arrived at the ski resort village of Brian Head. At 9,500 feet, it was nestled in a narrow alpine valley, wedged between Brian Head peak on the east and Navajo peak on the west. As I had predicted, there was indeed two feet of snow on the ground, maybe more. And of no surprise, Dry Lakes Road, the one leading to my cabin and also the one that ran parallel to Summit Overlook, was closed. As was customary during the winter season, it had not been snow plowed and was now impassible to cars. The only way in was either by cross-country skis or by snowmobile. Since neither Ziggy, nor Katya, admitted to any experience with skiing even though they both lived in Utah's ski Mecca, that only left snowmobiles.

We located a snowmobile rental right on Main Street, which doubled as State Highway 143, Thunder Mountain Rentals. Like a lot of seasonal businesses in Brian Head, the commercial operation occupied the ground floor of the two-story building with living quarters on the top floor. When the lifts shut down and the snow melted, the owner obviously spent his/her summers elsewhere, probably renting wave runners or surfboards at some beach in southern California.

Thunder Mountain Rentals offered brand new Polaris Indy 800 SP snowmobiles for daily use. They were powerful sleek machines with a lot more horsepower than we would ever need, but having no other choice, I ordered two. Unfortunately, the owner, for insurance purposes, would not allow three riders on one machine. Also, I rented a tow sled for Malachi. Sure he could probably run alongside and keep up, but he was getting old, the snow was at least chest-deep, probably deeper, and I thought he deserved to ride.

When the owner, Abe Eisemann (obviously German/Jewish) announced the rental fee would be a whopping two hundred and thirty-five dollars per day per Indy, I gulped and looked at the other two, hoping for some help. Ziggy immediately looked down and studied his shoes, and Katya simply informed me she had left her purse at the motel in St. George. Great!

To those exorbitant charges, the Eiseman also added the rental of three snowsuits, helmets, boots and gloves, insurance for the machines and of course the tow sled for Malachi. Grudging, I offered him a credit card.

The grand total came to a colossal eight hundred and forty dollars! No wonder he could spend summers at the beach drinking Mai Tai's and peddling surfboards.

That was a lot of dinero for a surgeon with no surgical privileges and who also was about to incur substantial costs, both legal and inventorial, when he and his ex-partner split their practice. Silently, I hoped when Katya was again in possession of her purse she would reimburse me, at least half. Though surgeons usually make more than psychiatrists, I suspected at this point in time her salary was much more than mine.

Even though it was just five thirty by the time we were completely outfitted and had received our mandatory safety and operating instructions, the sun had already started to dip behind Navajo Peak. And as if it were somehow attached to the setting sun, the temperature also began to plummet. I figured by time we got to the Summit Overlook, it would be too dark to see anything and too cold to do any exploring. Without consulting the others, I made an executive decision and headed straight for my cabin.

I operated one snowmobile and towed the sled that not only ferried Malachi, but also transported Katya and Ziggy's travel bags. Not expecting to spend the night, I had not brought an overnight bag, but I did remember to requisition my first aid kit from the pickup and stuff it in my snowmobile's rear storage compartment. No surprise, neither Katya, nor Ziggy offered to join me on my machine. Looking determined, Katya assumed the driver position on the other machine with Ziggy sitting close behind her and clinging to her for dear life.

Unexpectedly, I had another twinge of jealously. For some odd and inexplicable reason, I caught myself wishing I were the one clinging to beautiful Katya Kozlovsky. As fast as I could, I drove that absurd vision out of my head and fired up my machine.

I had, of course, operated a snowmobile before, but Katya had not. At first, I went slow, breaking a trail in the two feet of dry powder and giving Katya a chance to get the feel of her machine, i.e. how the throttle worked, how hard it was to steer and how easily it braked. She seemed to get the hang of it after a few minutes and I increased my speed a little. With a machine with this much power and going through this much powder, was a bit like water skiing, the rear ends of the machines often would skate/slide from side to side. From behind me, an angry Katya yelled and I slowed down a little, but not too much. With two feet of powder snow, you had to keep your machine moving. If you slowed too much, or stopped, the snowmobile would sink and mire, and then you would have a hell-uv a time getting it out.

The muffled orange twilight of dusk was rapidly morphing to the inky black of night when we finally roared up the hill to the cabin. On purpose, I circled the oval driveway adjacent to the cabin, then shut the machines down with the skis of the machines pointed back down the hill. That way when we got ready to leave in the morning we would not be mired in the deep powder. Katya and Ziggy grabbed their bags and I my first aid kit, then with Malachi leading we climbed the snow-laden stairs to the cabin.

Inside it was freezing. I rummaged around until I found some kindling and newspaper, then set about starting a fire. Kneeling before the native gray granite and blue agate fireplace brought back a flood of memories.

164

Samantha Rose and I had personally selected, hauled and stacked every single rock, both granite and agate, used in the construction of this fireplace as well as its companion chimney. Silently, I couldn't help but compare Samantha Rose to Katya Kozlovsky. They were both exceptionally beautiful women, but that's where the comparison ended.

Once, I had the fire cracking and flames jumping, I searched the pantry for something I could fix for dinner. At any moment, I expected Katya to confront me for coming to the cabin rather than going to the Summit Overlook, but she didn't. I suspect even she had enough sense to realize we would not have had enough daylight to accomplish anything and with the temperatures plunging it could have been downright dangerous.

From the pantry, not too surprising, I had very little to choose from. We, Tim, Wally, Ian and I, had pretty much depleted my stock of food during the deer hunt and I'd had no time to restock. Finally, I selected a large can of Dinty Moore stew and another can of Green Giant kernel corn. Lastly, I fished out a box of Bisquick; hot biscuits would go well with the stew. I could use the leftover batter for pancakes in the morning.

While I fixed dinner, unbeknownst to me as my mind was elsewhere occupied, Katya and Ziggy lay claim to the two bedrooms. Katya put her travel bag in the bedroom I usually used and Ziggy placed his in the guest bedroom.

I opened the cans, dumped their contents into two saucepans, then turned on the gas burners and pre-warmed the oven. As I mixed water with the powdered Bisquick, I could hear Katya in the bathroom freshening up. Ziggy, of course, was outside smoking. After returning, Ziggy snooped in the closet, locating an old chess set. He set it up on the coffee table in front of the fireplace and started playing a solo match. Periodically he punctuated his moves with his chronic hacking cough, occasionally expectorating phlegm into his handkerchief. Sometime, I decided, I would have to play him. I loved the game of chess.

Neither of them offered to help me. No real surprise there. While the biscuits baked, I set the table.

The aroma of hot stew and baking biscuits filled the cabin and suddenly I realized how hungry I was. The mountain air always improved my appetite, but oddly, for first time in months, the smell of hot stewed meat did not nauseate me.

When everything was done, I put some stew in a bowl for Malachi, then called the others to the table. I served each a steaming plate of stew, kernelled corn and biscuits, then loaded another for me. Without comment, I sat down and began eating. Instinctively, I began separating the vegetables from the meat. I still was not able to eat the meat. Even though the smell was okay, the texture in my mouth was not. I made a small pile of it on my plate, saving the beef for Malachi.

At first, we ate in silence, Katya and Ziggy concentrating on their food. Apparently, they were as famished as me. Unfortunately, after a few minutes Katya broke the silence.

"So," she asked out of the blue, "what's your story, Doctor Cooper?"

"W—what?" I nearly choked on my food. She was interested in my story! Why? Probably idle curiosity or maybe it was just small talk, even though she didn't seem the type.

"What's your story, Doctor Cooper?" she repeated. "You know more about us than we about you."

I suppose technically that was true, though I really didn't know all that much about either one of them. "W—what do you want to know?"

"Tell us about your life." Katya broke open a hot biscuit, releasing a cloud of steam.

"Uh—uh—there—there's not much to tell," I finally managed to dislodge the stuck food from the back of my throat without hacking it onto the table. "And, please call me Coop."

"Yeah, man," Ziggy added between bites, "tell us what makes you tick, Doctor Coop."

"Huh?" I had no idea where they were going with this.

"There must be a lot of things," Katya persisted. "Where did you grow up? Where did you go to school, both medical school and college? Are you married? Any kids? What about your practice? Group or solo? Is it successful? Start at the beginning."

"Yeah, come on, man, uh, I mean Coop," Ziggy paused for another paroxysm of coughing. This time he produced yellow/green sputum, which he hurriedly expectorated into a paper napkin. "Everyone's got a backstory."

I frowned and looked closely at Katya, then Ziggy to see if they were serious.

Apparently they were. They waited expectantly.

My frown deepened, but evidently they would not accept *no* for an answer. Finally, I sighed, cleared my throat again and began. At first haltingly and mechanical, I regurgitated, like I was dictating an operative note, then my delivery smoothed out and picked up momentum as I got into it.

"Uh—uh—I am a native southern Utahan, born in Washington County. In fact, where I live now was my childhood home. When my parents died I inherited the house and the ranch—"

For the next fifteen minutes, I told them about my life, both the good and the bad. Oddly, it seemed good, almost cathartic, to finally have someone to talk to, someone to unload on, someone to unburden my troubled soul. And after all, both were trained psychiatrists and like Catholic priests who hear confessions, I'm sure they had heard it all before. I told them about my childhood, including my initial dislike for ranching, and how I had ironically ended up back on the ranch. Briefly, I gave an outline of my formal schooling from grade school to residency and fellowship. Next, I related in detail, somehow I couldn't help it, the specifics of my three marriages and why they had failed—at least in my opinion. Surprisingly, and without hesitation, I told them about my past scrapes with law and my unwarranted malpractice lawsuits and how they were eventually dropped. Lastly, I confessed to my present problems, including the summary suspension of my surgical and hospital privileges and finished with the ugly particulars of my impending split with Tim Slade.

"To quote the incomparable Walter Cronkite," I forced a smile as I finished, "and that's the way it was."

Everyone was silent for a moment. I sighed and concentrated on mopping up the last bit of stew gravy with my biscuit, then transferred the meat onto Malachi's plate.

"So, what do you think?" Katya finally asked, turning to Ziggy.

"Probably a personality disorder," he answered immediately. "There is undoubtedly some covert and deeply embedded neurosis as well, as manifest by moderate depression, and maybe a bit of delusional thinking too. But primarily this strikes me as a personality disorder."

Katya nodded. "I agree, mostly, but I think the depression is a much more significant player, even bordering on clinical. I also agree there is a smattering of delusional thinking, but probably not enough to qualify as an overt psychosis, more specifically it has not yet advanced to full-blown schizophrenia. But without question, you are correct with your diagnosis of a personality disorder, but what kind? Please narrow it down, Ziggy. In which of the personality subcategories would you place Doctor Cooper?"

Needless to say, I was flabbergasted—actually more like stunned speechless! Sure, maybe this was a unique teaching opportunity for Ziggy, but they were discussing me like I wasn't even in the room. Like this was nothing more than a clinical setting and I was nothing more than a laboratory white rat, a mindless specimen in some Pavlovian experiment, and couldn't possibly understand what they were saying. Had they forgotten, I too went to medical school and had also successfully completed the mandatory six-week rotation in psychiatry?

"Well," Ziggy continued, unfazed, "he does have a healthy disregard for the law as manifest by his multiple arrests, his malpractice lawsuits and the charge of negligent homicide. Also, it appears he has difficulty in playing by society's rules as suggested by his multiple summary suspensions from the hospital and the present revocation of his surgical privileges. So, that coupled with his ongoing problems with interpersonal relationships and I would have to classify him as a classical antisocial personality disorder."

"Yes," Katya again nodded her head in agreement, "but to that I would add his blatant and callous disregard for others. For evidence of this, I submit my missing ex-husband Ian McKenna and his friend Wally Stroud. Also, he exhibits a real penchant for irresponsibility and seems to be totally devoid of remorse, also manifested by his response, or lack thereof, regarding to what has happened to Ian and Mister Stroud."

Ziggy nodded thoughtfully. "But you'll have to agree there are also some elements of narcissism and obsessive-compulsive behavior, as well as some overt signs of an avoidant personality disorder. This is confirmed by his obvious lack of social skills and his inability to make a strong commitment to his previous three wives. Man, take a look at him; he lives alone with just a dog--"

"--Malachi," I angrily interrupted, "is not just a dog!"

"That would be more typical of a schizoid personality disorder," Katya continued to argue, while totally ignoring me. "And the three failed marriage are more classical for a schizotypal disorder."

"But," Ziggy debated, "with the flashes of paranoia, the sprinkling of delusional thinking and the rogue disregard—"

"--Enough!" I shouted, standing up and gripping the lip of the table. "I can play that game too; I know all the psychiatric jargon. And believe me, both of you fit valid, unattractive and I might add much too common psychiatric syndromes."

"Pay attention, Ziggy," Katya said smugly. "This should be good."

Ziggy," I hissed, "you are a classical thumb-sucking Peter Pan Syndrome and Katherine you are a quintessential example of Sigmund Freud's common, but sad Penis Envy Syndrome!

# 15

I stormed from the room. Malachi hesitated for just a second, then thankfully decided to follow me. Maybe I did like dogs better than humans or at least these particular psychiatrist humans, but did that make me antisocial? I think not. It made me astute, discerning and appropriately selective. And I'm certainly not the only one who did not like psychiatrists; the general consensus was they were a weird bunch. Sure, me stomping out may be a little sophomoric, but right now I really didn't care.

After entering my bedroom, I immediately spied Katherine's overnight bag lying on the bed. Briefly, I considered grabbing it and throwing it back out into the living room, then thought better of it. Pivoting on my heel, I stomped from my bedroom into the guest bedroom, there I spotted Ziggy's bag. It perched on the bed like a rock cairn staking a claim and like a claim jumper I angrily snatched it from the bed. From the closet I grabbed a spare blanket and pillow, then tramped back into living room, angrily depositing the bag, blanket and pillow on the couch in front of the fireplace.

Out of the corner of my eye, I could see Ziggy, his eyes as big as coffee cup saucers. Katherine simply looked slightly bemused. Without uttering a single word, I returned to the guest bedroom and firmly shut the door and turned off the lights. After shedding my clothes, I draped them across the rustic pine dresser and climbed into bed. Unfortunately by then my adrenal glands had already pumped enough adrenaline into my venous circulation to keep me awake for hours. So in lieu of sleep, I tossed and turned, fumed and seethed.

Honestly, I don't think I'd ever met a woman quite as irritating as Katherine Kozlov McKenna, or Katya Kozlovsky, or whoever she was. Well, maybe my third wife, Claire Dubois was, at least at first. But at least with Claire, her annoying vexing behavior was without question a product of unbelievable stress; her daughter had gone missing from a youth wilderness boot camp. But as soon as we found her daughter those galling qualities rapidly disappeared—well mostly.

With Katherine, however, I suspected her infuriating traits were permanent, genetic, or were somehow imprinted at birth and would never disappear. The only silver lining I could manage to conjure, after tomorrow

I would be done with her. First thing tomorrow, I would take her over to the Summit Overlook to see were we assumed Ian and Wally disappeared. We'd look around for a few minutes, return to Brian Head, then on back St. George, hopefully beating the storm. And I would never have to see her again.

On the other hand, Ziggy was mostly okay, especially when he wasn't with her. With that humiliating psychiatric spectacle of a few minutes ago, maybe, hopefully, he was just showing off, or at the very worst just going along with Katherine. Why? I don't know. Maybe, he was hoping to wrangle a letter of recommendation from her. Whatever his reasons, at least personally he was likable, odd, but pleasant enough. I decided I could forgive him and would still help him secure a job at the hospital.

Finally, my mind turned to Ronnie Slade. What a pleasant change of thought! She was the complete opposite of Katya. She was radiant, smiled a lot, was always pleasant, was eager to please and was every bit as beautiful. I smiled at the thought. Yes indeed, I had to admit, I was happy, very happy, she decided to stay with me.

I suppose eventually I must have fallen asleep, I have no idea when, but a loud pounding on my door finally awakened me. Trying to block out the noise, I turned sideways and cupped a pillow over my head. It didn't work; the pounding persisted and even got louder.

"Jesus, go away," I mumbled.

"It's after eight o'clock!"

"So?"

"So, we've got a lot to do today."

"Like what?"

"Like you are going to show us where Ian disappeared."

That did it. Finally, I recognized the strident, no-nonsense voice of Katherine the Female Cossack.

"Geez, give me a friggin' minute," I growled, then added sarcastically, "and maybe you could cook some breakfast."

As I stumbled out of bed and headed straight for the shower, I realized I had no clean clothes. Oh, well, I smiled wryly, I would shower, mainly to wake up, then put back on my soiled and reeking clothes. Certainly, there was nobody here I was trying to impress.

When I finally entered the kitchen, needless to say, I was shocked. There sitting on the table were three plates, each stacked with two perfectly golden brown pancakes and on the floor a warm bowl of leftover stew for

170

Malachi. Instantly I concluded it must be the work of Ziggy, then I spied him still on the couch wrapped up in the blanket. He rose up on one elbow as I entered and immediately started coughing again. He looked lethargic and listless. His face was fever flushed, his eyes were puffy and his cough was chest deep, not bronchial, and was productive of phlegm he immediately sequestered in his handkerchief.

I felt his forehead. He was hot, probably somewhere around one hundred and two. By pinching the skin of his forearm, I checked his tissue turgor; his skin remained tented. No doubt about it, he was a little dehydrated. Next, I examined his handkerchief. It was daubed with yellow/green thick pasty sputum.

After locating my first aid kit, I placed a thermometer under Ziggy's tongue; his temp was 101.8 degrees. My initial guess was a little high, but not by much. Next, I fished out my stethoscope and listened to his lungs; there were no rales, or rhonchi and no dullness of the chest on percussion. It was probably not pneumonia, at least not yet.

From my first aid bag I fished out two aspirin and 500 milligrams of amoxicillin. Yes, I knew it was frowned on to give viral cold patients antibiotics, but with the green sputum I suspected he was getting a secondary bacterial infection.

With Ziggy taken care of, I turned back to the kitchen. That's when I noticed Katherine the Cossack was wearing Samantha Rose's apron. At first I was taken aback, even upset. That apron was kind of—uh—kind of sacred. But I had to admit she did look good in it, and somehow less threatening, and (I know this sounds sexist) a lot more feminine. Like a maître d', she ushered me to a chair, then retrieved a small pot of heated maple syrup off from the stove. As I buttered my pancakes, she drizzled hot syrup over them. Lastly, she filled my coffee mug, then still without comment the Volga River queen sat down opposite me and we ate in silence. When I was done, I insisted on doing the dishes.

"Well, I guess I'm ready go," I remarked as I put the dishes away.

"What about Ziggy?" Katherine asked.

"He stays right here by the fire. I don't think we'll be gone for more that two or maybe three hours."

"Will he be okay?"

"Yeah. What he needs is to spend the day resting and drinking fluids anyway."

"How far is it?" Katherine asked, her voice again returning to its usual chill.

Inwardly, I smiled. Though she'd cooked me breakfast, I imagined she was still stinging from my rebuke last night. Maybe, that's why she cooked breakfast, to make amends. Probably not. "Not far," I opened the guest bedroom door. "Maybe four or five miles."

In our separate rooms, we stepped into our snowsuits and coats, and Katherine pulled on her helmet. I preferred a ski cap. I liked to feel the wind and snow in my face.

Before we left, I dispensed two more aspirin and another amoxicillin for Ziggy to take in roughly four hours. Also, I set a bottle of juice next to him, instructed him to drink often and under no circumstances was he to leave the cabin.

As I stepped out on the deck, I checked the thermometer hanging on the wall. Even though it was almost ten o'clock, it nevertheless still flaunted a very chilly eight degrees. A light snow had started during the night and was still falling. A couple inches of new had accumulated on the deck and frozen ground. Silently, I hoped this was all we got and the bulk of the storm Sheriff Klein had predicted would miss us to the north. Fortunately, that was not all that unusual. Often weather forecasters predicted a lion of a storm for southern Utah and it turned out to be more of a tabby cat.

After firing up the two snowmobiles, I jerked up on all four skis to break the frost bond, then loaded Malachi onto the tow sled. Into the rear storage compartment, I added my first aid kit, my little-used hunting knife, a length of rope, a bottle of water, a solar blanket and a flashlight. Lastly, I lashed a pair of my snowshoes on the tow sled next to Malachi. In this country, you never knew when you might get your machines stuck or have a mechanical failure. From past experience, I knew it was wise to be prepared; winter in the mountains could be unforgiving. Once again, I operated one machine and Katherine and the other. Since last night we had the foresight to park the snowmobiles facing downhill, there was no problem with the powder. As usual, I led.

Once at the bottom of the hill, I turned right onto Dry Lakes Road and headed south. As opposed to earlier in October when we were using the pickup to search for Ian and Wally, now using snowmobiles we should be able to ride right up to the Summit Point Overlook. As I picked up speed, the falling snowflakes seemed to come in more horizontal, stinging my face and making my eyes water. Fishing my sunglasses from my front pocket, I put them on. That helped some to deflect the snow.

Twenty minutes later we were at the point where Dry Lakes Road angled as close to the Overlook as it would get, or at least I thought that's where we were. With this much snow, most landmarks were obliterated, including all evidence of the bulldozed road we had used in October. Picking what I thought was the right spot, we veered off Dry Lakes Road and headed due west, hopefully in the direction of Summit Overlook.

My path took me through the thick alpine forest; obviously I missed the dozed road. Deftly, I dodged white pine, balsam and quaking aspen trees, and also the occasional large granite boulder. Katya was doing fine, following strictly in my wake. After cresting the ridge top of a deep ravine, I headed down its steep seventy-degree slope, then increased my speed as I started up the other side. Once on top, I stopped, turned and watched Katya on her machine. Unfortunately when she started down the near vertical slope, she nervously squeezed the handbrakes. The slope was so precipitous even though she locked the brakes the machine continued to slide. As it slid, it angled sideways, slightly off the trail I had just broken, finally coming to a rest in the "V" at the bottom of the ravine. Now, with no forward momentum, the snowmobile immediately sank into the deep powder.

Suddenly realizing her plight, Katya immediately squeezed down on the gas feed lever, but she went nowhere. The rotating track simply spun in the loose snow and failed to gain traction, much like rubber tires on an icy road. She put it in reverse and tried to back up with the same results. Unfortunately, in either direction, forwards or backwards, not only was there deep powder, but both directions were uphill. She was hopelessly mired.

Briefly, and I admit a bit meanly, I thought about leaving her, at least for a while, so she would appreciate me, then I realized that was a classic example of antisocial behavior. That would only reinforce the earlier diagnosis from last night. With mixed emotions, I turned my machine around and started back down the hill.

Without stopping or even slowing, I came down the slope, then right in front of her snowmobile I executed a right angle turn and headed straight down the ravine, right in the bottom of the "V". After fifty yards, or so, the banks became less steep and I angled up the right slope till I reached the crest. Once back on top, I returned to the point above her machine, then completed the circuit again. After a couple of more loops, I had a pretty well packed track and on the next circuit, I stopped in front to her machine.

"Never stop at he bottom of a hill," I yelled above the clacking engine.

"I was sliding out of control," Katherine shot back.

"So, you should have let it slide. What would it hurt?"

"What if I hit something?"

"There's nothing to hit," I growled. "If you would have taken your hand off the brake and gave it some gas, you would have shot right back up the other side."

She scowled at me. "I thought I did pretty good."

She probably was right, considering she'd never operated a snowmobile before, but I wasn't in a charitable mood, particularly after last night. Without further comment, I had her get off her machine, then grabbing hold of both skis, I tried to lift and turn the five hundred pound machine ninety-degrees to get it facing down the trail I had just broken. Grunting and heaving, I barely moved it. Standing in almost waist deep snow, I could get no leverage. I tried again and again without much success, maybe moved it two or three inches. Just as I was about to give up, Katherine joined me. The Cossack took one ski and I took the other. In unison, we heaved and heaved and unbelievably we moved the machine a few more inches. After several more attempts, we turned the machine enough to direct it down the ravine, down the packed path. Surprisingly, Katherine The Great was much stronger than she looked and stouter than I had imagined.

Once we had her snowmobile aligned with the new trail, I hopped back on my machine and again led the way. We followed my previous path to the top of the ravine, then turned west again toward the Overlook. As we got closer to the rim, the more the wind seemed to pick up and the air got colder. After fifteen more minutes of dodging trees, downed logs and crossing ravines, we arrived at the rim, but unfortunately not precisely at Summit Overlook. Turning up the collar of my coat to protect from the wind, I took a minute to reconnoiter. Which way should we go along the rim, north or south, to find the Overlook? Finally, I mentally flipped a coin and we took off to the south.

Fortunately, I guessed right. After another ten minutes, I spotted the familiar mesa cliff jutting out like the bow of a ship into the blustery windstorm. We parked our machines right at the Overlook, about fifty feet from the edge. Even though now it was snowing a little harder, we were standing on bare rock. The wind had pretty much blown all the snow off the unprotected peninsula. Turning off my machine, I zipped my coat up

174

tighter and headed into a stiff breeze toward the rim. Leaning into the wind to maintain her balance, Katya followed.

"I think—is the place!" I shouted above the wind, while pointing down at the vast gray/white expanse directly in front and below us.

"This—where—last—seen?" Katya shouted back at me. Approximately every other word she spoke was blown away by the wind.

"No—this—where—headed—day—disappeared," I explained. "I—last—saw him—morning—when—left—cabin."

"But—this—where—" Katya yelled, "—the sheriff—camera?"

"Yes," I nodded and shouted back, "but—" I paused and inched closer to the rim, "—think—down there." Again I pointed downward and over the edge.

We were standing atop a hundred foot granite cliff, but because of the clouds and blowing snow any sunlight was mostly blocked. The visibility was so poor the base of the cliff was barely visible. What we couldn't appreciate, however, was how the terrain continued to drop off precipitously from that cliff base, in an almost uninterrupted series of shelving-cliffs and nearly vertical gradients until it reached the valley floor some three and a half thousand feet or three sloping miles below us.

"Is—there—way—down?" Katya shouted, also pointing down over the cliff.

"Maybe," I yelled back, "but—this—not—time—try."

"—Sheriff," she yelled, "must—gotten—down—get—camera."

"Yeah—not in—blizzard," I shouted, cupping my hands like a megaphone.

"Well—we—may--never—back." Katya turned and began searching for a way down.

"Let's—head—cabin." I grabbed her arm with one hand and with the other pointed back at the snowmobiles.

She shook loose of my grip and began picking her way down an almost perpendicular rock chute squeezed between two colossal upright granite slabs.

"Katherine—please!"

She didn't hear me, or at least pretended she didn't. Either way, she ignored me and continued on. Reluctantly, I decided I had to go with the willful Cossack. I brought her here; it was my duty to get her back.

"Damn psychiatrists," I muttered under my breath. "They don't have the sense God gave little children." Nevertheless, I called to Malachi and followed her, trying to stay in the path she had just broken in the fresh snow.

As we descended over and down from the exposed rim the, snow got deeper, much deeper. Apparently, the sheer cliff wall acted like a tennis backstop for the blowing snow, breaking the wind and allowing the snow to accumulate. By the time we were halfway down the chute it was waist deep, but at least now the wind had lessened a bit as it was feathering over our heads.

But even without the scourge of wind, the chute was still hazardous. Though invisible under the new layer of snow, the terrain consisted of nothing more than a jumbled and almost vertical rockslide. The footing was slick and treacherous. With each step, we ran a real risk of having a boot slip into a rocky slot, literally a granite bear trap, then the body's weight, coupled with forward momentum, would propel the body forward and downward, snapping the trapped ankle bones like a dry twig. The result, a very nasty trimalleolar fracture.

Also, Malachi, with his shorter legs, was particularly vulnerable to the deep snow. Wallowing down the slope, he looked a bit like a beached seal floundering toward the ocean.

Eventually, I realized it was easier to lie on my back and scoot/slide feet first, like a capsized river-rafter would down boulder-strewn Class IV rapids. With this maneuver, I easily passed Katya and arrived moments later at the base with a thud. Seconds later Katya, followed my lead. She and Malachi slid the rest of the way down steep slope, crashing into me just as I stood, knocking me over again.

Slowly, we disentangled, with each of us checking to make sure we still possessed all four limbs and testing to make sure all were still functional.

Satisfied I was indeed still in one piece, I grunted and I stood up, then brushed the snow from my face and neck.

"What now?" I growled at Katherine. I was still irritated with her, but at least now with the gale force wind tempered it was easier to communicate.

"We look around," she growled back.

"For what?"

"For clues."

"You mean for bodies."

"I mean for clues," she said curtly. "Ian's not dead."

I looked at my wristwatch, then relented. "Okay, it's just after one o'clock. Let's take an hour at most to look around, then we have to head back and check on Ziggy. I want to allow us plenty of time to get back. I really don't want to get caught out here after dark."

Katherine nodded, then with head down started kicking and sifting through the snow.

"And" I continued, "be careful. We're basically on a cliff here, a rock island, and not a very big one."

"*Islands in the Stream.*" She gestured toward the edge of the cliff and the ongoing current of passing clouds.

"What?" I shook my head. She certainly was not someone I would expect to quote from a Kenny Rogers and Dolly Parton song. "No—no," I countered, "this is more like a Normandy Beach minefield with the fog rolling in."

For the next thirty minutes, we worked the area in silence, both of us laboring in different directions. The way I saw it, not only was this a difficult and dangerous task, but it was also an exercise in futility. Not only had Sheriff Tiny Klein and Iron County Search and Rescue combed this area, but now more than likely we were searching in much worse conditions. Sure there was snow back then, but it was much deeper now. Also, the weather had turned colder and as we approached the winter solstice the days were shorter. If they had found nothing other than a camera, the odds of us finding anything else were next to zero. In my opinion, with these conditions, this whole endeavor smacked of a fool's errand.

Just as I was about to call a halt to the madness, Malachi started seriously sniffing, then with his front paws he started digging.

I stopped exploring and along with Katya gathered around the feverishly excavating chocolate lab. After just a couple of minutes, I heard his paws scratch the frozen ground. Abruptly, he stopped digging and thrust his entire face into the hole. When he came up, he held something in his jaws—something plastic.

"What is it?" Katya inched closer.

"I don't know." I called to Malachi. Like he was retrieving a downed mallard, he brought the object over and dropped it at my feet.

"Good boy!" I patted him on the head, then reached down, picked it up and turned it over. "It's just a Ziploc baggie," I informed Katya.

Indeed, that's what it was, but it was not empty. Though the interior was clouded and fogged from accumulated moisture, making it nearly opaque, I could nevertheless still feel several cylindrical objects. Puzzled, I continued to rotate the clouded baggie in my hands, trying to decipher its contents.

Katherine grabbed the baggie from me. Eschewing my careful tactile examination, she unzipped the baggie, reached in and pulled out something metal. It glinted like brass. "What is this?" She held it high.

I snatched back the baggie, fished out another brass object, rotating it in my finger. Clearly, it was a spent casing. Spinning it, I read the identification marking on the flat primer end. It was a .223 caliber Remington shell. I held it up to my nose. It still faintly smelled of burnt nitrogen and sulfur.

Finally, it dawned on me!

I knew exactly what these casings were. These were the shells Ian had collected from the site where Tim Slade had slaughtered that poor buck. These were his spent Bushmaster 90624 assault rifle casings!

Taking the shell Katherine was holding, I replaced both casings back in the baggie, then took a few minutes to explain to her the story behind them. I concluded, "this undoubtedly means Ian was here!"

Katherine was not nearly as excited by the find as I was. "We already knew that," she reminded me as she grabbed the baggie back again, this time placing it in her coat pocket. "Then this must be pretty close to where the sheriff found Ian's camera."

I remained silent, but felt a shiver tingle down my spine. These findings also more than likely meant Ian's body might very well be around here too.

"He's not here," Katherine snapped, reading my mind.

"More women's intuition."

"Call it whatever you like, but I know Ian better than you."

"Well, if you don't mind," I couldn't keep the sarcasm out of my voice, "I'll look around a little bit more."

Abruptly, I turned my back on her and went back to the spot where Malachi had found the baggie. Kneeling down, and with Malachi helping, we continued to dig and filter through the snow, ever enlarging our circle as we went. Our excavation took us right to the edge of the cliff. I brushed the loose snow over the rim and could feel the perpendicular face of the rimrock. Peering over the edge, I could see the slope dropped off, almost straight down. Were Ian and Wally down there? Probably, but this was as far as I could go. Checking my watch, I noted it was now almost three o'clock.

Sometime in the last few minutes, probably while we were absorbed with Malachi's baggie find, the wind changed directions, presently coming directly from the north. Now no longer blocked or backstopped, it howled in and around the ledges and rocky chutes, forcing me to move back from the edge. It was definitely time to head back to the cabin and Ziggy.

As I backed away from the rim, I called to Malachi. Instead of joining me, he suddenly started sniffing, then bolted right off the ledge.

"N-o-o-o!" I screamed.

I rushed back to the rim fully expecting to never see Malachi again. At the edge of precipice, I dropped to my knees and peered over. Ten feet below me on a small secondary ledge no more than ten to twelve square feet in area I spied the chocolate lab. Once again, he was furiously digging. The visibility was so poor from falling and blowing snow I couldn't tell what, if anything, he'd found. As I carefully backed away from the edge, I noted Katya had also inched over to the rim to watch.

Even trying to descend down those ten to twelve feet would be treacherous. Off to the left, there was what appeared to be another snow-covered, seventy-degree rockslide. It was similar, but smaller and on the opposite side of the ledge to the one we'd used to get this far. Finding no other route, everything else was essentially perpendicular, I headed for that secondary slide and began to cautiously pick my way down. Halfway to the bottom, I caught my foot in a hidden rock pocket and pitched forward and began sliding headfirst. Thankfully, my foot popped free of the potential fracture-trap and I did not bang my head on any passing boulders, but I did not stop till slammed into Malachi's little ledge.

With my heart pounding like a bongo drum, I picked myself up, dusted off the snow, then rejoined Malachi, who was still feverishly working. He was scratching at something under the fresh layer of snow. Kneeling, I used my gloved hands to brush and clear away the piled snow as he continued to work. I steeled myself for the macabre as I could clearly imagine why he was so excited and what he would find. Periodically Malachi would stop, thrust his nose into the hole, then immediately start digging again.

Above me, Katherine inched her head over to the edge. "What is it?" she screamed loudly enough to be heard above the swirling wind.

"I don't know," I shouted back. "Malachi's smelled something."

She said something else, which was blown away by the wind.

I turned back to the rock slab and my dog.

In that short period of time, Malachi had managed to scratch away the layer of loose fresh snow and was now feverishly clawing up and shredding the older ice. Pushing Malachi aside, I leaned in for a better look. Suddenly, a vortex of swirling snow engulfed me and I could see nothing. With a gloved hand, I scooped up Malachi's grated ice and held in close to my face. Surprisingly, it looked a lot like a cherry-flavored snow cone.

Suddenly, I knew what it was!

"What is it?" Katherine shouted loudly through cupped hands.

"Blood!"

"Whose?"

"I don't know. Probably Wally's or Ian's."

"Any bodies?"

"No," I paused to take a breath. "Not that I can see."

"What are you going to do?" She shouted from the ledge lip high above me.

"I need to save a sample."

"How?"

"In the back pocket of my snowmobile, I have a first aid kit." Again I paused for a breath. "To keep it from getting wet, I put it in a plastic bag. I need to go get the plastic bag."

"What?" she shouted.

As loud as I could, I repeated what I'd said, then started to climb back up to Katherine.

"Stay there!" she commanded, disappeared for a few seconds, then reappeared. "Why not use this?" She held up the baggie containing the spent Bushmaster shells.

Yes, indeed, why not? Fortunately, I doubted she could see my red face. "Take the shells out and put them in your pocket, then toss the baggie down to me."

"The wind will blow it away," Katherine yelled back. "I'll bring it down."

"No!" I shouted about the wind. "It's too dangerous. I'll come up." Once again, I looked for hand and foot holds.

She leaned over the edge. "And that's less dangerous? To go both ways, up and back?"

"You got a better idea?" I couldn't keep the sarcasm out of my voice.

Katherine was silent for a moment, then disappeared again.

Impatiently, I waited for a couple of minutes, then again began searching for a way back up to her level, to the higher peninsula.

Abruptly, she reappeared on the rim. "Here!" She tossed the baggie.

"No, don't--!" I fully expected the wind to blow it away, but it fell almost straight down, landing at my feet with a thud. Bending over, I picked it up and immediately realized why the wind had not taken it. Katherine

180

had stuffed it with small granite pebbles. Why hadn't I thought of that? Sheepishly, I had to admit there was probably more to the Cossack than just a pretty face.

Carefully, so as not to damage it, I emptied rocks from the baggie, then filled it with the crimson-colored snow. After again zip-locking it, I stuffed it in my coat pocket and with Malachi at my side again began searching for a way back up to Katherine. Unfortunately, there was no way except for the same way I came down. Calling to Malachi, I pointed the way upward. Now with the trail broken, he nimbly scrambled up the steep slope. Once on the upper ledge, he rushed over to Katherine who rewarded him with a congratulatory hug. Now it was my turn.

Cautiously, I picked my way up the seventy-degree rockslide. Footing was treacherous, so I used the three-point fixation technique. Before I moved a hand or foot, the other three appendages had to be securely fixed. With two hands and a foot secure, I could carefully move my other foot up, searching with it till I found another foothold. With two feet secure along with one hand, I could cautiously move the other hand till a higher safe handhold was found. This was followed another foot, then another hand and so on.

Fifteen anxious minutes later, it seemed like an hour, I was back on the upper ledge with Malachi and Katherine. Alas, there was no congratulatory hug for me. Breathing hard, I sat down on a rock slab, trying to catch my breath. God, I was out of shape. In between breaths, I eyed what we still had left, the other slope.

We still had one more precipitous, but much longer climb, then we would be back on top with the snowmobiles. I glanced up at the sky. Though it was cloudy and snowing heavily, I sensed we were losing light. Checking my watch, I was amazed. It was already nearly five o'clock. At most, we had an hour of daylight left! We really needed to keep moving.

"Let's go," I wheezed. Still breathing hard, I stood up and called to Malachi.

"Geez, Coop," Katherine objected, "take a minute to catch your breath."

Unbelievable! She actually sounded worried about my welfare, but unfortunately there was no time to bask in the sunshine of her concern.

"We're running out of time." I pointed to my wristwatch. "It'll be dark in an hour."

She started to argue, then changed her mind and nodded. "I'm ready whenever you are."

We worked our way back to the same rocky chute we had slid down earlier. Our tracks, both the boot and the furrow we'd made from sliding, were already nearly invisible from the falling snow. Looking up, I could barely see the lip of rimrock, but I knew the snowmobiles were up there, one hundred feet or so, almost straight above us.

"I'll go first," I said, "and re-break a trail."

For once, Katherine didn't argue and Malachi seemed happy enough to follow at my heels.

Using the same three-point technique, I started up the rock-jumbled snowy chute. About halfway up, I'd fixed both hands and one foot, then couldn't find a perch for my other foot. I replaced my foot and cleared a patch of snow with my gloved hand. The problem appeared to be a rectangular slab of granite at least as large as me and directly above me like a roof. It sported a smooth surface and was pitched forward at a severe angle. There was no way to scale it and it seemed to have no hand or footholds. Carefully, I worked laterally to my left, once again found the prerequisite three-point holds and began climbing upward.

After I had gained another ten feet or so, I found a relatively safe solid rock jetty to sit on, then turned around to watch the progress of Malachi and Katherine.

Malachi had no problem. He easily scrambled up the treacherous chute and joined me at the jetty. Now it was Katherine's turn.

Slowly, she worked up to the overhead, obstructing granite slab and like me couldn't find a hand or foothold.

"Work to your left," I shouted above the wind.

"What?"

"To your left!" I screamed. "You can get up from there."

Suddenly, she slipped, lost both her foot and handholds, then began careening back down the slope. Somehow, she managed to rotate onto her back, but then her right foot suddenly dropped and wedged into a rocky slot, the dreaded stone bear trap. Instantly, she pitched forward, but her trapped foot held fast.

Even though she was some twenty feet below me and the wind was howling, I could still hear the unmistakable sound of *cracking*, the fracturing of ankle bones.

182

# 16

Like tossing an anchor from a boat speeding through shallow water, Katya abruptly came to a stop, then pitched forward face down in the snow. Even though her lower leg was twisted and bent unnaturally, almost ninety-degrees, her foot remained trapped in the rocky vice.

"Katherine!" I shouted.

No answer.

"Katherine!"

Still no answer.

Malachi leaped off the rock jetty, bounded with amazing dexterity down the treacherous slope and nuzzled up to her, licking her face.

As rapidly as I could, I retraced my steps, working my way back to the motionless form of Katherine Kozlovsky.

It seemed like hours, but was probably no more than ten minutes before I reached her. She was totally silent and offered no voluntary movement of any kind. Lying prone and face down in the snow, her head was a good five feet below her trapped and grossly mangled ankle. This downward and prone position transferred all her weight to her chest and made breathing difficult if not impossible. For her chest to expand on inspiration, it had to move upward almost the full weight of her body. Also, the angle she came to rest, head down with her face and nose buried in the deep snow, blocked her air intake passages.

I suppressed the urge to rapidly clear her trapped foot and turn her over on her back. Instead, I nudged Malachi to Katherine's other side, then without moving her head or rotating her neck, I cleared her airway by scraping the snow away from her mouth and nose.

On a hunch, I held up a handful of snow that I'd extracted from under her face. It was red. Blood red!

Bending low, I observed the bleeding was coming out of the corner of her mouth, thankfully not from her nose or ears. Bleeding from both of those sites was a fairly reliable sign of a skull fracture. I palpated her frontal skull bone just to be sure; I could feel no shelving or depression of the bone. But were there other sites of hemorrhage? She might be bleeding inside her cranium even without a fracture and the blood would have no way to exit. That was an even worse scenario.

Backing off a bit, I watched her chest for any sign of movement, anything to indicate respiration. I could see no chest expansion, but with the bulking snow suit and coat on it was difficult to say for sure.

Ripping off my ski glove, I groped for her neck, trying to locate her carotid artery. There was no pulse! But my fingers were so numb I could hardly feel them.

I blew warm air on my cold fingers, then repositioned them on her neck. Wait a second! There was a pulse! It was weak and thready, but it was undeniably present. Jerking off my other glove so I could see my wristwatch, I counted—one hundred and twenty-six. That was fast, very fast, but that's what I would expect for severe trauma. At least she was still alive! But—but for how long? I still had seen no movement of her ribcage. Should I free her foot and turn her? Risk making her a paraplegic so I could begin CPR? Was being a paraplegic better than being dead? Jesus, I chastised myself, I had no time for this medical/philosophical debate. I had to do something and I had to do it now!

Instinctively, I looked to the heavens for help, to a God I didn't believe in. No surprise there—just silence and the continued howling of the wind. Sighing, I took in a deep breath, put my ski gloves back on, then reached for a boulder to begin freeing her foot. I decided to risk paraplegia and move her.

Suddenly, she groaned and took a quick short breath! Was that a death rattle? Nothing more than an agonal breath? I was not sure. Taking off my glove again, I placed my hand under her coat on her ribcage and waited. Five seconds passed, then ten, then twenty. Just as I was about to withdraw my hand, I felt her ribs move followed by a low muffled moan.

Removing my hand, I again checked her carotid pulse. It was still rapid, but the amplitude was a little stronger. She took another breath, fuller now and not quite so shallow. After a few seconds, she coughed, groaned again and tried to move.

"Katherine," I again kneeled by her head, still buried face down in the snow, and whispered into her ear. "Katherine, hold still while I free your foot."

Her eyelids fluttered, but she did not answer. Instead, she tried to lift her head.

Using both hands, I held her still, trying to immobilize her head and secure her neck. "Katherine," I pleaded, "please do not try to move!"

She moaned, but his time her eyelids fluttered opened and remained open. Gently, I tried to sweep the snow away from her eyes and dark lashes, then returned my hands to secure her neck. She continued to moan and her eyes remained glassy. For another couple minutes, she continued in this dazed state, then she attempted to speak.

"Wh—what hap—pened?"

"You slid down the slope."

"Slope?"

"What?" I asked. With her face down, she was speaking directly into the snow making it difficult to hear her above the wind. I bent down low, my ear next to her mouth.

"Wh—at s—slope."

I took a minute to reacquaint her with what we were doing and why, then silently debated whether to level with her about the extent of her injuries. Why not? After all, she was an MD and just like me had attended medical school. If it were me, I would want to know.

"Katherine, you are badly hurt." Again I got down low and tried to look her in one eye. "Undoubtedly, you have a lower tibia and fibula fracture, you know a skier's boot-top fracture. I also think you hit your head, resulting in possibly a grade-three concussion and—and I'm worried your neck may be injured."

"Is that all?" Katherine asked.

"As best I can tell."

"Oh," she said, "I thought it might be something serious."

I looked sharply at her to see if she was joking. She managed a half-smile.

She was joking! What a time for levity! I looked at her with renewed respect. She was showing some surprising grit.

She smiled again, this time in pain. "Actually, m—my foot hurts like hell."

Basically that was a good sign. At least, she wasn't already a para or quadriplegic.

"Can you move your fingers?"

She complied by fluttering both sets of fingers.

"How does your head feel?"

"Like it might explode."

"Your neck? Does it hurt?"

She paused for a minute. "It's kind of hard to say, but I don't think so."

With my back muscles about to spasm, I straightened my back and rested upright on my knees, then in the fading light examined the back of her neck. There was no obvious edema or ecchymosis. Next, I systematically palpated her vertebrae, starting with C-7 and working up to C-1 at the base of the skull.

"Tell me if there are any tender, or sensitive areas. How about here?"

She started to shake her head and I instantly stopped her. "Just tell me."

"No," she held her head still, "it seems okay."

I continued on to the next vertebrae and eventually all the way up from C-7 to C-1. At each level she denied pain. Maybe, hopefully, her neck was okay after all.

Again, I decided to level with her. "Katherine, I think your neck is okay, but without x-rays I can't be one hundred percent sure. If I try to move you there is a slight risk I will paralyze you, but—" I paused, trying to decide how to word what came next.

"—But," she finished my sentence, "but if you don't move me, I'll freeze to death tonight."

"Yeah," I nodded, though she couldn't see me, "we need to find shelter for the night."

"We're not getting out of here tonight?"

"No, it will be dark in another thirty or forty minutes. Even if I managed to get your foot free in the next few minutes, I still not sure how I would get you back up to the snowmobiles. Certainly, I couldn't do all that before nightfall."

She was silent for a moment. "Okay," she said decisively, "let's take the chance. Go ahead and free my foot and turn me. I'm not ready to die yet."

Again, she could not see my nod or the look of awe on my face. She was one tough Volga Queen. No—no, she deserved my respect. She was one tough all-American woman. Her foot and head must be killing her, yet rather than succumbing to the pain she was somehow holding it together. Not only was she holding it together, she was making rational life-or-death decisions.

And, I decided, she certainly deserved to be called by the name she preferred. No longer would I refer to her a Katherine Koslov McKenna, but from now on she was Katya Koslovsky.

"This may hurt," I finally said.

"Yes, I suspect it will."

Carefully, I worked the five feet up hill to her trapped foot. It would not do for me to slip and slide down this dangerous slope, also possibly breaking something or missing the small landing altogether and slipping away into oblivion. That would result in a death sentence for both of us.

First, I visually examined her leg. There was no obvious blood saturating the snow or her pant leg. That was a good sign. If it were a compound fracture (bone piercing the skin) I would expect significant bleeding. Unfortunately, that was the only good sign. The plane of leg and prone body compared to the trapped foot and ankle was more than ninety degrees! Anatomically, there was no way to achieve that kind of angle without fracturing bones, the tibia and fibula, or least their respective malleoli. With such severe angulation, the worry was not only for the bones, but also for the integrity of the ligaments, nerves and blood vessels. Ligaments and fractured bones could be repaired, but nerves were much harder to fix and if the vessels were disrupted and the foot tissue went very long without a blood supply it would die, necrose and rapidly decompose.

I brushed away the overlying snow from the rock trap, then took a moment to assess the situation. To free her foot without a lot of twisting, tugging and excruciating pain would require I remove some of the entrapping boulders. That seemed obvious and simple enough. Sadly, however, it was not quite that straightforward. It was more like a playing the stacked-block game of Jenga or Pick-up Sticks. Not only were some of the rocks very large, but they were also jumbled and wedged, and each one seemed to support the rock above it, and the one above it and so on. Like a jigsaw puzzle, the entire slope seemed to be interconnected in this seemingly random and precarious way. Remove the wrong one and I could trigger a rockslide, causing the entire slope above me to start moving and more than likely burying all of us, Malachi, Katya and me!

Like a carpenter remodeling an old house, I tried to identify which rocks were weight bearing and which were not. When I identified a likely structurally insignificant candidate, I carefully inched it out, then held my breath. One wedged stone I removed triggered a two-rock slide. I caught the bigger one, but unfortunately the smaller one, the size of baseball, hurled downward smacking Katya on her thigh.

She groaned out loud, but managed not move her head.

After apologizing, I redeposited the boulder I'd caught in a secure location, then checked her leg. When satisfied no further damage was done, I wiped the accumulated beads of perspiration from my forehead with a gloved hand. In spite of the frigid temperatures, I'd broken out in a cold sweat. Trying to steady my surgically trained fingers, I turned back to the rocky bear trap.

Snow gloves are certainly not like surgical gloves; they are bulky and clumsy, and allow very limited tactile sensation. In spite of the freezing temperatures, I finally jerked off my gloves, then returned to the tricky task using my bare hands.

Ten minutes later and with numb fingers, I'd removed enough rocks I figured I could free her foot.

"Katya," I said, staring at the back of her head.

"Y—yes," she replied, her voice was trembling with pain.

"I'm ready to move your foot."

She gritted her teeth. "Oh—are you still here?"

I couldn't tell if that was her usual sarcasm or once again an attempt to lighten the situation with humor. "Yes, and this is going to hurt."

"Really?"

I decided that was sarcasm.

She gritted her teeth. "I'm ready."

With her groaning loudly and me being as careful as I could, I extracted her right foot from the rocky vise. Unfortunately, however, this still required a bit of twisting and tugging.

With Katya crying out loud, and with one last firm tug, I popped her foot free. Abruptly, she stopped screaming and returned to softly moaning. Evidently, I concluded, she had lost consciousness again. That was an unintended, but probably welcome blessing. Hurriedly, I rolled up her pant leg and examined the injury. Her lower leg, ankle and foot looked terrible. They were remarkably swollen, misshapen, mottled purple and angled like the capital letter "L" instead of a normal lower case "l".

Taking advantage of her unconsciousness, I quickly tried to reduce her fractures and set the bones of her foot. This had to be done with extreme care. The serrated edges of broken bones were very sharp, like razors, and could easily slice through blood vessels, tendons, nerves or ligaments.

Once I had achieved a rough realignment, I gently set her foot down and waited for her to regain consciousness.

188

Within a minute or two, she started moaning louder and eventually opened her eyes.

"Are you okay?" I asked anxiously.

"So, is that how you treat all your patients?" Her voice was strained.

Again I wondered if this was an attempt at humor. "No," I replied, "just the ones who don't pay their bills."

"I—I'll pay," she groaned.

"Good. Let's try turning you on your back."

"Okay, I'm tired of being on top."

I smiled and once again wondered if this was her attempt at a slightly salacious joke.

"We've got to be careful," I cautioned, "I'm still worried about your neck, and the bones in your ankle are definitely unstable."

She quickly assessed the situation. "Are you trying to tell be you can't be two places at the same time?"

"Something like that."

"I think the neck is okay," she managed to croak. "I'll manage that if you'll take care of the leg."

"You've got a deal." I knew there was no other way.

Carefully, I took up my position next to her ankle. "We'll roll to your left."

"Tell me when. I'll help as much as I can," she said, speaking directly into the snow.

"Speak louder."

"Tell me when!"

"Okay, on the count of three."

Speaking loudly, I counted to three, then with her help I slowly rolled her perpendicular, upon her up on her left side, while still guarding her right leg. As we continued the roll, gravity took over and I lost my grip. She thudded over on her back, then immediately started to slide. I grabbed her pant leg and held on. Fortunately, she slid only a few inches, then stopped, her left shoulder butted up against the protruding roof rock. I held my breath and relaxed my grip. There was no further movement. At the moment, thank God, she appeared to be stable.

"Hold on to that rock by your left shoulder," I instructed her. "I going to try to pivot you so your feet are headed down the slope."

She squirmed around till she could grip the rock, then I incrementally rotated her, like correcting the time-hands of a grandfather clock, until her feet were directed downhill. Each movement of her leg was accompanied a low moan of pain.

Now that I had her supine, I noticed her forehead. It sported an ugly bluish-purple hematoma. The overlying skin was serrated and broken. Undoubtedly, she'd hit her head on a half-submerged rock when she fell forward on the steep slope. That, and of course the intense pain, had more than likely caused her loss of consciousness. Carefully, I palpated her forehead, again worried about a frontal bone skull fracture. Fortunately, I could feel no fissures, indentations or shelving, but then again there was so much swelling it was hard to say for sure. I would have to keep a close eye on her tonight for any sign of increased intracranial pressure. Severe headache, projectile vomiting without nausea, altered consciousness and unequal dilation of the pupils were all signs of a life-threatening subdural hematoma.

Sighing to myself, I looked up at the gray dumpling sky. Thankfully, it had stopped snowing, at least for the moment, but the wind continued to howl. Shielding my eyes against the gale, I tried to locate the approximate position of the sun. The clouds were so thick it was impossible, but it had to be getting late. Daylight was fading fast.

"Katya," now I could see and speak to her face, "I've got to leave you for a few minutes."

"Just like a man, and just when we were having a good time." She frowned, either in pain or at my announcement, then added softly, "and just like Ian."

I wished I had the time to follow up on that comment, but I didn't. "I'll be back," I shouted above the wind. "I've got to go up to the snowmobiles and get my first aid kit. Before we move you, I've got to stabilize your foot."

"Move me?"

"We can't spend the night here, exposed on this slope. We have to find some kind of shelter."

"No way for both of us to get back up to the snowmobiles?"

I shook my head. "No, not tonight. I can't carry you up this slope. I'll be lucky to get up and back myself without slipping—" My voice trailed off.

"Maybe you shouldn't come back." Her face was a mask. "There's no sense for both of us—" She didn't finish her sentence.

"Are you kidding me," I joked, "and pass up a chance to spend a night with the beautiful Katya Kozlovsky!"

She frowned, started to say something, then fell silent.

Geez, I said to myself, she really doesn't have a sense of humor.

190

Maybe I should leave just her. She may be right; if I stay there's a good chance we both could perish. I turned to leave.

"And," she moaned, "no girl could pass up a chance to spend a night with the legendary Doctor Cooper."

"Legendary?" I smiled. That's hardly the adjective I would have used, but instead of further entertaining those comments I told Malachi to stay, then turned back to the slope. Before I started my climb, I paused to check my watch. It was already five-fifteen. This time of year darkness came early in the mountains, particularly with cloud-covered skies. At most, I had no more than twenty to thirty minutes of visibility.

Thankfully, and without further incidence, I made it back to the Summit Overlook and the waiting snowmobiles. From the rear compartment of my machine, I fished out the first aid kit, a length of rope, the water bottle and the emergency solar blanket, then decided I might just as well take my hunting knife. After looping the knife scabbard and water bottle onto my belt and coiling the rope around my neck, I secured the first aid kit under my shirt and coat next to my abdomen and wedged the solar blanket under the waistband of my pants.

Back on the edge of the Overlook, the visibility was now so bad I had trouble seeing Katya and Malachi directly below me. Because I knew they were about halfway down the slope, I could vaguely make out some dark shapes, which was probably them. Briefly, I again considered Katya's suggestion to leave. I could be back to the warmth and comfort of the cabin within in thirty minutes, but then I thought of Malachi. There was no way I was going to leave him. And if I was completely honest, there was no way I could, or would, leave the gypsy woman either, no matter how much I wanted to.

Sighing to myself, I returned to the rocky chute, just to the right of the Overlook Point, and once again started down. Thankfully, as before, I descended without incidence. With this being my third time over the same snowy and rocky gauntlet, I had pretty much figured out which was the best route to take and where the best foot and handholds were located. As I descended, I worked on a plan for Katya.

As expected, Malachi was thrilled to see me, but unexpectedly Katya seemed equally happy, or at least relieved. Had she actually thought I would leave? Hurriedly, I checked her over. Her pupils were round and equal, she seemed alert, and her pulse was rapid, but strong. From my first aid kit, I took a 7.5-milligram hydrocodone pill and had her swallow with the water

I brought, gave her one more swallow of water, then I explained my plan. First, I would stabilize her fracture. Next, I would loop the rope under her arms, around her chest and tie it. Then lastly, I would brace myself and using the rope would lower her back down to the ledge, still some fifty feet below us.

"Ah, the best laid schemes o' *Mice an' Men*," she said uneasily.

"John Steinbeck." I promptly replied, again proud of my liberal education.

"No, actually Robert Burns from his poem, *To a Mouse.* Steinbeck borrowed it from Bobby Burns," she corrected me, then added with a tight smile, "if that's the best you can come up with, then let's do it."

I wanted to snap, 'if you have a better idea,' but I didn't. Cut her a little slack, I told myself. After all she was the one with the head injury, the very ugly leg fracture and the missing ex-husband.

So, showing great restraint, I bit my tongue and turned to my first aid kit. After rummaging around a bit, I located my SAM Splint and a role of Kerlix. I positioned the splint across the fracture, then wrapped it tightly, fixing it and the ankle in place with the Kerlix. Now, the leg seemed fairly secure, not weight-bearing stable, but not floppy either. Next, I looped the rope around her chest and under her arms, then tied it posteriorly just under her shoulder blades. At last I was ready.

"Can you hold your leg up, the injured one?" This part was critical.

She gritted her teeth. With supreme effort and groaning loudly, she used her hands to help lift and somehow managed to elevate the foot a few inches off the slope. She held it for no more than a five seconds, then with another loud groan let it collapse back onto the snow.

"Okay," I said, relieved at what I saw, "when we get going, hold the injured leg up and use the other leg to propel you forward. I'll keep you from going too fast with the rope. If you get tired, raise an arm and we'll stop and rest for a bit."

I located the rock protrusion, the same rock jetty that had stopped her earlier slide. Carefully, I positioned myself by sitting down on it, then pulled the rope taut. I felt a bit like I was sitting on Ike in my saddle and had my rope around a calf that needed branding.

"Okay, Katya," I flicked the rope a little as a signal, "whenever you're ready."

Again, mustering all her strength and using her hands, she slowly raised her right leg, then using her left foot pushed off enough--it didn't take much--to start sliding. Malachi bounded protectively alongside her.

Bracing against the rocky protrusion, I gripped the rope and carefully lowered her down the near vertical slope. Five or six seconds later, she abruptly raised her arm. I immediately gripped the rope and stopped her slide. Totally spent, she dropped her leg back down on the snow and groaned out loud. After a couple of minutes rest, she signaled she was ready to go. Once again, she raised her leg and I let the rope slide slowly through my gloved hands.

We repeated this maneuver two more times, then I came to the end of my rope.

"Are you there yet?" I hollered down at her through the gathering dusk.

"No!"

"How far?"

"Three, maybe up to six feet."

Damn, I muttered silently to myself, so close, but like Hall and Oats had aptly said, *yet so far away!* Now what? If I could pull her back up another three or four feet, I could tie the rope to the rock jetty, then work down to her and—and what? It would be very difficult to untie the circling rope with her weight pulling down on the knot. And if I did get it untied, then what? Just drop her? We would still be six feet above the ledge. If I could somehow leave her there, then I could go get the rope from the jetty, then we could start all over again. The problem, there was no fortuitous rock protrusion down there to serve as an anchor for her or me.

"Katya, I'm out of rope!"

She was silent for a few seconds, obviously working through what that meant and any other possibilities. "Drop me!" She finally shouted back.

I had reached the same conclusion; there was no other way. "Can you hold your broken leg up and break your fall with the other?"

"I can try."

"Tell me when."

"Now!"

Releasing the rope, I held my breath. In the gray and fast fading light it was hard to make out the details, but it looked like she dropped the six feet, landed on her good left foot, balanced there for a second, then momentum toppled her forward, once again ending up face down in the deep snow.

As quickly as I could, I made my way down to her, bobsledding the last ten feet. Again, Malachi was standing guard over her when I arrived.

"Are you okay?" I kneeled down beside her.

She used her hands and arms to push her face and torso up out of the snow. "You got any other bright ideas?"

I wanted to remind her it was her idea, but again I bit my tongue. "Let me help turn you over."

After rotating her to the supine position, I pulled her by the hollows of her arms over to a rock slab, propping her up in sitting position.

Once again I noted the open wound on her forehead was oozing from this latest fall. Now, at last I had time to tackle it. From my first aid kit, I located some Neosporin, a non-stick Adaptic dressing, a couple of four-by-four sponges and my last roll of Kerlix. As fast as I could, I dressed her head wound by wrapping her head. When I was done, she looked a little like Sinbad, wearing a white turban. With head wound finally dressed, I immediately turned my attention to our most urgent problem, finding some kind of shelter for the night.

In square footage, the ledge was about the size of a middle class house, but it was shaped like a small peninsula, protruding out from the cliff face into the vast and rapidly gathering black sea of darkness. The west edge peninsula dropped off abruptly into the gray of nothingness, while the east boundary was the sheer granite rock face. This perpendicular wall acted like a backstop, blocking the wind and allowing the snow to precipitate and accumulate in a large drift at its base. There was nothing else on the peninsula, no trees, no downed logs or even large bushes I could use to construct a shelter. In desperation, I left Katya and headed for the cliff face.

Just as Alaska's Muir Glacier routinely calves large slabs of ice into Glacier Bay, over the eons huge slabs of granite had calved (cleaved) from the sheer cliff wall. Some had tumbled onto the peninsula, lying at various angles and some had probably slid to the right or left completely off the ledge tumbling down the vertical slope, but one calf had not toppled or slid away. When it cleaved, it had remained standing. Its head was inclined at a thirty-degree angle, resting back against the vertical granite wall. Its foot was anchored about three feet from the base of the cliff and was buried in the deep snowdrift.

As I approached the rock face, the snow got much deeper. Struggling through the waist-deep snow, I waded toward the inclined slab. At the wedge-shaped aperture between the slab and sheer cliff wall, I stomped down the powdery snow, then kneeled down to size up the opening. It appeared large enough to admit me. Wallowing through the snow, I entered into the triangular-shaped cavity. Inside, it was mostly free of snow, but the floor was littered with small rodent droppings as well as an assortment of rock rubble: some pebbles, some chunks, but some faceted boulders as large as a basketball. As fast as I could, I cleared the debris from the floor, stacking the rocks adjacent to, but not blocking the opening. Then I backed out of the cavity and started back in the direction of Katya.

By now the light was so poor, I was afraid of walking straight off the edge of the cliff.

"Katya!" I yelled, trying to get a sound vector of her location. "Malachi!"

"Over here!" Katya shouted back as Malachi bounded over to join me.

With Malachi leading the way, I safely covered the remaining forty feet back to the sitting Katya.

"God," she shivered and tried to zip her coat up tighter around her neck, "it's getting colder."

"Yeah," I nodded, "the minute the sun goes down the temperatures up at this elevation drop like a--an overdosed fentanyl addict." I was proud of my simile, but when she didn't acknowledge it I decided it probably wasn't appropriate.

"A—and the w—wind doesn't h—help," she added, her teeth chattering.

"I found some shelter, but I need to move you."

"L—let's g—go."

Circling behind her, I put my arms under her shoulders. "I'll drag you, but do like before. Hold up your bad foot and help as much as you can with your good foot."

"Can you see where you're going?"

"No."

"T—that's comforting."

Slowly, we made our way back to the rock slab cavity. Katya moaned in pain with almost every step. Each time we stopped to let Katya rest her leg, I took the opportunity reassess our position and make slight corrections in our route. After a half dozen rest stops, we arrived at the aperture. Again, we rested for a minute, then somehow I pulled, pushed and dragged her into the cavity.

The interior of the cave was essentially a right angle triangle, with the back and floor shaped like an "L". The vertical limb was much longer and the horizontal limb much shorter. This allowed for enough space to sit up, our backs resting against the cliff wall and our legs extended straight out, but there was not enough room for all of us to lie down.

Once I had Katya and Malachi safely inside, I backed in, then used the same rocks I'd removed and stacked earlier from the floor to mostly close the aperture behind me. When I ran out of rocks, I simply sat back down next to Katya, our bodies touching. She instantly scooted three, or four inches, as far as she could, away from me, crowding Malachi against the cavity's far aperture, which remained closed with undisturbed ice and snow.

We sat in silence for a couple of minutes. Though we were only inches apart, I could barely see her, but sensed she was completely spent. Without warning, she slumped forward, banging her bandaged forehead against the tilted granite slab. Crying out loud, she sat up straight again and continued to moan.

Fishing my penlight out of my first aid kit and checked her pupils and forehead. Her pupils continued to be round and equal. Not unexpectedly, blood had soaked through her head bandage, but the goose egg hematoma on her forehead had not expanded any further. I checked her pulse, one hundred and two and strong. Next, I flashed the light on her fractured leg. It still looked to be fixed in good position by my SAM splint.

Even though everything looked stable, Katya continued to moan. Obviously, she was in great pain. It would be a miracle if she wasn't, considering she had a very nasty leg fracture, head trauma and probably a concussion. More than likely along with the leg pain, she was also battling a hellish headache.

No question, she needed better pain management, however trauma experts considered it ill advised to give narcotics to head injury patients. To accurately assess any possible increased intracranial pressure from an expanding subdural hematoma, the patient needed to be awake and alert. After giving narcotics, it would be difficult to say if any subsequent altered mentation or consciousness was from the drug or from the head trauma.

After listening to her moan for another minute or two, I made up my mind. I rummaged through my first aid kit until I found the brown vial of hydrocodone, then offered one to Katya along with the bottle of water.

She looked up at me and hesitated. "What about the protocol for head trauma?"

I shrugged.

She was quiet for a minute. "I guess if I do develop a subdural hematoma, there's nothing we can do about it anyway?"

196

I remained silent.

"So, I guess it really doesn't matter." She accepted and swallowed the pill with a sip of water. She rested her head back against the cliff wall, then almost immediately started shivering.

Finally, I remembered the survival, aluminum foil, blanket tucked in my waistband. Fishing it out, I unfolded it. Unfortunately it was only large enough to cover one of us. I spread it out over Katya.

"At l—least the w—wind is b—blocked," she said through chattering teeth.

"Yeah," I replied, peeking out through a small remaining gap in my rocked up wall, "but it looks like it's snowing again."

"G—great," she muttered.

In the dark enclosed space every sound was magnified and even though Katya quit talking, I could still hear her teeth chattering. Obviously, the survival blanket was not enough to keep her warm. With the looming specter of hypothermia, she was much more likely to go into shock.

"If we huddled closer together," I finally said, "it would be warmer. You know, if we shared body heat."

There was no immediate answer, nothing but clattering teeth and uncomfortable silence.

# 17

"S—so," she finally sighed with resignation, "how do you want to do this?"

I thought about it for a moment. There really was no ideal way. "If we could scoot your feet over where Malachi is and have Malachi move to where your feet are now, then you could lie down across my lap. Between me and Malachi, hopefully we can keep you warm."

The plan was simple; the execution was anything but. Finally after much grunting, groaning and pain, Katya was lying across my lap and Malachi was squeezed just below her in the narrow wedge-shaped part of the "V." I couldn't decide whether to gather her up in my arms or not. Would she would welcome such a move or take it wrong and snap off my head? Even with this new position and increased body contact she continued to shiver. Mustering all my courage, I gently rotated her toward me, then circled my arms around her and pulled her close. Lastly, I re-positioned the dislodged solar blanket back over her.

She did momentarily stiffen at the move, but surprisingly she didn't fight it or try to disengage. After a few seconds she relaxed and clung to me, burying her head under my chin.

I had to fight arousal and continually remind myself this was strictly a pragmatic maneuver, a lifesaving exercise. But regardless of all my attempts at logic, I couldn't help but note how good this felt. God, it had been a long time since I held a woman like this.

Eventually, she stopped shivering and some time after that her grip on my neck relaxed and she slept, as did Malachi. I tried to sleep, but my mind would not slow down or submit to autopilot. I hashed and rehashed the events of the last couple of days, trying to remember, collate and figure out where each fit into the ongoing, unsolved puzzle, the bigger picture.

What had we accomplished on this trip and at what cost?

First was our stop at the hospital's pathology department and our chat with Hank Bettis. The only thing mildly surprising about that visit was the DNA tests confirmed the blood to be both Ian and Wally's and—and of course there was Hank's less than subtle infatuation with Katya. But

198

even if the DNA tests didn't prove they were shot or murdered, what it did prove was they were together, even though they had not started out the day together. They must have at some time rendezvoused. Otherwise, it would be hard to explain the co-mingling of their blood. For them to both hemorrhage at exactly the same spot, but at different times was a bit hard to fathom. I don't think it is too big a leap of faith to assume the same fate befell both of them, whatever that fate may be.

Then we'd headed on to Cedar City and visited Sheriff Tiny Klein. He had informed us about finding Ian's camera and recovering Ian's damning photographs of the butchered buck. But even though the photos showed the buck had been shot multiple times, what it did not show was that it had been shot with a Bushmaster assault rifle and who fired the rifle.

Then lastly we found the casings Ian had collected from the site of the buck's massacre on this very ledge, then we found more blood one ledge down. As a point of interest, all of these items (Ian's camera, the baggie of spent shells and the second pool of blood) were all found in the same general area, the Summit Point Overlook.

So, what did this mean, all these clues? Did any or all of these samples, or any of the last two days of revelations provide any hints or answers to the ultimate question: what happened to Wally and Ian?

The only answer I could come up with was--hints, yes—answers, no. Nothing of the last two days definitively proved anything. The most I could say was something, maybe even something catastrophic, happened here at Summit Overlook. But what? Were their bodies somewhere close by? It was entirely possible. But with all the wind, snow and cold, there could be a body ten feet away and we would never know it.

If there were bodies did it mean murder? Not necessarily. In the storm and with poor visibility, Ian and Wally could have stumbled over the cliff and died, or maybe there was no catastrophic event, but they simply succumbed to the elements just like we almost had and still might. If I had not found this shelter we never would have made it though the night.

But on the other hand, could it have been murder? Just as I could not rule it in, there certainly was no way I could rule it out either. But if it was murder, who was the killer? Surely, I had to place Tim Slade, my soon to be ex-partner, at the top of the list.

So, what would it take to convict Tim? In order to make any murder case stand up in court, first of all one needed a body; we had none. Also, it was usually necessary to prove means and opportunity. Obviously, Slade had both opportunity and means, but without a body that probably would not be enough.

I sighed out loud in frustration. So, to summarize we'd gained all this non-incriminating and incomplete information, and at what cost? It nearly cost us our lives and it still could. Katya had a nasty trimalleolar fracture and brain concussion, and we were still far away from civilization. And these damages did not include my earlier losses, the suspension of my surgical privileges and the dissolution of my partnership with Tim Slade. But, I had to remind myself, my losses, and even Katya's, were nothing compared to what Wally and Ian had most likely lost—the ultimate and supreme loss, their lives!

Finally, my mind turned to the more urgent problem—getting out of here. Ultimately, I decided, it was not that complicated, Basically, I only had two options: either leave Katya here and go for help, or try to somehow get her out of this hellhole.

I hated to leave her. If I did, that would mean I would have to climb up that treacherous slope, snowmobile back to the cabin and pick up Ziggy, then snowmobile on to Brian Head. At Brian Head I would have to notify the sheriff and Search and Rescue in Cedar City. They would need some time to get organized and then transport their gear up to the Summit Overlook. Considering the weather and terrain, it would not be possible for a helicopter rescue; it would have to be a land rescue. All of this would take time and it was very conceivable she might have to spend another night up here alone. Not even taking the elements into consideration, only factoring in her ankle fracture and her head injury, I really hated to do that--by herself I was not sure she would last another night

The other option would be for me to get her out of here. Certainly, that sounded easier than it was. But was it even feasible? There was no way I could just load her up and piggyback her out of here. The slope was too steep and too unstable, and I was not that strong. Unfortunately, I did not have enough rope length to tie it around her, climb to the rim, then pull her up. And furthermore, that maneuver would be too traumatic considering her present injuries. I wracked my brain, trying to come up with a solution. If only I had some kind of sled, like the Ski Patrol used for transporting injured skiers, maybe I could figure out a way to get her out of here.

Even though I continued to work on the problem, I could no longer concentrate. My eyelids got heavy and my mind started to drift like snowflakes in a gentle breeze. Still clutching Katya Koslovsky to my chest, I slumped forward and slept.

Suddenly, there was a noise; someone was clawing at the rocks I had piled up to close the aperture. One by one, they were being plucked away. As the rocks were removed, the wind entering increased incrementally. Fumbling around, I tried to find something I could use as a weapon. Finally, I located my first aid kit, extracted a disposable scalpel, then held it up like a dagger. All the while the rocks continued to disappear from the aperture. When they were almost gone, I held my breath and waited. For a couple seconds nothing happened, then someone poked his head into our cavity!

I plunged my scalpel forward toward his neck, toward the carotid artery! The blade immediately broke, snapped off at the plastic handle, like I had hit solid granite. Frantically, I searched for my penlight; I also found it in my first aid kit. I focused on the intruder as he removed the last of the barrier rocks. It was Tim Slade! He was glacier blue and frozen solid, but nevertheless somehow was still able to move and was attempting to enter our shelter. Why? What did he want? I didn't know for sure, but I knew we had to get out of there! Rotating, I tried to punch him--.

"--Wake up, Coop!"

"Huh?"

Someone put a warm hand on my face.

"Coop, You're having a bad dream."

Subconsciously, I realized the only way to get away from a blue frozen Tim Slade was to wake up. Grudgingly, like a surfacing scuba diver who had just spent an amazing twenty minutes at Palancar Reef, I treaded upward toward consciousness.

Cracking open an eyelid, I spied a small hand rubbing my cheek. Following the hand down to its origin, I next spotted the beautiful Katya Kozlosky lying on my lap, then it all came flooding back. Though the light was muted, it was nevertheless bright enough for me to realize it was now morning. Indeed, I had slept, at least for an hour or two.

At that moment, Malachi also started stirring and somehow managed to wriggle into position to lick my face, then Katya's.

"You okay, Coop?" Katya asked as she hugged Malachi.

I nodded. "I should be asking you the same thing."

"My ankle is killing me and my head hurts like the fires of Hades," Katya forced a chuckle, "but other than that I'm fine." Somehow she managed a thin smile, then added, "At least I'm warm."

"Me too," I sighed, "but unfortunately we've got to get going. Somehow we need to figure out a way to get you out of here today."

"You should leave me," Katya said without hesitation.

Before falling to sleep last night, I had constructed a tentative plan, but now thought about changing it. Why? Because this morning I could not hear the wind howling, so possibly the storm had blown over and this might be a better day. Once I was outside, if it looked like the kind of weather Search and Rescue could fly their helicopter, then perhaps the smartest thing would be for me to leave Katya and go for help. With good weather, surely they could have her out before nightfall.

"Let's see what the weather's like," I said as I began taking down the rock barrier, which was still standing in spite of my dream.

Malachi exited our small cave first, then I had Katya sit up and I scooted out. Once I was outside, I turned around, grasped Katya under her arms and began pulling her out, her back down and headfirst. Groaning softly, she helped by pushing with her good leg and holding the injured one up off the frozen ground.

Indeed, thankfully, there was no wind and it looked like it would be a clear day. Though we were presently in the shade--the emerging sun's rays were still blocked by Navajo Mountain--Summit Valley far below us was aglow, bathed in glorious sunlight. I positioned Katya so she could sit up, resting her back against the cliff wall. Sighing, I sat down beside her and in silence we watch dawn break across the valley, sunlight inching ever closer to us.

After a few minutes, I cleared my throat and explained the two options to Katya: go for help or try somehow to get her up to the snowmobiles.

"You should go," she said after weighing the two possibilities. "I don't know if I could stand the pain of being dragged out of here and I don't know how you could do it. There's certainly no guarantee of success."

I nodded. "Then I probably ought to get going." I stood up and brushed the snow off my snowsuit. "I don't know if I can get Malachi to say with you, but I'll try."

After instructing Malachi to *stay*, I located the water bottle, handed it to Katya along with a couple more pills of hydrocodone, then covered her with the survival blanket and turned to face the rubble slope.

By now, after scrambling up and down this slope several times, I knew which route to take, where the good hand and footholds were and where the slope was the most stable. Fifteen minutes later I was back at the rim and the snowmobiles. Finally, things were going our way. With growing optimism, I straddled my Polaris and turned the key. Nothing. I turned it again. Absolutely nothing; the engine made no attempt to turn over. Maybe the battery was dead. I tried one more time, then got off my machine and mounted Katya's sled. Holding my breath, I turned the key. Again dead silence. I tried several more times with not even a single crank from the engine.

Dismounting, and though I'm not much of a mechanic, I released the latch and opened the hood. It took me several minutes to realize what the problem was. Finally I stuck my index finger into the empty holes bored into the engine block. There was no question about it, the spark plugs were gone—all four of them!

Almost in a panic, I opened the hood and checked my machine. Same thing. While we were stranded down on the ledge, someone had deliberately removed the spark plugs from both our machines. With the wind howling and the snow blowing it was no wonder we didn't hear or see them. But why? The only explanation I could come up with was someone was trying to kill us. Intentionally disabling our machines and leaving us stranded in a blizzard really could not be construed in any other way. This was no prank. This was attempted murder and came very close to succeeding, to becoming premeditated murder—*murder-in-the first-degree!*

But again, why? Logic would dictate it had to be related to our mission, our purpose for being here on the mountain. It could be a prank or a random act of insanity, but I doubted that. That meant in some way it also had to be related to the disappearance of Ian and Wally. But who? Who would do such a thing? Who would even care that we were looking for them? The only answer I could come up with was obviously it had to be the same person who made them disappear in the first place. I didn't want to jump to conclusions, but all fingers pointed to Tim Slade! By why? The only answer that made any sense: he was afraid we would find something here that was incriminating.

But enough of this unproductive musing! I was wasting time. There would be plenty of time for that later. We certainly were not out of the woods yet (both literally and figuratively.) This very well still could turn into a double homicide. We were still very much in a jam, but now there was no way I could leave Katya. Walking in two feet of fresh powder was difficult if not impossible without snowshoes, but even with snowshoes if I started out now there was no way I could get to civilization, mobilize Search and Rescue, and get back here before nightfall.

Katya needed a hospital and real medical care, not my crude back-woods medicine. With the storm gone and the skies now clear, the temperature would surely plummet tonight and I sincerely doubted she would survive another night in sub-zero temperatures. I had to get her out of here today. But how?

The tow sled that Malachi rode in on, along with my snowshoes, were still attached to my snowmobile. Maybe I could use the rope and lower the sled down to the ledge, then have Katya cling to it and pull her up. In theory it sounded plausible, but it reality it probably wouldn't work. The sled was too heavy for me to pull both it and Katya up that steep incline and the sled's runners (skis) rather than helping would probably hinder. Undoubtedly, they would jam or get stuck in the many holes, cracks and fissures in the rock-strewn rubble slope.

Sighing in frustration, I looked for something else. There was nothing, nothing at all.

Wait a minute! If I could manage to disengage or somehow rip the engine hood off one of the snowmobiles, it might work. It was shaped a lot like those cheap plastic snow sleds the kids use nowadays and with no runners it wasn't as likely to get jammed or wedged on the slope.

The hood was still open on my machine, as if begging for attention. I grabbed hold of it and hyper-extended it backwards until heard the plastic pop, then as hard as I could, I wrenched it to the right, then to the left. Finally, the hood broke free of its metal hinges.

I turned it over and placed it in the snow and dragged it through deep powder. It floated pretty well, but the windshield tended to drag, acting more like a rudder. Turning it back upright, I kicked out the windshield, then tried it again. It glided much better now. Lastly, using my knife, I cored a hole in the front at the point of the V to attach the rope, then with the modified hood in tow I started back down the rubble slope.

As I stepped back onto the ledge, without the wind and snow, I could clearly see Katya below. It looked like she was sleeping. For now I let her be and started down the rock incline. At the bottom, I searched for the rope. After scraping away six inches of new snow, I finally located it at the base, right were we'd left it. After tying it to my hood/sled and dragging it through the snow, I decided it might just work! Now it was time to wake up Katya and get out of here. Without question, we had a very long and difficult day ahead of us.

Walking over to Katya, I gently shook her.

At first she seemed dazed, then her eyes focused and she smiled. "You're back already."

"I never left," I admitted. "I just went up to the snowmobiles, then came back."

"What's wrong?"

"Someone disabled our machines. Took out the spark plugs."

She was silent for a moment. "Looks like someone really doesn't want us to get out of here," she finally concluded.

"Looks like," I agreed.

"We must be getting very close to something and that makes them uncomfortable."

I nodded my head in agreement, but said nothing.

"But that's attempted murder!" she blurted.

"Let's keep it at attempted," I said grimly. "We've got to get out of here."

"How?"

Instead of answering, I showed her my jerry-rigged hood/sled. "So, I'll climb with the rope up to that rock jetty, pull you up that far. While you rest there I'll climb the rest of the way up to the rim, then pull you up again."

"Remember, you don't have enough rope."

"We'll have to prop you upright and I'll tie my shirt to the rope to add length."

"Will it work?"

"Yes," I said confidently. Privately, however, I had my doubts. Even with the sled and enough rope, pulling her one hundred and twenty-five pounds or so up that steep rocky chute would be anything but easy, and—and she would have to hang on. If she got tired and let go, then—I didn't finish my thought.

"Well, let's get going," I said. "We've got a long way to go today."

With Malachi, supervising, I checked Katya's leg, making sure my SAM splint was still secure, then positioned myself behind her. Again looping my arms under her armpits, I grasp her around her upper chest, then began dragging her backwards through the snow to the sled and the rock chute. At the hood, I rolled her over, helped her stand upright on her good foot, then leaned her against the seventy-degree slope positioning the sled/hood under her.

Quickly, I stripped down to the waist (embarrassed by my lack of six-pack abs), took of my crew-neck long-sleeve shirt, then rolled it and knotted it to the rope.

"D—don't forget the evidence," she gasped. She was already out of breath from the exertion and intense pain.

"Huh?" I showed her where to grip the rope when we got going, just above where it was knotted it to the sled.

"You know, the brass shells and the blood."

"Oh, yeah," I grinned sheepishly.

With all that was going on, I'd totally forgotten about them. I inspected my coat pockets and fished out the baggie with the blood. Now it had thawed and looked thin and watery red Kool-Aid. My body heat had melted it, but that shouldn't matter. Carefully, I checked to make sure it was still properly sealed.

"I don't have the casings," I said after searching. "I think they're in your pockets."

"I can't let go," she said. "You check."

Bending over, I went through her pockets. Indeed she did have the spent casings. I put then along with the baggie in my coat pockets, then asked, "Are you ready?'

She gritted her teeth and nodded to the affirmative.

With rope in hand, I started climbing back up rubble slope to the rock protrusion positioned roughly halfway up the slope. Approximately a foot before reaching the protruding anchor rock, I ran out of rope. If I laid prone on the rock and dangled my arms, I had barely enough rope.

"Katya," I yelled, as I took out the slack, "now hold onto the rope."

"Here we go," I shouted down at her, then began inching her upward. "Help me as much as you can with your good leg."

Clinging to the makeshift sled and rope with both hands, and frantically working the slope with her left foot, we worked up the slope. Like a Secret Service agent guarding a presidential inaugural motorcade, Malachi scrambled protectively alongside of her. After we'd gone a foot or so, I carefully transitioned to the sitting position. Straddling the rock protrusion, I braced myself with my feet and continued winching her upward. My muscles ached and even with my gloves on the rope cut into my hands. After another fifteen minutes of backbreaking work, I had her high enough. Lying against

the sled and pinning it to the slope, she found a secure foothold with her good foot, then grasped the rock protrusion with both hands.

Gripping the slack end of the rope, I climbed the remaining distance to the top of the cliff. Once on the Overlook Point, I found a young scrubby foxtail pine, looped the rope around its trunk, then systematically ratcheted her up the slope. After stopping a couple times for a much-needed break to let my fatigued arm and shoulder muscles and her leg and arm muscles recover, I finally had her at the crest. Breathing heavily, I secured the rope to the stubby pine, then leaned over the lip, grabbed her under her arms and hauled her the rest of the way up over the rimrock. Using the last of my energy reserves, I helped her roll over onto her back, then we both lay spread eagle on the cold granite rock gasping for air. Malachi, who did not appear to be out of breath, joined us.

"N—now," she paused to take in another lungful of air, "what?"

"Now—we—get—out—of—here," I wheezed.

"That's—what—I—like—about—you," she managed a smile between breaths, "how—you—simplify—everything."

Now it was my turn to smile. "I didn't know there was anything you liked about me," I said breathing easier.

"That," she said, still smiling, "is a well-known literary device called irony."

"Thank God," I retorted, "you didn't resort to sarcasm."

"Seriously," she said after another minute, "what do we do now?"

I shrugged. "I'll make a harness out of the rope, we'll get you on the hood-sled, I'll put on my snowshoes and then just as if we were in Alaska's Iditarod we'll mush right on out of here. Like you said, its simple."

"I still think you'd make better time if you left me."

"You're not going to win this argument," I stood up and dusted the snow off my pants. "So let's get going. We've got a long day ahead of us."

"You heading back to the cabin or to Brian Head?"

"It's sixes," shrugged. "They're both about the same distance."

"Let's head back to the cabin," she decided. "I'm worried about Ziggy."

Ziggy! Geez, with all that had happened I had totally forgotten about him. When we'd left him over twenty-four hours ago he was suffering with a cold or the flu. Silently, I hoped he was okay.

"I'm sure," I said trying to reassure Katya, "he's faring much better than us."

"I hope so."

After putting my crew-neck shirt back on, I removed the snowshoes from where they were lashed to the tow sled, then fashioned a crude harness from the rope. Carefully, I positioned Katya prone on the tow sled, put on my snowshoes, shouldered the harness, then cheerfully shouted, *"mush!"* And we were off.

Of course our tracks from yesterday were totally obliterated by the violent snow and windstorm, but I knew the cabin was roughly north and east from Summit Overlook. Using my internal compass, I picked out a heading and started roughly in that direction. At the Point the snow was not very deep as the wind had swept it away, but unfortunately as we got back into the trees I discovered yesterday's storm had dumped another foot of powder to what we already had. Breaking a trail through this made progress slow, difficult and labor intensive. Determined, I put my shoulders to the harness and pushed on.

Mushing through the knee-deep snow was difficult for me, but almost impossible for poor Malachi. Even with his semi-webbed paws, he sunk in up to his chest and could only move forward by hopping or leaping. Soon he became exhausted and I worried for him. He was no longer a young dog. Finally, I managed to convince him to follow behind the sled, taking advantage of the trail that was already broken by the Katya-weighted sled and me.

About noon, when the sun was directly overhead, I stopped to rest. I found a downed quaking aspen log to sit on, took of my harness and coat, and rubbed my sore shoulders, checking for blisters. I would definitely need more padding for my shoulders. For the moment, I left my coat off; I needed to cool off. I was over-heated from all the exertion. Katya, apparently succumbing to the fatigue and pain, appeared to be sleeping. Malachi, also totally exhausted, curled up at my feet in the snow.

As I munched on a handful of snow to quench my thirst, I tried to reassess our situation. We had not even made it back to Dry Lakes Road yet, and from there it was at least another two miles to the cabin. At this rate, there was no way we would make it back by nightfall. If there was a moon tonight, and I was not sure if there was, as we spent last night in a cave, I could easily find my way in the dark, once we'd made Dry Lakes Road.

Katya did not look good and I was worried about her. Infection and/or pneumonia were always concerns and she was a prime candidate for a slow or delayed subdural bleed. I really should wake her and do a neurological check before we start moving again, but at the moment she looked so peaceful I hated to disturb her.

Also, poor Malachi looked totally spent. This excursion had taxed his eleven-year-old body to the maximum. I wished I could make room for him on the sled with Katya. I would gladly try to pull both him and her, even though he weighed nearly as much as her, but there was absolutely no way to get both of them on the sled. Well, at least we had good weather. Considering what we'd been through that was a plus.

Sighing out loud, I ate some more snow, then stood up and took off my crew-neck knit shirt and my t-shirt. After repositioning my t-shirt and long-sleeve knit shirt for shoulder padding, I donned my coat again. With the exertion of pulling the sled, I would still be warm enough. I re-shouldered the harness and for now opted to forego the neurological exam on Katya. Even if she did have a subdural hematoma there was not a damn thing I could do about it. Somewhere, long ago in medical school, they'd taught us not to perform tests purely out of curiosity. If regardless the results you were not going to act, then why do the tests? And certainly I had no way of drilling burr holes out here to relieve the increased intracranial pressure produced by a subdural hematoma. Sighing again, I leaned into the harness, called Malachi, then started moving the sled forward.

By the time I reached Dry Lakes Road, I was completely beat and had to rest again. Dropping the harness I found a suitable log to sit on. Malachi, also totally exhausted, dropped down at my feet. By now, I noted, the sun was well along its downward western arc, casting exaggerated, almost cartoon-like shadows of roadside quaking aspen across the road. The giant shadows loomed across Dry Lakes Road like an enormous picket fence.

After I'd caught my breath, I checked on Katya. She still had her eyes closed. Gently, I shook her.

"Katya," I whispered.

"Huh?" she mumbled and struggled to open her eyes.

"Thank God!" I blurted. That was purely reflex, a habit, the thanking of a god I'm not sure I believed in. A habit I was not proud of, but nevertheless I was happy she was conscious.

"Huh?" she repeated.

I smiled. "I'm just happy you're awake."

"Where are we?" She rose up on an elbow and looked around. "Are we at the cabin?"

"No, not yet." I tried to sound cheerful. "But we are on Dry Lakes Road."

"Will we make it to the cabin by dark?"

"No, not quite," I lied, "but it will be close."

She nodded, forced a tired smile, then collapsed back on the sled.

After giving her another hydrocodone pain pill with the rest of our water, I sat back down again. I needed another ten minutes before pushing on. Realistically, I knew there was no way we would make it back to the cabin by dark, so ten minutes would not make much difference. Soon I would have to start looking for shelter for the night. With no cloud cover, the temperatures were bound to be even colder than last night.

Re-shouldering the rope harness, I started north on Dry Lakes Road, looking for possible shelter as I went. At the junction of Dry Lakes Road and the Twisted Forest Road, we happened onto a bit of good fortune. Exiting from the Twisted Forest Road, a snowmobile had turned onto Dry Lakes Road also heading north. It had broken and compacted a path through the deep powder. This made a huge difference, not having to break trail through two feet of loose snow while pulling the sled.

Now, I made much better time. In another hour, I'd made it as far as Bear Flat, but even with this unexpected break, it was still unlikely we would make the cabin by nightfall. Gritting my teeth, I shoed on.

After another sixty minutes, I rounded a curve in the road and staggered to a stop. By my calculations, we still had roughly a mile to go, maybe a bit less, but it was nearly dusk and I was utterly spent. Not only could I not even proceed another ten yards, I also didn't have the strength to look for shelter. Without bothering to look for a place to sit, I collapsed on the road. Malachi shuffled over to lick my face.

I don't know how long I lay there in a semi-conscious state, but eventually I heard the low rumble of a combustion engine. Initially, I tried to ignore it. Not only was it a long way off, but more than likely it was a hallucination. Turning my head away from the sound, I closed my eyes again, but the sound got progressively louder. Probably because of the additive influence of the Doppler Effect, it soon became a roar. I staggered to my feet just in time to see the headlight of a snowmobile rounding the curve and bearing straight down on us.

It was coming fast, very fast! Stumbling to my feet, I hurried to protect Katya and Malachi, frantically waving my arms. The headlights blinded me and I instinctively stopped waving and used my arms to protect my eyes.

The snowmobile did not stop, swerve or even brake. In another instant it was right on top of me! I shouted, then along with Malachi I dove to the right, dragging the sled and Katya with me. The machine roared on by. Damn! He almost killed me and apparently still had no intention of stopping.

Suddenly, the snowmobile slammed on the brakes and skidded to a stop, coming to rest about fifteen to twenty yards away from us.

A man, at least I think it was a man, got off his machine and stared back at me. He was fully clothed in black. His snow boots, full body jumpsuit, Gore-Tex gloves and modular helmet were all charcoal back. I thought with his black helmet and rotating visor he bore more than a passing resemblance to Darth Vader. Without saying a single word, he flipped up the visor to get a better look at me. In the poor light of dusk, I could not make out his face.

Immediately, Malachi was up on his feet. Baring his fangs, he lunged forward and uttered a low threatening growl. Grabbing his collar, I managed to restrain him.

"Hey!" I shouted. "We could use a little help."

The man, still without speaking, abruptly turned from me and started rummaging in the rear storage compartment of his snowmobile.

"Hey!" I shouted again, "We could use some help. I've got a severely injured—"

I never finished my sentence. Suddenly, I was very nervous about this guy. If I had the strength, I would have shouldered the harness and with Malachi snowshoed out of there as fast as I could. But unfortunately, I didn't have the strength to go anywhere.

Shortly, the man stopped searching. Apparently, he'd had found what he was looking for. Pulling something from the compartment, he balanced it in his hand for a second, then turned and pointed it directly at me. At first, in the meager light, I couldn't tell what it was.

Then it dawned on me—*it was a handgun!*

# 18

KA-BOOM!

Simultaneously, I released Malachi as I dove to the left into the deep powder snow.

As I leaped, I heard report of the gun. The bullet screamed over my head, thudding into the trunk of a quaking aspen. By then Malachi was on him. The man desperately struggled to get away from the dog while trying to aim his handgun.

At that second, the roar of a combustion engine heralded the coming of another machine. As the snowmobile rounded the same curve, the on-coming headlight bounced, intermittently reflecting off the snow crystals.

With a vicious kick, the man booted Malachi away, then scrambled back onto his machine. Squeezing down on the throttle, his machine lurched forward, the rubber track spitting out chunks of snow like gravel from spinning tires. With in seconds he was out of sight, his red taillights occasionally winking through the aspen trees.

Almost immediately, the other snowmobile, actually it was a pair of machines, was upon us. This time I did not stand in the middle of the road and wave my arms, but the machines stopped adjacent to us anyway. Stumbling in the deep snow, I retreated backward to protect Katya and Malachi.

The rider in the lead machine dismounted and took of his helmet. He was just a longhaired kid, probably no more than twenty. The other rider was a young blonde female, probably his girlfriend. They looked anything but threatening.

"Y—you okay, m—mister?" he asked, his voice full of concern.

"No," I instantly sensed he was not with the other guy, "no, I'm not okay. I could use a little help."

"W—what's the problem?"

"This lady," I pointed at Katya, then quickly amended my words, "my friend here is badly hurt."

"W—what h—happened?"

He was obviously a stutterer, but seemed like a nice kid. "A snowmobile

accident," I lied, not wanting to go into all the details. "She got a broken leg and a rather severe head injury."

"W—where's your s—snowmobiles?"

"They were disabled in the accident."

"W—we can help," he volunteered. "W—where do you w—want to go?"

I took of my glove and extended my hand. "Lawrence Cooper," I said by way of introduction, "but please call me Coop."

"B—Brandon Telford," he took my hand, "but I go by T—Telly."

"Telford, huh, that's Scottish slash English, a variant of Telfer."

"Huh?" Telly looked confused.

"Oh, nothing," I replied as I shook his gloved hand.

He pointed to the girl on the other machine. "This is my friend, Bella."

I walked over to shake her hand.

As I grasped her hand, I considered his question. Where indeed should we go? At this point we were closer to the cabin than Brian Head, but now being without snowmobiles if we went to the cabin I would have no way to get Katya to civilization. She very much needed a hospital, an internist, an orthopedist and a neurosurgeon. On the other hand, Ziggy was not well when we left him, but it was probably just the common cold. It was a difficult choice, but at least in my mind Katya and her injuries took precedence over Ziggy's viral infection.

"Brian Head," I finally said. "It would be great if you could get us to Brian Head."

"O—okay," Telly said. "H—how do you want to do it? I don't have a hitch on my machine to pull a sled."

I thought about it for a moment. "I could tie the sled to the back bar of your snowmobile with this rope," I held up the harness, then added, "but you would have to go slow cause it will shimmy some with no runners."

Telly nodded.

"And I could ride double on one of the machines, but—but I don't know what to do with Malachi."

"M—Malachi?" Telly asked.

"The dog." I pointed. "That's his name."

"C—can't he walk?"

"He's beat."

We were silent for a moment.

"I can make room for him on the sled," Katya murmured. Obviously she had been awake and was listening. "I can turn on my side," groaning out loud she demonstrated by rolling over on her right side, "and make room for him."

She patted the space on the sled beside her and called to Malachi. He responded by immediately bounding through the snow and nestling in close to Katya.

I was both happy with this solution and oddly I was also disturbed by it. Malachi seemed completely, almost too completely, comfortable with Katya. It had been him and me against the world for years. Suppressing my surprising pang of jealousy, I used the harness rope to lash the sled to the back of Telly's snowmobile, then I decided I would ride with Bella, Telly's girlfriend. By following behind Telly, I could better keep an eye on the sled. I started to get on the snowmobile behind Bella, however she insisted that I drive, which was fine by me.

I signaled to Telly we were ready, then cautioned him once again, "go slow. They'll bounce a lot in that sled and I'm not so sure that rope will hold."

Telly nodded and started forward, the sled lurching behind him. Using a wide circle, Telly turned around and headed back down Dry Lakes Road. Our route would take us back across Bear Flat to the road that ascended over the northern flank of Navajo Mountain, then on down in a little alpine valley, which was also home to the ski resort of Brian Head and the town of the same name.

Brian Head, I knew, did not have a hospital, but it did have small clinic manned by physician assistants and nurse practioners. Obviously, it was a clinic that specialized in ski injuries, but it also had access to a helicopter operated by Life Flight. No doubt by the time we got to Brian Head the clinic would be closed, but surely they would have an after-hours emergency phone number.

Now it was almost totally dark as we moved forward. Mesmerized, I watched my headlight bounce off the Telly-towed sled, occasionally illuminating Katya and Malachi huddled together. Maybe it was a good thing Malachi was riding with her as it was decidedly colder now with no sun and no cloud cover. I knew in her fragile condition Katya would be more subject to hypothermia, but at least now she had Malachi to help keep her warm.

We turned on the road to Brian Head and started up the steep grade over the shoulder of Navajo Mountain. Everything seemed fine. Even though there was constant play between the snowmobile and the sled, the rope seemed to be holding and the passengers also appeared to be doing well.

Without further incident, we reached the apex of the shoulder and started down the far side. About three quarters of the way down the steep slope, the sled suddenly sped forward with gravity. Gaining momentum, it began go faster than Telly. On seeing this, Telly immediately accelerated, snapping the rope and freeing the sled. Instantly, it became a free-sliding toboggan. Unaware the roped had broken, Telly turned his machine to the left, following the road, but the sled went straight. Being behind, I saw the whole thing.

Damn! If the sled hit a tree, I sincerely doubted Katya could survive anymore trauma. Malachi, maybe, but not Katya. I gunned my machine down the slope and off the road, dodging trees. Within a couple of seconds my snowmobile roared adjacent to the sled, then I pulled ahead. Turning abruptly, I skidded crossways in front of the on-rushing sled.

"Raise up your leg!" I shouted to Bella as the sled crashed into us. On impact the sled angled obliquely allowing me to grab hold of the frayed rope with one hand and apply my snowmobile brakes with the other. Gradually, we slowed a stop.

Jumping off my machine, I rushed to Katya and Malachi.

"Are you okay?" Worry lines deeply furrowed my forehead.

She patted my hand. "You really are an adrenaline junky, aren't you?"

"And not just an antisocial personality disorder?" I quipped.

"The two are not mutually exclusive." She grinned and patted my hand again, then added, "thanks, Coop."

In spite of the dire circumstances and the plummeting temperatures, I suddenly felt warm. "Come on, let's get you to a hospital," I said, my voice husky.

I retied the sled to Telly's snowmobile, then we managed to cover the rest of the way to the Brian Head and the clinic without incident.

As I expected, the clinic was closed, but an emergency call number was posted on the door. I had to borrow Telly's cell phone to make the call, as my battery was now long dead. I touched in the number and after three rings a female answered.

"Brian Head Clinic."

"This is Lawrence Cooper. I have a friend with a head injury and a badly fractured ankle."

"A ski accident at this hour?" she responded doubtfully, then added, "the lifts have been closed for three hours."

"No," I replied, trying my best to remain calm, "a snowmobile accident."

"The clinic is sponsored by the ski resort. We only take care of ski accidents."

I decided it was time to pull rank. "Look," I snapped, "this is Doctor Cooper MD and I need an ambulance. Now!"

"Our ambulance has gone home for the night."

"Where?"

"To Cedar City."

"Get them up here!"

"Call nine-one-one." She hung up on me.

Still fuming, I dialed 9-1-1 and after a lengthy explanation, finally got patched to the appropriate agency. The ambulance service agreed to come, but said it would be at least an hour for them to get from Cedar City to Brian Head.

I gave Telly his phone back, bummed a bottle of water from him, thanked him and Bella profusely for their help, then untied the sled and let them go on their way. Now there was nothing to do but wait.

As they got on their machines and disappeared, I couldn't help but wonder where we would have been without their help. More than likely dead! Murdered by the first snowmobiler and if not that then dead from dehydration, exhaustion and hypothermia. Silently, I shook my head. In a little over an hour, they had renewed my rapidly-waning faith in humanity. Thank God there were still some good Samaritans left in this world.

After giving Katya and Malachi some water, I dispensed another pain pill to Katya, then we settled back to wait. I felt like I'd just gone ten rounds with M.M.A. fighter Ronda Rousey and I could only imagine how Katya felt. But though my body was totally spent, my mind refused to rest.

Who was the guy with the gun? Yes, I'm sure it was a guy, and try as I might I could come up with no one other than Tim Slade. Was I suffering from tunnel vision? Maybe, but I could think of no one else who had a grudge against us, me or Katya, and would even care we were up at Summit Overlook snooping around. Of course, I did not know a whole lot about Katya's personal life, so I couldn't say for sure she had no enemies, but I doubted she had people trying to kill her. Even more disconcerting, however, how did Tim Slade know we were up on the mountain? Either he had been surreptitiously following us, or he had an informant. Somehow,

216

I doubted Tim was that good at stalking; after all he was a doctor, not a gumshoe. When we left St. George, I had not seen him, or anyone, tailing us, but I wasn't really looking either. So, I guess technically it was possible, but I suspected someone must be helping him.

Katya stirred on the sled. "Where will they take me?"

"I'm going to request Dixie Medical Center in St. George," I replied. "The hospital in Cedar City does not have a neurosurgeon or a head trauma unit."

"Do you think I'm going to require neurosurgery?" She looked worried.

"No, but it's nice to have it available if needed." What I didn't say was I was still worried about a late subdural hematoma, but I didn't need to, I'm sure she knew. After all she had the same medical school training as me.

"But I will need orthopedic surgery?"

I nodded my agreement. "The ankle will need open reduction with internal fixation."

"The proverbial O.R.I.F.," she echoed, then added, "I remember that from my surgical rotation in medical school." She fell silent, then after a moment she asked, "What are you going to do?"

"Go with you, of course," I promptly replied.

"What about Ziggy?"

Geez, again I'd totally forgotten about Ziggy. When we'd left him— what had it been, a day and a half ago—he was sick and battling a bad virus. Furthermore, he was stuck. He had no way to get from the cabin back to civilization. We'd taken both snowmobiles and my Dodge pickup was still here in Brian Head. By now he was either over the worst, or seriously ill.

"Yeah," I instantly agreed. "You're right. I need to go rescue Ziggy."

"How you going to get there?" she asked. "Snowshoe?"

"Nah," I shook my head, "I'm too beat for that."

"I guess we shouldn't have let Telly and Bella go."

"Yeah," I nodded, then sighed out loud. "I guess somehow I'm going to have to rent another snowmobile."

"At this hour?"

"Yeah, either that or borrow—"

—The rhythmic flashing of an emergency vehicle's lights interrupted me. Not using the siren, but taking full advantage of the strobing red lights, the ambulance pulled up. I personally instructed the EMTs, because of Katya's head injury, she was to be taken to Dixie Medical Center in St. George, then as they started to load her I went to say goodbye.

She grasped my hand. "Thanks, Coop." Her voice was surprisingly husky. "You saved my life! I can never repay—"

"—Shsst." I impulsively leaned over and hugged her. And even more surprising she hugged me back.

"I'll collect Ziggy," reluctantly I disengaged, "and we should be back in St. George sometime tomorrow morning—probably in time for your surgery."

I watched the ambulance until its flashing red lights disappeared out of sight, then with Malachi headed directly over to Thunder Mountain Rental, fortunately only about a block away.

Of course at this hour the business was closed. Wearily, I trudged up the back stairs to the second story apartment. Though it was a short climb, only one story, my fatigued quadriceps protested by going into spasm. Groaning, I gave them a minute to relax, then managed to struggle the rest of the way to the landing.

The curtains of the door's half-window were drawn and it appeared dark inside. Under a sixty-watt porch light, I checked my watch. Was it really that late? It was eleven twenty-seven! The owner would not be happy, but what else could I do? I had to get back to the cabin, to Ziggy tonight. In the dim light, I could find no doorbell, so I rapped on the door.

I waited a couple minutes. There was no answer, so I knocked again—louder.

Still no answer, so I pounded, then I pounded continuously.

Finally the door opened.

"Jesus H. Christ!" Abe Eisemann cussed as he opened the door. He was wearing flowered boxers and armed with a handgun. "What the hell do you want?"

"Fine talk for a Jew," I quipped. Sometimes I just can't help it.

He recognized me and lowered his nine-millimeter Sig Sauer. "You can return your machines tomorrow," he growled, "during regular business hours, and yes I will charge you for another day."

"I'm not here to return machines."

He looked at me sharply. "Then what in *thee* hell do you want?"

"To rent a snowmobile," I smiled sheepishly, "of course."

"Where's the two you already have?"

"Disabled—over at Summit Overlook."

"Disabled!" he exclaimed, then looked at me suspiciously.

I took a minute to explain what happened, except for this latest

218

gunplay, then added, "when you go to get them tomorrow, you'll have to take extra spark plugs." I paused and added, "and one machine will need a new hood."

"You have to pay for all that."

"I know."

"Somebody out to get you?"

"It appears so," I replied.

"You better go to the police."

"They already know."

"So why to you need a machine tonight?"

I took a few more minutes to explain about Ziggy and how I was worried about his health and his welfare.

Abe grumbled to himself for a few seconds. "Okay, give me a chance to get some clothes on, then I'll meet you downstairs in ten minutes."

Nodding, I moved slowly, so as not to have a repeat of my muscle spasms, back down the stairs and waited, and waited. Twenty minutes later, don't ask me why it took so long just to pull on some clothes, I heard the double garage door grind open and I entered the lighted shop.

Abe selected a Polaris Indy 800 machine that looked like a clone of the other two I'd rented. After checking the gas and oil, making sure it would start, he then motioned me into his business office. Tiredly, he sat down on a padded chair behind his military green metal desk, then pulled out a pen and a piece of paper.

"Now let me see," he started write down figures, "for me to go retrieve a machine that is disabled through no fault of mine I charge a hundred and fifty dollars an hour. Over and back from Summit Overlook is two hours—that's three hundred dollars—times two machines that's six hundred dollars—plus let me see—" He paused, pulled out a parts catalog and flipped through the pages. "—Uh, lets say another couple hundred dollars for a new hood and spark plugs and another hundred for labor. That's a grand total of nine hundred dollars. Now to that we have to add an extra day rental to those two machines, they should've been back today. At two hundred and thirty-five a day, that's another four hundred and seventy dollars." He paused and worked an adding machine on the desk. "For a grand total of thirteen hundred and seventy dollars, and that's a bargain."

"What that is," I exclaimed, "is highway robbery!"

"Okay," Abe stood up and shoved the paper back in his desk drawer, "I'm going back to bed."

"Wait a minute," I quickly backtracked. "Okay, thirteen hundred and seventy dollars it is, now give me the key."

Abe sighed and sat back down. "That doesn't include the cost of the new rental."

I bit my tongue and sat down across from him.

"Now we add to that three hundred dollars rental for—"

"—Hold on," I barked, "the other machines rented for two hundred and thirty-five dollars per day."

"After hours charges are three hundred a day," Abe said indifferently, "take it or leave it."

I gritted my teeth. "Okay."

"Will you be needing another sled—"

"—No!" I blurted, "I've still got the one."

Abe looked at me oddly. "A sled but no machines—anyway, that's three hundred for the new machine added to thirteen-seventy—you owe me a grand total of sixteen hundred and seventy dollars."

Showing amazing self-control, I said nothing, pulled out my wallet and started to hand him a credit card, then hesitated. "You have a good day today renting machines?

He looked puzzled. "Yeah," he shrugged, "with the storm over, a lot of people went out today."

"You rent any machines to anyone from St. George?"

"That's confidential."

"How confidential?"

"Huh?"

"How confidential?" I repeated. "Fifty dollars worth?"

He looked at me slyly. "No more like a hundred dollars worth."

I groaned out loud, but nevertheless nodded my head. "Okay."

"Let's see," Abe did these calculations in his head, "that brings the grand total to seventeen hundred and seventy dollars even. I won't even charge you tax on the last item."

"That's big of you," I quipped, then added, "let me see your books."

"No, you pay first."

Groaning out loud, I offered him my debit card once again.

Abe ran the card, then shook his head. "This card is maxed out."

Angrily, I grabbed it back and handed him another one. This was becoming a very expensive trip.

He ran it, then nodded and handed me the receipt to sign.

"The books," I growled, a definite edge to my voice.

He rummaged through a metal file cabinet for a few seconds and finally he handed me his booking ledger.

"You don't book on your computer?" I asked, surprised.

"Don't trust 'em," he growled, handing me the register. "Up here in the mountains, the power is always going off."

Sitting down at his metal desk, I opened the ledger to today's date and ran my finger down the columns. Indeed, Abe did have a good day, even without my seventeen hundred and seventy dollars, but there were no rentals from St. George, Utah. Discouraged, I started to close the book. What a waste of a hundred dollars—

—Wait a minute! I found out that our snowmobiles were disabled this morning, but the act was probably done yesterday. Quickly, I thumbed back to yesterday's date.

Yesterday, the day of the storm, business was not nearly so good. Thunder Mountain rentals had rented only three machines. Slowly, I ran my finger over the names.

Bingo! There it was, St. George, Utah, but the name I did not recognize, Daniel Mahoney (obviously Irish), his listed address 2386 Anasazi Circle, St. George, Utah.

My spirits plummeted. I just threw away a hundred dollars I didn't have. As I closed Abe's book a thought occurred to me. Quickly, I opened the book again. "Abe, how did this guy pay for his rental?"

Abe hesitated, but before he could ask for more money I cut him off.

"Come on, Abe, I got not more money."

Abe bent over the books. "See that little 'c' after the guy's name," he pointed, "that means cash."

"Oh," I nodded, then copied down the name and address.

It was well after midnight when I fired up the Polaris. After going back to the clinic and picking up my sled, I attached it to my machine, coaxed Malachi onto it, then we left the lighted streets of Brian Head for the dark unlighted trail that went over the shoulder of Navajo Mountain to the cabin.

The Milky Way glowed fiercely, like fresh snow crystals inflamed by the slanted rays of an early morning sun. And by now, the Roman goddess Diana had managed to hang a quarter moon high in the sparkling rhinestone sky. As I had predicted, with no cloud cover the temperature had dropped to zero and even with my snowsuit and coat on I was freezing. Even though

I was in a hurry to get to Ziggy, I had to ease off on the throttle in an effort to minimize the wind/chill factor.

It must have been after one o'clock when I finally reached my property line and started up the steep incline to the cabin. It seemed like we'd been gone for weeks, but it actually it was less than two full days. As we the topped the crest, I noted the cabin was totally dark, but that was not too surprising considering the hour. As was my custom, I drove around the circle, then parked the machine with the skis pointed slightly downhill. Getting off the machine, I slapped my shoulders for warmth, stomped my feet to stimulate circulation, then with Malachi hurried up the steps and onto the deck.

Quietly, I opened the door and along with Malachi stepped into the kitchen. Not wanting to alarm Ziggy, probably sleeping on the couch, I avoided turning on the overhead lights. Instead I whispered, "Ziggy."

No answer.

I whisper a little louder, "Ziggy."

Still nothing. Even Malachi did not rush to his side.

I shouted, "Ziggy!"

Nothing but silence and the occasional creak of a milled pine log.

Giving up, I turned and flipped on the overhead lights.

Ziggy was not on the couch!

I whirled around—he was nowhere in the common room. I hurried to the guest bedroom. Not only was he was not there, but the bed looked like it had not been slept in. Next, I checked out my (Katya's) bedroom. Nothing there either, and again the bed looked unused. Taking them two at a time, I scrambled up the steps to the loft. No sign of Ziggy there. Now worried, I retreated back down the stairs and sat down on the couch. Even though I was completely exhausted, I had to try to think this through.

But try as I might, the only thing I could come up with was Ziggy must have become tired of waiting for us, or panicked, and struck out on his own. Maybe, hopefully, some snowmobiler, like Telly, had picked him up, otherwise on a cold night like this—I really didn't want to think about that. Should I go looking for him now? I checked my wristwatch, now it was a very late 1:37 a.m. I knew night searches were difficult at best, almost never productive and could be downright dangerous with a temperature--I paused to step outside and check my thermometer--with a temperature of minus two. Inadvertently get a machine stuck or suffer mechanical failure and you were as good as dead. Furthermore, I was totally spent. I simply didn't have the energy to conduct a search that night.

I hadn't slept much last night in the cave, then I'd spent the day pulling Katya up the rubble slope, then towing her sled all day through the knee-to-thigh deep powder. Physically, I was literally at the end of my rope; I had exhausted all my reserves.

Suddenly, I shivered. Damn, it was cold in the cabin. I needed to start a fire, then get a bite to eat and some sleep. Tomorrow, I would look for Ziggy.

Almost mechanically, I started a fire in the fireplace, then fueled it with a large pitchy pine log that should burn for hours. Taking off my coat, I heard the clink of the brass shells in my pocket, which reminded me to store the baggie of blood we had collected on the ledge in the fridge. Hopefully, we could preserve enough white cells that Hank Bettis could do another DNA analysis.

I wolfed down several peanut butter crackers, found a bag of teriyaki-flavored jerky for Malachi, then grabbed a couple of blankets from the bedroom and collapsed on the couch in front of the roaring fire. Also totally spent, Malachi curled up at my feet.

Even though I was utterly fatigued, I did not immediately fall asleep. As soon as I closed my eyes, my mind began replaying scenes of the day, starting with the gunman. Vividly, in my mind I could see him draw and point the gun. I could almost feel the bullet whistling past my ear and hear the distinctive thud as the bullet slammed into the quaky tree. Squinting, I tried hard to make out his face, but with the black helmet and fading I could not.

Suppressing a shudder, I forced my thoughts in a different direction. Obviously, well maybe not obviously, but more than likely the Dan Mahoney listed on Abe's rental book was a fake name. That's why he paid Abe in cash, so he would not have use a card that was embossed with his real name. That thought instantly prompted the questions of who and why? Who would have motive? The only name I could come up with was Tim Slade. To be fair, however, it was possible the guy who disabled our snowmobiles and took a shot at me didn't even rent a machine. He may have borrowed one, pinched one or already owned one. I knew the answers to the above riddles would not be forthcoming this night.

Sighing out loud, I forced my mind down yet another channel, Katya Kozlovsky. By now, she should be in St. George at Dixie Medical Center—nice and warm and hopefully out of pain. Her ankle surgery would probably be scheduled tomorrow, unless, of course, she displayed symptoms of increased intracranial pressure tonight. If so, that would require emergency neurosurgery. Needless to say, I would like to get back to St. George for her surgery, for moral support, but that would all depend on Ziggy.

In spite of our dire circumstances, I smiled in the dark. Now Katya didn't seem so bad. Certainly, she was not the Cossack bitch that I first labeled her—but she was indeed a Volga queen, in the very best connotation of the phrase. Not only was she beautiful, she was intelligent and had amazing grit. With the smile still lingering on my face, I finally drifted off.

I awoke before seven o'clock, not because it was getting light, but because I was freezing. Shivering, I got up with my blankets wrapped around me checked the fire. The pitchy pine log hand burned down to nothing more than a black wedge of smoldering charcoal. Using the fireplace poker, I stirred and stoked the coals to a bright orange, then added more wood.

Walking over to the window, I peered outside. A hint of light showed on the eastern horizon, just above Navajo Mountain. I opened the door and stepped out on the deck. It was bitter cold. Each inhaled breath stung my lungs and each exhaled breath resulted in foggy plumes of water vapor. Checking the outside thermometer, it read an alarming minus nine degrees. Then it all came back to me, I had an urgent mission. I had to find Ziggy today.

Back inside, I checked the pantry, looking for something I could eat. I was starving. Other than the peanut butter crackers of last night, it had been almost forty-eight hours since I'd had a real meal. From last October's hunt and our stay here a couple of days ago, the pantry was nearly bare, but I did find a can of peaches and a couple of granola bars for me. And luckily, I also spied a tin of tuna fish for Malachi. Opening up the can of peaches, I almost inhaled them in between bites of the chewy granola bars. Also famished, Malachi made short work of the tuna.

When we finished, the sun was barely peeking over Navajo ridge. It's slanted golden rays filtered through the quaking aspen trees, making it look warmer than it was. But regardless of the thermometer, it was time to go—I simply had to find Ziggy.

Quickly, I dressed in my snowsuit, coat and gloves, remembered to get the baggie of blood from the fridge, then headed back outside. Even dressed as I was, I could still feel the cold seeping through my insulated suit. Grabbing hold of the snowmobile skis, I broke the frost bond, then fired up the machine. After letting the engine warm for a minute or two, I persuaded Malachi back on the sled, then straddled my mechanical-purring machine. Squeezing the throttle, we lurched forward and down the slope.

The only thing marring the flawless, spotless snow was the broad track of my machine from yesterday. When I reached the junction of my private road and Dry Lakes Road, I paused. Now I had a decision to make. Should I turn right and head back over Navajo Ridge into Brian Head or turn left and head down the mountain toward State Road 143 and Parowan? The route to Brian Head I traversed last night and hadn't see anything, but it was in the dark and I surely could have missed something.

Finally, I decided to head down Dry Lakes Road toward S.R. 143 first, then if I found nothing I would backtrack and head toward Brian Head and turn in my rental machine.

This section of Dry Lakes Road was unblemished except for the occasion track of a wild animal. Two days ago it had snowed and was windy, very windy, but yesterday was calm. If Ziggy came down this road two days ago, it would have been during the storm and any sign would be completely buried. Involuntarily, I shuddered at the thought. However, if he came through here yesterday, I should see his tracks.

Cruising downhill was no problem, even with the two feet of new powder and coming back should not be a problem either, since I'd already broken the trail. I could just turn around and follow my tracks back.

Being vigilant, I slowly motored down the road past the point where Tim Slade had slid off during the ill-fated hunt, then on down to the intersection with S.R. 143. Nothing! No Ziggy and no tracks. Turning around, I started back. Still nothing. At the junction with my road I continued on, heading south by southeast toward Navajo Ridge and the town of Brian Head.

This section of Dry Lakes Road was well tracked. Several snowmobiles had been over it since the storm. Unfortunately, I could see no boot prints, but it was conceivable the snowmobile traffic had destroyed them. Throttling down my machine even more, I carefully surveyed both sides of the road as I went.

Just as I started up the grade over the shoulder of Navajo Ridge, I saw a flash of blue twenty yards or so off to the right. I stopped and tried to remember. Wasn't Ziggy wearing a blue snowsuit? Maybe. Suddenly, my anxiety snowballed. Turning my machine to the left, I headed off the road and in the direction of the blue.

I stopped ten feet away and stared. Indeed it was a body!

Lying prone in the snow, only the a bit of the back and shoulder was exposed. The head was completely buried in a drift, as were the legs and buttocks. Now with heart pounding, I turned off the machine and warily dismounted. Malachi, of course, beat me and was already off the sled and sniffing the body.

*Jesus, was it Ziggy?*

It had to be. Now I remembered, that was the snowsuit he was wearing.

He was frozen solid, solid as freezer meat.

'Why,' I asked myself, fighting to control my emotions, 'why did he leave the cabin in this weather? He should have known better. He must have been delusional.'

Fighting back the tears, I kneeled down by Ziggy and placed my hands on his rock hard, ice cold body. Damn, what a friggin' shame! I moved one hand to his hip, the other to his shoulder, then gently rolled he over.

*Wait a minute!*

The snow was red, a shocking Rorschach red!

Hemorrhage was not a common thing for someone freezing to death. Rapidly, I cleared the snow away from his head and face.

Suddenly, there it was—the cause of the blood and without question the cause of his death.

A small bullet hole, almost perfectly centered, was cored out in the middle of his forehead.

# 19

When life becomes as chaotic as mine had been for these last few weeks, routine activities are not only appreciated, but often necessary for one to regain his sanity, and his sense of balance and equilibrium.

It was good to be back at the ranch and once again involved in my usual daily activities, my normal routine. With Malachi at my side, I stumbled out of the house just as a splash of orange appeared on a darken sky, still sporting a few residual cirrus clouds from yesterday's storm--the ingredients, the promise of a spectacular sunrise. As I fed the horses, I again noted how badly their stalls needed cleaning. Somehow I needed find an entire day to get caught up on my ranch and household chores.

After feeding the horses, I hurried back to the house to eat breakfast and shower. I was scheduled to see patients in the office today, a good thing considering how much money I'd spent the last few days, most of it going to Abe Eisemann. Also, I must admit, it was somewhat surprising I had any patients left, considering how many times Ronnie had to reschedule them and by now word must have circulated my surgical privileges had been revoked. Well, apparently I did, so I better hurry. After feeding Malachi, I wolfed down a toasted bagel, gulped down a cup of coffee, then headed for the bathroom.

I climbed into the shower, turned the water to warm, almost hot, then leaned back against the tile wall and let the water spill over my head and shoulders. This was nothing short of heaven, just as the last three days had been nothing short of hell, particularly yesterday. Finding Ziggy like that was shocking and totally unbelievable.

Suddenly, I was hit with a pang of remorse; I should have been kinder to him. Sure he was a little strange, smoked too much and was a bit irritating, but who wasn't. I couldn't help but think he would have made one hell of a psychiatrist and probably just what St. George needed. I wished I could go back and tell him I would vigorously support his application for privileges at Dixie Medical Center, but alas it was too late. I sighed out loud, then as the hot water worked to relax my knotted muscles, I relived that terrible day.

After I realized Ziggy had not died from exposure, but was murdered, I began looking for clues. When rolling him over, the first thing I noticed, there was no exit wound, only a perfectly centered entrance wound. Also, at the same time I noted a gray/black smudge of powder burns roughly circling the wound. This probably meant he was shot at close range.

After finishing with Ziggy, I worked outward in ever increasing concentric circles, searching for any more clues: a collection of boot prints that would indicate where the shooter had waited in ambush or any spent shell casings that might match the ones I already had. Systematically, I checked the frozen ground to a radius of one hundred, even one hundred and fifty yards, and there was nothing. No boot prints, no casings, no nothing.

At first I was confused, couldn't figure it out, then I realized the only tracks in the snow were those from snowmobiles. So, that had to be it; Ziggy was shot right here from a snowmobile, much like I was, but with me fortunately the shooter had missed and fortuitously Telly and Bella had arrived. But maybe there was one other possibility. Perhaps, Ziggy had been shot elsewhere, transported here by snowmobile and dumped.

Finally, realizing there was nothing further to be gained, I'd left Ziggy and motored up over the shoulder of Navajo Ridge and down into Brian Head. Once in town, I went directly to the town marshal who immediately punted the ball to the Iron County Sheriff. Who could blame him? The murder did not actually occur within Brian Head's city limits and certainly with his small two-man office and even smaller budget, he was ill-equipped to handle a major murder investigation.

While waiting for Sheriff Axel 'Tiny' Klein to arrive, I went for an early lunch, purchasing a large pizza, half meat-lovers for Malachi and half cheese and veggie for me. In front of the restaurant, there was an outdoor table where we ate and waited for the sheriff. We were both starved and threatened to make short work of the pizza.

Sheriff Klein arrived just after noon with his entourage: a deputy, a photographer and two crime scene specialists. While he shared our last piece of pizza (actually Malachi's, as he preferred that over veggie) I filled him in on everything, everything since leaving his office three days ago. Was it only three days? It seemed like a lifetime.

First I explained how we'd arrived late, too late to go to the Overlook that day and spent the first night at my cabin. Then I told him how we, because of a cold virus, had left Ziggy behind when we went to Summit Overlook. Next, I told him how we found the shell casings and the blood on the drop-off ledge, then I promptly turned over the shells to him, but did not divulge I also had a sample of the blood. I wanted to save that for Hank Bettis.

Then, I described the details of Katya's accident, the head injury and ankle fracture, and how we'd spent the night. I told him how someone disabled our snowmobiles, but how we managed to get out of there anyway and eventually get Katya to a hospital. Next, I described, as best I could, the man on the snowmobile, how he fired a shot at me, and how we were saved by Telly Telford. Next, I related how today I'd returned to the cabin for Ziggy, found him missing, searched for him, then found him murdered. Lastly explained how I had systematically looked for clues and found none.

"You shouldn't have contaminated," Sheriff Klein growled, then paused to swallow the last bite of pizza crust, "the crime scene."

"There was nothing to contaminate," I snapped back, "just snowmobile tracks."

"That may or may not be so," the sheriff checked the pizza box for another piece--there was none, "but you should've left it for the professionals."

"Duly noted," I replied without contrition.

"So," he paused to wipe his hands and face with a paper napkin, "so, how do you put this all together?" He looked at me closely.

"Obviously, someone was trying to kill us and did kill Ziggy."

"Why? Why would anyone want to do that?"

"I don't know. Maybe they were afraid we had found something, or would find something."

"Something?" Sheriff Klein tossed his napkin in a nearby trashcan. "Something like what?"

I discarded the pizza box in a trashcan. "I don't know—more than likely something that would help us to identify and convict them of the murder of Ian McKenna and Wally Stroud."

"So, you got any suspects other than your partner, Tim Slade?"

"No," I shook my head, "everything still points to him."

"But we still got no bodies and no hard evidence."

"Now you do," I argued, "there's Ziggy and maybe those shell chasings will help."

"I doubt they will," Tiny replied. "Even if we found his fingerprints on 'em. But since you've been handling them they'll probably only find yours. And even if we could prove the shells were fired from Slade's gun, we still couldn't prove they were used in the commission of a crime, or for that matter even if there was a crime."

"Again, you're forgetting about Ziggy," I corrected him. "That certainly was a crime!"

"Yeah, well, I ain't seen that crime yet and there's no shells from it."

"You mean to say," I blurted, "we've got three people murdered and still can't even confiscate his assault rifle."

"I don't make the laws," Klein shrugged. "You can't take someone's gun away on a hunch. You know that. That's messing with America's sacred cow. Come on," he stood up, "and show me this crime scene."

"We'll need snowmobiles."

"Where can we get 'em?"

"There only one place I know of," I smiled thinly because this time I knew I wouldn't be paying, *"Abe Eisemann's Thunder Mountain Rentals."*

Of course, Abe Eisemann was delighted to have five more rentals. Surreptitiously, I asked him to add my last rental to the county's bill, since I was now helping them. He immediately turned the Sheriff, who vigorously shook his head no. Finally, after much haggling, I convinced them to reduce my charge for the day to a half-day rental and put the other half-day on the county's tab, since this afternoon we were doing county business. Tiny reluctantly agreed.

With me leading the caravan and still towing Malachi in the sled, we crossed back over the shoulder of Navajo Ridge to the murder scene. I sat back on my snowmobile and watched them work. Two hours later, to my surprise, they did come up with a single shell casing. They found it buried in the snow a dozen feet from Ziggy's frozen body and in and area I had gone over previously. I don't know how I missed it, but I guess that why they're professionals. Using what looked like hemostat, a technician picked it up, put it in a baggie, then into a hard-shell suitcase.

From there, the Sheriff wanted to go on over to Summit Point Overlook and have his team examine our disabled snowmobiles. Perhaps, his crime scene specialists would be able to lift some full or partial fingerprints from them.

Getting to Summit Overlook in good weather, no snow or wind, was a cakewalk. Today with no inclement weather and fast snowmobiles, it didn't seem nearly as far. Fifteen minutes later we parked the machines at the Overlook. While the crime technicians dusted the machines, particularly he hood and engine block, for prints, Malachi, the sheriff and I wandered around the Point. Peering over the edge I showed him where we spent the night and approximately where we found the shells and blood. Tiny did not seem inclined to climb down there and I didn't push him. I had no desire to go back down that slick rubble slope.

230

While the technicians were wrapping up, we left the Point and circled back toward the snowmobiles. Our path took us away from the edge, toward forest and through deeper snow.

Suddenly, Malachi bolted forward, stopped next to a foxtail pine and furiously started digging with his front paws. By now I knew that usually meant he'd found something. With Tiny following, I hurried over to see what he'd found.

I was shocked! The shredded snow he was digging up was crimson red—*blood red.*

As the sheriff shuffled over, I called Malachi off. As soon as Tiny saw the blood, he shouted for one of his technicians to come over and collect a sample. While the technicians obtained and preserved a sample of the ice and blood, Tiny circled the area, looking for other clues. A few minutes later, the sheriff located another single brass casing, not more than fifteen feet away and slightly behind a foxtail pine.

Along with the blood, the technicians also bagged the spent shell and stored both in their hard-shell suitcase. Apparently, they also had found some fingerprints on the disabled snowmobiles.

Whether the prints would be any help or not, remained to be seen. It was entirely possible they would be nothing other than my prints, or Abe's, or his mechanic's, but it was also possible they could be the prints of the murderer.

Back at Thunder Mountain Rentals, Sheriff Klein wrote down the names and addresses of everyone who rented a snowmobile the last couple of days and just as the sun was setting, he finally excused me and I headed for home.

Using my Bluetooth, on the way home I called the hospital. The floor nurse reported Katya was presently in surgery. Fortunately, and after some coaxing and pulling rank, she informed me Katya's CT scan was negative for skull fracture or subdural hematoma. "Thank God!" I whispered, looking to the heavens, then was immediately annoyed. Why did I continually thank a God I didn't believe in and really had nothing to do with Katya's favorable prognosis. Oh, well, some habits are hard to break.

When I got back to St. George, I rushed to the hospital, going directly to the ICU. At the nurse's station, I located Katya's chart and read the details. No one tried to stop me. Apparently, they had not yet heard of my suspension, either that or they were afraid of me.

Regardless, it was clear from the chart Katya's ankle surgery went well, thank God. And as advertised, the report on the C.T. scan did not show a subdural hematoma, intracranial bleed or skull fractures. Again I subconsciously whispered a thank you to a God.

Setting down her chart, I hurried into Katya's room. She was, however, still too groggy from anesthesia and pain medicine to communicate. Leaning over, I kissed her forehead, said goodbye and that I would see her tomorrow, then exited the hospital. It was well after dark by the time Malachi and I arrived home.

—Abruptly, the water went cold. Shivering, I realized I had daydreamed through an entire tank of hot water. Turning off the cold water, I shivered again as I stepped out of the shower and grabbed a towel. While toweling off, I checked my wristwatch—7:38 a.m. I still had a little time. I wasn't due to start seeing patients until nine.

Quickly, I gathered up my arsenal of guns: my .3006 deer rifle, my .22 Winchester rifle, a semi-automatic Browning shotgun, another Beretta over/under shotgun, a .45 Desert Eagle handgun and a 9-millimeter Smith & Wesson handgun. It was time to make good on my pledge to make my life and my house a gun-free zone.

Once I'd collected my arsenal, I set them on the kitchen table so I would remember to take them when I left for work. On my way, I would drop them off at the St. George P.D. headquarters on the north side of town just at the base of St. George's signature red sandstone bluff. With task finally completed, I rechecked my wristwatch. That little chore took more time than I'd thought; now I really was running late. I hurried into the bedroom to get dressed.

On the way to the office, I dropped off the baggie of blood Katya and I had collected from the ledge under Summit Overlook and was informed by my buddy Hank Bettis it would cost me another seven hundred dollars to do DNA analysis. Fortunately we already had the DNA of Ian McKenna and Wally Stroud on file for comparison or it would have been a lot more. Reluctantly, I agreed. What else could I do? Since I had none, money was beginning to mean nothing to me. It was almost like I was playing with Monopoly money.

On the positive side, the turnaround time to receive DNA analysis results had gone down considerable. I remember when it took at least a couple of months, but now Hank informed me he would have the results in a couple of days.

It was at that moment, I realized I forgotten to bring in my guns I was going to turn over to St. George P.D. Oh, well, I guess there was no real hurry. Nothing was lost and they certainly weren't going anywhere. I would remember to do it tomorrow on the way to work.

When I walked in the office it was a very tardy nine twenty-six. As usual, Ronnie looked simply stunning. Her pink low-cut knit blouse seemed to highlight her platinum blonde hair and her tight designer jeans most assuredly highlighted her terrific figure. Almost like Malachi when I came home after being gone for a few days, she likewise seemed overjoyed to see me. Discretely, she pecked me on the cheek and I promised to fill her in on the details of my ordeal when I got a minute. As it turned out, I didn't get a break until the noon hour, actually twelve-thirty.

Just before I finished with my morning patients Ronnie slyly suggested we meet for lunch at a discreet soup and sandwich restaurant in the neighboring town of Sana Clara, some five miles away. How could I refuse?

Not too surprising, she arrived before me. Sitting at a corner table, she had her compact mirror out and was putting the finishing touches on her already impeccable blonde hair and touching up her already flawless makeup. When she saw me, she waved cheerily, put away her compact and motioned me over. Once again, I caught my breath. She was hands down the most beautiful woman in the café. As I started to sit, she stood and again pecked me on the cheek.

"God, how I missed you!" she gushed as we both sat down.

"I missed you too," I replied, suddenly realizing how nice it was to be with her. Not only was she easy on the eyes, it was great to have someone to talk to and make a fuss over me. It had been a long time since anyone did that—well at least a beautiful female. Malachi regularly made a fuss over me.

"So what happened?" she asked, sitting down again. "I had to re-schedule patients two days in a row."

"I know," I replied, sitting down, "I'm sorry. I would have called but where I was there was no cell phone—"

I paused as our waiter arrived to take our order. I ordered a salad and a portabella mushroom sandwich. Ronnie looked at me oddly, so I explained I was off meat. She shrugged and ordered homemade taco soup and a small smothered pork burrito.

While we were waiting for our food, I described in detail my ordeal of the last few days. When I got to the part where the rogue snowmobiler fired his gun at me, I paused a moment to consider, then thought better of it. Skipping that, I concluded with, "anyway, that's about it." On a hunch, I deliberately withheld that information and at least for now the horrific fact that Ziggy was murdered. I gambled Ronnie had not yet read the morning paper or listened to the local news.

"Katya had surgery yesterday and is still in the hospital," I finally said to break the silence and to continue the conversation.

"Oh," Ronnie said, then insincerely added, "I do hope she gets better."

The waiter arrived with our food, then mistakenly set the burrito in front of me, probably a natural mistake, and the portabella sandwich and salad in front of Ronnie.

"Was Tim busy while I was gone?" I asked as nonchalantly as I could while redistributing our food.

Ronnie nodded. "With you gone so much and not doing surgery, his days have been more than full."

"So, he worked every day that I was gone?"

"Yes, everyday." Ronnie stirred her taco soup with a spoon."

"All day every day?"

"Yes, Coop. Why the twenty questions?"

I didn't answer; instead I filled my mouth with mushroom sandwich and silently chewed. Something was not quite kosher here; the math just didn't add up. If Tim Slade worked in the office all day every day, then there was no way he would have to time to go seventy-five miles up to Brian Head, rent a snowmobile under the name of Daniel Mahoney, disable our machines, take a shot at me and kill Ziggy. On the other hand, though certainly not conclusive, all the evidence gathered over the last three days pointed the finger at him.

In my mind, there were only two possibilities: either I was dead wrong about Tim Slade, or Ronnie Slade was lying. Of course I could check the office computer to verify Tim's schedule, to see if his last three days really were full. Schedules, however, were relatively easy to fake; apparently the veteran's hospitals were quite adept at this. To further validate, I could cross-reference the names on the computer schedule with the patient's medical charts, checking to see if office notes were dictated for each patient listed on the schedule. That, of course, could be faked too, but it would be much harder and take a lot more time. However, if Ronnie said he worked all day for those three days, then I suppose I had to believe her—

"—So," I suddenly blurted out, "what's Tim's middle name?"

Ronnie looked at me quizzically. "Why?"

"I don't know," I labored to come up with a logical explanation. "All

234

this time I've been working with him and I still don't know his middle name."

"Daniel," she shrugged. "His middle name is Daniel."

Daniel, huh? Was that just a coincidence? Maybe. But why not swing for the fences? "How about his mother's maiden name?" I asked, thinking if it were Mahoney I'd just hit a home run.

"I don't remember," she replied, blowing on her soup to cool it. "I've never met either of his parents. Apparently, they've been dead for sometime now."

We ate in awkward silence for a few minutes, then Ronnie asked, "did you see that letter from the hospital?"

"No." I took another bite of portabella sandwich. It wasn't that bad.

"I set it on your desk. It looks official."

At first I couldn't think of any hospital correspondence I was expecting, then I remembered I had sent a letter appealing the suspension of my hospital privileges. More than likely it was related to that. Hopefully, I'd been reinstated. With my bills piling up, like plowed mountain roadside snow after a blizzard, I really needed to start doing surgery again. As my friend Russ Spielman reminded me the other day, *if a surgeon doesn't cut, he doesn't eat.*

We finished our meal with mostly small talk. Ronnie informed me that in a recent poll ran by our local newspaper, *The Daily Spectrum*, Tim was leading all other candidates running for county commission and unfortunately I came in dead last. This came as no big surprise to me and to be honest I was relieved. Not because now it looked like the Lake Powell pipeline would be built, I still opposed it, but I was relieved I would no longer have to worry about campaigning.

As we got up to leave, Ronnie quickly leaned over and kissed me, then as she walked away, she said, "see you at the office. You better hurry or you'll be late."

I was late, but before I started with the patients, I went into my private office and found the letter from the hospital Ronnie had told me about. Ripping it open, I extracted a single sheet of paper and read.

*Dr. Cooper, this letter is to inform you that the Executive Committee has convened and voted to reinstate your operating privileges. You will be on probation for one year and Dr. Kenneth Kees has been assigned to proctor/monitor your work. If there are any questions you can call or fax me. Sincerely, Jeremy Faux.*

Finally, something was going my way! Hopefully this was the beginning of a trend, a harbinger of things to come.

Since I started the afternoon patients late, consequently I finished with them late. As you might imagine, I was still troubled by the events of the last few weeks and the lack of concrete answers, so it was hard for me to concentrate on my work. What I really needed was guidance, some sage advice. Immediately, I thought of my longtime friend and mentor, Doctor Jacob Heinz. As soon as I finished with the patients, I picked up my cell phone to call him. Unfortunately it was dead. I hadn't charged it in days. Undeterred, I used the office landline.

Without hesitating, Jacob invited me over for dinner and of course I couldn't refuse a Sophie dinner. Her dinners were infinitely better than my microwaved frozen veggie dinners. Also without asking if I wanted to do it, Jacob informed me I would have time to run home and pick up Malachi. I suspected he secretly wanted to see Malachi more than me.

*"Guten Abend,"* Jacob greeted me at the door, then immediately ignored me in favor of Malachi. And, of course, Malachi played it up, like he always did, wagging his tail and making a big fuss over Jacob.

Dinner was a vegan curry that was actually very good. Sophie used chopped summer squash, spinach, onion and kale, and spiced it with curry, ginger and garlic cloves. Malachi was treated with white rice and hotdogs, which he wolfed down like it was steak. After dinner, Jacob grabbed a pot of coffee and headed out on the patio. Even in the winter, early evenings in St. George are usually mild with temperatures normally above forty degrees. Also, Jacob had a large outdoor propane heater, which he immediately turned on. The heater, plus the hot coffee actually made it quite comfortable.

*"Was sie zu belästigen?"* Jacob asked, pouring two cups of coffee. He was shaking so badly from his Parkinson's disease, he spilled about as much coffee as he poured into the cups.

"Jacob," I smiled and shook my head, "I don't understand. You're speaking German again."

*"Ja, Ja,"* Jacob nodded and smiled. "The older I get the more I seem to revert back to my native tongue. Drives poor Sophie crazy."

I nodded. "That makes sense. The older you get, your remote memory gets better and present memory gets worse."

*"Ja, Ja,"* Jacob laughed. "The other day I lost my car keys. It took me

two days to find them. I finally discovered them in the refrigerator."

"So what did you say?" I smiled at his story.

"I didn't say anything, just cursed *ein bisschen*," Jacob laughed again.

"No," I shook my head, "what did you say in German that I didn't understand.

"*Ein bisschen*—a little bit."

"No, before that."

"Oh, I just asked vhat vas troubling you?"

"It's still this Wally Stroud and Ian McKenna thing. Both are still missing and we are no closer to finding out what happened than when I talked to you last."

"Vell, any new developments?"

After taking another a sip of coffee, I brought him up to date. I told him the DNA on the blood I found early confirmed it was both Ian and Wally's. Then I told him about the harrowing trip to Brian Head with Katya and Ziggy and Katya's near-death accident. Also, I described how someone had disabled our machines, took a shot at me and murdered Ziggy. Finally, I informed Jacob of the new evidence we'd found, the blood on the drop-off secondary cliff ledge as well as the shell casings and the blood we'd found on top the next day with Sherriff Klein and we were presently waiting for the DNA analysis on all those new blood samples. "And," I concluded, "that's about it. It has to be Tim, but I just can't prove it."

"*Es wird puzzingling*," Jacob frowned, then quickly rephrased in English, "it is puzzling, but it still bothers me that Vally and Ian's wives are not more heartbroken by their disappearance and probable death."

"Well, apparently neither of them had good marriages. In fact Katya and Ian had filed for divorce and Wally's wife was thinking about it."

"Do you know vhy?" Shakily, Jacob sipped his coffee. "Vhy vere there marriages no good?"

I shook my head. "I really don't know."

"Vell, *das ist ein guter Anfang*," he said, then translated, "that's a good place to start. There is something not quite kosher there."

We sipped our coffee in silence. Yes, Jacob was right. There was something odd about the wives reactions to the losses of their husbands. I made a mental note to talk to Katya and Susan Stroud further about that.

"And," Jacob continued, "keep an open mind about Tim."

I frowned. That would be hard to do, particularly when all evidence stacked against him.

"Jacob, I'm sure it's Tim."

"It may be," he nodded, "but there's no hard evidence yet."

We finished our coffee in silence, both lost in our own thoughts.

"Well," I finally said, standing up. "Jacob, I got to go."

"Ja, Ja," he said also standing and reaching for his cane. "You be careful, Coop. There is a murderer some vhere out there."

After thanking Sophie again for the excellent dinner, I kissed her goodbye on the cheek, waved to Jacob, then called to Malachi. We climbed back into the Dodge and headed straight for the hospital to check on Katya.

She was sleeping when I arrived at 1-West, so I headed straight for the nurses' station to check her patient chart. Fortunately, her vital signs were good: EKG strip - NSR (normal sinus rhythm), pulse - 78, BP - 115/70, O2 sat - 92 and most importantly her temp was 98.8. I peeked at her through the door. She looked comfortable. Her face looked relaxed, not drawn in pain, as it had been the last couple of days. I decided I would not wake her, but make a point to come see her first thing in the morning.

After the hospital, it was time for Diamond Valley, the ranch and bed. I still had horses to feed and frankly I was still exhausted. Right now, all I wanted was a good night's sleep and for this to all go away—at least for eight hours.

It was after ten when, we, Malachi and I, finally entered the house. However, the second we stepped through the back door the phone started ringing. Glancing down at my answering machine I noted I had three unanswered messages. At the moment I was so tired I wanted none of it. I simply unplugged the ringing phone and ignored the unanswered messages. After turning out the lights and locking all the doors, Malachi and I dropped onto the bed. It felt good to be home and to spend a full night in my own bed. Sighing contentedly, I closed my eyes and almost immediately dozed off--.

--Suddenly, the doorbell rang.

Groaning, I rolled over and pulled the covers over my head. If I ignored it, maybe it would go away.

The doorbell rang again, followed shortly by loud banging on the door.

"Jesus," I shouted, "go away."

They probably couldn't hear me, anyway the pounding continued. Groaning, I got out of bed and grabbed a robe. Malachi, now fully awake, also jumped off the bed and followed. As I started for the door, I suddenly remembered Jacob's admonition from earlier in the evening, *"You be careful, Coop. There is a murderer some vhere out there."*

Abruptly I stopped and tried unsuccessfully to suppress a shiver. After all, it was just a couple of short days ago someone had tried to murder me! Were they back to try again? Perhaps the prudent thing to do would be to take a gun with me. Suddenly all my resolve to make this house and my life a gun-free zone vanished, disappeared like spooned sugar in hot coffee.

I hurried back to the bedroom and dialed the lock combination and opened my gun safe. It was empty! Where the hell were my guns?

Oh, yeah, I remembered I took the guns out of the safe this morning. I was going to turn them in at the St. George Police Departments, but when I left the house I'd neglected to take them. They must still be in the kitchen scattered on the table.

Without turning on a light, I crept into the kitchen and found my guns. Feeling around in the dark, I finally selected my Desert Eagle .45 handgun manufactured by Kahr Arms. That should be enough firepower for even the most determined intruder. After another couple of seconds of blind groping, I located a magazine and a box of bullets. Fumbling some in the dark, I loaded the magazine, then inserted it into the grip of the gun. As I started for the door, I remembered I hadn't cocked the gun; that meant there was no bullet in the chamber. With my left hand, I quickly pulled back on the slide, then listened for the mechanical click as the slide snapped back and a inserted bullet. Now I was fully armed!

And just like that my solemn vow to never pick up a gun again had vanished, just like a magician's disappearing act. Poof, and it was gone! With just a hint of danger and what did I do? Go straight for a gun! Right now, however, I didn't have the time to be disappointed with myself. With my heart pounding, I opened the back door and slipped outside. With less than a quarter moon, it was very dark. Most of the light came from the Milky Way, glowing like an enormous galactic burl of rhinestones.

Meanwhile the infuriating pounding on the door started again. If nothing else, they were determined. A reasonable person would have given up by now.

With gun in hand and Malachi at my side, I quietly shuffled through the backyard, then staying to the shadows I circled around to the front of the house.

In the dark, I could barely make out the person standing on my porch and still periodically pounding on my door. Was it the same guy who took a shot at me on the mountain? I couldn't tell, but I could tell instead of a black snowsuit he was wearing an expensive-looking, fleece-lined suede leather coat. However, the coat, with the collar turned up, also made it difficult to make out detailed physical characteristics. At least I could tell he was not that big. Thank God!

Being as quiet as I could, I crept up behind him and shoved the barrel of my Desert Eagle .45 hard into his back, right between his shoulder blades.

"Don't move a muscle!" I growled.

# 20

"And keep your hands where I can see them," I added, then barked, "and raise 'em higher!"

While he raised his hands, I quickly appraised the man standing on my porch with his back toward me. Obviously, it was not Tim Slade, too small, but hopefully by identifying him it would lead me to the man, probably Tim Slade, who tried to kill me a couple days ago. And with any luck, it might also go a long way in solving the puzzling disappearance and probable murders of Ian McKenna and Wally Stroud. In my mind, all those crimes had to be connected. It would be too much of a coincidence if they were not and I wasn't a big disciple of coincidence.

"Now turn around slowly," I commanded, "and no sudden movements." With my index finger still cupped around the concave trigger, I held my breath.

Doing precisely as told, the man, still holding his hands high, slowly turned around.

Suddenly Malachi rushed him.

Simultaneously my jaw dropped, as did my gun!

In that brief second, Malachi was on him. But rather than tearing him apart, he was wagging his tail furiously and begging for attention.

"Oh, hi, Ronnie!" I said sheepishly.

Instead of looking frightened, she looked slightly amused. "Aren't we being a little paranoid, Coop?"

"Yeah," I laughed nervously, as I hid the gun the gun behind my back, "yeah, I guess I am."

"Well," she smiled sardonically, "if you're not going to shoot me, how about inviting me in?"

"Sure," I said, happy to change the subject away from my gun-happy paranoia, "let's go around to the back door. It's unlocked."

With me leading the way, we retraced my path to the back door, then on through the kitchen into the living room. On the way, I deposited the Desert Eagle back on the table and turned on the lights. Ronnie sat down on the sofa, then immediately got up again and removed her fleece-lined suede leather coat.

"Nice coat," I remarked as she handed it to me to hang up. Indeed, it was a nice coat and looked particularly good on her with her blonde hair, her tight designer jeans and her Carlos Santana boots.

After hanging up her coat, I asked, "can I get you anything?"

"Yeah," she laughed, "after having a gun shoved into my back, I could use a stiff drink. What you got?"

"Not much," I admitted, "nothing very strong, maybe a little white wine."

"Then that will have to do," she laughed again, then turned to Malachi who was still begging for her attention.

For just a second I watched her play with Malachi and once again was struck by her beauty. Having her here almost instantly brought a different feel to the house. I searched for the word—home. Yes, now it felt more like a home.

Feeling oddly content, I returned to the kitchen and in the pantry located a single bottle of Chardonnay. How long it had been there, I could only guess, but I suspected it dated back to my last marriage with Claire Dubois. She loved wine. I was not a big drinker, seldom bought alcohol and almost never wine. Oh, well, at least it ought to be properly aged.

After some searching, I found an opener and as usual butchered the cork while attempting to remove it. Easily frustrated, I gave up and used the blunt end of a butter knife to push the mangled cork back down into the bottle. There it floated forlornly, like a battle-damaged seventeenth century frigate.

Gurgling the wine around the cork frigate, I managed to pour two glasses, then after picking out little shards of cork I carried the wine glasses into the living room and offered one to Ronnie.

"Thanks," she said, immediately draining nearly half the glass. "Maybe," she blushed, "you should bring in the bottle."

I returned with the bottle, set it on the coffee table, then started to sit down in the love seat facing the sofa and Ronnie.

Expressly she patted the sofa next to her. "Why don't you sit here by me, Coop?"

Simultaneously, it seemed like both a good and bad idea. I wavered, then like I was being controlled by an alien power, got up and sat down next her. I could feel the tingling of static electricity as our thighs touched.

As usual around beautiful women, I was tongue-tied and could think of nothing to say. Ronnie didn't seem to mind; she was too busy finishing her drink.

Eventually, I stammered, "so w—what you doing here, R—Ronnie?"

"Huh?" she handed me her empty glass.

Getting up, I refilled it and handed it back to her, then sat back down, this time on the love seat facing her.

"So, what you doing here, Ronnie?" I repeated, more evenly this time.

"Oh," she laughed, "actually, Tim asked me to deliver a message."

Talk about pouring cold water on the hot fire of passion. My lust for her disappeared like bath water down a drain. Just the mention of Tim's name reminded me Ronnie was still married.

After fortifying myself with a first sip of wine, I asked, "so, what did he say?"

"A couple of things. One he wants you to know he had nothing to do with the disappearances of Ian and Wally," she paused to take another sip of wine.

I snorted dismissively, then asked, "and the other?"

"He wanted me to tell you he's rented a cabin up at Brian Head--"

"--I knew he was up there!" I blurted, cutting her off.

"So?" She looked confused. "He's taking his annual ski vacation. Anyway, he said if you want to come up, you and he can conclude your business."

"What business?" I asked suspiciously.

"Geez, Coop, what you been trying to do--the business of separating your practices."

"Oh! With or without lawyers?"

"Without," she said promptly and once again offered me her empty wine glass.

"But I have office tomorrow."

"Tomorrow is Saturday, Coop."

"Oh, yeah. Why the sudden change of heart?" I asked warily, accepting her glass.

"I don't know," she shrugged. "But I wish he was that agreeable when it comes to giving me a divorce."

"He still won't budge on that, huh?" I replied, unable to keep the disappointment from my voice.

As I refilled her glass and again picked out the tiny cork shards, I processed what she had just said. To say I was surprised by this proffered olive branch, if indeed that's what it was, was a huge understatement. Somehow this whole thing didn't sound or smell right, even though in retrospect I did know Tim took annual ski vacations to Brian Head. Nevertheless, to me it was all too convenient. It had all the hallmarks, all the warning signs, of an ambush!

Was I overreacting? Was I once again being consumed by runaway paranoia? Probably. However my gut feeling, my strong gut feeling, was to be skeptical and cautious, very cautious.

Also if I was honest, I was disappointed that Tim would not grant Ronnie a divorce. Even though I knew it was foolish, I'd started to imagine us, Ronnie and me, as couple. It was time for me to settle down again and I could do a lot worse than Ronnie Slade.

I handed her a half full glass of Chardonnay. "You got an address?"

Setting down her glass, she fumbled in her purse for a few seconds, finally producing a Post-it scrap of paper. She offered it to me.

"Did he say a time?" I asked as I stuffed the address in my robe pocket.

"Anytime in the afternoon, but he wants to ski in the morning." Ronnie took another long sip of Chardonnay, then pounded the couch next to her. "Why you sittin' waaay over there?" She pounded the couch again. "Come sit by me, Coops. I'm lon-a-ly." Obviously, she was starting to slur her words.

I hesitated a moment, then somehow once again my feet started moving without permission from my head.

It might have been the wine; or perhaps the subsurface need for some kind of emotional catharsis; or maybe it was just the accumulated loneliness from years of living alone; or maybe it was just yet another fla-grant manifestation of my weak character; or perhaps all four, but even though I kept telling myself it was not a good idea, I somehow ended up on the couch, sitting next to the incredibly beautiful Veronica Slade!

"Uh—uh are you still going to stay?" I asked, suddenly noticing my robe had gapped open exposing most of my left thigh.

Before I could close the "V" in my robe, I felt Ronnie's hand glide over to my thigh. Her hand was soft as silk and her touch was simply arousing.

"I can stay all night if you want," she purred, her hand inching higher.

"N–no," I stammered. "I meant are you still going to stay at the office? Work for me?"

"What do you think?" she murmured, then as if for confirmation she slowly slid her hand to my upper thigh.

I could only withstand so much. I'm no man of steel and when it comes to this sort of thing. I admit, I am very weak, but—but in my defense it had been such a long time. God, how I wanted to take her in my arms and carry her into my bedroom—

—Abruptly, I stood, her hand falling away from my thigh. "Ronnie, I just can't do this! Not while you're still married to Tim and we, you and me, still have all this unfinished business with him."

She looked and sounded wounded. "Well, we may not be divorced, but we are separated."

"Are you still living in the same house?"

"Well, yes."

"Then you're are not separated."

"Maybe not physically," she countered, "but we've been separated emotionally for years."

"Ronnie," I softened my voice, "not tonight. Honestly, I would like to sometime, but under different circumstances."

Without another word, she got up, gathered up her purse and headed for the door.

"Don't forget your coat," I said, hurrying to retrieve it from the closet.

"Are you okay to drive?" I asked, handing her the leather coat. "I can take you home."

Still not answering, she donned her coat. Angrily she unlocked the front door, stalked through it and slammed it behind her.

I sat for a moment in stunned silence. What had I done? Almost instantly I wished I could take it all back. What would be so wrong with spending a night with Ronnie? Physically, I ached for her. I surely didn't handle that very well. Not only had I lost a potential lover, but possibly also a superb employee. I hated the thought of an office without Ronnie Slade.

Groaning out loud, I stood up, then suddenly sat back down again. It was, however, a bit bizarre that she continued to be Tim's messenger boy, especially if their relationship was as strained as she'd led me to believe. Perhaps, their relationship was not that bad. If it wasn't, then why the big show? Suddenly, a troubling thought occurred to me. Was Ronnie Slade playing me? If so, why?

Involuntarily, I shivered! Was she a spy for Tim? Was she feeding him information about me? Is that how Tim found Katya and me up on the mountain, at the Summit Overlook, and nearly killed us? And he did kill Ziggy! I shivered again. Was Ronnie an accessory to murder?

"Nah," I laughed out loud and once again stood up. This too was a classic example of my galloping paranoia. Not Ronnie. She was much too classy for that.

Calling to Malachi, I headed for the bedroom. Maybe I would get some answers tomorrow when I met with Tim. But—but I'd better be careful, very careful. Tim had already demonstrated how dangerous he was and of what he was capable. And—and he knew full well I was on to him, plus now he had the additional advantage of picking the terrain. Any general would tell you how important that was, to fight on familiar land.

Needless to say, though I was exhausted I didn't sleep much that night. My thoughts Ping-Ponged from Ronnie Slade, to Tim Slade, then back to Ronnie again. Though I looked at it from every angle, I still did not come up with anything new, no concrete answers.

Tired of thinking about that I thought about Katya. She was not at all what I'd first thought. Not only was she a pretty face, but she also had a fair amount of grit. Mentally, I compared her to Ronnie. Any man would be lucky to end up with either one of them, but I had to remind myself they were both still married. Maybe neither were happy marriages, but nevertheless they both were still married! Sighing, I looked at the clock.

Well before sunrise, I got up, put on a pot of coffee, then went outside to feed the horses.

Since Tim wanted to ski in the morning and morning skiing ended and one o'clock, there was no need for me to be up to Brian Head before two o'clock. It would take me approximately an hour and a half to get from the ranch to Brian Head, so by doing the math, I figured that would leave me five or six hours idle morning hours with nothing to do but fret and worry. From past experience, I knew there was nothing better for anxiety than physical labor. It looked like this would be a good morning for me to finally clean out the horse stalls.

After my usual breakfast of coffee and a toasted bagel, and a can of dog food for Malachi, I grabbed a light jacket and with Malachi tagging along we headed for the barn.

The manure in the stalls was deep with some wet and some desiccated. Unfortunately, I hadn't cleaned them in some time. Taking off my jacket, I rolled up my sleeves and got started. First, like collecting autumn leaves, I raked the manure from each stall into a large central pile. Unfortunately, each stoke of the rake created a fine plume of excrement dust, much like wheat dust in a tower silo. To protect my lungs, I had to briefly stop, find and strap on a surgical mask, then I continued at a frenetic, anxiety-consuming pace. Using a snow scoop shovel, I pitched the accumulated piles it into the bucket of the frontend loader of my Kubota tractor. When it was full, I transported the manure out into the pasture and tried to scatter it evenly. And even though it was hard work, it felt good to finally do something physical, to get some exercise. Also as a secondary benefit, it temporarily took my mind off my Tim Slade, Ronnie Slade, Katya Koslovsky and Brian Head Mountain.

It was almost straight up noon when I finished and I headed directly for the shower. Once done with showering and dressing, it was time to head up to Brian Head. Calling to Malachi, I grabbed a coat, then walked through the kitchen on my way outside to the Dodge.

In the kitchen, however, I paused and eyed my pile of guns still resting on the table. Should I take a gun? That would break my vow of no more guns. But hadn't I already broken that vow last night with Ronnie? Well, yes and no, but technically no. I hadn't fired the gun. Suddenly, I realized I was splitting hairs and rationalizing my actions, but I couldn't help it.

On the other hand, wouldn't Tim have a gun? The answer was a most assured, yes! He never went anywhere without a gun and usually more than one. So, wouldn't that put me at a distinct disadvantage if I did not have a gun? The answer was obvious—and I really did not have a death wish.

Still I hesitated, vacillated for another couple of seconds, then abruptly grabbed my Desert Eagle .45 again along with a couple of full magazines. Thoroughly disappointed with myself, I headed for the back door. As soon as the door opened, my vow and all my lofty intentions vanished in the brisk winter air like heat escaping from a chimney. Even though I tried to justify that I was only being practical, my conscience whispered, 'this is just another example of your weak character.'

On my way out of town, I briefly considered stopping at Dixie Regional Hospital to see Katya, but by now I was running a little short on time. I made a mental note to see her on my way back.

It was the same problem with Sheriff Tiny Klein. When I passed Cedar City, I wanted to stop to check on the DNA test from the blood we'd recovered from the top of the Summit Overlook, but unfortunately I didn't have enough time. I wanted to make sure I had plenty of time for Tim. As I drove, I made another mental note, I needed to check with Hank Bettis on the blood sample Katya and I had found at the bottom of the cliff the day before. Well, to be fair, it was Malachi that found both blood samples, but right now I had to concentrate on Tim.

After an hour and a half of driving, I arrived at the small ski village of Brian Head. Fortunately all streets were plowed, but the cornrows of snow on each side of the highway were nearly four feet high. The tall snow banks afforded only tunnel visibility. From the Dodge, I could only see the top half of most of the buildings.

By the time I arrived, afternoon skiing had started, so street traffic was sparse. I pulled into a mostly empty condo parking lot, pulled out my cell phone and punched in the address Ronnie had given me, then waited. After a few seconds, the smart phone came up with a prescribed route. From the map, it looked like Tim's cabin was on the outskirts of town. Following both verbal and visual cues, I fired up the Dodge and started down the road.

Our recommended GPS route took us down State Road 143, which also doubled as Main Street, then up the steep west shoulder of Brian Head Peak. After approximately one mile, I was prompted to turn left onto Bristlecone Lane, then left again onto Sleigh Circle. From Sleigh Circle I turned onto Snowmobile Road, then left one last time onto Toboggan Lane.

The entire subdivision had surprisingly few cabins. Apparently, this was due to a couple of factors: one, this was a relatively new development, and two, the location was fairly far from downtown and the slopes. In fact, on Toboggan Lane there was only one cabin and evidently that was where Tim Slade was staying. It was so remote a gunshot probably would not be heard downtown or the ski slopes, and maybe not even by the neighboring cabins.

Turning around, I parked the Dodge on Snowmobile Road. Perhaps it would be wise if I scouted the cabin and determined, if possible, what I was getting myself into. After pulling on my snow boots, I instructing Malachi to stay, grabbed the Desert Eagle .45 along with my two full magazines and got out of the pickup.

Once outside, I immediately felt the cold and pulled my coat tighter around me. I found it odd that in spite of the cold there was no smoke wafting from the cultured rock chimney of Tim's log cabin. Maybe he was not there, or had just arrived. Or perhaps unlike my cabin, he had some other source of heat. Hopefully, he was inside and waiting, but somehow it just didn't feel right. With a growing sense of foreboding, I took a deep breath and headed toward the cabin.

The lot to the left of Tim's cabin was not only vacant, but also heavily wooded with stands of quaking aspens and an occasional Colorado blue spruce and foxtail pine. Leaving the pavement, I headed in that direction. The snow was knee-deep, making walking difficult, very tiring. By the time I arrived at the grove of quakies, my quadriceps were aching and were again on the verge of spasm.

Taking a minute to let my quads recover, I mapped out a route. The copse of quaking aspens continued from this lot onto Tim's, being particularly thick right behind his cabin. This was the route I decided to take. The grove offered good cover and hopefully I could work all the way to the back of his cabin without being seen.

Fifteen minutes later, I was in Tim's backyard and within thirty feet of the cabin. I hunkered down for five minutes and watched the cabin. There was nothing. No activity to indicate I'd been spotted.

Taking deep breath, I hurried, as best I could in two feet of powder snow, to the back wall of the cabin, then flattened out against it. Inching to my right a couple of feet, I peeked into a window. It appeared to be a bedroom and was unoccupied. Systematically, I worked to the front of the cabin, checking out each window as I went.

When I arrived at the front of the cabin, I paused at the corner of a large picture window. I took a quick glance and saw nothing. This was puzzling. I had checked out the entire cabin and still not located Tim. My internal alarm went off. Something was not right here! Quickly, I dropped down and looked around once again. Still I did not see anything. No activity on the road and no movement in the forest.

Cautiously, I rose to a half crouch and peeked in the picture window once again, this time taking my time. I was looking into what was obviously the living room and could see dead smokeless coals in the fireplace. Systematically, I scanned the room, then scanned it again. There was nothing other than a La-Z-Boy recliner facing the fireplace, but I could only see the back of the chair. Perhaps, there was someone in the chair; I couldn't tell for sure. I needed to change my angle, my line of sight. I started to leave then paused.

Suddenly I noticed something else. On an end table next to the recliner was what looked to be a handgun! From this distance, I could not discern the make or caliber. I was pretty sure it was a gun, but I needed a better look, a better angle.

Once again, I labored through the deep snow to a window located on the south wall, the same wall as the chimney and fireplace. Again, I cautiously stood up and peered in. From this angle I couldn't see the fireplace, but I could see the dining table, it was right in front of me. There still were a few dirty dishes scattered on it as though someone had just finished lunch.

I shifted my gaze to the La-Z-Boy chair. Indeed, it was occupied! From this angle I could not see the face, only part of one shoulder and one leg, but it had to be Tim. Slowly, I lowered my head, then sat down in the snow to consider my options.

Actually, they were very few. I could simply turn around and leave or I could go knock on the front door, knowing full well I would have to be ready for anything.

I'd not come this far just to turn around again and leave. Pulling the Desert Eagle .45 from my Levi's waistband at the small of my back, I ratcheted back the slide inserting a bullet in the chamber, then replaced the gun, pulling my coat down over it. Taking a deep breath, I stood up and walked straight for the front door.

At the door, I hesitated again, then knocked loudly on the door, waited a few seconds, then knocked again. Nothing. I knocked even louder, then waited some more. Still nothing. No one answered the door. Maybe Tim was sleeping. I literally pounded on the door. Nothing. Snatching my Desert Eagle from my pants, I used the butt to rap on the door, this time loud enough to wake even the deepest sleeper. Still nothing.

Leaving the front door, I returned to the south window and looked in. The person in the chair had not moved. I could still only see part of one shoulder and one leg. Again with my gun, I rapped on the window. Still nothing. Returning to the front door, I tried to open it; it was locked. Systematically, I once again circled around the cabin, checking all the windows. All were locked. I tried the back door, the same result.

The back door, however, was a window door, glass on the top, wood on the bottom. Again using the butt of my Desert Eagle, I shattered the glass in the left lower corner, close to the door handle, then with the barrel of the gun I swept away any clinging shards.

Once again I paused, thinking all the racket would bring Tim running, gun in hand. Nothing. Carefully reaching inside, I slid back the deadbolt and unlocked the door. With my gun in the ready position, I opened the door and entered the kitchen. Feeling a little foolish, I simulated the actions I'd seen the T.V. cops use. Quickly, I glanced right with my gun leveled in that direction, then using the same action I looked and pointed the gun to the left. Nothing. Next, with the gun trained straight ahead, I advanced into the living room.

The man in the La-Z-Boy still had not moved! And the handgun still rested undisturbed on the end table next to him.

"Tim," I said cautiously.

He did not answer.

"Tim!" I said more loudly.

Still nothing. I couldn't shake the feeling I was waking into a trap.

With my gun still in the ready position, I warily circled the recliner, all the while keeping my eyes glued on the handgun. If he reached for it, I was ready.

Suddenly it occurred to me; Jesus, he may have more than one gun!

Quickly I lifted my eyes from the gun on the end table and focused on the man in the recliner.

Then I gasped and dropped my gun.

# 21

Now I saw the reason Tim Slade had not moved. There was a small bullet hole perfectly centered right in the middle of his forehead, ringed with black power burns. His face was contorted and forever frozen in a grimace of horror, or recognition, or both.

Other than he was a much bigger man, he looked a whole lot like Ziggy Ziegfeld. Carefully, I tried to move his head forward, looking for an exit wound. With his *rigor mortis* now fully advanced, this was not easy. His neck would not bend. Finally, I tilted his whole torso forward just enough to see behind his head. There was no exit wound. Gently, I returned him to his previous position.

As I continued to examine Tim another though occurred to me, was I alone? Anxiously, I raised my gun again and looked around. Was I being paranoid, or was the murderer still here? I held my breath and tried to listen for sounds. Nothing. Nothing but the raspy dry sound of my own respiration. Once again looking like a T.V. detective, I decided to check out the other rooms.

The floor plan was much like my cabin. There was a large open studio-like kitchen, dining and living room area and four other rooms: two bedrooms, a bathroom and a loft. With heart pounding and gun in the ready position, I cautiously investigated all four rooms. Again there was nothing. At last I was convinced I was alone. There was absolutely no one in the cabin other than Tim and me.

Sitting down on a full-grain leather sofa, I consciously tried to slow down my breathing and contemplate my next move. Actually, there was not much to consider. My next move had to be to inform the authorities. I had to get hold of Sheriff Tiny Klein.

Fishing my cell phone from my coat pocket, I flipped through *recent contacts* till I found the sheriff's number, then punched it in. No cell service. Looking around, however, I spied a phone on the lamp table next to the sofa. Using the cabin's landline, I called the Iron County Sheriff Department. After going through the receptionist and waiting for a full five minutes I finally got Tiny on the phone. He sounded grumpy, particularly when I told him I had another murder for him to investigate. After giving him the address, he sighed out loud and agreed to meet me in forty-five minutes.

"And don't touch anything," he growled before hanging up, "and don't leave. You better be there when I get there. You've got a lot of explaining to do."

Forty-five minutes was a long time to wait in a room with nothing to do other than stare at a corpse. Suddenly, I remembered Malachi was still in the pickup. While I waited for the sheriff, I should let Malachi out and give him a chance to stretch his legs and relieve himself.

As I gripped the couch arm to help boost me up, I felt something that did not feel like full-grain leather. In fact if felt a lot like marbled ewe fleece. Puzzled, I stood up, then turned and picked up the wooly article.

Indeed, it was fleece, a fleece-lined suede leather jacket. Understandably, with all my attention focused on a murdered Tim Slade, I had not noticed it. Picking it up, I looked at it more closely, while rotating it in my hands. Still baffled, I tried it on. It was too small, much too small for Tim or me. It had to be a lady's coat. Shrugging, I started to set it down again. After all, the sheriff had told me not to touch any—

—Wait a minute! Wasn't that the very same coat Ronnie Slade was wearing last night, just a few hours earlier at my house? And my house was a full seventy-five miles away. Maybe she had two identical coats—but probably not.

It surely looked the same to me. I tried to put it on again. No question about it, it was too small for a man and too large for a child. It had to be a lady's jacket! I set it down again on the arm of the couch, then on a hunch went into the larger bedroom and opened the clothes closet. I had hoped I was wrong, but I wasn't. Just as I expected, the clothes racks contained both men and women's clothes. What did it all mean? I wasn't sure. After all this was a rental and it could be the owner's clothes, or maybe Tim had a girlfriend on the side. That certainly would not surprise me. Or—or they could be Ronnie Slade's clothes! They appeared to be the right size, but I was no expert on women's sizes or clothes.

Still trying to make sense of it all, I left the bedroom, went through the living room, and without looking at Tim, unlocked the front door and stepped outside. God, it felt good to be out of that place. I took a deep breath of cold untainted air and tried to clear my head. Pulling back the slide on the .45, I ejected the bullet from the chamber, replaced it in the magazine and headed for Malachi.

Back at the Dodge, I let Malachi out, then with his wagging tail turned up, like a gravity-defying pendulum, we wandered down Toboggan Road. For the moment, I tried to block the macabre scene in the cabin from my mind. Instead, I watched an oblivious and happy Malachi darting ahead of me, racing from scent to new scent. I marveled how much alike and at the same time how dissimilar we were. We both thoroughly enjoyed our hikes, but for me they were all about sights, for Malachi all about scents. While watching him, my mind returned to the cabin, I simply couldn't help it. My mind hated chaos and insisted on some kind of logic. I tried to make some sense of it all.

Who would want Tim dead? And why? They must have had a pretty compelling reason to go to such extremes. Certainly, I did not know much about Tim's personal life and it was entirely possible he had enemies I knew nothing about, but I couldn't help but wonder if this had something to do with the disappearance of Ian and Wally. Either we had a rash of isolated, unrelated murders, (Ziggy, Tim and probably Ian and Wally), which was hard for me to believe, or in someway they were all connected. But try as I might, I couldn't come up with plausible string theory that would connect them all.

Finally, in frustration I switched mental gears. What about that fleece-lined leather coat? Where did that fit in? Or did it? I would be willing to bet the ranch that was Ronnie Slade's coat. If so, what did that mean? I tried to think it through.

There was no question she was wearing the same coat last night at my house, so that meant she must have left my house and immediately drove up here to Tim and this cabin. Why? Was she two-timing me? Playing me for a fool? Reporting my every move to Tim?

Or—or even worse, was she the one who murdered Tim? Obviously, they had not been getting along, were contemplating divorce and previously I'd seen Tim get physical with her. Maybe she came up here, they got into a fight and somehow she killed him. Or maybe it was self-defense. On second thought, in the heat of a battle it was highly unlikely anyone could fire a shot and center it so perfectly in the middle of the forehead. To me, though certainly I am no expert, this looked more like an execution-style killing. It was entirely possible Tim was shot while he slept.

But Ronnie, beautiful, vivacious Ronnie a murderer! I simply could not believe it. Though I didn't know many killers, actually none, Ronnie just did not have the look of a murderer to me. I sighed out loud. I'd come to another dead end, so I switched channels again.

So, if I didn't subscribe to the random killing theory was there a common thread connecting all these deaths? The only thing I could come up with was they all seemed to be in someway linked to me. All but Ziggy were part of that ill-fated deer hunt and even Ziggy was down here with Katya to investigate the disappearance of Ian, which occurred on that hunt. So not only were all the murders connected to me, they were also connected to the hunt.

Suddenly a disconcerting thought occurred to me. Was Katya next? Or even me? I was the only one left who was on that hunt. I tried to suppress a shiver and failed. But who would have a vendetta for us four deer hunters? Who would want us all dead? And why? So many question and so few answers. And try as I might, I could only manage to come up with more questions, but not any new answers.

We continued to wander.

Finally calling to Malachi, I turned around and headed back toward the cabin. Sheriff Tiny Klein should be arriving soon and he would be very annoyed if I was not there. As I rounded the corner, however, I realized I was already late.

"So, where were you?" Tiny demanded, looking at his wristwatch as Malachi and I approached. He and his crime scene team had already assembled in front of the cabin.

"I'm sorry," I said sheepishly. "I took Malachi for a walk."

Looking at my wristwatch, I couldn't believe he was already here. That was a fast forty-five minutes. Apparently, I was so absorbed in my deliberations time had gotten away from me.

"Have you been inside?" I asked, trying to divert the conversation away from my tardiness.

"No," the sheriff growled, " we've been waiting for you."

"The front door is unlocked," I pointed, "we might just as well get this over with."

"You lead," Tiny said, "and show us what you've got."

I took another minute to put Malachi back in the truck, then opened the front door and led the entourage into the cabin and stopped right in front of Tim Slade.

Tiny Klein was silent for a few seconds, studying the corpse, then observed, "this looks a lot like that other fellow from a couple of days ago."

I nodded. "Ziggy Ziegfeld."

"Doesn't look fresh," Tiny continued, as he put on latex gloves.

"Why?" I asked, though I probably already knew the answer.

"The blood's already clotted and dried and the body's already cold," the sheriff answered. "And we have full *rigor mortis* even in the larger muscles, but it has not converted back to flaccidity yet. It probably happened sometime last night."

I had nothing to add, so I remained silent.

Still gloved, Tiny picked up the gun on the nightstand. "It's a Colt three-fifty-seven Magnum," he observed, then looking a lot like Malachi, he sniffed it. Next, he opened the revolving cylinder and counted out loud as he ejected six-unfired bullets. Without further comment he handed the gun to a technician who immediately bagged it.

Like he was going through a pre-flight checklist, Tiny continued. "Looks like he was killed right in this chair."

"Why?" I asked again; this time I hadn't a clue.

"See how his arms and legs conform to the natural curves of the chair. That means the *rigor mortis* set in while he was sitting in this chair. If he was killed somewhere else and brought here, we wouldn't have that."

I nodded. That made sense.

"And, the Medical Examiners will be able to confirm this if they find *livor mortis*. When someone dies the blood settles to the most dependent part of the body before it clots. With this fellow, considering he's sitting in a chair, that means the blood would be in his buttocks, the back of his thighs, and his feet and ankles. I suspect the medical examiner will likely find the purple line of demarcation characteristic of—"

"—I know what *livor mortis* is," I cut him off.

"Oh," Tiny shrugged, then continued on as though he was talking to a medical student taking a forensic pathology elective. "And it was definitely not a suicide."

"Why?" I decided to play along.

"Hard angle to shoot oneself," Tiny replied, then added, "and the gun lying nearby had not been fired, and there was no suicide note."

The sheriff studied Tim for a couple more seconds in silence, then abruptly turned to me. "Are you packin', Doctor Cooper?"

"Huh?" Mentally I had to mentally switch gears.

"Are you armed? You got a gun on you?"

"Nah—" I started to say, then I remembered the Desert Eagle in my waistband. "—Uh, yes," I admitted. "I've got a forty-five."

"May I see it?" Tiny held out his huge paw.

Suddenly it occurred to me, I too was a suspect! Reaching behind me, I pulled the Desert Eagle from my waistband, rotated it so the barrel was pointing toward me, then handed it butt-first to the sheriff.

As with Tim's gun, he immediately put the barrel to his nose and sniffed.

"It hasn't been fired," I said lamely.

Tiny grunted, then slid the slide back, locked it in place and checked the chamber for a bullet. There was none. Thankfully I'd remove it earlier. Next, ejected the magazine and silently counted the bullets. Grunting again, he replaced the magazine and gave the Desert Eagle back to me.

"You getting a little paranoid?" he asked, nodding at my Desert Eagle.

"You bet I am," I admitted. "Everyone related to that hunt is dying."

"Seems that way," Tiny agreed. "While the technicians work on the body, why don't you show me the rest of the cabin?"

Nodding, I led the sheriff from the large studio-like room into the kitchen. Immediately, he spotted the glass shards on the floor and the broken window in the back door.

"Looks like this is how the murderer got in," he commented, immediately going over to investigate.

"Nah," I admitted, "I did that. Couldn't find any other way to get into the cabin."

"So, we'll probably find your fingerprints on the doorknob?"

"Yes," I nodded, "and a lot of other places too."

"I thought I told you not to touch anything."

"Well," I gulped, "I had to make sure the killer wasn't still here."

"So, you don't think the perp broke in?" Tiny asked.

"No," I shook my head, "it doesn't look like it."

"Maybe it was someone he knew," the sheriff suggested.

"Or, someone he was expecting."

"Maybe. So did you find anything else in your wanderings?"

I hesitated for only a second. Should I tell him about Ronnie's fleece-lined coat? If I did, she would instantly become a person of interest and sometimes that was a label that was hard to shake. I hated to point a finger at her without first talking to her, getting her side of the story.

"Nah," I finally said, "nothing."

"Any shell casings?"

"No," I shook my head again, "but I didn't really look."

"Well," Klein said, "we will. We'll turn this cabin upside down before we're done."

I nodded and showed him the rest of the cabin. He paused at the walk-in clothes closet in the master bedroom.

"Looks like Mister Slade had a lady friend staying with him," Tiny observed as he rifled through the outfits in the closet. He turned to me, "his wife?"

"How should I know?" I replied defensively.

"She works for you doesn't she?"

Apparently, Tiny had been working this case, at least doing background checks.

"Today's Saturday," I said curtly. "I don't know what she does on weekends."

"Oh, yeah," he smiled, "it is Saturday. With this job I never get a day off, so weekends makes no difference."

"Almost like a surgeon," I smiled, trying to lighten the conversation.

"If you see his wife, tell her I need to talk to her," he said without smiling.

Next he went through the dresser drawers. Holding up a lacy black bra, he turned back to me. "Slade have a girlfriend?"

"Nah—I don't really know."

"It's amazing," he remarked, eyeing me closely, "how we can work side-by-side with someone for years and never really know 'em."

"Yeah," I shrugged, "it is incredible."

Finally, the sheriff finished with the master bedroom and I showed him the rest of the cabin, the guest bedroom and the loft, then we finished back in the living room.

"Well, I guess I'll shove off—"

"—What's you hurry," Tiny cut me off. "Let's sit down," he nodded toward the couch, "I've got a few questions for you."

Silently, I groaned, but what choice did I have. Following the sheriff's lead, I sat down on the sofa, my arm resting on Ronnie's coat.

"So, where were you last night?"

I frowned. So, he really did consider me a suspect. "After ten, I was at home."

"All night?"

"Yes, all night," I barked.

"Can anyone corroborate that?"

Briefly, I though about telling him about Ronnie's visit, but still was reluctant to drag her into this mess. Was I being foolish? Probably. Was I letting my love/lust for her cloud my judgment? Probably.

"No, only Malachi."

"Malachi?"

"Malachi's my chocolate lab," I explained, then added, "no, I was home alone all night."

"What about before ten o'clock?"

I thought about it for a second. "Oh, I had dinner with Jacob and Sophie Heinz in St. George. You can check with them."

"I will."

"Am I a suspect?" I finally blurted.

"I just think it's curious that every time we have a murder, you're the one to discover it."

"I would use a different adjective than curious," I replied, "more like unnerving."

Sheriff Tiny Klein sighed out loud, then slapped his knees. "Well, I guess you can go, but it goes without saying, don't go on any long vacations until we've figured all this out."

Nodding, I got up to leave. Just as I reached for the doorknob, a crime scene technician hurried over to Tiny.

"Found this behind the wood box." He held up a single shell casing in a plastic baggie.

The sheriff accepted it, held the baggie up to a window, while rotating it in the light. "Good work," he said, handing it back to the technician.

From my vantage point it was impossible to say for sure, but it did look a lot like the other shells Katya and I had found on the ledge. The ones we'd already given the sheriff.

"You can compare it to the shells from the ledge," I volunteered, "and with the one found where Ziggy was murdered."

"Really," Tiny said sarcastically. "Gee, I never thought of that."

I turned back to the door. Right now what I didn't need was his sarcasm. Opening the door, I stepped over the threshold.

"Oh, by the way," the sheriff stopped me again, then paused a minute and silently eyed me for a couple of seconds. "I guess there's no good reason not to tell you this."

"Tell me what," I growled. I hated these cat-and-mouse detective games.

"Well," the sheriff continued, "we've already done ballistics on the casings from the ledge and compared them to the one found by Ziggy."

"And," I demanded.

"And some match, some don't. The gun that fired and expelled the shells on top, the one from the Overlook, was the same gun that fired the bullet that killed Ziggy."

"Oh," I said, trying to decide what that meant. "And what didn't match," I asked.

"The casings you and Katya found below the Overlook on the ledge. The ones you said Ian collected from the butchered deer."

That revelation did surprise me. I'd never suspected we were looking for more than one killer, one gunman. I had expected all casings would match, that they were all fired from the same gun.

"And," he continued, "the casings from Ziggy and the top of the Overlook were twenty-two bullets and the ones below the Overlook on the ledge were two-twenty-three bullets."

"Those are Bushmaster bullets," I blurted.

"Very good," Tiny said derisively, then added, "but the other two were fired from a twenty-two. Definitely not the same gun."

"But that doesn't necessarily mean it was not the same person," I quickly added. "Most people in Utah have more than one gun."

"I agree," the sheriff said, "but on the other hand, we now know something else is at work here."

"Huh?" I was not following him.

"Tim Slade is dead."

"Oh," I said, awkwardly.

He was right, of course. Maybe, I had been focusing too much Tim as the killer. Without comment, I turned back to the door.

"And," he stopped me one more time. "I got the DNA analysis back on that blood we found on top of the Overlook."

"Oh," I turned back. "Actually, it was Malachi that found it."

"Who?"

"My dog."

"Yeah, well anyway it was from your buddy, Ian McKenna."

I arched an eyebrow. "And none from Wally Stroud?"

"No," the sheriff shook his head, "only McKenna's."

Frowning, I thanked Tiny for sharing that information, then closed the door. So, what did that mean, only Ian's blood? The DNA analysis that Hank had done on the blood I'd found earlier, the day after the disappearances, showed both Ian and Wally's blood. Now, this sample from the Overlook showed only Ian's blood. What was the significance of that? I didn't know for sure, but I didn't like the implications either. But now with Tim's death, all my previous working theories were completely destroyed, in an instant summarily disproved. Tim was most likely not the murderer.

I sighed out loud and turned away. It looked like I was back to square zero.

Trying to make some sense of it all, I hurried back to the Dodge and Malachi. I still had things I wanted to accomplish before this day was over. First, I wanted to stop at the hospital and check on Katya Kozlovsky, then I wanted to track down Ronnie Slade and have a serious discussion with her. Finally, even though it was Saturday and even though I would probably have go to Hank Bettis' home, it was critical I find out the results of the second DNA test, the one from the blood Katya and I (actually it was Malachi once again) had found on the ledge below the Summit Overlook. Shoving the Dodge in gear, we started down the mountain.

Ninety-minutes later, I parked the pickup in the parking lot of Dixie Medical Center. Taking the stairs two at a time, I sprinted up to the second floor, then using my keycard, I swiped the electronic lock, opened the doors and entered the ICU.

She was gone!

Her room was empty. Had something terrible happened? Immediately, my anxiety ratcheted up several notches. As a surgeon, I know in the post op period several catastrophic events could happen. Had she suffered a pulmonary embolus, stroke or a post op M.I.?

At the nurses' station, I grabbed the nearest nurse and asked. She informed me, thank God, Katya was doing well. So well, in fact, they'd transferred her to s standard floor, 1-West. I thanked the nurse, then rushed down a flight of stairs to that floor.

As I walked into her room, Katya grinned when she saw me. No, it was more that just a grin, it was a smile, a radiant smile. Malachi excluded, I'd had no one look that happy to see me in a very long time.

I pulled up a chair and sat down at her bedside. Reaching over, she searched for my hand.

"So, how you feeling, Doctor Koslovsky?" I asked, engulfing her small hand in mine.

"Fine," she replied. "Actually, other that a little headache and a sore ankle, I feel good."

"I'm glad," I said. "I was worried."

She patted my hand. "What did my tests show?"

Quickly, I reviewed her CT scan, ankle X-rays and lab tests with her, then finished on a lighter note, "so, it looks like you're going to live."

"Thanks to you," she smiled again. "So, how's Ziggy?"

So much had happened since I last talked to Katya, I'd forgotten she didn't know about Ziggy. Should I tell her, or wait till she was recovered and out of the hospital? I really hated to destroy the closeness, the ambience I was feeling right now.

But, even hospitals have newspapers and televisions, and with two murders only one county away, more than likely it was headline news already. Certainly, I'd rather her hear it from me than read it in the newspaper, or hear it on the evening news. It was a small wonder she hadn't heard about it already.

"Well," I took a deep breath and paused. There was simply no good way to do this. "Well, I don't know how to tell you this, but—but he's dead!"

There was total silence.

"I'm so sorry," I added softly.

Katya was silent for another full minute. "The flu?"

"No," I shook my head, "he was murdered."

"Murdered!" She looked horrified. "How?"

There was no need to sugarcoat it now, I decided. She would find out anyway. "He was shot in the forehead."

"Oh, my God!" She again lapsed into silence, trying to digest it all. Finally she simply choked out, "why?"

"I'm not sure."

"Does it have anything to do with Ian's disappearance?"

"I'm not sure."

What the hell, I finally decided, give it all to her. "Tim Slade, he was on that deer hunt too. Anyway, he was also found murdered today up at Brian Head."

Katya suddenly looked worried, very worried. "So, what's going on, Coop?"

"I'm not sure."

"Well, what do you think?" she asked, bluntly. "And give it to me straight."

"Well, like I said I don't know for sure," I replied, "but there have been four recent murders, if you count Ian and Wally, and the only common threads I can think of is in someway they were all related to me and in someway were all associated with the deer hunt."

"No, not Ziggy."

"Yes, he was, but in a more roundabout way. He was down here with you checking on the disappearance of Ian."

"So, are we in danger?" Her dark eyes darted from me to the door, then the window.

"Maybe—I don't know."

"Then I need to get out of here," she concluded. "Here in the hospital I'm a sitting duck."

She was right. Of course, I could go to the St. George PD and ask them to put a guard on her, but would they? I had not been threatened and no real proof we were in danger, only a hunch, and furthermore none of this had happened in St. George. Perhaps, I could ask Iron County's Sheriff Klein to talk to his Washington County counterpart, but then again would he? It was doubtful, since I was high on his list of suspects and maybe the only one on his list. Protect me from me. That made no sense.

Slowly, I nodded my agreement; she was right. "Okay, but I've got a couple of other things to attend to this evening, then I'll come back and we'll bust you out of here."

"I'd feel better about that." She looked relieved.

Now, it was my turn to lapse into silence.

"Something bothering you?" Katya finally asked.

Nodding, I took another deep breath, then blurted, "Katya, for some time now I've had a feeling you were holding back, not telling me everything about your relationship with Ian."

She sighed out loud and nodded. "We were in the process of getting a divorce."

"I thought you told Hank Bettis in his office the other day you were already divorced."

"Well, we are mentally and emotionally, but it seems the paperwork takes forever."

"Why?" I asked, thinking of my previous divorces. Actually, all three were pretty civil, almost no bickering and all accomplished in a very short period of time.

"Mainly," Katya explained, "it was that we couldn't agree on how to divide our assets."

"Why?"

"I had a feeling Ian was holding out on me," she divulged. "We were married for eleven years and every year the books just didn't add up."

"Didn't add up?"

"At the end of the year, our income and expenditures just did not match, or even come close. I couldn't figure out where all the money was going. And it was not just his money that was missing. We had joint bank accounts."

"Maybe he was having an affair?"

"I'm sure he was, but we're talking about large sums of money here," she disclosed. "Not just date money."

"Do you think he was squirreling money away somewhere?"

"I'm sure of it, but I couldn't find it and neither could my lawyer."

"So--so why? What do you think was going on?"

"I think, but I can't prove it," Katya quickly added. "I think he was smuggling money into foreign banks and was planning on leaving the country."

Suddenly a thought occurred to me. "So, that's why you were suspicious when I first told you he was missing. Why you thought he was faking his own death."

She simply nodded.

Bewildered, I shook my head. Even though that made some sense, it nevertheless managed to confuse me even more. "But obviously you still care for him."

"Yes," she nodded, "we did have some good times together, some good years. They weren't all bad."

I just couldn't see it. I couldn't understand why any man who was married to the beautiful, intelligent Katya would feel the need to stray.

"I still don't understand," I finally blurted out. "He had you!"

Once again she was silent for a long moment, then sighed out loud.

"Well, you see, Coop, Ian was gay."

# 21

I was stunned!

For a long moment, I could think of nothing to say.

In retrospect, however, this should have come as no big surprise. Obviously, I knew Ian was a little effeminate, but—but being effeminate didn't always equate to being gay. Clearly, when it came to Ian I had on harness blinders, resulting in myopic tunnel vision. I wished he had told me; it would have made absolutely no difference in our friendship.

"So, you think he had a lover?" I finally asked.

"I'm sure of it."

"Who?"

"I don't really know," Katya replied, "but I think it was someone out of town."

"Why?"

"I guess it was a couple of things: all his mysterious business trips, which consistently seemed to last for two or three days longer than they should, and of course all his strange credit card purchases."

"So, I gather you don't think his lover was from Salt Lake City," I reasoned, "but did you ever figure out where he was from?"

"No," she shook her head, "I don't think they ever rendezvoused in his town, or Salt Lake City, but probably met at a some neutral location."

"How did you come to that conclusion?"

"There was no consistent pattern," she explained. "The credit card charges were all over the place. They never seemed to come from a single location."

"Maybe his lover was married too."

"Maybe," she shrugged. "He probably was."

"Anything else I should know." I looked at her closely to see if she was lying.

"No," she shook her head firmly. "That's it. Now you know everything."

"Everything?" I said doubtfully.

"Well," she laughed, "at least everything about Ian."

"What about you?" I smiled.

"That would take years," she smiled slyly, her dark gypsy eyes flashing.

I wanted to say, 'I hope I have years to find out,' but instead I stood up and said, "okay, sit tight for now and I'll be back."

"How long will it take?" Once again she looked worried.

"Not more than a couple of hours," I replied, turning for the door. "Probably not that long."

As I sprinted across the parking lot toward the Dodge, I was greeted by the glow of a rapidly aging sunset. I stopped to watch. Suddenly, that scene seemed to be a metaphor for me, and even Malachi. Already faded to a sangria purple, the thin carpet of clouds must have moments ago been a brilliant glowing pink. Now dipped well beneath the western horizon, the dying sun's rays would soon be totally extinguished. Soon the faded purple of dusk would blend into the blackness of night. So, it was with Malachi and me.

Still thinking of the sunset, I continued on toward the truck. Finally forcing my mind back to the present, it occurred to me it might be better for me check with Hank Bettis first before it got too late, then I would attempt to track down Ronnie Slade.

On the way to Hank's house, I took a moment to review what I had learned in the last few hours. Actually, quite a lot. More than I'd learned in the previous two months.

One, the big one, Tim Slade was murdered! Not only was that a huge shock, but it put a much different slant on everything. For example, that meant Tim probably was not the killer. Sure, he had machine-gunned down the regal buck, and that was reprehensible enough, but he probably didn't kill Ziggy, or Ian, or Wally. Why do I say that? Because the shell casings from Ziggy and Tim's murder were not from Tim's Bushmaster assault rifle, but rather from a twenty-two. Though that didn't completely exonerate Tim of Ziggy's murder, it certainly did not implicate him either, and in my mind made him a most unlikely candidate.

Two, the DNA tests from the blood sample taken from the top of the Overlook confirmed only Ian's DNA (blood) and none from Wally. What that meant, I wasn't entirely sure, but it might be very helpful to see what the DNA test showed on the second blood sample I'd given to Hank, the one Katya and I had obtained from the ledge below the Overlook. If that again showed only Ian's blood, then certainly I would have to look at that differently than if it showed both of their blood.

Three, tonight I'd learned Ian was gay and he had a lover, probably from out of town. And furthermore, Katya suspected he'd been stashing

266

away money in some foreign bank and was planning on leaving the country. Apparently he didn't make it, but it would be nice to retrieve that money for Katya and maybe critical to know whom his lover was.

That was a lot to absorb and digest, and right now I didn't have the time to thoroughly think it through or evaluate it logically as I was pulling up in front of Hank Bettis' house. After cracking a window, I again told Malachi to stay, then got out of the truck and hurried up the steps to the front door of Hank pueblo-style house.

Jenny Bettis, Hank's wife, answered the door. She was a small woman, no more than five foot-two inches tall, but she was surprisingly robust for her size. Her blue eyes sparkled with a glint of mischief. According to Hank, she spent most days gossiping or chatting on Facebook, discussing or disclosing some new turpitude or failing she'd discovered in her neighbors.

"Oh, Coop," she smiled brightly, "come in. It's been a long time."

"Too long," I agreed, trying to be amicable. "Is Hank in?"

"I haven't seen you since you brought, oh, I can't think of her name, to dinner."

"That would have been my wife, Claire," I said brusquely, not wanting to get in a long conversation.

"Oh, yes, Claire," Jenny forced a thin plastic smile. "What ever happened to her? She was such a dear. I haven't seen her around lately."

"We got divorced."

"Oh, I'm so sorry to hear that; she was such a sweet thing, and smart. You have such bad luck with women, Coop, don't you?"

"I'll admit my record is not great," I agreed, then added more forcefully, "Is Hank in?"

She ignored me again. "How many does that make for you, Coop?"

"How many what?"

"How many marriages?"

"Oh, three," I replied curtly, then for the third time I asked, "is Hank in, Jenny?"

"Hank? Oh, yes, he's in his den watching T.V."

"Would you tell him I'm here?"

"I'll show you to him."

Again employing her best faux smile, Jenny showed me into the Hank's den. As we walked down the hall, I couldn't help but think Hank probably spent as much time as possible holed up in his den just to get away from his annoying wife.

As soon as Hank saw me, he flipped off the T.V. and stood up. As opposed to Jenny, he sported a genuine grin. He pointed to the leather couch for me to sit, then fetched two beers from a nearby half-fridge.

"So, how you been, Coop?" he asked as he popped the tab on his beer.

"The usual," I said vaguely, deciding I did not want to take the time go through everything that had happened since I last saw him.

"You still with," he paused, "I can't remember her name. That Russian beauty?"

"Yes," I nodded, still not going into detail, "I'm not really with her, but she's still around. And though her name is Russian, she is very American."

"All-American!" Hank grinned lecherously, then added. "Man, what I wouldn't give to be single like you."

"It's not all it's cracked up to be."

"Neither is marriage," Hank nodded toward the door, his grin more doleful now.

"Well," I began, anxious to change the subject, "have you heard anything on that latest DNA test? The one labeled: *Below the Overlook*."

Hank nodded and took a sip of beer. "I tried to call you two or three times today on your cell phone, even left a text-message, but never heard from you."

"Oh," I said, pulling out my cell phone. Sure enough there were three messages from Hank Bettis, one from Sheriff Tiny Klein and the last one was from Ronnie Slade. "Oh," I said again, replacing the phone back in my pocket, "I've been out of cell phone range for most of the day. What did it show?"

"Come by my office tomorrow," Hank said with a straight face, "and I'll give you the report. Home time is for personal time, time for family and friends. I never mix business with pleasure."

"Oh, come on, Hank," I pleaded, "give me a break." Silently I added, 'if you only knew what kind of day I've had!'

"Okay," Hank's straight serious face was replaced by his usual affable grin. "I'll show pity on you this time, but only if you agree to come to dinner sometime."

I almost asked, 'does that include Jenny,' but instead I nodded my okay, then out loud said, "well—"

"—Well," Hank continued after on more sip of beer, "without the report, I can't give you the actual gene sequencing and the matching data,

268

but in a nutshell I can tell you the blood was from Ian McKenna."

"All of it?" I asked, subconsciously rotating the beer can in my hands. "And none of it from Wally Stroud?"

"No," Hank shook his head firmly, "none of it was from Stroud. It all belonged to McKenna."

I was silent for a minute, trying to think through the implications of that revelation.

"You seem surprised," Hank said, breaking the silence. "Not what you expected, huh?"

"No, it's not what I expected," I agreed. "I just assumed it would be like the first sample we ran, showing DNA for both of them."

"So, what does it mean?" Hank asked. "What's the significance of first finding DNA from both of them, then the second DNA from just one of them?"

"I'm not sure," I replied truthfully, taking a small sip of beer.

"Well anyway, I hope it helps," Hank grinned, "cause it sure is going to cost you a grundle of money."

"Yeah, I'll come by this week and give you a check." I set aside my mostly full can of beer. "Hank," I stood and checked my wristwatch, "I hate to be unsociable, but I've really got to go."

Hank winked. "The Volga queen is waiting, huh?"

I didn't even try to reject his romantic assumption. Loosely, it was true; she was waiting for me, but not in the way he thought.

"Thanks again, Hank," I said. "I owe you one a big one."

"Yeah, you do," he grinned. "Bring the Russian, uh I mean the American, cover girl and go out to dinner with Jenny and me sometime."

Nodding, I headed for the door, but privately I thought, 'I don't owe you that much!'

Back in the Dodge, and after Malachi welcomed me back, I pulled out my cell phone and listened to my messages. After skipping through Hank Bettis' text and voice messages, the next one I came to was from Sheriff Tiny Klein. It was a voice message:

*"Doctor Cooper, this is Sheriff Axel Klein. We've run matches on all the fingerprints we found in Tim Slade's rental cabin. There were a ton of yours, big surprise, but there were also a lot of Tim's wife, Ronnie Slade. We need to talk to her, but can't find her. She seems to have disappeared. We also know she works for you. Do you know where she is? Give me a call anytime, day or night."*

Considering how well we'd gotten to know each other over the past few weeks, I thought Tiny's message was strangely formal, addressing me as Dr. Cooper and identifying himself as Sheriff Axel Klein. I guess that meant I was still a suspect.

The next message, also a voice message, was from the very person the sheriff was looking for, Ronnie Slade. She sounded nervous, maybe even frightened.

*"C—Coop, this is Ronnie. I—I need to talk to as soon as possible. Don't go to my h—home, I'm not there. I—I'm at the La Quinta Motel on South Bluff Street, room three forty-one. M—make sure you're not followed."*

She sounded nervous, almost panicky, I thought as a put my cell phone away. At least now I knew where she was. That should save me a lot of time. I fired up the Dodge and started down the street.

Suddenly, the thought occurred to me, *'Ronnie really is a suspect in her husband's death!'* Not only is Sheriff Tiny Klein looking to interrogate her, but maybe even arrest her. Not just Sheriff Klein, but earlier at the cabin I had considered she might be a suspect as well. And also I had entertained the possibility, and still did, that she might be playing me for a fool.

Driving by instinct, I turned onto Bluff Street and headed south toward the freeway interchange. If I were totally honest with myself, I'd have to admit I really didn't know Ronnie Slade that well, or of what she was capable. But I did know I'd better be careful, damn careful around her.

Still trying to make sense of it all, I pulled into the La Quinta Motel and parked in the shadows, well away from the lobby, then realized I would have to go through the lobby to get to the third floor. This time of night all outside doors would be locked and I would need a cardkey to enter. After attaching a leash to Malachi's collar, I knew all La Quinta Motels were dog friendly, we got out of the pickup and headed for the lobby, stopping long enough for Malachi to relieve himself on a Japanese boxwood shrub. An overhead bell tinkled as we entered the lobby.

"May, I help you?" a young woman with frizzy red hair asked pleasantly from behind the check-in counter.

"I'm just here to see a friend," I said, reluctantly stopping.

"Which room?" She smiled, marked her page, then set down her leather-bound *Book of Mormon*.

"Huh? Oh," I pulled out my cell phone and quickly thumbed to and played Ronnie's message. "Uh, room three forty-one."

"She has requested no visitors without me checking with her first," the clerk said firmly.

"Well," I explained, "she's the one that gave me the room number."

"I still have to check."

"Well," I snapped, not at all trying to keep the irritation out of my voice, "then do it."

The clerk scowled at me for a moment, then picked the phoned and punched in the number. "A man's here to see you." She paused to listen, then turned to me. "Your name?"

"Coop," I said curtly.

"A Mister Coop," she said into the phone, listened for the answer, then hung up. "Through that door," she pointed, "then up the stairs to the third floor."

"Thank you," I said insincerely, then with Malachi leading, headed in the direction she'd pointed.

Hurriedly, we climbed the stairs, shuffled nearly halfway down the hall and stopped in front of room #341. There I hesitated for a moment, tying to gather my thoughts. I had no idea what to expect. It could be anything from spontaneous heartfelt embrace to a gun in my face.

At that thought, I checked to see if my Desert Eagle .45 was still in my back waistband; it was, thank God. I thought about pulling out, but then decided that might be a little over-dramatic. Briefly I was again hit with a pang of guilt, having to resort to guns again. I really would quit guns, I promised, but not right now. Taking a deep breath, I raised my fist and rapped on the door.

As Ronnie slowly opened the door, I held my breath with my right hand behind my back, resting on the .45. I was ready for anything. With the open doorknob still in her hand, she paused for only a second, then rushed to me, throwing her arms around my neck.

As I held her close, Malachi jumped up on her, wanting his share of affection. After a couple of seconds, she backed away, quickly pulled me and Malachi into the room, then shut and locked the door, including the safety lock. Once again, she pulled me close and I could feel her trembling under my arms.

As I embraced her, I looked over her shoulder and checked out the room. It was pretty much a standard motel suite with a bathroom, a kitchenette and two queen beds. On the far wall adjacent to the only window was a table/desk with two chairs, and in the opposite corner a small-overstuffed couch, actually more like a love seat. Centered above the beds was a mass-produced oil painting of a quaint Spanish plaza and at the foot of the beds was an armoire, housing a silent T.V.

I held her at arms length and eyed her closely. She looked worried, even terrified, and with her swollen red eyes it was obvious she had been crying. But in spite of her apparent state of anxiety, she took a moment hug to Malachi, who was still demanding attention, then she took my hand and guided me over to the closest bed. The instant we sat down on the bed's edge, she again grabbed and clung to me like a reformed sinner to the Rock of Salvation (an odd simile for a professed atheist).

To me, she did not look, or act, like someone who had just committed a horrific murder. Either I was a poor judge of character, which I admit I often was, and she was totally blameless in the death of her husband Tim Slade, or she was staging an Academy Award performance. But on the other hand, I had to remind myself, she did flee from the cabin, leaving her coat behind. Did someone that was totally innocent bolt from the scene of the crime? Why didn't she just call 911 and get the authorities?

"I'm so afraid, Coop," she whimpered, still clinging to me.

"Afraid of what?" I asked, making no attempt to disengage. Actually, it felt pretty good.

"I think someone is out to get me!"

"Get you?" I didn't expect that. "Why?"

"I don't know."

"Ronnie, you're making no sense."

She didn't immediately answer, but continued to cling to me and weep softly. This almost seemed to be some kind of an emotional catharsis. Something she had to do.

"Tim was murdered!" she finally blurted between sobs.

"I know," I replied, "I found him."

"You found him!" Ronnie pulled away, giving me a confused look.

"Remember, last night at my house you told me Tim wanted to meet with me this afternoon. We were going to try to figure out how to separate our practices." At that moment, I decided not to tell her about the fleece-lined jacked and that I knew she'd gone up to Tim's cabin after she'd left my place.

"Oh, yeah," she sniffled, "with all that's happened, I guess I'd forgotten." She paused for a minute, then blurted, "so, the police know?"

"Yeah," I nodded, "and they want to talk to you."

272

"To me?" Now her voice was trembling. "W—why me?"

"I don't know," I fibbed. "I think anytime a married person is murdered, they want to talk to the spouse. It's protocol."

"Am I a suspect?" She looked physically ill.

"Like I said, until the murderer is caught, the spouse is always a suspect." I paused, saw her blanche, took pity on her and added, "but so am I."

"You are?" She managed to look both puzzled and worried.

"Yeah," I nodded. "I found the body, and apparently my ongoing feud with Tim was well-known to Sheriff Klein."

"Are they going to arrest you?"

"Not yet," I replied, then added with more confidence than I felt, "they really don't have enough evidence to arrest me."

Clinging to me once again, Ronnie was quiet for a long moment. I suspect she was trying to collate and make sense of all this.

"So," I finally continued, breaking the silence, "I suppose we should call the sheriff. I promised him I'd call if I saw you." I fumbled to retrieve my cell phone.

"No!" she grabbed my phone. "You don't understand."

"No, I guess I don't." I took my phone back. "Why don't you tell me?"

She hesitated for another long moment, then blurted, "I was up at Brian Head!"

I acted surprised. "You were? When?"

She hesitated again. "Last night, after I left your place."

"I don't understand," I said, and I didn't. "Why?"

"Uh, I—I," she stuttered, apparently searching for the right words, "uh, I—I had to let Tim know you were planning to come up there to meet him."

"You didn't need to drive seventy miles in the middle of the night to do that," I broke free of her embrace and slid a few inches away, "that's what telephones are for."

"But—but," she stammered, still trying to come up with a reasonable explanation.

"Come on, Ronnie," I said coldly, "cut the crap! For once be honest with me."

She eyed me closely, then sighed out loud. "Things were not as terrible with Tim and me as I'd led you to believe."

"Go on," I snapped.

"But t—that doesn't mean I don't care for you."

I ignored her. "So, why did you go to the cabin?"

273

"Well," she looked away and mumbled, "when Tim goes on ski vacation, I usually go with him." She paused again, then added as apparent justification, "I love to ski."

"So, you were staying at the cabin?"

She nodded, still without looking at me.

"So, that means," I couldn't keep the disgust out of my voice, "you were going to make love to me that night, then head straight up the mountain and do the same with Tim?"

"No," she sobbed, "that didn't happen."

"Obviously," I growled, "but it might have."

"No," she vigorously shook her head, "I would never let it go that far."

I took a second to absorb Ronnie's confession. My mind was whirling. I couldn't decide rather to be repulsed, relieved or offended.

"So," I said, slowly meting out my words, "it appears you've been playing me for a fool."

"No! No I wasn't," she continued to sob, "I love you!"

"But you also loved Tim."

"Yes," she conceded, "you can love more than one person at a time."

A thought suddenly occurred to me. "So, Tim had affairs too?"

She nodded.

"And you knew about them?"

Again she nodded, but remained silent.

"And you were okay with that?"

Still she said nothing.

"And you've had affairs, other than me?" I asked, though I really didn't want to know. Actually, I wouldn't classify me as an affair, but more of a flirt.

Ronnie shrugged, which I took to mean yes.

"So," I took it one step further, "you and Tim were swingers?"

"No," she finally spoke, "not so much swingers as we had an open marriage."

Now we were both silent. While the physical distance between us remained the same, less than a foot, the emotional gap between us widened exponentially.

She broke the silence by scooting over that eleven inches and embracing me again. This time I didn't reciprocate. "But I'm ready for a change. Now I really want a serious monogamous relationship. I want you Coop."

At first I said nothing, but did not try to disengage either. Finally I pushed her away. "Did you spy on me for Tim? Did you report my comings and goings to him?"

She nodded. "But it was a two-way street. I told you about him too."

"Uh-huh," I said, "but I just don't get it." I looked at her closely. "To me, this seems more than just sadness of Tim's death. You seem frightened, you're trembling!"

"I—I saw him."

"Who?"

"The killer. I'd just got out of the shower."

"Who was it?"

"I didn't see his face."

"But he saw you?"

She nodded.

"So, why didn't he kill you?"

"I ran and at the moment three or four snowmobiles roared up the cul-de-sac and stopped. I jerked open a door and screamed. The guy must have gotten spooked and left."

"Who was on the snowmobiles?" I asked, suspicious of her story. I remembered there were no neighboring cabins.

"Just some midnight partiers. Probably kids. They were drunk. They thought I was crazy."

"And since you're a witness, you think the murderer will come after you?"

"Yes," she nodded. "I don't think he knows I can't really identify him."

So, far she was making some sense. "Okay," I nodded, "I get that, but why don't you want to talk to Sheriff Klein?"

She hesitated, then instead of answering she reached for her purse. Opening it, she fished around, eventually producing a handgun!

My heart started pounding. Was this it? Was she going to kill me?

Reflexively, I reached behind me for my Desert Eagle, but simultaneously she flipped her gun around and handed it to me butt-end first.

I relaxed my hand and accepted her gun. Rotating it in my hands, I looked at it from every angle. It was a hot pink Walther P-22. At no more than six inches long, it weighed less than a pound and sported a ten-round magazine. In other words, it was a .22 caliber woman's handgun. The very same caliber that had killed Ziggy and her late husband Tim!

"So," I deduced, "you're afraid the sheriff will find out you have a handgun?" Though I'd figured that much out, I was still confused.

"Yes. You see, in the past Tim and I have had some very public fights. He was even arrested once for getting too physical with me."

At least that part was true; I'd seen it. "And still you stayed with him?"

"What can I say," she smiled ruefully, "sometimes I like it rough."

"Well," I snapped, "if that gun is registered, they're going to find out you have it anyway. Is it?"

"Is it what?"

"Is it registered?" I was beginning to lose patience with her.

"Yes," she nodded, "I think so. It was a gift."

"Well, if you're telling the truth, then they can clear you of the murder in about a day. There is such a thing as ballistics, you know, forensic science."

"Huh?" She looked puzzled.

I sighed and had to remind myself that after all she was a blonde. Then I took a moment to explain to her about ballistics, that the sheriff had collected spent shells from both crime scenes and they could easily tell if her gun had fired those shells.

Ronnie looked so relieved I almost decided to believe her. Either she had no idea the sheriff had shells from both crime scenes for comparison, or she really did not have an understanding of ballistics, or both.

"So," I finally said, "shall we call the sheriff?"

She let out a sob, probably of relief, then nodded her assent.

After again fishing my smart phone from my pants pocket, I touched in the number. When he answered, I told him, without going into the particulars, I had found Ronnie Slade. He sighed tiredly, then told me he was still up at Brian Head working the crime scene. When done there, he still had to chase down a couple of leads, so he more than likely would be staying the night up there. He paused for moment to think, then said, "why don't I meet you two at the Brian Head Town Marshall's office tomorrow at nine o'clock sharp."

I lobbied for ten, and he reluctantly agreed.

After turning off my cell phone, I stood up. "Ronnie, I 've got to go. You stay right here tonight and I'll be back tomorrow at seven-thirty."

"You're going?" Again she looked like she might cry. "You can stay right here." For emphasis she tapped the bed we were sitting on. "And Malachi can have the other bed."

"No," I shook my head. "I don't think that's a good idea." Silently I added, 'and I'm not exactly feeling romantic toward you right now.'

It was as if she read my mind. "Okay, then you can sleep in the other bed with Malachi."

"No," I shook my head again, thinking of Katya waiting in the hospital, "I still have things I've got to do tonight."

"B—but what about the murderer," she stammered, "he's still out there."

"Lock your doors and don't answer the phone unless it's me."

"But," she shivered, "w—what if he comes here? W—what if he finds me?"

"If anything at all suspicious happens, call nine-one-one first, then call me," I instructed her, then added, hopefully sounding more convinced than I was, "and anyway, the murderer is still up on the mountain."

"I—I hope so," she said, latching on to me again.

After a moment, I managed to disengage from her, then gave back her pink Walther.

"And," I reassured her, "and you have your gun. You'll be alright."

She still looked nervous.

"You do know how to use it don't you?"

She nodded. "Tim gave me lessons and even took me to the gun range a few times."

"Good." I gave her a quick hug, then grabbed Malachi's leash and turned to leave.

"Wait!" she blurted. "There's something else, something I haven't told you."

"What?" I growled, trying to, but not succeeding in hiding my annoyance. I thought she'd told me plenty already.

"T—that night, right before he died," she mumbled, "right before I went to shower, Tim told me something, something else—"

"—Well?" I growled impatiently.

"I know this sounds strange," she admitted, "but Tim thought--no he was convinced--that Ian and Wally are still alive!"

# 22

"Alive? Why?" I asked, my voice heavy with skepticism.

"Why what?"

"Why did he think they are alive?"

"Really two, no three reasons," Ronnie replied. "One, he swears he didn't murder them. Two, he can't find anyone else with a motive. And three, he's pretty sure he's seen them since their disappearance."

"Pretty sure?" I still was not convinced.

"Well, he wasn't one hundred percent sure."

"Where?"

"Where what?"

I gritted my teeth. "Where did he see them?"

"I think somewhere up around Brian Head," she shrugged.

"Where specifically?"

"He didn't say, but he spent a good bit of time up there looking for them. Even rented a snowmobile one day.

At least that part rang true. I'd already figured out he'd rented a snowmobile from Abe Eisemann.

"Why? Why would he go to all that trouble?" I asked, before I'd thought it through. If I had, her answer would have been obvious.

"I guess," she replied, "he was trying to prove his innocence."

"Anything else?" I asked.

"No," she shook her head, "now you know everything."

Once again I gave her a quick hug of encouragement, said goodbye, then Malachi and I left her room and returned to the Dodge. On the way back to the hospital, I mulled over all of what she had just told me.

Before Tim's death, I never would have believed her story, but now he was dead it seemed possible, even plausible. Were Ian and Wally really still alive? Certainly, we had not been able to find any bodies, and it hadn't been from lack of trying. Of course, we had attributed the lack of bodies to the rugged terrain and the difficult winter conditions, and fully expected to find them after the spring thaw, after the snow had melted.

Moreover, this new revelation also added some new traction to Katya's story. Was this whole disappearance fiasco staged like she'd suspected? Was

Ian really trying to disappear to some foreign country where he'd stashed a small fortune? If so, why was he still here? And was he in someway associated with the murders of Ziggy and Tim? If so, why?

In the dark, I pondered this, then silently shook my head. I had a hard time believing that last part. Ian just did not strike me as a killer. Unless he was scamming me, I didn't think he even knew how to use a gun, let alone put two bullets dead center in Tim and Ziggy's forehead; that was some pretty damn good shooting. But on the other hand, how well did I really know him? Honestly, I did not know him well at all! Sure we'd been college roommates, but I hadn't seen him in twenty years until recently and even that had been for less than two days. Were those two days long enough to make an accurate appraisal of his character? Probably not, but nevertheless I still could not picture Ian McKenna putting a gun to someone's forehead and pulling the trigger. Try as I might, I could not see him as a cold-blooded killer.

Lastly, I considered the possibility that Ronnie and Katya were also targets. If Ronnie really had seen Tim's killer, then it was entirely possible, even probable she was at risk. With Katya the risk was not so obvious, but certainly with Ziggy's murder, and her relationship to him and Ian, I could not fully discount the possibility. Also, that day at the Summit Overlook, when Katya and I were stranded on the ledge, someone had disabled our snowmobiles. Certainly that would qualify as attempted murder. So, obviously someone was out to get her, or me.

And what about me? Not even taking into account the disabled snowmobiles, someone had tried to kill me on Dry Lakes Road, and probably would have succeeded if Telly Telford and Bella had not shown up. So possibly there had been two attempts on my life. My head hurt from trying to figure it all out. Why? With my determined and dogged investigation, was I getting to close to figuring it out? Is that why I had two attempts on my life?

Somehow I ended back at the hospital parking lot. I must have driven twenty or so blocks instinctively, as I don't remember making any turns or stopping for a single red light. That always gave me an eerie feeling. I fully expected to hear the wail of a siren and see the flashing strobe lights of a police cruiser pull up behind me, but thankfully there were none.

Once again, I cracked a window, instructed Malachi to stay, then hurried toward the hospital. Eschewing the elevator, I scrambled up the stairs to Katya's room. I almost never took the elevator, as that invariably meant running into patients, which meant questions. Then while I danced around their personal health questions, I tried to figure out exactly to whom I was talking. My memory was good, but not that good. I simply could not remember the details of the health histories of a couple of thousand people. That's what computers were for.

Also, I shunned the nurse's station and hurried straight to Katya's room. Cracking open her door a couple of inches, I peeked in.

She was alone and I was relieved to see she was all right!

The lights were dimmed and she was in bed, though she did not appear to be asleep. With her head turned toward the shadeless window, she seemed to be staring out at the black night. I couldn't help but notice, even under these circumstances, with hair mussed and no makeup, she was still incredibly beautiful. In my opinion, maybe even more so than when she was made-up.

Rapidly, I did hallway medical assessment. She had an I.V. running, probably for antibiotics and maybe pain meds, and her fiberglass-casted right foot protruded from underneath the hospital blanket. Also, she had wire leads exiting from under her hospital gown, traveling directly to an overhead oscilloscope, which displayed continuous EKG, blood pressure and pulse data. On her right index finger a pulse oximeter was clipped, but fortunately there was no sign of a Foley catheter or drainage bag hanging from the bed rail. And that was it, I could see no other lines or tubes.

Taking one last look, I rapped lightly on her door.

"Come in," she said nervously.

Opening and closing the door behind me, I entered.

"Oh," she sounded relieved, "it's you, Coop!"

"Are you okay?" I asked. When she nodded, I added, "you ready to go?"

"Are we going to tell them or just leave AMA (against medical advice)?"

"AMA," I confirmed. "I don't want to attract any attention and I doubt that they are ready to release you."

Nodding, she immediately began removing her I.V. First, she ripped the tape from her wrist, then extracted the plastic angiocath, instantly placing her thumb over the puncture site to prevent significant back-bleeding.

"Can you find a Band-Aid or some tape?" she asked.

Searching the bedside console, I found a 2x2 gauze pad and some paper tape, then applied both to the puncture site.

"Did they give you a walker or some crutches?" I asked, when finished.

She nodded. "There are crutches in that closet."

I retrieved a set of aluminum crutches from the closet and set them at her bedside. "You sure you can do this?"

She nodded determinedly, then using the electronic remote control, raised the back of her bed up to the full sitting position. After throwing back the covers, she grunted as she used her hands to help swing her casted leg over the side of the bed, then without a moment's hesitation she jerked the leads off her chest and unclipped the pulse oximeter.

Instantly, I spotted a problem. She was still wearing a rear-tie hospital gown. She couldn't leave the hospital like that.

"Where's your street clothes?"

"They should be in the same closet as the crutches."

I checked again. "They're not here."

Katya frowned. "How about the bottom drawer of the nightstand?"

I pulled open the bottom drawer of the nightstand and found and removed her street clothes. They were the same ones she had on when we'd left St. George. The very same day she and Ziggy ambushed me in my waiting room, and had fought with Ronnie, right before we headed up to Brian Head. Smiling ruefully, I thought about how much had changed since then. It had been less than a week, but it seemed like decades ago.

"How do you want to do this?" I held up her red cargo shirt and designer jeans.

"Isn't there a bra in there?" she asked, ignoring my question.

After searching again, I came up with a lacy black brassiere and handed it to her.

"Do you mind?" she said, motioned for me to turn around. I complied and after a moment, she added, "okay."

Turning back around, I gasped. She was sitting before me with nothing on, but a black bra and black panties. This was cruel and unusual punishment for someone like me. Someone who had been single for over five years!

"I'm going to need some help with the rest of it," she admitted.

Trying to control my breathing and with my hands shaking, I helped her don the red cargo shirt, but the designer jeans were a problem. There was simply no way to fit them over the cast. Finally, I gave up and used a pair of bandage scissors to slit the pant leg up to about the knee, then she easily slipped into them. The jeans fit too easily, I suspected. Conservatively, I estimated she'd lost eight to ten pounds in the last week. Next, I put a sock and hiking boot on her left foot, then I managed to stretch the other sock over her casted foot. Lastly, I placed the spare right boot in a plastic garbage bag to make it easier to carry and helped her put on her winter coat.

Again I asked, "You ready to go?"

Nodding, she grabbed her crutches and immediately started hobbling toward the door. She opened it and shuffled out into the hall.

Against my better judgment, I decided in Katya's condition it would be better to use the elevator. I pushed the button and we waited. Fortunately, when the cab arrived, it was empty. We hobbled on board, then just as I pressed the down button a man blocked the closing door with his out-stretched hand and hurried on board.

Not wanting to engage in conversation, Katya and I looked straight ahead, focusing on the closing door.

"Doctor Cooper!" the man beamed. "Is that you?"

Inwardly, I groaned and turned to look at him. Immediately, I recognized the face, indeed he was a patient, but on the spur of the moment I could not come up with his name or his medical history.

"Hi," I finally said, "how are you?"

"Looks like your wife had an accident?" He smiled and nodded at Katya's foot.

"Yeah," I replied, purposefully keeping my answers short, "a ski accident."

"That's too bad," he laughed, "I guess we're not kids anymore."

I smiled and nodded my agreement.

"Anyway, I'm glad I caught you."

I gritted my teeth.

"I think I might be allergic to that medicine you gave me."

Of course I drew a blank. "What medicine?"

He looked at me oddly. "You mean you don't know?"

I shrugged and forced a smile. "Without my peripheral brain, my office medical records, I'm afraid I don't remember. Why don't you tell me?"

"I don't know," he sulked, "it started with a 'C', or something."

Fortunately, we'd arrived at the ground floor and the elevator doors opened.

"I'll tell you what," I said as we exited the elevator cab, "call the office tomorrow and tell my nurse which medicine. I'll review it and get back to you. But for now stop it."

I said a firm good-bye, then helped Katya out of the hospital and into the Dodge. The second Malachi saw her he was overcome with joy and smothered her with kisses. Feeling a sharp pang of jealousy, I watched her eagerly hug him back. Sometimes, I thought, I would gladly trade places with Malachi.

Still envying Malachi, I fired up the Dodge, put it in reverse, then was hit with a pang of conscience. For some reason, at that moment I thought of Ronnie, huddled in her motel room, frightened out of her mind and sitting on her bed with the pink Walther pointed at the door. Sure we were all potential targets, but right now she seemed to be the one most at risk. And she was the only one that was alone. Though she couldn't identify him, she had seen the murderer! Could I in good conscience leave her there by herself all night?

Pushing the gearshift back in park, I turned to Katya and sighed deeply. "There's something I need to tell you."

"Okay," she replied, eyeing me closely.

I paused for a second, then blurted, "I'm worried about Ronnie."

"Who?"

"Ronnie Slade."

By her frown, I could tell Katya had made the connection.

"You mean your receptionist," she said curtly, unable to totally keep the venom from her voice.

"She was also Tim Slade's wife."

"You mean the guy that was murdered?"

"Yes," I nodded, "and unfortunately she saw the murderer."

Katya was silent for a moment, obviously trying to comprehend. "So, you think she's in danger?"

I nodded.

"What do you want to do?"

"She's frightened out of her mind," I explained. "Do you mind if we stay with her tonight?"

"Do I mind might be the wrong question." Katya also sighed out loud, then nodded. "But I know what it's like to be frightened and alone. Let's do what we have to do."

Instead of thanking her, I gave her hand a grateful squeeze, then picked up my cellphone. Rapidly, I thumbed through my directory until I came to Ronnie's name, then pressed on the touch screen.

The phone rang six times, then routed me to voicemail. What did I expect? After all, I had given her strict instructions not to answer the phone.

"Ronnie," I said into the phone, "it's me. I'm going to hang up and call again. This time answer me."

I called again, this time she answered on the first ring. "Coop?" she almost sounded both relieved and hysterical, "is that you?"

"Yeah," I replied, "are you all right?"

"N—no, not really."

"Have you had any visitors?"

"N—no, b-but I keep hearing someone outside."

"You're on the third floor," I said doubtfully.

"S-so?"

"Nothing. Ronnie, I've got a proposition for you."

"O-okay."

"I'll come over and spend the night with you on one condition."

"W—what?" She suddenly sounded suspicious.

"That Katya and Malachi come with me."

"Katya?"

"Katya Koslovsky. You met her that day in the office."

She was silent for a full five seconds, then finally blurted, "the Russian bitch?"

I was glad Katya could hear. "Well, I guess that depends on your point of view, but yes."

"You won't come without her?"

"Look Ronnie," I said impatiently, "she's just as much a target as you."

Again she was silent for a second. "O—okay, just come!"

As I turned off my phone and replaced it my pocket, Katya said dryly, "Doesn't sound like she was too thrilled about Malachi coming over."

"Huh?" I glanced sharply at her.

She grinned and grabbed my hand. "Come on, let's go."

On the way to the motel, I decided that was a first; Katya did indeed have a sense of humor.

Ten minutes later we arrived at the La Quinta Motel. After parking the Dodge, I put Malachi on a leash, and the three of us headed for the front door. Hoping to avoid the night clerk, I opened the door for Katya and we hurried across the lobby as fast as her crutches would allow. We'd just reached the hallway, when the she looked up from her *Book of Mormon* and spied us.

"May I help you?" she said loudly.

"No thank you," I replied, turning around again. "We are just going back up to see three forty-one."

"Is she expecting you?" the clerk asked, sweeping an unruly lock of frizzy hair out of her eyes.

"Yes," I nodded my head. "Call her if you like."

She ignored my suggestion, looked at her wristwatch and asked bluntly, "at this hour?"

"Yes," I replied firmly, "at this hour."

She looked from me, to Katya, then back at me. I could almost read her thoughts. I almost expected she was going to start in with a morality lecture.

"Are you planning on spending the night?" she asked almost contemptuously.

"This is not a *ménage a trios*," I snapped.

She ignored me and repeated, "are you planning on spending the night?"

Gritting my teeth, I nodded to the affirmative.

"Miss Slade only paid for one guest," she said coldly. "For two more guests," she paused to look at her computer, "that will be another fifty dollars plus tax."

I started to argue, but somehow managed to hold my tongue.

As I pulled out my wallet, she added, "and a twenty-five dollar deposit for the dog."

Scowling instead of answering, I gave her a credit card. After signing the receipt, I returned it to her and put the card back to my totally empty wallet. I really needed to get back to work.

With her pink Walther in hand, Ronnie opened the door on my first knock. Even though she looked haggard and distraught, she still managed to glare at Katya and give Malachi and me a welcoming hug, pausing to cling to me. Somewhat embarrassed, I managed to disengage, usher in Katya and Malachi, then closed the door.

"Are you okay, Ronnie?" I asked, doing my usual visual assessment. Physically she looked okay; mentally I was not so sure.

She nodded, the Walther still wavering in her hand. "Y—yes, but I'm still hearing those sounds outside."

"Probably the wind," I said, taking the Walther from her, then added, "you already know Katya."

Ronnie tersely nodded, but offered no greeting. An awkward silence followed.

"Well," I finally said, "it's late and we've got a big day tomorrow. Let's try to get some sleep."

"How do you want to do this?" Katya finally joined the conversation.

"Do what?" I asked blankly.

"The sleeping arrangements," Katya replied with a tight smile.

Yes, I thought, how indeed. "Well, since it's Ronnie's room," I said, " she should have one bed and since you have a bad ankle, you should have the other."

"Where are you going to sleep?" Katya asked.

"He can sleep with me," Ronnie blurted.

Both ladies looked at me, waiting for my decision. This was kind of a Sophie's Choice, though certainly not with the same devastating consequences. I looked at both women. Any man would be happy to share a bed with either of them and certainly I was no exception. Was God toying with me again? For a man who had been single for five years to suddenly be presented with two beautiful women did indeed seem like the work of a sadistic god, or at the very least a cruel twist of fate.

I sighed out loud. "I'll take the couch."

Both women shrugged and each seemed satisfied that I had not chosen the other. Katya hobbled over to the far bed and I helped her turn back the cover and get in. Ronnie managed the same feat without me. After saying a general goodnight, I turned off the lights and sat down on the overstuffed couch.

In the faint light, I watched Malachi. He was used to sleeping on a bed, usually mine, but there was not enough room for me, let alone him, on the couch. I was curious to see which of the girls he would choose. I guess like me, he did not want to offend and was not ready to choose. To my great satisfaction, the previously traitorous dog picked me, curling up on the carpeted floor beside the small couch.

The couch, however, was never meant to be a bed. If I stretched out supine, my feet hung out over the one arm and my head and neck draped and kinked up against the other. My only other option was to ball up in the fetal position, which eventually made my back muscles go into spasm. Eventually, I decided it was my fate, my mission was to stand guard for the night.

I passed the night by sitting on the couch, watching the door, occasionally getting up to peer out the window and listening to the others softly snore. Even though it was an incredibly long night, thank God it passed without incident.

When morning arrived, I left the girls to get breakfast, hoping they would not kill each other while I was gone. At the closest fast food restaurant

I ordered four breakfast sandwiches and three coffees (Malachi did not drink coffee), then returned to the motel. The girls, though still not behaving like sisters, or maybe they were, seemed to have managed to share the bathroom and get ready for the day.

With very little conversation, we ate our breakfast sandwiches, drank our coffee and got ready to leave. I'd already decided that all three of us would go up to Brian Head. I hated to leave Katya alone for the day and I thought Sheriff Klein might profit from her perspective, might benefit from what she had to say. So far she'd been right on almost everything.

After breakfast we all headed out to the Dodge. Before I closed the room door, I reminded Ronnie to bring her gun. At the pickup another tense moment occurred as we tried to figure out seating arrangements. Even though the truck had a bench seat, it was not meant to accommodate three adults and a large chocolate lab. I immediately climbed into the driver's seat, deciding to let them sort things out. After some hesitation, some shuffling and some shoving, Ronnie ended up next to me, Katya took the window seat and Malachi seemed happy enough to sprawl across both of their laps. Lucky dog!

Almost immediately on leaving St. George, I noticed a white Ford Explorer settle in the lane behind us. At first I didn't think anything of it, but it was still in the same position when we passed Leeds and Kanarraville. At Cedar City, I pulled off on the freeway shoulder, let the SUV pass, then stomped on the accelerator and coaxed the Dodge in behind it. I breathed a sigh of relief when I noted it had rental plates. Undoubtedly it was a skier who flew into St. George, rented a car and was now on their way to the resort at Brian Head. To confirm this, I followed the Ford, at a safe distance, all the way up the mountain to Brian Head, then saw it turn off at Giant Steps (ski resort) parking lot.

With all that maneuvering, it took us an hour and forty-five minutes to get from St. George to Brian Head. We arrived at the Town Marshal's office at precisely 10:14 a.m., almost fifteen minutes late. A deputy/receptionist showed us back to the conference room and to an impatient Sheriff Axel 'Tiny' Klein.

"You're late!" the sheriff barked as we walked into the room.

I shrugged and offered as way of explanation, "one man, two women and one bathroom."

"Huh?" he looked baffled. "Coop, sometimes I just don't follow you."

I shrugged and smiled. At, least I was again Coop and not Doctor

Cooper. Maybe that meant I had once again had been demoted from suspect back to a person of interest.

"You remember Katya, Ian's wife, don't you?" I said.

Tiny smiled broadly and stood to shake her hand. "Of course I do. It's good to see you again Missus McKenna."

"Call me Katya, please." She smiled radiantly as she shook his hand.

"What happened to your ankle?" He nodded at her casted foot.

"I injured it the over at the Overlook."

"Oh, yeah," Tiny nodded. "Coop told me about that."

"And," I continued my introduction, "this is Ronnie Slade, Tim's—uh—Tim's widow."

"Call me, Ronnie," she said, employing an appropriate grieving half-smile.

The sheriff took her hand. "I'm so sorry about your husband."

"Me too," Ronnie replied, the smile quickly disappearing from her face.

"Well," Tiny said, finally taking his eyes off Ronnie, "why don't we all sit down. I have a few questions—"

"—Before we get into that," I interrupted, "Ronnie has something she wants to give you."

"Huh?" she looked at me blankly.

"The Walther," I nodded at her purse.

"The what?"

"The gun, the one in your purse."

"Oh," she exclaimed, smiling inanely. She fished her gun out of her purse and handed it to the sheriff.

"What's this?" Tiny stared at it for a moment, then grabbed a pencil, speared it through the trigger guard, transferring the pink Walther to the desk in front him.

"It's my gun," Ronnie said.

"So," the sheriff said. "I assume you have a concealed-carry permit."

"Sheriff," I jumped in, "if you'll notice, it is a twenty-two caliber, the same caliber that killed Tim Slade."

"And Mister Ziegfeld," Sheriff Klein added, then turned Ronnie. "I guess this is your way of telling me you didn't do it."

Ronnie nodded nervously.

"Well, nevertheless," he said, "we'll have to do ballistics on it." Tiny got up, found an evidence bag, carefully placed the gun in the bag, then sat down again. "So, Missus Slade—"

"—Please," she cut him off, "call me, Ronnie." She was smiling again.

"Okay, Ronnie," Sheriff Klein was suddenly all business, "give me your version, the whole story of what happened. Start with the day of the murder, and finish with today."

For the next thirty minutes, Ronnie supplied the details. Sheriff Klein frequently interrupted her with probing or clarifying questions. To her credit, Ronnie did not vary her story in the least from the version she'd told me last night in the motel and at my prompting she also told the sheriff that Tim was convinced Ian and Wally were still alive.

"Okay," Klein finally said, "we'll check out your story." He turned to me, "anything else?"

"Yeah," I nodded. "Katya also thinks Ian is alive." I turned to her. "Katya, why don't you tell the sheriff what you told me last night?"

For the next ten minutes, Katya told Sheriff Klein about her rocky and recently estranged relationship with Ian, and her theory of his disappearance.

"Well," Klein said thoughtfully, "you two surely have given me a lot to think about." He stood up. "And believe me we will check it all out."

"So, that's it?" I said, also standing.

"Yeah," Tiny nodded, "for now. But I don't want any of you taking long vacations."

"What about some protection," I asked. "These girls could be targets!"

"Well," Klein said doubtfully, "I don't know if the investigation has progressed far enough to warrant that. I haven't even checked out their stories."

"So, you're going to do nothing?" I asked, dumbfounded.

The sheriff hesitated for a moment. "You heading back to Washington County?"

I nodded.

"I can't promise you nothin'," he said, "but I will call Sheriff Beatty down there and see what he can do. Check with him when you get back to St. George."

With me feeling less than satisfied, we left the Town Marshall's Office and rejoined Malachi at the pickup. Again there was another brief round of musical chairs, but this time Katya ended up sitting next to me. Ronnie took the passenger window and Malachi was more than happy to again stretch across their laps. Firing up the Dodge, I started out of the parking lot.

Ronnie broke the silence. "Are you in a hurry to get back to St. George?"

"No, not really," I answered. "Why?"

"It's just I think the murderer is probably waiting for us in St. George."

"So?"

"So, I'm not in any hurry to get back to St. George."

"Me, either," Katya added. "What will we do when we get back? Hide out again in a motel room and wait for the murderer?"

Well, that may, or may not be the case, I thought. The murderer could be anywhere, not necessarily in St. George, but it wouldn't hurt to give Sheriff Klein a little time to set something up with Sheriff Beatty.

"Have you ever seen Cedar Breaks," I asked, then added. "This time of year they close the road, but it's just a short hike to the first observation point overlooking Labyrinth Canyon."

It was probably the only thing they'd agreed on all day, but both girls insisted they wanted to go. Neither had seen Cedar Breaks. After leaving the parking lot, instead of heading north to Parowan and I-15, I headed south on Highway 143 toward Panguitch and Cedar Breaks.

The road climbed sharply toward Brian Head peak, leveling off at approximately eleven thousand feet. We continued on across a relatively flat snowy meadow for another mile, then turned off onto Highway 148 toward Cedar Breaks. In another two hundred yards, the highway abruptly ended, blocked by a huge mound of snow. In the winter, UDOT (Utah Department of Transportation) only plowed the road this far, thus effectively closing the road. From this point we would have to hike another hundred yards to the observation point.

Not too surprising for this time of year and considering the road was closed, there were no other vehicles. We would be afforded something that was never possible in the busy summer tourist season. We would have solitude; we would have Cedar Breaks to ourselves.

I parked the truck in front of the huge snow mound, then we all scrambled out of the truck, trudging through the snow to the observation point. Fortunately, here, close to the precipice, the wind had blown most of the snow away, making the trek relatively easy, even for Katya on her crutches.

From the observation point, the rugged terrain dropped off precipitously, at least a thousand feet. This cliff edge, known as Cedar Breaks, was in the shape of a vast natural amphitheater, roughly three miles wide.

But the view was unparalleled! Indeed, it was a magical enchanted winter scene. Wind, rain and frost had carved into the rather soft Clarion

Formation of salmon pink sandstone, creating a fairyland collection of eroded freestanding columns, thin ribbony canyon walls and knobby-layered hoodoos, which looked a lot like Nature's totem poles. A pillowy mantle of white snow added contrast to all these incredible crimson pink sandstone features.

At the observation point, the National Park Service had strategically placed three observation benches. Facing the panorama spread out below us, they were constructed of weather resistant concrete. No surprise, Ronnie and Katya selected separate benches. Ronnie chose the far north bench; Katya sat down on the middle one. Not wanting to show favorites, I selected a third bench, the one furthest south, sitting down with Malachi lying at my feet.

For a few moments everyone was silent. Words were not adequate, seemed intrusive, and really were not needed. For the first time in a long time I felt at peace. Up here it was easy to forget one's troubles, to forget all the unanswered questions, all the murders and the fact that there was still a killer out there somewhere.

I gave my mind permission to temporarily overlook, block out, all of life's pressing troubles and I immersed myself in the astounding beauty of nature. The girls, I could tell, felt the same way and even Malachi seemed silently content.

For a full twenty minutes we gazed out over the incredibly sculpted terrain of pink and white, then finally Ronnie sighed out loud and broke the spell.

"Is anyone hungry?" she asked.

"Yes," Katya nodded he agreement.

I heard my stomach growl and reluctantly we stood up with the girls and we prepared to go.

KA-BOOM! A single shot rang out!

KA-BOOM! Then another.

# 23

The first shot missed high, flying harmlessly out over the rim and dropping into the canyon maze of Cedar Breaks.

With the second shot, however, Ronnie cried out in pain, dropping to the frozen ground in front of her concrete bench.

KABOOM! As she was falling, the gun barked again and a third bullet screamed through the cold air. This one also missed, striking one of the concrete planks of the bench in front of her. As the impact pulverized a dime-size crater in the slat, it was accompanied by small puff of cement dust and tiny impact-exploding shards of concrete.

Instantly, I was on my feet and running. Just as another shot rang out, I leaped over the bench and tackled Katya. Together we tumbled to the frozen ground in front of her concrete bench.

"Are you okay?" I gasped, rolling off of her.

"Yes." She nodded, still clinging to me.

Looking up between the concrete slats of the middle bench, I tried to assess our situation. The shots came from the direction of parking lot. Fortunately, that area was higher, meaning the shooter had to shoot down on us. That slope created just enough of an angle from horizontal to effectively close the apertures between the concrete slats, making the benches a fairly good protective shield.

Lastly, I noted with a start there was an Arctic white SUV over in the parking lot, which was certainly not there when we'd arrived. I was amazed we had not heard it pull up, but I suppose we were so focused, so engrossed with nature's fairyland, like veteran Zen masters we'd blocked everything else out. From where I lay, I could not tell for sure if it was a Ford Explorer, but I strongly suspected it was and I was willing to wager it was the same rental that had followed us from St. George earlier that morning.

Suddenly, it seemed strangely quiet, made all the more apparent when contrasted with the battlefield chaos of the recent rifle blasts. At the moment, there were no more solitude-shattering rifle shots or whining bullets. The only noise to reach my ears was the bellows-like rasping of my own hyperventilation and the pounding of my runaway heart. While trying to slow my breathing, I crouched behind the bench and waited for the next barrage.

However, no more shots rang out, but on the other hand the white SUV did not leave either. In the eerie, but expectant silence I tried to think, tried to anticipate the shooter's next move. Really, in my mind he had only three options. One, he could simply wait for us at the parking lot; we had no other way out. Two, he could circle through the forest around our right or left flank in order to get an unimpeded shot at us, one not blocked by the concrete benches. Or three, he could merely get into his SUV and leave. The latter I did not think he was likely to do. Why should he? He had not accomplished everything he wanted, Katya and I were still alive, and at the moment he had us at a huge strategic disadvantage. Why leave when he had everything working in his favor?

Nervously, I scanned the forest to our right, then our left. For whatever it was worth, I could see no movement, but the forest was very dense and would make great cover. It was entirely possible he was moving out there and I would not see him. Glancing to my left, I could see Malachi still crouched at the south bench where I had been sitting.

Suddenly, he jumped up and bolted from the cover of the bench toward Katya and me.

"No!" I screamed.

KA-BOOM! The gun barked again! A bullet screamed toward Malachi! It missed him by no more than an inch, striking the frozen ground with a thud.

"Son-of-a-bitch!" I was incensed.

Firing at people was one thing, but shooting at an innocent blameless dog was plain damn mean, downright despicable and totally unnecessary. The dog was not a threat as a witness, or in any other way. As I grabbled Malachi and pulled him to safety, I silently vowed I would get the shooter, whoever he was. And I was sure it was a he. This was not the sort of crime women usually resorted to.

'But,' I thought as I hugged Malachi, 'get him? Get him how? Get him with what?'

Suddenly, I remembered I was armed. I still had the Desert Eagle .45 tucked in the waistband at the small of my back. Somewhat sheepishly, I remembered my ongoing failure to live up to my *no guns* resolution, my repeated failure to turn in my guns. But—but now I was happy that I still had a weapon. Reaching behind me, I lifted up my coat and shirt and gently removed the handgun. The odds had instantly gotten much better. They were not yet even, he still had a rifle (considerably more accurate at distances), the advantage of higher terrain and he still had us pinned down, but at least now I could fight back. Taking a deep breath, I pulled back the slide, cocked the gun and inserted a bullet into the chamber.

Since it looked like we had a moment of reprieve, I glanced over to where Ronnie lay. Unfortunately, I could see no respiratory or voluntary muscular movement. Was she still alive? I certainly hoped so, but there was no question she had been hit. I'd seen her fall. Somehow, I had to get over there to check on her.

"Katya," I whispered, "I've got to go check on Ronnie."

She frowned at first, then nodded. "Be careful!"

"Keep Malachi here," I whispered again, guiding her hand to his collar, then to Malachi I added, "stay, Malachi, stay. I will be right back."

Katya nodded and I squeezed her hand for courage. Hers or mine, I was not sure.

Replacing the Desert Eagle behind my back in my waistband, I jumped up and ran. Crouching low like a marine on Omaha Beach, I sprinted toward Ronnie, then dove, tumbling behind her bench.

To my surprise, no more shots rang out. Did that mean the shooter was not interested in me? Probably not, I grudgingly decided. More than likely it just meant at the moment he was not ready to fire. But why? Could it mean he was on the move? Certainly, that was possible. I shuddered at the thought. Or maybe he was just distracted, or reloading his rife. Once again I anxiously scanned the forest on both flanks and once again I saw nothing.

For whatever reason, right now it was quiet. Taking advantage of the lull, I rolled over to Ronnie. She was lying at an odd angle face down. First I felt for her neck, checking for a carotid pulse.

There was a pulse, thank God! It was strong, of good amplitude and with an acceptable rate of approximately 90. I could see no obvious wound on her head, neck or back. Rolling her on her back, I dropped my head down on her chest, listening for respirations.

"I—m okay," she whispered so softly I would not have heard her if my right ear was not resting on her upper chest next to her vibrating vocal cords. "I'm playing dead."

Turning my head slightly, I looked at her closely. Indeed she was alive! She looked frightened, but surprisingly composed.

"Where are you hit?" I whispered, my head still resting on her chest.

"Right leg, just about the knee."

Raising my head from her chest, I checked out her leg, rotating it slightly so I could see both anterior and posterior surfaces. There was no exit wound, but it appeared the entrance wound was about ten centimeters above the knee, slight lateral to midline. It probably went through the *vastus lateralis* muscle, the lateral arm of the quadriceps, but fortunately it likely missed the bone. Also fortunate, it appeared also to have missed the major nerves and arteries (the femoral artery, vein and nerve.) In fact, the wound had already clotted and the bleeding had mostly stopped.

"Can you stand?" I asked.

"I don't know. Probably," she whispered back.

Briefly, I considered our options. There was simply no way we could make a run for it. "For now," I whispered softly to her, "continue to play dead until I get this guy neutralized."

"O—okay," she agreed without moving her head.

"Good girl." I said, surreptitiously squeezing her hand as I turned to go.

"Is she alright?" Katya shouted from the middle bench.

"No," I shouted back, "she's dead."

I heard muffled gasp from Katya. I wished I could tell her that Ronnie was okay, but there was no good way to do that without blowing her cover.

Suddenly, another shot rang out from the north. The bullet screamed past my left ear, missing me by no more than an inch or two. Instinctively, I dove around the south edge of the northern bench, leaving a motionless Ronnie behind and exposed. Fortunately, there were no shots directed at her.

"Katya!" I screamed from behind the north bench. "He's shooting from the north." Frantically, I pointed his direction.

Instantly, she understood. Just as another shot rang out she scrambled with Malachi behind the south end of her middle bench. The whining bullet thudded into the armrest of her chair just above her head, again kicking out bits of dust and concrete.

Apparently, however, he must have bought Ronnie's performance, as he fired no more bullets at her. But it was just a matter of time; she could not remain perfectly still forever, nobody could. Human muscles simply would not allow it. Eventually, they would fatigue, spasm and demand to be moved.

This definitely was no good! I had to do something and I had to do it now. Eventually he would pick us off one by one.

I took a couple of seconds to catch my breath and to think it through.

The last shots came from the north. That mean from the parking lot, he'd circled through the forest to the north. If I headed north, I would probably run right into a hail of bullets. On the other hand, if I headed south and he saw me, which he probably would, he would know I'd left Katya and Malachi unprotected. It was a classical Catch-22, as in Joseph Heller's novel, damned if I do, damned if I don't.

But—but maybe there was another way. When you are at a major disadvantage use deception—he didn't know I was armed. However, before I resorted to that, I decided I would give it one more try. I would try to end this thing peacefully. Certainly, that was a lot less risky than what I had in mind, the plan I'd just worked out.

Rolling over on my abdomen, I rose up to my knees, being careful to stay well behind the shielding bench. Cupping my hands, I yelled, "What do you want?"

No answer.

"You've killed, Ronnie," I shouted again, "and Katya and I can't identify you."

Still no answer.

"Why don't you just leave? We'll give you a half-day's head start before we tell Sheriff Klein."

Still no answer.

I waited.

Still nothing.

KA-BOOM! Another shot rang out, the bullet screaming over my head.

That was it? That was his answer! Apparently, there was no way I was going to convince him to leave. It was time to put my scheme in motion. It was risky, very risky, and there was a good chance one, or all of us would get killed, but on the other hand if I did nothing we would all surely die.

Taking one more deep breath, I jumped up and sprinted back for Katya and Malachi, and the protection of the middle bench. Just as I lowered my shoulder to dive, I heard the rifle bark and felt a bullet tear through the fabric of my coat, almost simultaneously burning and tearing the skin of my right shoulder. Luckily, it did not actually penetrate the underlying muscle.

I landed in a heap next to Katya and Malachi, then rapidly scooted behind the south end of the bench. One more shot rang out, harmlessly striking the hard ground next to the bench, kicking up bits of dirt and ice.

Katya immediately grabbed me and pulled me in close. A joyful Malachi licked my face.

"Are you alright?" Katya asked anxiously, her face lined with concern.

"I'm fine. He just hit my coat," I fibbed.

She sighed softly as she clung to me.

"Ronnie's okay," I whispered.

Puzzled, she pushed me back at arm's length. "But you said—"

"Shsst," I whispered. "She's just playing dead."

"Oh," she nodded, pulling me close again.

"We can't stay here," I added. "Eventually, he'll pick us off, one by one."

Katya nodded.

"I've worked out a plan." Then I took a couple of seconds to explain my strategy, and finished by adding, "I don't think he realizes I'm armed."

"I don't know," she said doubtfully.

"It's the only way," I insisted.

"Please be careful."

"I'll be fine," I said with more confidence than I felt, then added, "keep Malachi with you, okay?"

Again she nodded and I got ready to leave.

Abruptly, I jumped up, and again crouching low, sprinted south, directly away from the shooter. A bullet thudded at my feet, but I didn't stop. Zigzagging, I ran past my south bench, continuing on toward the trees. When I reached the forest, I immediately darted to my left just as another bullet pounded into the trunk of a huge Englemann spruce.

Quickly, I disappeared deeper into the forest, but stayed close enough to the edge that I could periodically see the observation point, the benches, Katya, Malachi and Ronnie through breaks in the trees.

Almost immediately I started circling to the north toward the parking lot and circling in the general direction of the shooter. The snow was deeper away from the exposed point and I worked slowly through it, stopping often when there was a window through the trees. Malachi and Katya remained crouched behind the southern edge of the middle bench. Ronnie had not moved and still remained sprawled adjacent to the north bench. Fifteen tense minutes later, I had progressed far enough to reach the parking lot, approximately halfway in the arc to the shooter.

I paused to check the Dodge. All four tires were flat!

On closer inspection, all four tires had been slashed with a knife! Obviously, the killer was serious about getting us. He was taking no chances of us escaping.

I continued on. A couple minutes after leaving the parking lot, I stopped once again at an opening in the forest, which afforded a good view of the observation point. Resting behind a foxtail pine, I watched and waited for a few seconds. Everything looked the same. I started to leave.

Suddenly, the man appeared at the edge of the forest to the north. He was dressed in a dark snowsuit, topped with a charcoal black-hooded coat and dark sunglasses.

Who was it? I wasn't sure. Was it Ian? Probably, he had Ian's build, but I couldn't tell for sure with his hooded coat shading his face and his dark sunglasses.

Now he was moving out in the open, confidently striding through the snow toward Ronnie, Katya and Malachi, his rifle held in the ready position.

I held my breath. Was he just going to walk up a shoot the girls and Malachi point blank? I surely looked like it. With me gone did he think he would get no resistance? Did he think I had done the cowardly thing and ran off, trying to save my own life? With the Dodge's tires slashed, he knew I wouldn't get far.

He resumed his apparent death march toward the girls and Malachi. With my heart pounding, I continued to watch him. Now he was much closer, no more than sixty yards. I almost thought I could see a grim tight smile of triumph on his dark face. I had to do something and I had to do it right now. I was out of time. I had to put my plan in motion!

Steeling myself, I walked out from behind the foxtail pine, right out in the open.

"Ian!" I shouted, reaching behind my back and gripping the comforting handle of Desert Eagle .45.

Jerking his head up, the man glanced over at me. He looked surprised to see me, but still said nothing.

"You don't have to do this," I yelled, while still walking slowly toward him. "You can leave right now."

He said nothing, but once again started his beeline toward Ronnie, Katya and Malachi.

Suddenly Malachi snarled and lunged, but Katya held him tight.

He looked at Katya holding Malachi and grinned. "Don't get impatient doggie," he growled. "I'll get to you soon."

"We'll give you a full day head start," I shouted, picking up my pace, now a brisk walk, "before we notify the sheriff."

Still he said nothing. Malachi continued to snarl and lung at him.

298

Holding fast to his collar, Katya managed restrain Malachi.

By now the killer had arrived at Ronnie. He toed her with his boot. Nothing. No movement, not even a twitch of her finger. He toed her harder. Still nothing. He then literally kicked her in the abdomen. Somehow how she managed not to move.

Jerking the Desert Eagle from my waistband, I started running toward him.

Ian ignored me. He was now totally focused on Ronnie. Raising his foot he stomped down on her wounded leg.

Unable to continue the ruse, Ronnie groaned out in pain.

Grinning with satisfaction, he then raised his rifle, aiming at her head.

"Now!" I shouted.

Katya released Malachi. With fangs bared, he charged.

The killer looked up, redirecting his rifle toward Malachi.

Even though I was still at least eighty feet away, too far for a good shot, I stopped, put two hands on my .45, raised it to the shooting position and fired.

The bullet struck Ian in the right shoulder, spinning him around. Stumbling, he managed to regain his balance enough to face me. Seemingly unfazed by the pain, he raised his rifle to his wounded shoulder and pointed it toward me, cupping his finger around the trigger.

By then, Malachi was on him. With his most deadly weapon, his canines, he latched onto Ian's right calf.

Crying out, Ian use the butt of his rifle to club Malachi away, momentarily stunning the dog.

All the while, I continued my charge forward. Now I was at no more than thirty feet, a much easier shot.

Finally free of Malachi, Ian looked up, saw me coming and quickly elevated the rifle to his shoulder.

Simultaneously, I also aimed the Desert Eagle .45, firing a millisecond before Ian. My bullet struck him in the abdomen, slightly throwing off his aim. Fortunately, his bullet whizzed harmlessly past my head, but mine spun him to the frozen ground. The rifle fell from his left hand, clattering loudly to hard ground beside him.

Once again on the move, I rushed over and kicked the .22 rifle well out of Ian's reach, then pulled Malachi off of him. Rapidly, I examined my chocolate Labrador. He was all right. He may have a broken rib, maybe two, but he was breathing freely and without too much effort. Convinced he would be okay, I turned back to the wounded and bleeding Ian.

Suddenly, I was a doctor again; instead of a murderer lying before me on the frozen ground there was a patient, a badly injured patient, who needed my help. Setting the Desert Eagle aside, I dropped to my knees to examine Ian.

The bullet had entered the abdomen to the right of the midline just below the ribs. Fortunately, that meant it had probably missed the major vessels, the aorta and vena cava, so death was probably not imminent. With this type of wound, more than likely he would not bleed to death in a matter of seconds, but rather in a matter of hours.

Also, more than likely, the spinal cord had been spared, meaning no long-term paralysis, but, I paused to think, what organs were conceivably in the bullet's path? What had it possibly injured? I studied the location of the wound again and the trajectory the bullet had taken. Well, I hastily concluded, it could have struck the gall bladder and more than likely it hit the liver. Also, small bowel and the proximal transverse colon injuries were a possibility as well as damage to the right kidney and maybe even the ureter.

Undoubtedly, Ian would need surgery and the sooner the better. He would likely lose a kidney and maybe the gall bladder and a portion of the right lobe of his liver. Without question, his recovery would be stormy with the real possibility of peritonitis, abdominal abscesses and even a colostomy, but more than likely he would eventually recover.

Acting on habit, I reached up to his neck to check his carotid pulse. I couldn't immediately find it. Was his blood pressure that low? Maybe my bullet had struck a major artery, like the right renal and he was bleeding out. Still groping, I glanced to his neck, then up to his face.

Wait a minute! This was not Ian McKenna!

I jerked off the dark glasses and snatched the hood from his head.

No, indeed it was not Ian McKenna.

It was Wally Stroud!

# 24

## Seven Months Later

It was early June and much warmer now, but not quite yet the furnace-like heat of July. With daytime high temperatures hovering close to one hundred degrees, it was still possible to ride a bike, a horse or take a hike in one of the many nearby state or national parks as long as it was early morning or late afternoon. Come July all those activities would move indoors under air conditioning or become nocturnal.

Up at Brian Head, Cedar Breaks and the Summit Overlook, the deep snow of winter had also faded, except in shady patches above 11,000 feet. The snowfields were rapidly receding, being replaced by the vivid fresh green of spring and variegated meadows of mixed wildflowers.

For me down in the desert, down in St. George at a mere 2,500 feet, life had pretty much returned to normal, or at least I had no impending calamities of which I knew. Dixie Medical Center had reinstated my hospital and operating privileges, but as a precondition they had also tacked on a one-year probation. That was okay by me; surely I could keep my nose clean for a year. However, to keep the loan sharks and collection hounds at bay, I had to immediately go back to work, but not today. Today, even though I was still very much in need of money, I'd taken the day off to help the incredibly beautiful Ronnie Slade move.

With Tim gone, she had decided their home in the trendy Sunbrook Subdivision was much too big, too expensive and was haunted with too many memories, both good and bad. Five months ago, she'd put the house on the market. On my recommendation, she listed with my friend and realtor Russ Spielman. After it sold, Ronnie bought a smaller home, also using Russ, in the Morningside Subdivision, which was still very nice, but from that single transaction she was able to save and bank a substantial amount of money. As a secondary bonus, this new location was closer to our office, allowing her to walk or ride her bicycle to work. Then add to that the money she will eventually receive from me for buying out Tim's share of Urology Associates and she should be okay, at least financially

Yes, I had pretty much forgiven Ronnie for her duplicity, for her playing both sides of the fence with Tim and me. She was going through a pretty rough patch back then, just as I was, and she was simply trying to survive the best she could. Perhaps her judgment could have been better, but who am I to talk. But regardless of that, I found it next to impossible to stay angry with the effervescent, gorgeous and the occasional *dumb blonde act* of Ronnie Slade.

With my pickup loaded with as much as it could hold, Malachi and I drove from her old Sunbrook home to her new Morningside home. Standing on the curb, and I might add looking glorious in the morning sun, Ronnie waved to us as we rounded the corner. In her tight denim shorts, white tank top shirt and flip-flops, I must admit she never failed to take my breath away.

As I pulled up, she smiled and walked over to greet us. I couldn't help but look at her long sexy legs, but also noted she seemed to be suffering no residual limitations from Wally Stroud's bullet and her scar was next to invisible.

This time, however, as I pulled up I also noted Ronnie had a new companion. Standing beside her and looking every bit as happy to see us was a dog. From the cab of my truck, I couldn't be sure, but it looked like a yellow Labrador retriever. Other than the color and size, he/she looked a lot like Malachi, but was a little smaller. Just from the size, I suspected the new dog was a female and even before I'd brought the truck to a full stop, Malachi was clamoring to get out to say hello.

This load was mostly small stuff: coffee tables, end tables, nightstands, lamps, bedding, kitchen articles and personal knickknacks. Yesterday after work, I had coerced my friend Russ Spielman to help me with the heavy stuff. Coerced may be the wrong word; he actually rushed to volunteer.

As we worked, Russ and I once again got into an argument over the Lake Powell pipeline. Of course, Russ was still in favor and likewise in favor of more growth. Being in real estate, that's how he made his living. But as a native southern Utahn, I had already seen St. George grow from a sleepy desert town with a meager population of just under five thousand to a busy metropolitan community boasting a population of well over a hundred thousand. Of course, along with this extraordinary growth came the triplet traveling companions: crime, congestion and air pollution. However without more water this exponential growth could not, and would not, continue. St. George had pretty much exhausted all local recourses of water, so if this kind of growth was to continue that meant the Lake Powell pipeline. As usual, Russ and I agreed to disagree, even though I suspected with the passage of time, when water rationing was eventually initiated, I might very well end up on the losing end of this argument.

Today my helper was not Russ Spielman, but Malachi, and we almost never argued. Today, however, he seemed less interested in helping me than in making the acquaintance of the new dog. Ah, Malachi, my beloved but fickle dog.

Turning the Dodge around in the cul-de-sac, I waved to Ronnie, then backed up over the curb, across a small patch of lawn and right up to the concrete landing of her front door. The moment I opened the door Malachi scampered across my lap and jumped out truck to greet his new friend.

"I see you've got a new companion," I nodded at the dog as I got out and joined her.

Grinning, she introduced me. "Coop, this is Callie." At the mention of her name, Callie came over to say hello, ducking her head and wagging her tail vigorously. As with Ronnie, I couldn't help but love her--what a little flirt!

"Where did you get her?" I asked, petting Callie's head, then added, "she's a great dog!"

"Actually," Ronnie replied, "she's a rescue dog. With Tim gone, I could stand the thought of being totally alone, especially in a new house and--and I've always loved Malachi."

I looked at her and nodded. "Good idea," I agreed, while privately thinking, 'when the word gets out you're single you won't be alone that often.'

Ronnie ushered the dogs into the backyard, closed the gate, then with her carrying the lighter items and me the heavier we began unloading the pickup.

As was typical for this time of year the temperature rapidly began to rise and by ten o'clock the thermometer had already risen to an uncomfortable ninety degrees. Ronnie escorted a panting Malachi and Callie inside where it was cooler and we continued to work.

After we'd finished with that load, Ronnie, Malachi, Callie and I hopped in the Dodge (yes, it was crowded, but by now I was used to that) and drove to the Sunbrook house where we loaded the pickup one more time, then returned to Morningside.

We worked for another half hour, but when the thermometer had jumped to a sweltering one hundred degrees, hottest day of the year so far, Ronnie suggested we take a break. With a handkerchief I wiped the sweat from my brow and readily agreed. Retreating to the air-conditioned kitchen, I sat down on at the table and Ronnie opened the fridge.

"I'm sorry," she laughed, "but it looks like all I have is water, one cola and one beer."

"Water is fine," I said, stuffing my damp handkerchief in my shirt pocket.

She handed me an eight-ounce plastic bottle of water, then took one for herself. "Hot work, huh?" she grinned, taking a long swallow.

"Yeah," I agreed, "but at least we're done with all the heavy stuff."

She smiled her patented smile, the one that compelled men to do almost anything she asked. "You don't know how much I appreciate your help."

"No problem." I also took a big gulp of water. "How many pickup loads do you think after this one?"

"Just this one," she replied. "I can get the rest in my car."

"I talked to Katya earlier. She said she's coming over to help."

"Is she up to it?"

Sure," I replied, "she's all healed up now. They took the pins out of her ankle last month. Now she walks without much of a limp."

"Good," Ronnie said, filling a bowl of water for Malachi and Callie.

I couldn't help but smile. Even though they had started off at each other's throats, like Shakespeare's Montagues and Capulets, they were now friends. Through the hot fiery furnace of a life-and-death struggle, Ronnie and Katya had somehow bonded and forged a friendship. Certainly, that made my life easier.

"Well, anyway, I'm glad she got the job at the hospital," Ronnie continued. "It will be nice to have her around." She smiled slyly. "Someone I can have girl-talks with."

"What's wrong with me?" I jested, pretending to be hurt.

"What do you think?" Ronnie quipped. "You know nothing about women."

Considering my record, that was probably true. "Anyway," I continued, "she moved down from Salt Lake City last week and I think she starts at the hospital next Monday."

Katya had accepted a psychiatry position with Dixie Medical Center; the very same position the now deceased Elijah 'Ziggy' Ziegfeld was interested. Though it probably didn't help much, I wrote her a glowing letter of recommendation, just as I'd promised to do for Ziggy, but sadly never got the chance. It was a decent job and the salary was competitive for the intermountain area, but she was leaving an even better job with a higher salary at the University of Utah Hospital. She said she was tired of the cold, snow and smog of Salt Lake City and tired of the internal politics at the University of Utah.

"Well," Ronnie sat down at the table across from me, "maybe this weekend the three of us could grab some chicken and head up to Pine Valley for a picnic."

"Yeah," I agreed, "it would definitely be cooler up there in—"

—We were interrupted by a knock on the door and Ronnie excused herself and went to answer.

Now left to myself, my subconscious mind began to wander, eventually ending up back on Brian Head Mountain and Cedar Breaks. Mentally I began to relive the events of seven months earlier.

The man I'd shot at the Cedar Breaks observation point was indeed Wally Stroud and not Ian McKenna. To say I was shocked was an understatement. He was a longtime friend and hunting companion! And though he'd just tried to kill us, I immediately started offering first aid, medical assistance.

He was in considerable pain, there was nothing I could do about that, but I could care for his abdominal wound. Jerking off my coat and sweatshirt, I removed my t-shirt, then managed to tear it into long strips. A couple of the strips I wadded into a ball of cloth, positioned it right over the entrance wound, then tied the remaining strips tightly around Wally and over the cloth ball to create a pressure dressing. This seemed to stem the flow of blood, at least that which was exiting from the wound, and I hoped it had also tampanoded and stopped the hemorrhaging inside. Unfortunately, I had no way to verify this or to check on any internal bleeding.

While I worked, I couldn't help but ask, "why, Wally, why? What in the hell is going on? Why were you trying to kill us?"

Instead of answering, he continued to moan. The more questions I asked, the louder he groaned. And even though I persisted and asked him several times, I never got a straight or a coherent answer.

Once I had his wound adequately dressed, I asked him if he could stand with help. He nodded, indicating he would try. With my assistance he struggled to his feet, then with his right arm draped over my shoulder I walked (dragged might be more accurate) him back to the parking lot. Limping badly, Ronnie tried to help, but it was all she could do to get herself back to the parking lot. Katya, hobbling on her crutches with Malachi trotting at her heels, followed close behind.

At the parking lot, I suddenly remembered Wally had disabled the Dodge by slashing all four tires and realized we would have to use his rental SUV.

After searching his pockets, I eventually found the keys to the white Ford Explorer. Fortunately, it was a new one with three rows of seats. I opened the tailgate, lowered the back row of seats as well as one of the second row seats, then with Ronnie and Katya's help managed to wedge/scoot Wally through the open tailgate and onto our newly created cargo bay. Ronnie limped up onto the remaining upright second row seat and though he was not happy about it Malachi had to squeeze in next to Wally. Lastly, I helped Katya with her crutches climb onto the first row passenger seat and I took the driver's seat.

I fired up the SUV, backed out of the parking lot, then raced down the hill toward the ski village of Brian Head. On the way, I had Katya call Sheriff Klein. Fortunately, he was still in Brian Head and agreed to meet us on Highway-143 next to the Giant Steps parking lot. With sirens wailing and lights flashing, he then escorted us down the mountain to Interstate-15 and on into Cedar City. We exited the freeway at the north interchange, then delivered a semi-conscious Wally to the Cedar City Hospital emergency room.

On arrival at the E.R., his blood pressure had dropped precipitously to an alarming 54/32 and his heart rate had skyrocketed to 148 beats/minute. All this was an indication he was indeed bleeding internally, resulting in substantial blood loss. The E.R. staff immediately started an I.V. of Lactated Ringers, typed and crossed him for eight units, sent a blood sample for a stat hematocrit and ordered a couple units of O-RH negative (universal donor) blood. His blood count came back critically low at 16%, but they had already started transfusing the untyped blood by then.

In less than an hour, the E.R. doctors and staff had Wally stabilized, evaluated by the trauma surgeon and was on his way to the O.R.

After Wally was taken care of, I had the E.R. docs evaluate Ronnie's wound. An x-ray confirmed the bullet had not struck the bone and was not adjacent to any vital nerves or vessels. Consequently, they simply cleaned, disinfected and dressed the wound. She would probably carry that bullet for the rest of her life.

While we waited for Wally to get out of surgery, I told Sheriff Klein, with Katya and Ronnie's help, all that had happened up at Cedar Breaks. He nodded, then said that helped to clear up a few things, but he also indicated we still had a lot of work to do to fill in the missing pieces, to understand rest of the story. Lastly, he asked for my gun.

Gladly, I handed it over and told him I really didn't want it back. He looked at me oddly, but nevertheless accepted the Desert Eagle .45.

All of this, the murders and the slaughtered deer, had only strengthened my resolve to get rid of my guns, to quit hunting and go vegan, or least to limit my animal protein to cheese, milk and fish. Of course, I would still purchase red meat for Malachi. Once again I resolved as soon as I got back to St. George I would turn in the rest of my arsenal to the St. George P. D.

Wally was in surgery for almost four hours. After surgery was over and he was safely in the recovery room, the trauma surgeon, Dr. Enrique Ibarra (Basque - a habitational name from ibar, meaning meadow) came out to talk to us. I knew Enrique from medical meetings, from talking to him on the phone and from sharing common patients. After exchanging greetings and introductions, he filled us in on the surgery.

My prediction of potential injuries turned out to be fairly accurate. Wally had sustained a transverse colon injury, resulting in gross fecal abdominal contamination, an absolute requisite for a colostomy. Also, he had a shattered right kidney, requiring a total nephrectomy, and had a couple of puncture holes in the small bowel, which of course had to be repaired. Lastly he had suffered injuries to some smaller arteries, the vertebral and the gonadal, which were simply tied off. Wally had lucked out, if you can call it that, in that my bullet had indeed missed the spinal cord and major abdominal vessels, the aorta and vena cava.

"So," Dr. Ibarra finally concluded, "he has a long road ahead of him, but more than likely he will live."

To this Sheriff Klein added, "if he lives he more than likely he will spend the rest of his life in jail. That is providing the County Attorney does not seek the death pen—"

"—Do you want a piece?" Ronnie asked, jarring me out of my reverie.

"Huh?"

"Do you want some pie?"

Now fully back to the present, I noticed she was holding a pie wrapped in a white kitchen towel with steam still wafting up from its golden crust.

"Where'd you get the pie?" I guess I really had spaced out.

"Oh, the next door neighbor," Ronnie smiled, "a welcome-to-the-neighborhood gift. Do you want some?"

"Oh, sure. As long as it's not mincemeat."

"Huh? No it's apple," Ronnie frowned. "Sometimes I just don't get you, Coop."

"Never mind," I replied quickly. Now was not the time to explain my aversion for meat. "Sure," I said again, "but just a small slice."

"What were you thinking while I was gone," she asked as she cut the pie. "You seemed a million miles away."

"Oh," I grinned sheepishly, "I was thinking about all my ex-wives!"

She fired daggers at me. "Now I can see why they are all *ex-wives*."

"No," I laughed, "actually I was thinking about seven months ago, up at Brian Head."

"Do you think we'll ever know the full story?" she asked, now suddenly serious as she placed a paper plate with a piece of apple pie in front of me.

"I don't know," I shrugged. "Sheriff Klein says that Wally, on the advice of his attorneys, isn't talking. Not a peep—"

—Again we were interrupted by a knock on the door.

"My," Ronnie smiled, "I didn't know I was so popular."

She left to answer the door and returned a minute later with Katya Koslovsky. Once again, I was struck by how lucky I was just to be in the same room with those two.

Katya smiled at me, her patented gypsy smile, accepted a piece of pie from Ronnie, then pulled up a chair, joining Malachi, Callie and me at the table. "What were you two talking about?"

"My previous marriages," I joked.

"That should take a while," she retorted, dark eyes shining, as she pretended to settle back in her chair for a long discussion.

"No," Ronnie corrected, as she cut an even tinier piece for herself, "really, we were discussing Brian Head."

"Oh," Katya replied, her demeanor instantly changing. Her eyes misted over and she added, "they finally found Ian's body, huh?"

"Yes," I nodded, "about a week ago. It took that long for the snow to melt and that area was very difficult to search anyway."

"But that should give them some clues," Katya insisted, wiping her eyes, then forking off a small piece of pie.

"Yeah," I nodded, "the autopsy showed Ian was shot in the forehead with a twenty-two, exactly the same M.O. as Ziggy and Tim. And of course Wally Stroud owned a twenty-two rifle."

Now it was Ronnie's turn. Her eyes also misted at the mention of

Tim's name. "Seven full months later, with a decomposing body," she asked, wiping away a tear, "how can they determine anything?"

"Determine what?" I asked.

"That it was the same M.O. for all the murders," Ronnie said, "and that it was a twenty-two gun?"

"Well, they all had similar wounds in the skull, an entrance wound, but no exit wound," I replied, then added, "that's consistent with a smaller caliber gun, like a twenty-two, and then of course there's the ballistic evidence. Like a fingerprint, each gun's firing pin strikes the bullet a little differently. They've recovered spent shells from all the murders and can compare those with ones fired from Wally's gun."

"So they found the shell from Ian's murder?" Katya asked.

"Yeah," I said, "the sheriff thinks he was murdered up at the Summit Overlook. They found an empty cartridge up there some time ago. I was with them."

"Then," Katya continued, "in retrospect, I guess that's why the DNA tests showed only Ian's blood at the Overlook and down on the ledge where I was hurt."

"Yes," I agreed. "The sheriff thinks Wally killed him right at the Overlook, then pushed his body over the edge. Apparently, Ian's body bounced a couple times on the ledge before its momentum took over that edge too."

"Every bone in his body must have been broken," Katya shook her head, then added, "I'm just glad he wasn't alive for that."

"Yes," I agreed, "there were a lot of broken bones, but there was something else."

"What?" Ronnie and Katya asked simultaneously.

"Well," I turned to Katya, "remember how Hank Bettis told us Ian had prostate cancer?"

She nodded.

"His bones were riddled with it."

"So," Katya said, again brushing away a tear, "even if Ian and Wally had made it to the Cayman Islands, Ian wouldn't have had much time to enjoy it."

I nodded and we ate in pensive silence.

"So, why?" Katya finally blurted. "Why would Wally do such a horrible thing?"

"Like I said, Wally isn't talking, but Sheriff Klein has a working theory."

"What's the theory?" Ronnie asked. "I think we'd all like to hear it."

"We may never know for sure," I began, "but like Katya suspicioned Ian was gay and did have a lover. That lover, of course, was Wally Stroud. They'd actually met years ago when they were both students at Dartmouth." I paused long enough to give the remainder of my piecrust to Malachi.

"Go, on," Katya insisted, giving Callie the rest of hers.

"Also, Sheriff Klein thinks Katya was correct about the foreign bank accounts. He's actually traced one to the Cayman Islands and he also thinks she was right about their plans to disappear and leave the country."

"So, was framing Tim," Ronnie asked, again with wet eyes, "part of their plans?"

I nodded. "Unfortunately, they needed an alibi, a way to disappear. Tim kind of fell into that role when he and Ian didn't get along and he slaughtered that deer. Of course, Ian strengthened the alibi by continuing to fuel their feud. He snapped pictures of the butchered deer and collected the assault rifle's spent shells."

"What about that blood you found on the first day after their disappearance?" Katya asked. "The one we checked on with your pathologist buddy, Hank Bettis. I think that showed both Ian and Wally's blood."

"Yeah," I replied, "again this is pure conjecture, but the sheriff thinks somehow they staged that, probably by inflicting small cuts on each other, to strengthen their alibi."

"Oh," Ronnie suddenly saw the light, "if everyone thought they were dead, then no one would come looking for them or their money."

"Yes," I agreed, "apparently Wally had been stealing from his wife as well."

"Okay, I can buy all that," Katya sighed, "but I still don't understand why Wally had to kill poor Ian. Certainly he had his faults, but he was such a gentle soul."

I shrugged and shook my head. "Nobody but Wally knows for sure, but Sheriff Klein thinks it was simply a lover's quarrel. Perhaps one of them, probably Ian, was getting cold feet and wanted to back out. Maybe even expose the whole scheme."

"Yeah," Katya nodded, "that I can believe, but what about Ziggy? He wasn't involved with either Ian or Wally."

I frowned and handed Ronnie my empty paper plate. "Katya, didn't you tell me once that Ziggy had met Ian?"

"No," she paused to think, "no, I don't recall saying—"

"—No," I cut her off, "now I remember. It was Ziggy who told he had once met Ian with you at a department Christmas party."

"That may be so," Katya frowned, "but what's that got to do with anything?"

"When Sheriff Klein was trying figure out a connection, I relayed that information to him."

"So?" Katya still looked confused.

"Well," I continued, "he thinks when Ziggy was sick, and we failed to come back, he left the cabin looking for help."

"Oh," Ronnie jumped in and helped me with the rest. "So, when he left the cabin he ran into Ian and Wally."

"Yes," I nodded my agreement, "that's the theory. Ziggy instantly recognized Ian and Wally killed him. Perhaps, that's what precipitated Ian's and Wally's dispute."

Katya held back a sob. "It never would have happened, Ziggy would still be alive if we'd returned when we said we would."

"We are not to blame," I insisted. "We would have returned except you had a broken ankle and Wally, or Ian, or both of them disabled our snowmobiles."

We lapsed into silence once again. Each of us was lost in our own personal pain.

"Well," I said, slapping my knees, "time to get back to work."

"So," Ronnie stopped me, "what's going to happen to Wally? Do they have enough evidence to convict him without a confession?"

"Yes, Sheriff Klein is convinced they have plenty. They did recover Wally's fingerprints on our disabled snowmobiles. With that, along with the ballistics, the DNA evidence and our testimonies of his attempt to murder us at Cedar Breaks, they should have no problem putting him away for life, maybe more."

"Well," Katya also handed Ronnie her empty plate, "I'm just glad it's over."

"Me too," Ronnie chimed in, her radiant smile returning.

"Time to go to work," I repeated, then with Malachi and Callie at my heels, I headed out of the door to the pickup. A couple minutes later, I returned with a cardboard box full of knickknacks. "Where do you want these?"

"In the bedroom," Ronnie said, "I'll show you."

Two hours later we were done. Not only was the pickup unloaded, but we'd helped Ronnie put everything in its proper place.

"Is that it?" Katya asked, straightening a picture that I hung a bit crooked.

"Yes," Ronnie nodded, "and I can't thank you two enough for helping me."

"It was our pleasure," Katya gave Ronnie a hug, then with dark eyes flashing and sporting her most sultry gypsy smile she grabbed my hand. "Come on, Coop, let's go home."

As I reached for the door, once again someone knocked, then knocked again.

"Go ahead," Ronnie instructed, "open it." She held an excited Callie back by her collar.

Opening the door, I was surprised to see my buddy, Russ Spielman.

"Oh, hi, Russ," I said, still holding Katya's hand. "More papers for Ronnie to sign?"

"Nah," he said, shifting his gaze down at his shoes.

"Well, you're too late to help with the moving. We're done."

"I'm not here," Russell looked up at me and smiled slyly, "to help with the moving."

# Readers Guide

1. At the time of this book's publication, there are three books in the Dr. Cooper series. *Hemorrhage* was written in third person from two different points-of-view: Dr. Cooper and Samantha Rose. The first half of *Mountain Mayhem* was written in third person from three different points of view: Doc, Mack and Harvey. The second half was written entirely in first person. *The Reluctant Carnivore* was also written entirely in first person. What are the advantages and disadvantages of each format? What method do you like best? Why?

2. The title, *The Reluctant Carnivore*, is actually a metaphor. Name at least two different ways the title serves as an analogy to the plot.

3. As the series progresses, Dr. Cooper's personality has evolved. In what ways has he changed?

4. In what ways has he remained constant, the same?

5. Coop, Tim Slade and Ian McKenna all have distinctive personalities. Describe the unique traits of each including their flaws.

6. How would you describe Ronnie Slade? Her appearance, personality and flaws?

7. Coop has several hobbies, which are consistent throughout the series. What are these non-medical interests?

8. Initially Ian McKenna is not scheduled to go on the hunt. Why is he eventually included?

9. How and when did Coop and Ian first meet and become friends?

10. Though it is not apparent at first, Ian and Wally are old friends. Where and how did they first meet?

11. There are several reasons Ian McKenna and Tim Slade did not hit it off. Name as many as you can.

12. Other than being a friend of Coop, what is other purpose/reason the author wrote in the Russ Spielman character?

13. Why is Coop not in favor of the Lake Powell pipeline? Why does Russ Spielman favor its construction?

14. Coop's friends, Jacob and Sophie Heinz, have aged in this book; both have acquired new health problems. What are their illnesses?

15. Initially, Coop and Katya do not hit it off. In what ways are they total opposites?

16. Other than her looks, what is it about Katya that Coop eventually finds attractive?

17. What eventually attracts Katya to Coop?

18. Why did Katherine Kozlov McKenna change her name to Katya Kozlovsky?

19. What is Ziggy Zeigfeld's job/profession?

20. Why did Coop, Ziggy and Katya go to Brian Head and rent snowmobiles?

21. The next day Coop and Katya leave Ziggy behind at the cabin. Why?

22. How is Katya injured? What is the extent of her injuries?

23. Coop and Katya are stranded at the Summit Overlook. What happened to their snowmobiles?

24. Why is Ziggy murdered?

25. Why is Tim Slade murdered?

26. Coop has his pathologist friend Hank Bettis do DNA analysis on the blood he found the second day of the hunt while looking for Ian and Wally, and later on the blood he, Katya and Malachi found on the Overlook ledge. How were the test results different? What did they prove?

27. Why is Wally Stroud trying to kill Ronnie Slade?

28. How would you describe Ian MeKenna's relationship with Wally Stroud?

29. What are Ian and Wally's long-term goals and plans?

30. Sheriff Axel "Tiny" Klein has a theory of why Ian was murdered. What is his theory?

31. Though Ian McKenna is murdered, even if he had lived he would not have had much time left. Why?

32. Why did Coop eventually forgive Ronnie Slade?

33. In this book, the author wrote in a love interest for Malachi. Why do you suspect he did this?

www.ingramcontent.com/pod-product-compliance
Lightning Source LLC
Chambersburg PA
CBHW031154050726
47495CB00019B/1736